SENTINEL

LOST

MIND SWEEPER 5

AE JONES

GABBY READS PUBLISHING

Sentinel Lost AE Jones

Copyright © 2015 by Amy E Jones

Publisher: Gabby Reads Publishing LLC

Cover Art: theillustratedauthor.net

Editor: demonfordetails.com

PRINT

ISBN-13:978-1-941871-09-6

Barb H –
You are one of my biggest cheerleaders. Thank you for your unwavering friendship. I'm truly blessed to have you as my lucky charm.

CHAPTER 1

How many supernaturals does it take to screw in a lightbulb? In this particular case, way more than I had backing me up.

I walked around the outside of the Cleveland Museum of Art. Even though the pole lights in the parking lot were on, reflecting eerily in the puddles, the inside of the building was pitch dark.

And the museum was never dark.

I pulled Stanley, my .9 millimeter, out of his holster and clicked off the safety. I didn't need supernatural senses to know something was hinky.

Damn. This was supposed to be a quick drive-by. Misha was *so* going to owe me for this one. He'd detected some sort of energy surge on his equipment. *Go check it out, Kyle. We'll be right behind you, Kyle.* Ugh. Normally Misha's energy spikes amounted to nothing.

But then, when could I rely on anything being normal?

I reached for my phone to find out how far he, Jean Luc, and Talia were from my location. Before I could call, a loud *thump* made me slip into the shadows and then slink along the side of the building until I reached the back.

A metal door slammed open, and a huge man darted down the stone steps, his footfalls echoing across the lagoon in front of us.

Come on. Give me something, big guy. Are you a norm or a supe? I hesitated for a second. If he was a human burglar, I had no jurisdiction here. *Screw it.* He was getting away, and my gut told me to take a chance.

"Freeze!" I yelled, walking into the light of the full moon and aiming Stanley at the guy.

He jerked to a halt, turned toward me and stared. His eyes glowed like lighthouse beacons. Supe it is. *Now we're talking.*

"Bureau of Supernatural Relations. Hands where I can see them," I barked while I moved closer.

He stood there glowering.

"Did you hear me? Hands up!"

He raised them slowly, and I stepped closer. He clenched his right fist, and I gasped. Even though he was several feet away, invisible fingers clamped around my wrist like a vise. I tried to yank out of his hold. He frowned at my resistance, and as he closed his left fist, I aimed and shot. He howled, clutching his left shoulder. When he pulled his hand away, blood ran down his arm. *Green* blood.

What. The. Hell?

He flung his right arm outward, and Stanley flew from my grip. Then he raised his hand, palm down, and I dangled in the air, my feet jerking beneath me in a futile attempt to touch the ground. His upper lip crooked up like an evil Elvis. He studied me for a moment like I was a lab experiment.

This was what I got for listening to my gut. *My stupid, stupid, gut.*

After a few seconds, his forehead wrinkled, his expression changing from evil to confused. What was he confused about? The best way to kill me?

"Kyle! Where are you?"

The supe jolted at Misha's voice and flicked his fingers, catapulting me through the air, my stomach lurching as I helicoptered backward. I braced for impact, praying I didn't land on the marble steps.

Instead of stone, I landed on a wall of water that opened up and sucked me under.

Misha leaned over the marble banister at the edge of the lagoon. "You okay, Kyle?"

I nodded, wiped my face, and coughed up some more water. "Yeah...There's a supe running around out here. I winged him."

"We saw something run off. Jean Luc followed him, and Talia went inside to check on the guards." His mouth hitched up slightly on the right. "How'd you end up in the lagoon?"

I glared at him. "It's springtime in Cleveland. Balmy weather. You know me, anything above forty-five degrees, and I'm off to the beach."

Misha's ice blue eyes twinkled. "Do you need me to come in there and save you?"

"I can save myself." I stood, water cascading off my jacket and soaked jeans. I slogged to the side of the lagoon, and Misha leaned down and plucked me out like I weighed nothing. His demon strength did come in handy in a pinch. Would have been handier if he'd gotten here a few minutes earlier.

I tipped my head right and left and bumped it with the heel of my hand to drain the water from my ears, and then we walked back toward the building, my boots squelching with every step. I cringed. Good work boots were hard to come by, and I'd lost more than one pair to demon slime alone.

The air churned around us like a mini-cyclone. Seconds later, Jean Luc flashed into view in front of us.

I frowned. "All that vampire super speed, and you didn't catch him?"

"No, *ma petite*. He vanished. You should not have tried to confront him alone."

I almost argued that I could take care of myself, but water still dripped off the tip of my nose, which made the claim seem pretty ridiculous, even to me. "I was just going to detain him until you guys got here. I didn't know he was a supernatural on steroids."

"We need to get out of here before the cops show up," Misha cut in. "I can't figure out why the alarms aren't going off."

Talia joined us on the terrace. "We're not going anywhere. I found two security guards. One is dead, and the other took a bump to the head and is groggy."

"Let me see if I can help him," Jean Luc said, and he and Talia went inside.

Misha grimaced. "I'll call Captain Morrison to fill him in on what's going on." He checked his cell. "No reception. The building must be blocking it. I'll be back in a minute," he mumbled as he jogged away.

I stood on the terrace alone. "No problem, guys. *Really.* I'll just hang out here and...drip for a while."

CHAPTER 2

The Cleveland PD swarmed the scene like frantic ants. Cop cars littered the parking lot alongside a CSI truck and a coroner's van.

I pulled the police-issue blanket tighter around me while Misha and I waited next to the yellow tape blocking the building's entrance, which was guarded by a huge cop. He was almost as big as Misha, so no one was getting inside the building without permission. But several seconds later, Captain Morrison walked up to the yellow tape and motioned to let us through.

Morrison was in his sixties with graying hair, but he was still fit, and his eyes were the eyes of a cop. Always watchful. Absorbing the details of people, place, and evidence at all times.

He held up the yellow tape, and we ducked underneath. Then he herded us to the coroner's van, where Talia and Jean Luc were already waiting. Morrison nodded to the technician standing next to them, and the man flipped open the top of the body bag. The victim was a middle-aged man. His head sat at a weird angle, and his neck bulged on the right. I took a jerky breath and looked away for a moment. I'd managed to avoid seeing him earlier. Not so lucky now. I *definitely* hated this part of my job.

"Give us a minute, John."

The technician put down his clipboard and left.

Chief Morrison looked at me. "I should have warned you we were jumping right into things. I don't have much time before I have to let the ME start the autopsy. The victim is Carl Willis."

"Human?" I asked Jean Luc.

"*Oui.*"

"The ME's preliminary examination on scene states that Willis' neck was broken, but he'll do a full autopsy tonight." Morrison turned to me. "I understand you tangled with the perp."

"Yep." I went on to describe what happened, leaving out the green blood, 'cause I had no idea what to make of it. Maybe a trick of the moonlight? At least that was my hope.

"So you hit him?"

"Yeah. He'll have to lie low for a bit, but he'll heal."

A plainclothes officer interrupted us, and Morrison excused himself for a moment. I leaned over and whispered in Talia's ear. Her eyes widened at my request, but she nodded and left.

Misha spoke up again once Morrison returned. "Did the thief get away with anything?"

I shrugged. "I don't think he was carrying anything."

Morrison chimed in. "The museum director is going through the building as we speak, but as you know, there are a lot of objects housed here. Since only the most valuable items have sensors protecting them, it might take a while to figure out if anything was stolen, or if the guard's interruption stopped the robbery."

"What about security tapes?" Misha asked.

"The security feed was jammed."

"Has EMS finished checking the other security guard?" Jean Luc asked.

"David Heller," Morrison replied. "Practically a kid. I just spent a couple minutes talking to him. After hearing Kyle's story, I think your team needs to question him. You know better than I do what to ask in cases like this."

He led us around the back of the building, through a maintenance entrance, and down the hall to a small break room. A young guy barely old enough to shave with a crew cut and washed-out green eyes sat at the table. He had the beginnings of a wicked black eye and gripped a mug of coffee like a lifeline. Maybe it was the only normal thing he had to hold onto right now. A cop stood behind him, leaning against the wall with his arms folded. When he caught sight of the captain, he jerked away from the wall and practically stood at attention. *Suck-up.*

"Smith. I want to speak with the witness," Morrison said.

The cop nodded, but didn't move.

"That will be all for now."

Smith's eyes narrowed a bit on the rest of us, but he had enough sense not to ask questions before he left the room. "Yes, sir."

Morrison closed the door. "How are you doing, David?"

David gulped and fiddled with the mug. "I'm okay. When can I get out of here?"

"I need you to run through the story you told me one more time for my colleagues, here. Can you do that for me?"

"I keep thinking I'm going to wake up and realize it was a nightmare. A twisted *Night at the Museum*, you know?"

Misha propped his hip on the table. "Great movie."

"Yeah. Carl and I joked about it all the time since we pulled the night shift." He gulped again. "I can't believe he's dead."

"Can you tell us what happened?" Misha took a seat across from David.

I was more than happy to have Mish lead the interrogation. Even though his size, blond buzz cut, and Russian accent could be intimidating, he had a way of drawing people in.

"We'd just finished our rounds and were sitting in the control room when the video feed went dead. We waited for sixty seconds, and when the camera system didn't reboot itself, Carl went to check it out."

"Why didn't you go with him?"

"That's not the protocol. Carl went to check, and he was supposed to keep me posted on his headset. If he found something wrong, he would radio me to call the cops and then the security supervisor."

"Did he call?" Misha asked.

"Yeah. He called each time he finished checking an area of the museum. The first two calls were fine. But when he called the third time, he sounded panicky. Like he knew someone was there, but he couldn't find them."

Misha coaxed. "What did you do?"

"Before I could call 911..." He stopped and closed his eyes.

I stepped closer. "What happened, David?"

"Carl screamed. And...I grabbed my club and ran after him."

"You don't have a gun?" I asked, surprised.

He shook his head. "No. I haven't passed the security course yet that allows me to carry. But Carl has a gun."

"Did he shoot it?"

"He didn't get a chance. I ran into the special exhibit room and saw Carl dangling in the air with nothing holding him up. He was fighting for air and had his hands up by his throat. His gun was lying on the floor.

"I...I didn't know what to do, I froze for a second, and then I ran up and swung my club, and it connected with something. Something that grunted. Then Carl's neck twisted to the side, and he fell in a heap on the ground."

David blinked hard several times before he got to his feet. "Then the guy appeared in front of me. His eyes were glowing. And I swung at him again, but the bat flew out of my hands like he was controlling it with his mind or something." He planted his fists on his hips, lifted his chin, and leaned toward us a bit, like he was ready to do battle if we doubted him.

"What color were his eyes when they glowed?" I asked.

David's hands fell limp at his sides. "You believe me?"

"Yes."

He shuddered. "They were white with no pupils."

"And his skin?"

"He was white with brown hair."

Sounded like the same one I'd tangled with. "Think you could help us put together a composite drawing of him?"

"Yeah."

I glanced at Jean Luc, who'd been observing quietly. He walked out of the room.

Misha continued the interview. "What happened next, David?"

"I thought I was dead. He took a step closer, punched me in the face, and knocked me to the ground. I made a grab for Carl's gun. I mean, if he was going to kill me, I wasn't going to go easy, right? But the gun shot across the room, and then the lights went out."

"Was he carrying anything?"

"He had a backpack on, and it looked like it had something heavy in it."

I closed my eyes for a second and thought back to the supe running down the steps. Now that David had mentioned it, it was possible the supe had been carrying something on his back.

Misha smiled at him. "You did a wonderful job, David."

David sank into his chair again. "Carl is dead. I should have gone with him."

Misha shook his head. "From what you've told us, you did everything you could have done under the circumstances. You're lucky to be alive."

"So I'm not going crazy?" His eyes widened to the size of half dollars.

"What's wrong?" Misha asked.

"If I'm not going crazy...then this really happened. *Holy Shit.*"

Which summed up my thoughts quite nicely.

Before David and I could have a mutual breakdown, Jean Luc returned with Misha's laptop, which he set on the table.

Misha flipped it open and started typing. "David, I'm going to pull up a software program to help us create a picture of this guy. Hopefully it won't take long. Are you still with me?"

David nodded, and I raised my eyebrows and tipped my head toward the door, inviting Jean Luc and Morrison to leave the room with me. We convened in a cleaning supply storage space next door.

"That kid is amazing," I said.

"He sure is," Morrison agreed. "I should recruit him for the academy. So...what do you think?"

"His description and story certainly make sense based on what I saw. I'll look at his composite and add anything he missed," I replied.

"So how the hell are we going to cover this up? I don't want David sent for a psych eval."

I cleared my throat. Even though Morrison was aware of the supernatural, and called us in to help on cases, he didn't know I could manipulate memories. "We, ah, have the ability to make David forget about the supernatural aspects of what he saw."

Morrison frowned. "I don't want you drugging him."

"No drugs."

"And the composite? I can get one of my people in here to help with it."

I turned to Jean Luc, and he gave me a nod, so I continued. "To be safe, I don't think we want to share it with anyone outside this group. We're going to make David forget he saw his face."

"Why?"

"Because it would be safer for him if his statement said the assailant was masked," I answered.

Morrison opened his mouth to argue, but Jean Luc cut him off. "Captain, you are allowing us to help with this case because it is a supernatural containment issue. If we release the assailant's picture on the police wire, we may create a situation where your officers confront him without having any concept of how truly dangerous he is. We do not want anyone else to be hurt. Let us do our job."

Morrison stared at Jean Luc for several tense seconds before saying, "Okay. You've got forty-five minutes tops with David, and then you have to get out of here."

Thirty minutes later, Misha had the composite, a dead ringer for the supe who chucked me into the lagoon.

I sat across from David and reached for his hand. He flinched at the contact, then blushed. I smiled at him. "I need you to think about what happened one more time, David. Just for a moment."

I stared into his light green eyes. I pictured the supe David had seen, but I covered his face with a mask. I reworked the memory. David ran into the room and saw the man with his gloved hands around Carl's neck. David hit him with his club, and the man recoiled but still was able to break Carl's neck before he turned on David and knocked him to the ground. Then David lost consciousness, and when he came to, the cops had arrived.

I packaged the memory in tendrils of warmth, which I then eased into David's psyche. The tendrils braided around his synapses and made themselves at home. Tingling bubbled along my scalp, and I stayed connected with David for a moment longer until I was sure the new memories had taken hold.

We said our goodbyes, and then Misha, Jean Luc and I walked out of the room and met Morrison in the hall.

"Well?" he asked.

"It's done. He remembers a masked man now, and getting punched, which made him dizzy, and the guy escaped."

"I just got off the phone with the Mayor." Morrison's mouth turned down. "The Feds are going to step in. Art theft is their bailiwick, and with a murder on top of it, I'm not going to be able to keep them away from this."

Jean Luc interjected, "It would help immensely if we were able to determine what the thief was after."

"As soon as I hear from the museum director, I'll let you know. I'm also going to see what favors I can call in to help with the Fed situation. In the meantime, you need to figure out how we're going to contain this. And I want to be kept in the loop."

We trudged out of the building and climbed into the van.

I rubbed my tired eyes. "Shit. The last thing we need is some *X-Files* team coming here."

Misha's eyes lit up. "Even though they got most things wrong, I loved the show until David Duchovny left."

"*Focus*, Misha."

"Sorry, little one."

"Where did Talia go earlier?" Jean Luc asked.

"She went to look for blood samples on the terrace. I didn't want the cops to see them." I swallowed before I continued. "Because when I shot him, he bled green."

Misha smirked. "Green? We're not talking about Vulcans, Kyle."

"I know that! I hope I'm wrong. Either way, Talia's making sure there's not any supe DNA lying around for those CSI techs to stumble on." I took a deep breath. "Do we think our perp is a vamp?"

Jean Luc frowned. "The glowing white eyes do not make sense to me. And David did not mention fangs or claws, which would have been evident if the vampire was on the attack."

"He didn't show any to me, either. Add the telekinesis, and it doesn't sound like shifter, which leaves demon."

"A high-level demon," Misha added. "He can both dematerialize and use telekinesis."

I bit my lip. "Plus, he blocked the cameras and shut off the lights. I tangled with a Haltrap in Nevada who could black out cameras."

Misha frowned. "Haltraps wouldn't have enough power to match what you and David described."

"Then which demon clans do?"

"On earth it would be Pavel, Shamat, or Traman. They can have one of those powers, but usually not all of them at once."

My stomach twisted. "On earth? Do you think we're talking about someone from the demon realm? Like the Majock who helped Sebastian last year?"

"It's a possibility," Misha replied.

The somersault in my stomach graduated to a full-blown Cirque de Soleil performance. Memories of what Sebastian did to Dalton as part of his brutal quest for the Key of Knowledge flooded my brain. The torture, Dalton almost dying, and me erasing his memory of our time together to save his sanity. *Damn.*

Jean Luc watched me in the rearview mirror. "Are you okay, *ma petite*?"

"Yep. Started down bad memory lane but put the car in reverse and got the hell out of there."

The back door opened, and Talia climbed in holding an evidence bag, her mouth set in a grim line. "Sorry it took so long. I had to flash a few times while I was collecting the evidence so the cops couldn't see me."

"Well?" I asked.

She held up the bag with a small vial inside. "I was able to collect the blood. Which is a good thing, because you're right. It's green. I don't know how we would have explained that away."

Misha lost his smirk, and I pinched the bridge of my nose in an attempt to stop a lurking headache.

"I wish I'd been wrong. What the hell are we dealing with?"

"Something not from earth," Jean Luc said.

The setup was too perfect. Misha looked at me, and I sighed, dreading what he would be unable to stop himself from saying next.

"Live long and prosper."

CHAPTER 3

"*Knock, knock.*"

"Stop it, Marie," I groaned, pulling my striped comforter up to my ears and snuggling deeper under the covers. I had barely gotten three hours of sleep since leaving the art museum, and the sun was already taunting me through the window.

"*Knock, knock.*"

"I'm not answering you."

Marie's head appeared through my closed bedroom door, her gray hair in tight curls. "I can do this all day, you know. Since I'm dead, I don't have to be anywhere anytime soon. *Knock, knock.*"

"Fine. What's there?"

"Don't you mean who?"

"Not in my world."

"You're no fun," Marie huffed and floated the rest of the way through the bedroom door and over to the bed.

She was wearing her signature yellow sundress. Didn't ghosts ever get to change clothes? She continued, interrupting my tripped-out thoughts. "I've been spending time with Groucho Marx and decided to try out some jokes he taught me."

Heaven must be an interesting place. "Marie, you didn't show up just to tell jokes. What's up?"

She hesitated, and I sat up a bit to get a good look at her. "Is something wrong with Dalton?"

"No. Last time I peeked in on Joe he was fine."

I blew out a breath. "Then what's wrong?"

"How are you doing?"

"With what?"

Marie huffed at me, *again.* "With this Key business. You know. Girl meets boy. Boy absorbs supernatural knowledge. Girl erases boy's memory to save his sanity. Girl loses boy, but gains knowledge. Supernatural seizures result."

"Wow, Marie. Have you ever considered writing personal ads? You might have a knack for it."

"You need to work on your displaced aggression, Kyle McKinley. It's not healthy."

"I suppose you've been talking to some heavenly therapists, too?"

Marie shrugged and floated closer to me. "Maybe. How are Jean Luc and that new vampire doing?"

"That new vampire's name is Talia, and she and Jean Luc are finally together after wasting too much time denying their vampy feelings. I'm glad Jean Luc finally listened to my advice."

Marie frowned. "And I'm mad about that, young lady."

I stifled the urge to laugh. "Did you honestly think you were going to have a relationship with him? You're dead, and he's a vampire."

"Exactly! He's a vampire, which means he wouldn't be judgmental about me being a ghost."

"You're not corporeal, Marie. How exactly would this have worked?"

"Love finds a way, dear."

I flung my arm over my eyes, hoping she would take the hint and go away. How was I supposed to rein her in? I had no frame of reference. My own mother was a train wreck, and although I'd never known my grandmothers, I certainly didn't need a bossy, ghostly one. "Marie, can you give me some privacy?"

"I give you plenty of privacy when you're playing with your kitty cat."

I growled and lifted my arm to glare at her. "Stop calling Griffin a kitty cat. He's the leader of the US shifter contingent."

Marie's eyes twinkled. "Whatever you say, dear. Where has he been lately, by the way?"

"In Europe, meeting with international shifter leaders."

"Why didn't you go with him?"

"Because it would have been boring, and they sure wouldn't have let me attend the meeting."

"Right, we don't need you causing any international incidents."

"Funny."

Marie giggled. "I am, aren't I? Now let me try out some of these jokes."

My phone rang—*thank God*—and I made a grab for it, not even checking to see who it was. Even if it was a telemarketer calling at the butt crack of dawn, I was grateful for the save. "I have to get this, Marie. Hello."

"Kyle, are you up?"

I glared at Marie some more, and she smiled innocently at me.

"Yes, Misha, I'm awake. What's up?"

"Jean Luc and I just checked the museum to see if we could find out anything else about our green-blooded visitor now that the sun is up, but we came up empty. Since we're close by, why don't we pick you up?"

"Sure. I'll be ready in five."

I flung off the comforter and scrambled out of bed. "I've got to go, Marie. I can't talk about Jean Luc anymore. Now go away, so I can get dressed."

"Kyle, sweetie, we have the same lady parts."

"Marie!"

She chuckled and faded away. I brushed my teeth and dressed quickly in jeans and a turtleneck. I pulled on thick socks and rummaged in my closet to find my backup work boots. I crammed my foot into the first boot and then hopped on one foot out into my hall while I yanked on the other one. I hopped right through Marie floating in my path. Icy pinpricks skittered over my skin.

"Holy crap! I thought you left." I frowned at her. "Are you haunting me? Do I need to burn something of yours to set you free? Maybe a priest could get rid of you."

She floated a little higher and glared down as if she wanted to intimidate me. "What in the world are you talking about?"

"Well, unless you're tied to me for some strange reason, I can't figure out why you'd spend your undead days in Cleveland, Ohio."

Marie beamed. "It's not the place that attracts me, dear. It's the people. Now your teammate, Misha, is a Shamat demon, right?"

Warning bells rang in my brain. "Yes."

"Is he single?"

"We are so not going there."

"Russians are a very passionate people."

I shuddered. "It's official. I'm going to need therapy."

Tires squealed outside, and I ran to my window to check the street below. The team van sat in front of my apartment building, smoke still rising from the tire burns on the street. One of these days, my neighbors were going to call the cops on Jean Luc.

"See you later!"

I grabbed my coat, locked up, hustled down the stairs, and hopped into the back of the van. Once I snapped my seatbelt on—because you never rode anywhere with Jean Luc without buckling up—I let out a hard breath.

Jean Luc peeled away from the curb. "Rough morning, *ma petite?*"

"You could say that."

Misha stared longingly as we passed the all-night bakery, like a child stared under the tree on Christmas morning. "I would have loved some donuts."

"Maybe tomorrow, big guy. So, no luck at the museum, huh?"

"No," Misha said. "I also called Nicholas earlier to fill him in on what's going on."

I shrugged, not giving a flying fig if Nicholas knew what was going on or not. Even though he ran the Bureau of Supernatural Relations—or BSR, like all the cool kids called it—I didn't consider him my boss anymore. Not after he threatened me last year. There would be no Boss of the Year mug forthcoming.

"Where's Talia?"

Jean Luc turned the corner. "She took the blood sample to the lab so Doc can look at it after she has finished her shift at the hospital."

Twenty minutes later, we pulled into the empty parking garage and trooped upstairs to the office. Since it was 6:00 am, Dolly wasn't manning the front desk yet, so Jean Luc unlocked the door to the reception area. With its heavy wooden furniture and high ceilings, the room looked like something out of a 1940's mystery novel, but newcomers were in for a shock when they went into our back office, which was populated by rejects from the 1970's. An almond-colored faux wood table and lime green sofa were the highlights of the seriously out-of-date décor.

Jean Luc hustled to the kitchen to make coffee, God help us. Misha and I plopped down at the table, and he started hammering away on one of the laptops before I could take a deep breath. Our technology guru hard at work.

"What you doing, Mish?"

"Trying to match up the drawing with pictures from our supernatural database. I doubt it's going to be that easy, but we have to start somewhere."

"Right. Are you cross-referencing demon powers as well? Maybe we can narrow the suspects even more."

Misha grinned like a proud papa.

"What? You think I don't pay attention to what you say? Okay, so I don't pay attention to a lot of your techno-babble 'cause it's so geeky, but I still pay attention."

"And I'm proud of you. Next thing you know, you'll be spouting factoids like Abby from *NCIS.*"

The office door squeaked open, and Talia bustled in. Even first thing in the morning with no sleep, she was all pulled together. She reminded me of a prettier version of Halle Berry, if that was even humanly possible. Between her and Jean Luc with his long black hair and sexy good looks, I felt like I was surrounded by Calvin Klein underwear models.

Talia strolled in and gave Jean Luc a quick kiss. "Doc said she'd call us when she had information about the blood."

I groaned. "Dear God, no PDA. My eyes are burning."

Misha giggled, which was quite disconcerting coming from a six foot six, two hundred and forty-pound demon.

Talia smirked. "You must be cranky because you miss your cat."

"Griffin's not my cat. You're starting to sound like Marie." *Oh, crap.*

Misha stopped typing. "Marie who?"

Now I'd done it. How was I going to answer and keep them from going ballistic? I mean, I'd opened up to Misha and Jean Luc about the Key of Knowledge and how it seemed to be in me now, hadn't I? I'd told them I would not keep secrets going forward. But I hadn't gotten around to telling them about Marie yet. *So sue me.*

"Ahhh, do you remember when Dalton was talking to his dead grandmother last summer?"

Jean Luc walked out of the kitchen. "*Oui.*"

"Well, she kind of never left, and she talks to me now."

As far as reactions went, it was about what I had expected. Jean Luc carried on a conversation with himself in rapid-fire French, and Misha's Russian curses were very colorful. Talia sat next to me and waited for the international tirade to peter out.

When silence finally descended, she said, "Is she haunting you? Do you feel like you're in danger?"

"She's more annoying than scary."

"And what does she want?" Jean Luc demanded.

"She says she wants to be my guardian angel, since I have a tendency to get into trouble."

"Smart ghost," Misha muttered under his breath.

Jean Luc sat across from me. "Why is she still here?"

"She's got the hots for you," I blurted, the whole honesty thing apparently turning off the common sense filter in my brain.

Jean Luc's eyes widened, and he opened his mouth and then closed it again. I'd never seen him at a loss for words before.

Misha guffawed. "I thought I'd seen it all, my friend. Now even the ghostly females are after you."

"I wouldn't laugh, if I were you. She's set her sights on you now that Jean Luc's taken." Yep, my filter was no longer functioning.

Now it was Misha's turn to imitate a guppy.

I held up my hands. "I'm sorry, guys. I wasn't trying to keep it a secret, honest. If I'd felt threatened, I would have told you."

Jean Luc frowned. "I do not like it, *ma petite*."

"Why? She's harmless."

"If she is harmless, then why are the angels allowing her to come to earth now that her mission is complete?"

As usual, Jean Luc cut right to the straight and pointy of things. My *something's-rotten* meter started to ding. I would be asking Marie that very question the next time I saw her.

CHAPTER 4

"So where are we?" I asked.

I stood in front of the clean whiteboard in the back office and reached for a black marker. I wrote "Art Museum," "Break-in," and "Murder." Then I listed the powers the supe used on Carl and David and finished off with the word "Demon," and added "Green Blood" underneath it with a series of question marks.

Misha looked up from his computer screen. "So far I haven't found a match for the drawing in our database."

"What about the powers?"

"I'm compiling a list of demons that have shown at least one of these powers. I haven't found anyone yet able to do all of them."

"That we know of," Talia added. "The database is only as good as the info we've been given. I'm sure there are demons out there that hide their abilities."

I stared pointedly at Misha, who had hidden his own telekinetic abilities from me for years. Hell, he still hid his powers from his family.

"What have you found out, Jean Luc?" I asked.

"I am still completing the background check on Carl Willis. So far, I have discovered nothing abnormal. He was married with two grown children. He was a security guard at the museum for ten years, and does not have a prior record."

"And David Heller?"

"Heller's parents were killed five years ago. He and his younger sister live with their grandmother. Heller graduated from high school last summer, and from what I can ascertain, he is now supporting the three of them with his security guard salary."

"Of course he is." This kid was on the short list for sainthood. There had to be something they could do for him. I wrote the name David on the board, but as I wrote the letter H, my hand shook so hard I dropped the marker. I stared at the floor, watching it roll away.

Talia jumped to her feet. "Kyle?"

Jean Luc flashed and caught me before my body seized up fully. Muscles locked in my legs and had me whimpering like a whipped puppy. He picked me up and laid me on the couch while Misha fetched a blanket and covered me.

"Should I call 911?" Talia asked.

"*Non.* She will be all right." Jean Luc turned to me. "Breathe through it like we practiced, *ma petite*. With me now. Deep breaths."

He rubbed my shoulders, and his vampire thrall rushed through me. I closed my eyes and let the warmth envelop me, and as I'd learned, I didn't fight the names bouncing around in my cerebellum. I had to let the Key show me what it needed to, and when the names lit up, two came to the forefront, and I sighed as my muscles unclenched.

After a few minutes of deep breathing, I opened my eyes to find Jean Luc sitting on the coffee table next to me, smiling. Talia and Misha hovered close by, both wearing worried frowns. Misha was holding something wrapped in plastic.

"She will need some protein now," Jean Luc said for Talia's benefit while Misha unwrapped the stick and gave it to him. "This is beef jerky. Are you ready for a couple of bites?"

I pushed myself into a sitting position slowly, and Jean Luc tucked the blanket around me. I took a bite of the jerky, chewed, and swallowed the salty meat.

Talia scowled and put her hands on her hips. "Is someone going to tell me what the hell is going on?"

I nodded at Jean Luc, who launched into the story.

"Last summer, when Sebastian and the Pavels were looking for the Key of Knowledge, we found it. Or rather the Key found Joe."

"What does that mean?"

"The Key is not a physical object. It is knowledge that is absorbed by its keeper. In this case, it was supposed to be Joe."

I set the jerky down, my stomach souring. "Sebastian tortured Dalton because he believed Dalton had stolen the Key. He didn't know it was a part of him. And when we finally rescued Dalton, he was badly damaged. Nicholas felt the only way to save his life was to change his memories of being the Key and knowing us."

Jean Luc frowned. "Nicholas forced you to erase Joe's memories."

"He might have threatened me, but he wasn't wrong. It saved Dalton's sanity. But when I finished, I had somehow not only absorbed Dalton's memories, I had absorbed the Key."

"Does Nicholas know you have the key?" Talia asked.

"No. And I want to keep it that way. You're only the sixth person who knows about this. Jason, Doc, and Griffin do, too. Oh, and Marie, which makes seven, but she's a ghost."

"She can still tell people," Misha groused.

Talia sat on the coffee table next to Jean Luc but directed her question to me. "And what hit you just now was the Key at work?"

"Yeah. I have all of this stuff floating in my mind, and I can't interpret it, so the Key forces the issue sometimes. I see phrases and names like some sort of giant rolodex in my brain. Jean Luc's been trying to help me access the information without all the drama."

"Through his thrall with you," Talia replied.

"Uh, yeah." This was going to get awkward real quick. Only I would end up in a position where I had to explain why a vampire bit me and placed me under his thrall. And to his vampire girlfriend, to boot. It was like a supernatural version of *Days of Our Lives*. Cue crescendo music and long, drawn-out stares.

Talia reached out and grasped my hand. "Jean Luc's explained that he bit you to protect you from Sebastian. I'm fine with it. And if it also helps you with these episodes, then so much the better."

Misha was still hovering, so I moved my legs so he could sit on the couch next to me. He put his arm around my shoulder. "What did the Key have to say today, little one?"

"David, the museum security guard, is on my list of names. I'm not sure why I didn't respond to his name when I first heard it, but when I started to write it on the board, the Key walloped me."

"Better here than at the art museum," Jean Luc said.

"True. While it was at it, the Key gave me another name, Marlene Thompson."

"Do you think she has something to do with the case?" Talia asked.

"Maybe."

Misha kissed me on top of the head and rushed to his laptop. "Let me do a search on the name and see what I get."

Jean Luc held up the jerky. "You need to eat some more of this or your headache will not go away." He looked at Talia. "Protein seems to help her after an attack. As well as sleep." He turned back to me. "Close your eyes for a few minutes and rest."

I pouted like a petulant child, but he simply stared at me until I reached for the jerky. He was never intimidated by petulance.

"Fine," I said, "but I'm not sleepy."

I stretched and sat up. I couldn't tell how long I'd been asleep, but my stomach rumbled loudly. Which was probably what woke me up to begin with.

Misha chuckled from his perch at the table. "I've ordered Thai food for dinner. It should be here shortly. How are you feeling?"

"Better." I pulled the blanket off and sat up, flexed my still-tight shoulders, and then ran my fingers through my short hair to smooth it down enough that I didn't look like a punk. Now that I'd dyed it blonde instead of my neon color of the week, I was at least attempting to look respectable. "Any breakthrough on the case?"

"It's only been a couple of hours, Kyle. I'm good, but not *that* good."

"Did you find anything out about the name Marlene Thompson?"

"There are three hundred and thirty six in the US. Three in Ohio."

"Anything interesting about them so far?"

"One of them is a pharmacist in Columbus, one is a retired teacher in Ashtabula, and the third is a phlebotomist in Dayton. I'll set up an alert to track any news items involving the name."

I nodded, my nerves jumping. I'd done the same thing for Dalton after I changed his memory. I basically cyber-stalked him until Misha found out, talked me into letting him watch over Dalton, and promised to tell me if anything important happened.

My phone rang, and I picked it up from the table and glanced at the screen. Griffin. I held up the phone and showed it to Misha. Griffin wasn't supposed to call me until later today. I glowered at Misha, who held up his hands, palms out, in defense.

"Don't look at me. I didn't call him."

I went into my office and closed the door to escape Misha's big ears. "Hello."

"Hello, my sweet."

My heart beat a little faster at his endearment. "How are things going?"

"Good. I'm packing now and will leave shortly."

I sat at my desk. "You don't have to come home early on my account."

"I'm not. Our meetings ended early. What's wrong, Kyle?"

Crap. "Nothing."

"You're lying to me."

I let out a huff. "You can't smell my emotions through the phone, shifter."

"No, but I can hear them in your voice."

I hesitated. This "being honest" stuff was taxing my nerves. "I had another incident."

"With the Key?"

"Yes."

He growled.

"I'm fine. I was with Jean Luc, and he helped me. It wasn't as bad as the time in Vegas."

"We need to find a way to stop this."

I ran my palm along the pockmarks on my wooden desk. "We will."

"What triggered it?"

"We have a new case." And I spent the next few minutes filling him in.

"Be careful, Kyle."

"I'm glad you're coming home." I took a deep breath. "I miss you."

A low rumbling sound came through the phone.

"Did you purr?"

"Yes."

"*Awww.* Does Lion King need some nooky?"

He groaned. "Don't play with me on the phone, Kyle. I can't handle it."

I laughed. "I'll find *some* way to make it up to you when you get home."

He groaned again. "You're going to pay when I get my hands on you."

"*Promises, promises.*"

CHAPTER 5

Could a person explode from eating too much Pad Thai? I stuck my chopsticks in the takeout box and set it on the table. Misha gazed at the box like it was a long lost lover, and I pushed it to him to finish. I had never seen anyone eat the way he did. He chalked it up to his demon metabolism.

Talia snickered from her spot on the couch next to Jean Luc. "Watching him eat is like watching a *Three Stooges* movie. You keep telling yourself it'll be over soon, but it just keeps going."

"Hey! I like the Stooges," Misha protested.

I grinned. "Of course you do, Mish."

Jean Luc's phone rang, and he answered it. "Yes, Captain. We are all here. Let me put you on speaker." He set the phone on the table. "Go ahead, sir."

"I just finished talking to the museum director, and she can't find anything missing from the exhibits."

"I don't buy it," I said.

Morrison paused for a second before answering. "Do you think she's lying?"

"I'm not sure. What's her name?"

"Cynthia Hamilton."

Misha entered the name into his laptop.

I continued. "David told us the assailant's backpack seemed heavy. I think they need to dig a little deeper and figure out what's missing. And fast."

"Have you gotten results from the autopsy?" Jean Luc asked.

"Pending the blood work sent off for testing, the ME has ruled the cause of death as a broken neck. We found no trace evidence of the assailant on Carl Willis or in the special exhibits room where Carl was killed."

"Can you send us some samples from the scene?" Jean Luc asked.

"It'll be tricky, but I'll work on it."

"And can you email me a copy of the autopsy results?" Misha asked.

"Sure. I'll also put a fire under the director's rear and see if she can figure out what the perp stole."

I smiled. "I have a better idea. Misha was just about to run me home, and since the museum is on the way, why don't we stop by and talk to the director ourselves?"

"She should still be there. With the investigation going on, the museum is closed today. I'll tell her you're coming so she doesn't give you the runaround. Let me know what you find out."

Morrison hung up, and Misha chuckled next to me. "I was running you home, huh?"

"Eventually. All I did was move the timeline up a bit."

Misha clicked on the laptop keys. "Okay, a real quick look at Director Hamilton tells me she has a PhD in Art History. She is originally from Chicago and moved here to take the job at the museum. I doubt she has a record, but I'll run her name through the database to be sure."

"Do you want me and Jean Luc to come with you?" Talia asked.

"Nah. I'll keep Misha in line. We should be fine."

Jean Luc frowned, almost as if he didn't trust me or something. "Maybe we should go with them."

I picked up my coat. "Go home and have some vampire alone time. We'll bring you up to speed tomorrow."

Twenty-five minutes later, Misha and I walked through the main museum entrance and into the atrium, which always takes my breath away with its three-story glass ceiling. We followed a guard into an employees-only area, where he knocked on a glass door. A middle-aged woman with her hair bundled into a makeshift ponytail glanced up and motioned for us to enter.

Cynthia Hamilton walked around her desk, and I tried not to gape at her. She was a tall woman, as in NBA women's basketball tall. Standing between her and six foot six Misha, I felt like a shrub in a grove of giant sequoias.

"Ms. Hamilton, I'm Kyle McKinley, and this is Misha Sokolov. I believe Captain Morrison told you we would be stopping by?"

"Yes. He said you were helping with the case." She frowned slightly. "I'm not sure what I can tell you that I haven't already told the police. I don't know what was stolen at this point, if anything at all."

Her office was chock-full of books and various museum pieces spread out on a long conference room table across from her desk.

"I can imagine taking inventory is pretty overwhelming," I said.

She grimaced. "You could say that. Our building is almost six hundred thousand square feet. The CMA has approximately forty-five thousand objects on display, not counting the pieces in storage."

"Holy crap."

The director laughed harshly. "Exactly what I've been thinking since the day began."

"Did you know Carl Willis?"

Her smile faded. "Yes. We have more than four hundred employees, but I try to meet all of them. Carl worked here for ten years. I can't imagine why anyone would kill him."

Misha nodded. "Would you tell us how you're going through your inventory?"

"I have our staff methodically checking through every room to ensure nothing is missing. For some of the smaller gallery spaces, which are filled mostly with paintings, it doesn't take long to take inventory. But most of our rooms have multiple pieces in display cases, and many of the cases are linked to sensors that trigger an alarm if they're opened."

"Were any of those cases disturbed?"

"So far we haven't found any. I have no idea what this thief was after. I confirmed that our more priceless pieces are still in place. It was first priority, and they're all still here. Then I moved on to the special exhibits room, since it's where Carl was killed."

"What is currently in the special exhibits room?" Misha asked.

"We're between exhibits at the moment. We were supposed to be opening a new one next week, an exhibit of ancient Mayan artifacts. The room isn't completely set up yet."

"And nothing is missing from there?" I asked.

Cynthia shook her head. "The pieces set up so far are all still there."

"What about the pieces that haven't been set up yet? Where are they being kept?"

"Some are crated in the room. Others are in the storage area."

"Could you have your people look through those items next?"

"Are you following a hunch, Ms. McKinley?"

"I think the thief took something from that space and Carl died because of it. And if it helps, Captain Morrison mentioned the other security guard saw the thief carrying a backpack that appeared to have something heavy in it. I would think whatever he stole would need to fit inside, and almost fill, a backpack."

"Interesting. That means we can exclude some of the bigger pieces."

Misha handed her his card. "Call us if you find out anything, no matter how minor."

Once we were in the car, I rested my head against the seat and took a deep breath. "Well, that was a bust."

When Misha didn't respond, I peeked over at him. He was sporting an impish grin.

"What?"

"You were the model of diplomacy in there, little one. I think you are growing up a bit, yes?"

I stuck my tongue out at him. "Oh, stuff it, Mish."

"Maybe not so diplomatic after all."

"I wasn't going to give the woman a bad time. She's got her hands full. I can't imagine cataloging all the items they have on a normal day, let alone in the middle of this chaos."

"Let's go get some cannoli from my favorite bakery and think about next steps."

"Misha we just finished dinner!"

He grinned, and I rolled my eyes. How could I have forgotten who I was talking to?

I took a sip of the cappuccino Misha had talked me into buying and propped my feet on my coffee table. "So what do you think we should do next?"

Misha reached into the pastry box for his third cannoli and bit into it, the powdered sugar falling like snow onto his chin. "As soon as Morrison sends the autopsy results," he said, "I'll forward them to Doc so she can see if anything stands out. And I'm going to keep digging into potential demons that could have killed Carl Willis."

"I can help with that." I made a wiping motion over my chin.

He reached for a napkin and cleaned his face. "You hardly slept last night, and you need to get some sleep."

"And you don't?"

"I'm a demon, little one. I can go for days without sleep."

I huffed out a breath. "It's more than likely all the sugar you inhale."

He chuckled. "I'm sure it doesn't hurt. Jean Luc and Talia don't need much sleep, either. I'm surprised you didn't want them to come along with us."

"I want them to have some private time together. Talia's only been here a few weeks, and I don't want them to screw things up again. Plus, someone on the team should be getting lucky."

"Griffin will be home soon, yes? You'll be getting lucky in no time. Unless he is not good in bed?"

My face heated. "Mish! We've had this conversation before. My sex life is not up for discussion."

"I don't understand why you're so squeamish about sex, Kyle. I've told you I'm simply curious about human mating practices."

"What are you, the demon version of Freud? I'm not squeamish about sex. I'm squeamish about *describing* sex to *you*."

He tilted his head and stared at me until I blew out a hard breath. "Griffin is good in bed, and that's all you're getting out of me."

"You seem more content lately, Kyle. I'm glad you've been able to move on."

My heart stuttered, and I nodded, since I was at a loss for words.

His knowing gaze tightened on me. "As I promised, I'm watching out for Joe. He's still working with the FBI in Chicago."

I set my cup on the table, the coffee churning in my stomach. "I know you are. If anything happened to Dalton you'd tell me."

CHAPTER 6

Someone was knocking. I squinted at my bedside clock. Two in the morning, and I had a visitor. Was I destined to never sleep a full night again?

I reached behind my headboard, grabbed Stanley, and stalked to the door. I peeked through the peephole, and my heart went pitter-pat while I flipped Stanley's safety on and opened the door.

"Hello."

Griffin grinned. "Hello, beautiful."

I looked down at my tank top and boxer shorts. "You must be suffering from jet lag."

Griffin walked into my apartment, shut the door, and locked it. He stepped toward me. I stepped back away from him. His green eyes held a mischievous glint, and even in rumpled clothes he was ridiculously handsome. For once his brown hair wasn't tied back in a queue. Instead it hung loose, almost reaching his shoulders.

"Did you come straight from the airport?"

His mouth curved up even more. "Yes. I had to see you."

"Why didn't you call?"

"I tried. It went right to voicemail."

I shrugged. "It probably needs to be charged."

"If I had a key, we wouldn't have this problem. I would have crawled into bed, and we would be snuggling right now."

"If you had tried to crawl in bed with me while I was sleeping, I would have shot you."

He chuckled. "I won't take it personally."

"At least when Booger lived here, I felt like he watched my back. He was the best watch-cat."

"Because he was a shifter, of course."

"Minor detail. Maybe I'll ask him to move back in with me."

Griffin's eyes flamed amber. "I don't think so. Would you consider putting Stanley down so I can kiss you?"

I sighed for effect. "I guess so." I set the gun on the hall table.

He leaned in and kissed me softly on the lips but ducked away before I could latch onto him.

"I thought you were here for a kiss."

The corner of his mouth quirked up. "Didn't we just do that?" He pulled off his coat and hung it on the rack by the door. "How's your case going?"

Apparently he was staying for a while. "It's still early. Not much has happened since you called. How was your trip?"

"It went well. I think relations between the US and European shifter nations were improved by the summit."

I wiggled my eyebrows. "Relations, huh? What type of relations?"

His eyes heated, and he took a step closer. "The boring kind. Business relationships. But it'll help make our pack stronger if we can form treaties with other packs."

"That's what makes you a good leader," I said. "You're always looking out for your people." I ran my palm down his shirt buttons.

He grabbed me and pulled me against his chest. "God, I missed you."

He kissed my eyelids, which had become his normal way of greeting me, and then his lips roamed along my jawline, until he rested his nose in the crook of my neck for a few seconds.

I smiled and sank my fingers into his hair. "It's been a long trip. I think you need a shower."

"Only if you help me scrub my back."

"What a tired pick-up line that is. Next you'll be wanting to show me your etchings."

He growled and nibbled where my neck met my shoulder.

I groaned. "Not fair. You're cheating."

He laced his fingers with mine and pulled me toward the bathroom. "I'm not cheating. I'm making love to you."

"Is that what you call it?"

He pushed me up against the bathroom wall and ground his hips into my belly.

"Okay. You win. Let's get you clean, Mufasa."

"I should have never shown you my animal self." He nibbled my chin.

I ran my hands up his back, pulling his shirt up over his head. "You didn't have a choice in the matter."

He let me go long enough to turn on the shower and strip.

I stared at him appreciatively. "You are one fine specimen."

He stepped into the shower, and I yelped when he yanked me inside. The warm water quickly soaked through my tank and boxers, and he smirked at me before lowering his lips to mine.

I woke to warm arms around my waist, and I snuggled back against Griffin's chest. He was normally a hotbox. I wasn't sure if it was his shifter nature or just him, but I appreciated it, since Cleveland springs were damp and cold. After we played in the shower for a while, we had finally tumbled into bed, played some more, and then fallen asleep.

I turned in his arms, and he smiled at me, his green eyes drinking me in.

"Can we stay in bed all day?" he asked.

"I want to, but I'm working that case."

Griffin's hands drifted lower. "I don't have to tell you to be careful, right?"

"Of course not. I'm the new-and-improved Kyle, remember?" I placed my hand over my heart. "I no longer try to do everything on my own and I tell my team—"

"And me."

"...and *you*...when I'm in trouble."

"Good girl."

He squeezed my bum, and I lost the ability to think for a bit. When we finished our morning calisthenics, I glanced at my alarm. 8:00 am. *Crap!* The new-and-improved Kyle was running late.

I kissed him on the nose and climbed out of bed, pulled on my fuzzy robe, and stumbled into the kitchen to brew a pot of coffee. The dark liquid flowed into the carafe, and I took a deep whiff as the smell of java filled the air. This was one of my favorite times of day. The quiet time right before I had to jump into the thick of things.

Except my quiet time suddenly ended with pounding on my door. When the hell had I become so popular? As a general rule I was antisocial, for God's sake.

I opened the door. "Morning, Mish."

"I've been trying to call you for the last hour."

"My phone's dead, and I forgot to charge it." I padded into the kitchen, poured myself a cup of coffee, and sat at the table.

Misha helped himself before sitting across from me. "You're normally at work by now."

I shrugged. "You said it yourself last night. I was tired."

Just as I finished with my flimsy excuse, Griffin came waltzing into the kitchen with his pants on—thank goodness—but his shirt hanging open.

"Good to see you again, Griffin." Misha grinned. "When did you get back in town?"

"Late last night."

Misha slugged me lightly in the shoulder. "So someone else got lucky."

"Misha!"

"*Kyle!* I don't get it. Why you're so hung up about sex?" He looked at Griffin. "We were talking about the two of you yesterday."

"Really?"

"No worries, my friend. She told me you are good in bed."

Griffin's eyebrows rose. "Did she?"

My forehead clunked on the table. "Why are you here, Misha?"

"The Captain called and wants us to meet him at the PD at nine this morning. Since I couldn't get ahold of you, I came to pick you up."

"Let me get dressed." I made the mistake of glancing at Griffin, who winked at me. I ignored him, instead pointing my finger at Misha. "No sex questions while I'm gone."

Misha's lip actually stuck out in a pout.

"I mean it. If I hear any sex talk while I'm getting ready, I'll never bring you pastries again. *Ever.*"

Misha pulled into the lot of the main Cleveland PD precinct and parked the van. "Jean Luc and Talia should be here any minute."

"Did Doc have a chance to review the blood and autopsy results?"

"She's running a bunch of tests on the blood and wants us to stop at the lab later for a chat. She didn't see anything out of the ordinary with the autopsy results. Carl's neck was broken after sufficient pressure was applied. The coroner assumed actual hands did the breaking, although, from David's description, I'd say Carl was killed telekinetically."

I stared at him for a moment, wondering if I should ask the question that had bubbled to the surface of my consciousness.

"What is it, little one?"

"Could you do the same thing with your telekinesis?"

He frowned for a second before responding. "I guess it's possible, although I have never hurt anyone using my power. I seldom use it, and when I do, it's for defense."

"Don't you want to use your power more?" I asked.

His eyes widened.

I held up my hands. "Not to hurt anyone. I mean don't you want to see what your powers could do?"

He shrugged. "I have seen what the quest for power can do to supes and norms. I've never felt the need to fixate on my abilities."

"But what if you're meant to use your powers to help people?"

His gaze narrowed on me. "Somehow I think we're no longer talking about me."

I banged my head against the seat. I was being psychoanalyzed by a Shamat demon. "I hate it when you get all intuitive on me."

He chuckled. "I do have it in me, you know."

"I know."

He waited in silence for me to continue.

"I used to wonder all the time why I had my ability. When I was young, it was more a curse than a gift. But then I met Nicholas, and he showed me supes exist, and I came to the conclusion that what I could do made sense in a freaky, kismet kind of way."

"Go on."

"But then last year, when my power changed and went from simply manipulating a memory to absorbing it as well, it scared the hell out of me. And now with the Key invading my brain and kicking my ass whenever it wants to send a message, I can't help but wonder if I'm going to self-combust at some point."

Misha scowled. "We'll figure out what all this means, Kyle. There has to be a reason why you're now the keeper. Maybe the prophecy can help explain it. Has Father Brown been able to translate any more of it?"

"No. Father's been on a sabbatical in Greece. He's supposed to be coming home any day now. Hopefully he'll have something new to share with us."

Misha patted my knee. "We won't let anything happen to you."

I rested my hand on his. "I know." Although I wasn't convinced any of us could control the Key. I sure hadn't figured out how.

CHAPTER 7

A red vintage Mustang skidded to a stop in front of me and Misha as we headed into the precinct. Talia rolled down the driver's window and grinned while Jean Luc climbed out of the car.

"Since it's almost nine, I'll go find a spot and meet you there."

She zoomed away, and I gave Jean Luc a deliberate, wide-eyed look. "Talia drove?"

"It is her car," he growled.

Misha chuckled.

"And?" I pushed.

"And she will not let me drive it."

Misha's chuckle morphed into a full belly laugh.

We made our way into the front reception area, where the desk sergeant buzzed the door open and directed us down the hall to the Captain's office. The Captain's assistant greeted us and then led us into an interrogation room to wait, he said, until the Captain finished his meeting.

Five minutes later, Talia opened the door and joined us.

"We could have waited for you," I said.

"It's okay. I just careened into a man in the hall. But it was worth it. He was one fine-looking human."

Jean Luc frowned, and Talia gave him a hip bump. "You're so cute when you're jealous."

"Isn't the honeymoon stage over with you two yet?" I mock groaned.

After ten minutes of waiting and not discussing anything too relevant, since we were in an interrogation room and the walls had ears, my antsy came to the forefront. Morrison said we needed to be there at nine sharp, and now we were twiddling our appendages.

I stretched and walked around the table to the mirror, where I stared at my reflection. Maybe I should let my short hair grow out? Change the color again? It hadn't been blue for a while, and blue looked good with my gray eyes.

The longer I stared in the mirror, the more my skin tingled. Either someone was watching us, or my usual paranoia had kicked in. I winked at the mirror. If someone was watching, I wanted them to know I was on to them.

A minute later, Morrison came into the room. *Coincidence?*

"Sorry to keep you waiting," he said. "Have we learned anything new?"

I smiled. "Before we get started, why don't you invite whoever's watching us to come in too so we can get this party started?"

He nodded at the mirror and then walked to a switch on the far wall and flipped it on. "No one can hear us now." He rubbed his hands together and beamed at us like a proud parent. "I was able to pull some strings and bring in someone from the Feds who knows about the supernatural and will help us hide it as best he can. Added bonus is, he used to work for me, so he knows Cleveland, too."

Oh, God.

The door opened behind me, and I turned slowly, knowing, but not wanting to believe, who would be standing there.

I locked onto his face and my vision narrowed, black closing in until I was staring down a long tunnel. And at the end of the tunnel was Dalton.

He studied me while I stared right back at him. He was still lean, and his dark brown hair was shorter than I remembered. Maybe it was a regulation Fed haircut.

And, of course, front and center were his iridescent turquoise eyes. But they were different. They lacked warmth and recognition. They were the eyes of a stranger. The eyes of a cop who was busy assessing who he was dealing with. Eyes that took in every angle so he could accomplish whatever was needed to get the job done.

I had wanted so much to see him again. But not like this.

I took a slow, deep breath to stop the tunnel vision from closing in on me completely. *Not now. You can't lose it now.*

After a moment, he turned to the rest of the group and gave them a once-over. Both Misha and Jean Luc pushed their chairs back with loud scrapes and got to their feet. Talia watched their reactions and got up as well, obviously sensing something was wrong, but since she'd never met Dalton, she was clueless about what a cluster this was.

Morrison clapped Dalton on the shoulder and grinned. Of course he had no idea we all knew Dalton, since I'd also changed Morrison's memories relating to the Key case. The case that had almost cost Dalton his sanity. And was about to make me lose mine.

"This is Special Agent Joe Dalton. He used to be my media relations contact for the department and helped keep the press from finding out about some sticky cases involving the supernatural. He'll be working with you on the case. Joe, let me introduce you to the team."

Talia's eyes widened, and she gaped at me. I looked away from her to keep from crying, laughing—hell, I didn't know which.

Morrison gestured. "Jean Luc Delacroix and Misha Sokolov."

He shook their hands. "Gentlemen."

The sound of his voice sent my memories into overdrive. The deep tones reverberated along my spinal column, waking up my nerve endings.

"Talia Walker and Kyle McKinley."

"We've met."

I flinched. *He remembered me?* But he offered his hand to Talia.

"Sorry about almost flattening you in the hall."

She glanced at me before shaking his hand. "No worries. We both should've been watching where we were going."

He nodded and then turned to me with his hand outstretched. The last thing I wanted to do was touch him. His eyes narrowed on me the longer I paused, so I grasped his hand and then dropped it quickly. Too quickly, as if his touch burned me. But that wasn't the case. There had been no heat between us.

Dalton scanned the group. "If the Captain hasn't already told you, the FBI has jurisdiction in this case now. Because of the supernatural angle, the Captain was right to call me in on it. But I can't promise to cover up everything. A man died, and the government will be watching closely to make sure I handle things the right way."

Jean Luc answered. "Of course."

"The Captain has filled me in on the museum incident." He looked at me again. "You had a run-in with the perp and ended up in the lagoon?"

"Yeah." I swallowed. "Wasn't expecting to deal with tele-kinetic powers."

Dalton frowned. "I wanted to talk to the other witness, but you somehow changed his memory?"

"I was able to change it with my thrall," Jean Luc replied.

I barely stopped my mouth from dropping open at the lie.

Dalton focused on Jean Luc like he was a specimen under a microscope. "What are you?"

His tone made me grind my teeth. "Just to clue you in on supernatural etiquette, that's a rude question."

He frowned. "We have a murder to solve. Etiquette is not a top priority."

I opened my mouth to retort, but Jean Luc looked at me and gave his head a small shake.

"I am vampire."

"And what is your thrall?"

"Some vampires have the ability to make suggestions to humans, and they follow them."

"And you used your thrall to make the security guard forget?"

"Yes."

Except Jean Luc was leaving out an important piece of information. Namely his thrall only worked on humans he'd bitten. I struggled for a breath. The lies had begun. Who would be the keeper of these lies? 'Cause at some point they always had a way of biting you in the ass.

"And you made him forget because you wanted to cover up the supernatural?" Dalton's mouth flattened as if he had eaten something bitter.

"Didn't you do the same thing—cover up the supernat-ural—when you worked here?" I wasn't sure why I felt the need to defend our actions to Dalton, but I couldn't seem to help myself.

Before Dalton could answer, Jean Luc continued, "Yes, we wanted David to forget, but we also did it to protect him."

Morrison nodded. "Heller would have been sent for a psych eval if I had taken his testimony as is. Or, worst case, he would have been considered a suspect since his story was so far-fetched."

"What do you think killed the security guard?" Dalton asked Jean Luc.

"Based on David and Kyle's description, we believe it might have been a high-level demon. We are attempting to cross-reference demons with the abilities David described to us to see if we have any matches."

Dalton asked. "And what else have you discovered so far?"

Misha jumped in to tell about our visit with museum director Hamilton while I watched his lips move. At some point, his words no longer made sense to me, as if he were an adult from a Charlie Brown cartoon "wah-wah-wahing."

Misha stopped, and then Dalton said something, and the room went quiet. After a few more seconds, all the faces in the room turned my way. Whatever he'd asked had been directed to me. *Shit.*

"Sorry?"

"I said, do you have anything else to add regarding your visit with the museum director?"

"No. Misha told you everything."

He stared at me for a moment, and now *I* felt like a specimen under a microscope. *Not now. Hold it together a little while longer.*

"I'm going to review the autopsy results and the police case notes, and then I think we should regroup later," Dalton said in clear dismissal.

As everyone else said their goodbyes, I hurried out the door. I had to get out of the building. I shoved open the precinct door and sucked in damp air. It had started to rain, which was no surprise since it was springtime in Cleveland, and I rushed across the parking lot, my boots smacking the wet pavement.

I reached the van and yanked on the door handle. Pain shot up my fingers into my hand when it wouldn't open. I laid my forehead against the cold window, waiting for Misha to come out and unlock the damn door.

Footsteps thundered up behind me and stopped a few feet short of me. "Are you okay, little one?"

He touched my shoulder, and I jerked away and spun. He held both palms out in front of him, as if trying to calm a trapped animal. Jean Luc and Talia watched from behind him.

"I'm fine."

Talia came closer. "I'm sorry, Kyle."

I shrugged. "There's no need to be sorry. He doesn't remember me, which is a good thing. Everything is hunky dory."

Jean Luc and Talia exchanged a cryptic vampire look.

"Okay. I'll meet you all at the office," Talia said and walked away, but Jean Luc remained.

I glared at him.

"I am going to ride with you."

"I'm fine, Jean Luc."

He opened the door and held out his hand. "Kyle, get in the van. You are soaked."

I climbed into the backseat. Jean Luc sat next to me, and Misha clambered into the driver's seat and pulled out of the lot. I reached up and wiped the rain off my face and rubbed my hands on my damp jeans. And I kept rubbing them, letting the repetitive motion distract me. He was fine. I was fine. Everything was fine.

"*Ma petite*, are you okay?"

"Stop asking me that!" I yelled, my nerves jangling up my spine so hard that I shuddered in my seat. I knew what was coming next.

I hadn't had a panic attack since I was sixteen and first discovered my gift. All these years later, it felt like it was yesterday—heart pounding up into my throat, blocking my ability to breathe.

Jean Luc pushed my head between my knees and rubbed his hands along my back, his thrall warming me and slowing my heart to normal. At the rate I was going, I would need to bottle his thrall and keep it on me at all times.

I don't know how long I stayed with my head between my knees, but when I started to breathe easier, Jean Luc helped me sit up. At some point, we had pulled to the side of the road, the rear door was open, and Misha was now squatting in front of me.

I stared into his worried face. "He's different. So guarded now."

Misha cradled my hand. "He works for the Feds."

"It's more than that."

Jean Luc nodded. "In his mind, he remembers being attacked by a serial killer last year and barely escaping with his life. That would profoundly change anyone."

"So you're telling me I screwed him up by changing his memories?"

"No, *ma petite*, I am telling you he has much to work through. The real memories of his torture almost drove him insane. You saved him by changing his memories. Do not lose sight of that."

CHAPTER 8

Claustrophobia alert, line one. Misha and Jean Luc hovered while we walked into the office, like they were afraid I was going to have another meltdown.

I acknowledged Dolly, who sat perched behind her reception desk wearing a designer red dress with her blonde hair twisted up to enhance her supermodel face. She set down her *Guns and Ammo* magazine to greet us, and once again, I wondered what she did in her spare time, but was oh-so-afraid to ask.

"Boss man is here," Dolly announced.

I closed my eyes. Of course he was. Nicholas never stayed away for long, and he seemed to have a sixth sense about trouble. And he wasn't shy with his opinions, but then neither was I.

Misha opened the door to the back office and ushered me inside, probably to keep me from bolting in the other direction.

Nicholas took up the center of the room as if he owned it. And technically he did. He was the same as always. Impeccably dressed and oozing a Cary Grant type of vibe—except he had blond hair. I was not impressed.

Before any of us could get a word out he said, "Joe's back."

"How the hell could you already know?" I blurted.

"I have my sources. Why is he here?"

"Didn't your 'sources,'" I said using air quotes, "tell you why?"

I leaned forward to get into the boss's face, but Jean Luc put a calming, thrall-charged hand on my shoulder. I forcibly tamped down my anger and continued, "The FBI was going to horn in anyway, so Captain Morrison requested him because he knows how to control the fallout from the museum break-in."

Nicholas' lips flattened into a harsh line before he spoke again. "Have we learned anything new?"

Misha answered, "Nothing since my last call to you."

"How do we get him to leave again?" Nicholas asked.

"We solve the case," I bit out.

"I don't need to remind you how dangerous it is to have Joe here, do I?" Nicholas pushed.

"He did not recognize us," Jean Luc responded. "The mind sweep is holding."

Nicholas frowned. "For now."

I parked behind our facility by the river. It looked, from the outside, like an abandoned building, which was our intent. Keeping humans away was an important part of not exposing the supernatural. I'd volunteered to find out what Doc had discovered from the blood samples. I could have phoned her, but after Nicholas left, I couldn't sit still, since the hovering had intensified. Once Talia arrived, she'd fussed as much as Jean Luc and Misha about my mental stability.

And being the overprotective bunch they were, they insisted on having one of them accompany me. Misha got the short straw. I was expecting a lecture from him but had a merciful reprieve, since he was involved in a phone call the entire drive. A call he conducted in Russian.

He finally hung up when I cut the engine. "Sorry, little one."

"I'm fine, Mish. If you have somewhere else you need to be, just let me know. I don't need a babysitter right now."

He clucked his tongue at me. "Jason told me once that you are one of the most stubborn people he ever met. I told him I already knew."

My stomach bottomed out at Jason's name.

"Have you talked to Jason lately?"

The grin left Misha's face. "Yes."

"Is he going to come back to work with us?"

Misha stared out the window for so long I didn't think he was going to answer me. "He's not ready yet."

"It's my fault."

"Kyle—"

"It is. I should have told him Griffin suspected he was part shifter. Instead, he had to hear it from William, the sick bastard. And of course he taunted Jason about it. Now he's keeping us all at arm's length. Doc hasn't heard from him, either."

"He'll return when he's ready, Kyle. He's strong, and once he accepts who he is, he'll want our help."

I opened my mouth to argue, but Misha's phone rang again. He looked at the screen. "I have to get this. It's my father. He's been working to find out if there are demons on earth with the powers we're seeking." He clicked on the phone and spoke in Russian again.

I handed him my keys. Since the only Russian I knew was swear words, there was no point in eavesdropping.

I walked through our storage facility to the lab door. After I entered numbers on the keypad, the doors swished open, and I went in. Doc was examining something under a microscope on the other side of the room. Even with her blonde hair in a ponytail and wearing scrubs, Sabrina was gorgeous. Of course, being a Succubus demon went hand in hand with beauty. If sex was the way *you* fed, you wouldn't last long if you were ugly.

She frowned and came around the table toward me. "Kyle."

I hung my head. "Shit. It was you Misha was talking to on the drive here."

She feigned surprise. "What are you talking—"

I interrupted her with some choice Russian curse words, and her eyes widened. *Busted.*

"You speak Russian."

She sighed. "Fine. He called me and told me what's going on. He's worried about you."

"I'm fine."

Sabrina propped her fists on her hips. "Don't give me a line of bull."

I usually loved that Sabrina never pulled her punches. *Usually.*

"Okay. I lost it for a minute when I saw Dalton. It was shock more than anything. But he's fine, and I'll be fine."

"You must be hurting."

"We need to solve this case. Then he will go away, and everything will get back to normal." And if I said it a few thousand more times, maybe I'd actually believe it.

Doc pointed to a chair. "Sit."

"Why?"

"Because I want to check you over."

"Don't be ridiculous."

"Misha told me you had another episode with the Key yesterday."

"How do you say 'big mouth' in Russian?" I grumbled as I plopped onto the chair.

She ignored me while she poked and prodded. After a few minutes, she looked at me and frowned.

"What?"

"I think your reflexes are a little sluggish. How do you feel?"

"I feel fine."

"I want you to call me if you have any more incidents, got it?"

The door swished open behind me, interrupting my response. "You can come in now, Misha. It's okay. I won't hurt you *this time*."

At least he had the good grace to blush.

I gestured at the microscope. "Do you have something for us, Doc?"

She scowled, more than likely due to my change of subject. "Yes. I've been examining the blood samples. It's demon, but they're not cells from any of the demon clans currently on earth."

"What's with the green?"

Doc grinned. "It's interesting, isn't it? I think it might have to do with the atmosphere in the realm. I would imagine after the demon has been on earth for a while the color would change to red."

"So you believe we're dealing with a recent arrival from the demon realm?" I asked.

"Yes."

I looked first at Misha and then Doc. "Isn't the demon realm locked down? How do they even get to earth?"

"The portal between the realm and earth is guarded," Misha answered. "But given enough motivation, folks will find ways to get past most any kind of barrier."

"That doesn't make me feel secure."

"The average human is much more likely to die from heart disease, cancer, or accidents than a run-in with a rogue demon."

"Misha. Don't give up your day job to become a counselor."

Doc sighed. "Are you two done squabbling?"

We both nodded.

"We need to figure out who this demon is and if he's still on earth."

"I know someone who might be able to help us," I said. "Doyle."

Misha scowled. "He's a con-demon. Do you honestly think you can trust him?"

I considered it for a second. "He's gone legit now, but I bet he still has contacts. Let's go fill in Jean Luc and Talia and then pay a visit to Doyle."

CHAPTER 9

I plowed through the reception area and into the office. "Time to hit the road. We…"

My words and steps faltered, and Misha ran into me from behind. If he hadn't wrapped his arm around me, he would have knocked me flat on my face.

Jean Luc and Talia sat at the table while Dalton watched us from in front of the whiteboard. He took in our less-than-elegant entrance, including Misha's arm around my stomach.

"You have something new on the case?" he asked.

I untangled myself. "Doc reviewed the demon blood samples."

"Doc?"

"She's our Medical Examiner," Jean Luc volunteered.

Dalton folded his arms across his chest. "I read the report. The only blood samples gathered were from the victim."

I folded my own arms across my chest. "In point of fact, we gathered some samples of our own, and here's the kicker. He's from the demon realm."

"What the hell is a demon realm?"

I looked at Misha, who took over. "Only certain demon clans are allowed to live on earth. Those who have been deemed too dangerous remain in the demon realm."

"And you're saying one of those demons was at the art museum?"

Misha and I nodded.

"How do we find him?" Dalton asked.

Jean Luc stood. "He might not be on earth anymore."

"Right," I agreed. "But he's found a way to escape the realm and come to earth. More than likely someone's helping him. I was going to talk to Doyle. See if he can hook us up with an informant or two."

"I'm coming with you," Dalton announced.

Alarm bells pealed in my brain. "That might not be a good idea. We can talk to our contact and report the results to you."

"This investigation is hands-on for me. I will not sit on the sidelines."

I dug in my heels. "Well, our contact is going to spook. You're wearing a suit, for God's sake. You might as well have Fed stamped on your forehead."

"I always carry other clothes with me. I'll get them from the car and change, and we can be on our way."

"Fine."

Dalton walked out of the room, and I flipped into pace mode. "Misha. After we leave, would you get hold of Doyle and let him know we're coming? And for God's sake, tell him to act like he doesn't recognize Dalton."

Thirty minutes later, I parked my car and looked at the man sitting next to me. Dalton was now dressed in jeans and a Henley shirt with a brown leather jacket. We hadn't spoken during the drive, and the awkward silence was choking me.

"Let me do the talking in there, since he's my contact."

He opened his mouth as if to protest, and then he gave a quick jerk of his chin in acceptance. That had been easier than I expected.

Dalton held open the door of the Auto Emporium, and I glanced around in awe. The building was the size of a small hangar bay, and it was full of cars. Dalton came in behind me and picked up a brochure next to the door, paging through it slowly. Then he walked up to the truck sitting to our right and studied the price sticker. He looked like he was shopping for a car. Which I guess was the point.

He was a natural. Since when was he comfortable under cover? The last time he had to play a part, he'd stammered like a junior high boy asking a girl to go steady. Of course, he had been talking to his ex and I was listening in at the time.

An older guy wearing a polo shirt with the Auto Emporium logo rushed up to us. "Have you been helped?"

"Not yet," I said. "I'm here to see Kevin Doyle."

The wattage of his smile dimmed. "Hang on a second." And he left.

A few minutes later, Doyle arrived. His eyes still had a bit of a buggy quality, but I was happy to see he hadn't let his comb-over grow back.

"Hello. I understand you asked for me. How may I help you?" He spoke in a loud voice, as if announcing to everyone in the building that he was unfamiliar with me.

"I was given your name by a friend who bought a car from you. I'm looking for a new car."

He peered around like a shoplifter watching out for mall security, and then leaned forward and hissed, "Why are you here? I'm not in the business anymore."

"I know, but I have an issue, and you could probably point me in the right direction."

Dalton walked up to us, and I tensed, hoping Misha had been able to reach Doyle.

"Are you two together?" Doyle asked, his right eye twitching.

"Yes," I replied through gritted teeth. Doyle was terrible at lying, which was why he'd been a mediocre con-demon. His tic was a sure sign he might fold under the pressure.

"Can we talk somewhere more private?" I asked.

Doyle led us to a small room with a table and chairs. He gestured to the chairs and shut the door. "I'm legit now, Kyle. I don't want to get into trouble with the boss."

I held up my hands. "I don't plan to mess things up for you. But we have a big problem, and I need your help."

He leaned against the door. I took it as a sign to keep talking.

"We have a demon that's crossed over from the demon realm and killed a human."

"And?"

"And I want to know how a demon is able to get to earth when the portals are supposedly blocked."

Doyle stopped leaning and pulled on his collar. "I never dealt in demon trafficking."

"I'm not saying you did. But I bet you can direct me to someone who does. Come on, Doyle. Help me out, here."

"You've fallen into some serious sh—stuff this time, McKinley. Crossovers are dangerous."

"But there are border patrols."

Doyle grimaced. "Oh, yeah. The demon border patrol makes the US Border Patrol look like the *Mickey Mouse Club*."

"If they're that tough, how are the demons getting through?" Dalton asked.

"When you tell someone, human or demon, they can't do something, they try all the harder to prove it can be done. For enough money, there are ways to open temporary portals to earth. By the time the patrol senses the break, the portal is closed, and the demon is through."

"Who do we need to talk to, then?" I asked.

Doyle hesitated. "If I tell you, promise me you won't go in there half-cocked by yourself."

"She's not going anywhere without me."

"No offense, human. But she's going to need more protection than you."

"I promise. Misha and Jean Luc will be in on the meeting," I said.

"You're going to need to involve that new vamp you have working with you, too. The more supe power the better."

I didn't bother asking how he knew about Talia. He was gifted that way. "Spill, Doyle."

"Talk to Eli Miller. He's a Traman. He owns a bar in Shaker Heights."

"And what's his connection to all of this?" Dalton asked.

"He's the go-between on the earth side. He schedules the meetings with the demons and the Abstatholm."

"Abstatholm?"

"They're the supes who can open the portals back to the demon realm. Eli is going to demand to know how you found out about him. Give him the name Charles Jenkins. Jenkins has his fingers in all kinds of supe dealings."

"I owe you one, Doyle."

"Nah. Just don't keep coming here and getting me in trouble with the boss. She's a real taskmaster."

"She can't cut you any slack?" I asked. "She's your mother-in-law, for crying out loud."

Doyle snorted. "Which makes it worse. I've been married to her daughter for eighty-five years, and she still doesn't have any grandbabies."

I laughed, and he smiled briefly before his expression turned serious. "Be careful, Kyle. These supes are not the kind you want to mess with."

I pulled out of the Emporium's parking lot and drove toward the office. Dalton sat quietly for a few minutes. I looked over at him and could almost see the wheels spinning. He finally turned his attention to me, and I was glad I had to watch the road and not look into his eyes.

"How do you know Doyle?"

"He used to be a con-demon. Petty stuff, mostly. His real talent is intel. He finds out pretty much everything that's going on in Northeast Ohio."

"You two seem pretty close."

I nodded. "If you'd said that to me a year ago, I would have laughed. But now? You're right. He's helped me, multiple times."

"And he was concerned about you going to see Miller alone. I would think you would be able to take care of yourself. With your powers, I mean. What are you?"

I stopped at a light. "I thought we covered this before. It's rude to ask that."

When he didn't answer, I made the mistake of glancing toward him again. This time, his eyes locked onto mine. His beautiful turquoise eyes. *Damn.*

"I'm not anything."

He frowned and opened his mouth, more than likely to argue with me, but I spoke first.

"I'm human."

His eyebrows rose. "How did you end up on the team, then?"

"It's a long story."

A horn sounded, and I looked up. The light was green. I kept driving while the silence stretched between us. I wasn't sure if he was trying to use some sort of cop technique—maybe sweat it out of me—before he swooped in with his questions, but I needed to think fast and come up with something to tell him.

Why *would* a human work on the team? I didn't dare tell him too much for fear it might trigger his memories. If anything could trigger his memories, that is. Hell, this was all-new territory, and I didn't have a clue how to find my way.

"How long have you been working on the team?"

Okay, he had just been figuring out how to go at this from another angle. "Ten years."

"*Ten years*. How old were you when you started?"

"Twenty. I saw my first vampire when I was twenty and got pulled into a case with Jean Luc and Misha. After it was solved, they asked me to stick around." Which was sort of the truth.

"And so you help them hide the truth from us?"

"Us?" I asked, although it was obvious where he was going, and I didn't like it.

"Humans."

I turned into a Chipotle parking lot and put the car in park. "Are we really going to have an us versus them conversation?"

His eyes narrowed. "No. I just want to understand why you work for supernaturals."

"I work with supes because I don't want the kind of pandemonium that is sure to break out if the truth is revealed. And it would break out. Humans are close-minded as a whole and scared of anything different. They would persecute supernaturals."

"You have a pretty cynical view of the world."

"One that's been reinforced over the years. I've seen it again and again while we're working cases."

"So you help them forget?"

"What?" My throat tightened.

"Jean Luc uses his thrall to make them forget."

"Right. If we have someone we think is going to cause trouble, we help them forget." I turned off the car. "I'm going to run in and get some food to go. Are you hungry?"

"You don't even know if I like Mexican food."

He loved Mexican food, and I knew it, but it wasn't something I could tell him. "Come on. You're a cop. It's in your DNA. I've never been in a Chipotle that doesn't have at least one cop eating there."

Ten minutes later, we piled into the car with our takeout bags. I laughed as a state trooper parked and went into the restaurant. "Told you."

Dalton shook his head, and just for a second, time fell away. I fumbled with the key and turned on the car.

"Why did you only get three burritos?"

"What do you mean?" I asked, a bit thrown by the question.

"There are four of you at the office, right? Talia, Jean Luc, Misha and you."

"Actually there are five of us. You probably haven't met Dolly yet. Jean Luc and Talia don't eat, and Dolly brings her own food to work. Two of these burritos and the order of chips and guacamole are for Misha."

Dalton's eyes widened. "How can he eat all that?"

I shrugged. "It's his demon metabolism."

"And I understand there are different kinds of demons here on earth?"

"Yeah. Twelve clans are allowed on earth. Misha is a Shamat. They're pretty powerful."

"And who decides who gets to stay on earth and who has to go?"

I pulled out of the parking lot. "Good question. I would say the demon council has the final say, but Misha can tell us for sure."

"So what's the deal with you two? Are you and Misha a couple?"

I felt a strange sense of déjà vu. Dalton had thought Misha and I were a couple the first time we met. "No. Why would you think that?"

He shrugged. "He's very protective of you."

I looked away. "He's my teammate, and one of my best friends." I frowned. "Do you think it would be the only reason they would keep a human around?"

"No."

"Here's the deal. Sometimes it's helpful to have a human on the team. I serve as a liaison between supes and norms when it's needed. The fact that I don't have powers doesn't mean I'm useless."

"I never said you were useless. I'm done with that line of questioning."

He didn't say the words "for now" but they hung in the air between us.

CHAPTER 10

"Kyle McKinley, you are the love of my life."

I rolled my eyes at Misha from across the table. "I think that's a bit of an exaggeration."

His ice blue eyes twinkled at me. "I think not." He picked up his second burrito and took a bite.

Jean Luc chuckled next to me while keeping his eyes on the laptop. He was running a background check on Eli Miller while Misha inhaled his dinner.

"Elijah Miller runs The Dante Club. He has no police record, and the supernatural database shows some minor incidents, but nothing in the past fifty years."

Dalton interrupted him. "You have access to the police database?"

Misha grinned. "We have access to a lot of things."

"So we go in there and, what, confront him?" I asked.

"He'll run scared if we do that." Talia walked out of the kitchenette. "We should go in as prospective clients. We can be the go-between for a demon who wants to cross over."

"A sting." I announced. "I like it. Who's going in?"

Jean Luc answered. "Misha and I can start the conversation with Eli."

The door leading to the reception area opened, and Dolly sauntered in with her coffee mug. She'd changed her clothes from earlier and now wore black spike boots and a polka-dot mini dress, her hair hanging in loose curls now. Hot date, maybe? She dumped the liquid from her mug into the sink and then faced the room. "Your plan isn't going to work."

"How do you even know what we're talking about?" I asked.

Dolly shrugged. "I could say it was my shifter hearing, but I've been listening in on the intercom."

I looked at the phone. The green intercom light blinked back at me. I narrowed my eyes at her.

"Hey, it gets boring up front. A girl's got to do something to keep herself occupied."

"Why isn't the plan going to work?" Dalton asked.

"Because Dante's isn't a bar. It's an exclusive club. Invitation-only for males. But females are free to come and go."

I smirked at Talia. "Looks like we're in for some undercover work, partner."

Dolly snorted. "Not in those skater-boy outfits you wear, McKinley. You need to find a pair of heels and a dress, the shorter the better, before you set foot in the place. Otherwise, you'll stick out like a sore thumb."

Dalton frowned. "We're going to send them in alone?"

"We know how to work under cover." Talia assured him. "We'll be wearing ear pieces and trackers, too."

"So we go in later tonight?" I asked.

Dolly replied. "Nope. It's Monday, and the club is closed."

Misha crumpled his food wrappers. "You sure do know an awful lot about the place, Dolly."

She gave him a sly grin. "I used to spend time there a while back."

"Have you met Eli Miller?" Jean Luc asked.

"Not personally. Eli is quite picky about who he spends time with. But he's partial to humans."

Maybe I was useful after all. I peeked at Dalton out of the corner of my eye, and his scowl told me he wasn't happy with the situation. At all. At least some things hadn't changed. His alpha male was still front and center.

The team spent an hour plotting our next steps. Afterward, since our plan to meet Eli had been waylaid for the moment, I decided to call it a night. I drove home and parked in a spot mercifully close to my apartment building and trudged up the stairs. I stopped at the top of the landing. Griffin was leaning against my door reading something on his phone. *Crap.* I'd forgotten he was coming over tonight. His face lit up, but in a matter of seconds, his expression morphed into a frown.

"What's wrong, Kyle?"

"I'm okay."

He shook his head and took a step toward me. "You're *not* okay."

"Sometimes I wish you could turn that nose off and stop sniffing my emotions." I unlocked my door, and he followed me inside.

"Tell me what's wrong."

"It's Dalton."

"Has he been hurt?"

"No." I took a deep breath. "He's back."

Griffin's eyes widened for a second, but then he quickly schooled his face into a neutral mask. "Does he remember you?"

"No." I sank down onto the couch, since my body had decided it was done standing.

Griffin sat next to me. "Tell me."

"The Feds handle art thefts, so Captain Morrison pulled some strings and asked for Dalton to work the case. He thought it was a great solution for us, since Dalton knows about the supernatural and would help keep it quiet. Of course, the Captain doesn't remember Dalton worked a case with us last year since I made them both forget."

Griffin's eyebrows knitted together. "I'm confused. I thought you changed Dalton's memory. How does he remember about the supernatural?"

"I changed his memory of the case he worked with us. But Dalton knew supernaturals existed before he met me. I couldn't erase all of his long-term memory. There was no way to be sure what Morrison had told him over the years. What cases Dalton covered up while he worked media relations for the police department."

He ducked down so he could get a good look at my face. "How are you holding up with all this?"

I touched my finger to his nose. "You already have the answer, right?"

He gripped my hand, and I let the warmth of his touch soothe me.

"I'm sorry this is hurting you, Kyle."

"*You're* sorry? This has got to be more than awkward for you. *I'm* sorry."

He pulled me against his side, wrapping his arm around my shoulder. "Never apologize for your feelings, Kyle."

"I just...I never got to say goodbye to him, and now he's back but he's a different person."

"I know, my sweet."

I took a deep breath. "But as soon as we solve this case, he'll leave again, and things will go back to normal."

Griffin didn't answer. Instead he kissed my temple and rested his chin on top of my head.

"I didn't sign up for a girls' day," I grumbled from the back seat of Talia's Mustang.

Doc laughed from the front passenger seat. "Humor us, Kyle. You need to get out more."

"I get out plenty."

"Right," Talia answered.

"I don't need you two ganging up on me."

Doc swiveled in the seat and pinned me with a glare. "You need some time away or you're going to drown in self-pity."

"Has anyone ever told you your bedside manner sucks?"

"Yes. But normally it's a patient who's being a baby."

"Touché."

Doc smiled and turned to face the windshield again. "In any case, we need to find you a dress. Do you still have the silver heels I got you?"

"No."

Doc huffed. "Kyle!"

"I lost them when I was being firebombed by demon assassins. So sue me."

Talia turned into a parking lot, and I glanced around. "This isn't the mall."

"Nope," Talia answered. "The mall isn't going to have what we need."

"How do you even know about this place? You've only been living here for a few weeks."

Talia shrugged and opened her door. "A vampire knows how to Google."

I stopped myself from groaning. Could I make a break for it when I got out of the car? Nah. Talia could flash, and she'd be on me in a second. *Damn vampire super speed.*

I climbed out of the car and walked behind Doc and Talia into the exclusive-looking shop. A clerk met us at the door with a gracious smile. "How may I help you?"

Doc smiled right back and gestured toward me and Talia. "Need some party dresses for my friends here. The sexier the better."

The clerk looked at Talia first, and then me. "Let's see what we can do. Follow me."

Talia and Doc high-fived each other, and my stomach sank. I was not looking forward to this *at all*. First, we were herded into an area with chairs and a three-way mirror. The clerk suggested we relax, and then she hustled through the store, pulling dresses and placing them on a small rolling rack.

When she returned, she crooked her finger at Talia. "You first."

Talia followed her to the dressing rooms, and I let out a sigh.

Doc growled. "We're not torturing you."

I shrugged. "Depends on your definition of torture."

Talia tried on three dresses, and every one was amazing on her. But a burlap sack would look good on Talia. With each new dress, Doc circled her like she was prey. Both women were stunningly beautiful. As in ridiculous, super-model beautiful. Doc was blonde and fair, like a Nordic goddess. And Talia's brown skin was flawless, as were her gold-flecked eyes. *I am not feeling insecure...I am not feeling insecure...*

"What do you think, Kyle?" Doc asked, interrupting my fit of self-doubt.

"Any of them work. It's quite sickening." But I said it with a sincere smile.

Talia laughed. "I think I'll hold my decision until we see your dresses."

The clerk motioned for me next, and I followed her like I was being led to the gallows.

Doc sighed. "If you're a good girl, I'll buy you dessert."

I grinned. "Promise?"

I entered the small dressing room. Three dresses hung on hooks. I swallowed hard once I got a good look at them, but then squared my shoulders. If I could face rogue shifters, I could try on some skimpy dresses. I flipped over the price tag on the first dress, a deep purple, and swallowed hard again. *Holy crap!* What were these dresses made out of? Silk? Sewn by fairies?

I stepped into it and checked myself in the mirror before I moved aside the curtain and walked a few paces to the three-way mirror.

Doc's eyes narrowed on me. "Not too bad. What do you think?"

I shrugged. "Okay."

"I was talking to Talia."

Talia stared at me for a moment. "Kyle is not comfortable in it, so we should look at something else."

Doc nodded, and I went back into the dressing room. The second dress never made it out of there. No way was I wearing it anywhere in polite society. I reached for dress three, which was a deep burgundy, and slipped it on. It actually looked pretty damn good in a-way-too-short kind of way. The thin straps showed off my shoulders, and at least my bum was covered this time. But I would have to remember not to reach up for anything, or all my secrets would be exposed.

I opened the curtain, and the saleswoman grinned while she held out a pair of slinky black sandals. I slipped them on and presented myself for Doc and Talia's inspection.

Doc smacked her hands together. "That's the one!"

"It's perfect, Kyle," Talia agreed.

"That it is," Doc agreed. "Talia, you should buy the gold one. Those two dresses will knock 'em dead, if they aren't already."

Talia and I changed while the clerk rang up our purchases. Then we all climbed back into Talia's car.

"Now, on to the beauty shop," Doc announced.

Oh, hell no! "You didn't say anything about a beauty shop."

Doc grinned. "Of course I didn't. You wouldn't have come."

"I'm not going to any beauty shop."

"Did I mention there's an old-fashioned ice cream parlor across the street from it?"

"You have no shame, woman."

Doc laughed. "And you need to sow some oats, Kyle."

"I agree, you need to have some fun," Talia said.

"I don't need to sow any damn oats. What are you two, the supernatural version of Thelma and Louise?"

"Hardly," Talia scoffed. "This car is a classic. No way would I drive it off a cliff."

CHAPTER 11

I stared at my reflection in the office bathroom mirror. It was probably good I'd stuck with the smaller sundae instead of the banana split I really wanted. The burgundy dress fit like a second skin. And the rest of my actual skin wasn't covered up very well. The dress was open to the small of my back, and the skirt hit mid-thigh, exposing my legs to my open-toed sandals. Toes sporting burgundy nail polish to match my dress and the couple of burgundy highlights added to my blonde hair.

I didn't look like me. Or rather, I didn't look like the old me.

Talia stepped out of the bathroom stall where she had changed and straightened her dress. "Are you ready, Kyle?"

"As ready as I'll ever be." I opened the door, and we walked down the short hall into the main office space where Misha and Jean Luc waited for us.

Misha whistled. "You two look amazing."

Jean Luc nodded and reached for Talia, but she shook her head and backed up a step. "Don't want to smell like you, my dear. I'm supposed to be on the prowl for a male, remember?"

Jean Luc growled, and she laughed lightly.

"Where's Dalton?" I asked.

As if in answer to my question, the office door opened and Dalton walked into the room. His eyes tightened on me for a second, and then he looked away. An irrational stab of disappointment surged through me. What had I expected? He wasn't the same person anymore. And I wasn't either. Once this case was resolved, he would return to Chicago, and I would be here with Griffin.

Talia and I drove to the club in her Mustang while the guys followed in the surveillance van.

"Can you hear me, Misha?" I asked, checking our earbuds.

"Loud and clear, little one."

"How about the trackers?" Talia asked.

"Yep. Two little blips are showing on my monitor. But you two are going to behave tonight so we don't have to worry about trackers, right?"

"Absolutely," I answered. "This is a fact-finding mission."

We parked and hustled to the club entrance as fast as our heels could carry us. Springtime in Cleveland meant it was still God-awful cold and wet. And we were outside in sandals and barely-there dresses supplemented with nothing more than short, light wraps. I'd never asked if vamps could feel the cold, but I was going to freeze to death before we got inside. Hypothermia was definitely *not* sexy.

The bouncer looked us over, eyes locked for a long time on Talia—big shock—before nodding for us to enter. We walked into the small alcove and were greeted by a blast of heat and music. We slid off our wraps and handed them to the smiling coat room attendant.

"First time here, ladies?"

"Yes," Talia said.

"Welcome." She looked us over too, and already I felt like a piece of meat. "You should both fit in here quite nicely. In the main salon you'll find a bar. There are several rooms branching off of the main salon, but please don't enter those. They're by invitation only."

We walked into the main room, and it took a few seconds for my eyes to adjust to the low light. The bar was some kind of dark wood with a brass runner around the top. Leather high-back chairs surrounded the bar, and several clusters of sleek tables, chairs, and sofas were scattered throughout the space. It was definitely high-end, but that didn't conceal its true purpose. Especially when the men in the room started to stare. And they weren't subtle about it. And the more overt stares we got, the more I wanted to laugh. Whether human or supe, males had never been a subtle breed.

I followed Talia to the bar, and the bartender appeared as soon as we were seated. "What can I get you ladies?"

"I'll have a chocolate martini." Now, I'd never so much as sniffed a chocolate martini, but it seemed like the right thing to order as part of my undercover persona.

He reached for a glass and then turned to Talia. "I have a special red for you."

I arched my eyebrow at her when he turned away, and she leaned closer and whispered. "Shifter."

Which made perfect sense for a bartender. He would be able to sense what you were right away. My life would be so much easier if I could tell when someone was a supe. A lot of times I could guess, depending on the situation, but at times like this, I was clueless.

The bartender placed the drinks in front of us. My martini had a curl of chocolate on the rim. Talia's glass looked like it held a deep, red wine, but I knew better. I reached for my purse and the bartender shook his head. "Taken care of."

"That was fast."

He skimmed his eyes over both of us. "Not really. You two won't have to worry about paying for a drink tonight."

Jean Luc growled in my earbud. Talia chuckled.

I smiled at the bartender even though what I wanted to do was go home and take a shower. I glanced sideways at Talia and murmured, "Let the games begin."

She chuckled again and spun her chair so she was facing the room. I blew out a breath and did the same.

Thirty minutes later, my wish to take a shower had morphed into visions of being sprayed down by a biohazard team. Talia was handling the attention quite well, and I was faking it as best I could, but my face hurt from all the smiling. I hadn't smiled this much in...well, ever.

When an enormous male, I was guessing demon, came lumbering toward us, my smile faltered slightly. He was bigger than Misha, which was saying something. But while Misha's demeanor was welcoming, this guy's was frosty. With grim lips and a glare that would melt glass, he set off my scary meter.

He stopped in front of me. "Someone would like to meet you."

I widened my eyes. "I think the proper greeting is 'hello.'"

His mouth dropped open slightly, but he recovered his frown and continued. "My boss would like to meet you, follow me."

"And who would that be?"

"Eli Miller. He owns the club." He crossed his arms as if to intimidate me, but I stayed on my barstool.

I smiled sweetly at his bluster. "I'm flattered, but if your boss wants to meet me, then he should introduce himself."

The behemoth gawked at me for a moment—maybe he had never heard the word "no" before—and then he turned away and lumbered back to the corner alcove.

Talia leaned over and muttered, "What are you doing?"

"I'm playing a hunch. If we're setting up a deal with Eli, he wouldn't expect us to be all giggly and gushing, would he?"

"I hope you're right, McKinley." Dalton's voice sounded in my ear, and I closed my eyes for a second, breathing carefully.

"Can you see what he's doing?" I asked Talia.

"He's talking to a man in the back corner booth and gesturing toward us."

"Does Eli look pissed?"

Talia picked up her drink and casually glanced back. "He's frowning."

Crap. Please let me be right. I set my martini glass down and smiled at no one in particular. The *Jeopardy* theme song played in my brain, counting down the minutes. I hated the *Jeopardy* theme song. When the buzzer sounded, would it mean I'd blown it?

Hmm hmm hmm hmm—hmm hmm hmmmmmm. Hmm hmm hmm hmm, HMMM, hm hm hm hm hm...

"Eli's walking this way," Talia whispered.

"I'd like to bet it all, Alex," I mumbled.

Talia stared at me like I had two heads.

I watched him approach. It was a bar after all, and I wasn't playing the shy debutante. He was around six feet tall, stocky, and his black hair was slicked down with too much product. Maybe he and his bouncer worked out together. Hell. His bouncer could probably bench press a Mack truck.

When he finally stopped in front of me, the other men who'd been circling us seemed to slink away at the same time. *Interesting.* Definitely the alpha in the room, even if he wasn't a shifter.

He showed his teeth and ran his eyes over me. "I understand from Johnny that you weren't inclined to join me without an introduction."

"He's correct."

"What about now?"

I shrugged. "Still waiting for the intro."

He barked out a laugh. "I'm Eli."

"Hello, Eli. I'm Carly. And this is Shauna."

He dipped his chin in Talia's direction as a greeting. "You two friends?"

"Yes. We do *everything* together," I said.

Eli's eyes flared for a moment, and then he grinned. "Good to know."

Eli Miller was a slimy, slimy demon. Why was I not surprised?

"Will you both join me?" He held out his hand to me, and I took it.

Talia joined us, and we wound our way through the people until we were in the back alcove. He gestured to the corner table with burgundy leather, and Talia and I slid into the booth. Which wasn't easy in extremely short dresses. At least for me. As usual, Talia handled it with aplomb. Of course a waitress appeared as soon as we were seated.

"Would you like something to drink?" Eli asked.

"I'll have a white wine," I answered.

"I've got a special supply of AB neg you might like, Shauna."

"That sounds great," Talia said.

The waitress hustled away, and Eli settled back into the booth. "I haven't seen you in here before. Are you two new to the area?"

"I've lived here for a while. Shauna moved here a couple of weeks ago. I'm introducing her to everything Northeast Ohio has to offer."

"And what made you decide to visit us?"

"We heard it's a great place through the grapevine." I stopped talking while the waitress placed our drinks on the table. I picked up the wine and took a sip before continuing. "We also were hoping to discuss a little business venture with you."

Eli's eyes tightened on my face. "I don't deal in drugs or prostitution in my club."

"McKinley," Dalton growled in my ear piece, but I ignored him.

I shook my head. "Not even close to what I'm talking about."

"What type of venture?"

"We hear you also deal in transportation."

Eli sat up straight, and his guard took a step closer to the table. "Who told you that?"

I hesitated, and he grabbed my arm and squeezed. I managed not to gasp, but Talia flashed her fangs and hissed.

"Is she your bodyguard, too?" Eli asked.

I pulled my arm from his grasp and didn't rub it. No way would I show him any weakness. "It pays to have your friends close."

Eli looked pointedly at his bodyguard. "I couldn't agree more. Who told you about me?"

"Charles Jenkins." I held my breath waiting for his reaction.

After a moment he seemed to relax.

"What type of transportation are you looking for?"

"I have a friend who needs to travel to the demon realm."

He nodded. "I'm only the front man for these deals. I do the negotiations. Which start at 100K."

I didn't blink at his number. "We have the funds."

"When does your friend need to cross over?"

"As soon as possible."

Eli frowned. "It takes time to set these things up. We don't want the border patrol to get a whiff of it."

"We're not looking for trouble with them, either. Our business is urgent."

"Let me see what I can do for you. But a rush job costs more."

"Fine." I pulled out a fake business card. "Contact me when you have an idea of when this will be a go."

I started to slide out of the booth, but he laid his hand over mine. "How about you stick around for a while?" He rubbed his thumb over the back of my hand, and I bit my lip to stop it from curling up in disgust.

I smiled. "My rule is business before pleasure. If you're able to pull this off for me, then I'll pay you another visit with pleasure in mind."

I finished sliding out of the booth, praying my butt wouldn't stick to the leather. Because that wouldn't be sexy, and I was trying my damndest to be confident and sexy.

Talia and I collected our wraps from the coat room, the bouncer at the door smiled at us, and we smiled right back as we stepped out onto the street.

Talia grabbed my hand and I jumped. "Slow down, Kyle. Don't blow it now."

I glanced back at the bouncer who looked at our joined hands and then at our butts. When he looked up at me, I winked at him, and he chuckled. I was so pulling off the sultry right now.

"Meet us at the office," Dalton barked in my earbud.

My sultry deflated like a day-old balloon.

Chapter 12

"I'm confused, McKinley." Dalton paced back and forth in front of the whiteboard like an irate schoolteacher.

"Confused about what?"

"Do you not understand what a fact-finding mission is?"

"Of course I do. And we found out a lot of facts on our mission."

"We talked about this before you went under cover. You were to casually ask around, not set up a meeting with Eli."

"How exactly was I supposed to find out if Eli was dealing in crossovers if I didn't set up a deal with him? He wasn't going to blurt it out during polite conversation."

"She's right," Talia chimed in.

My eyes widened. I was so used to fighting the overbearing sea of testosterone that it was a nice change of pace when someone agreed with me. Apparently having another X chromosome handy was a good thing.

I reached down and pulled off my sandals. "If I'm stuck torturing myself in four-inch heels, I'm going to find out the truth and fast."

Misha chortled. "You both did a good job."

Jean Luc nodded, and I pointed at him while I glared at Dalton. "Even he thinks we did a good job, and he's ridiculously overprotective of Talia."

Jean Luc's gaze narrowed on me. "You and Talia will not be going to the next meeting alone."

"We won't need to. Now that Eli knows we need to send a demon over, we can bring Misha into the picture."

Talia sat at the table and pulled off her own heels. "They're going to probably want a down payment to prove we have the cash."

"No problem," Misha said.

Dalton's eyebrows climbed. "You've got that kind of cash available?"

I gestured at the lime green sofa. "I know the seventies décor here screams cheap, but we're not a nickel-and-dime operation."

"I knew that when I saw the surveillance equipment you use," Dalton fired back.

I opened my mouth for a retort and then stopped. *What was the point?* Being snarky with him didn't help, and I was committed to being the new and improved Kyle. He wasn't the same Dalton, either, and he sure didn't need to deal with my baggage. Hell, he didn't even remember I *had* baggage—namely him.

I got up, holding my heels dangling by their straps. "I'm going to go change out of this getup, and then we can discuss next steps."

My phone beeped as I walked down the hall, and I pulled it out. Misha had hooked up the number I gave Eli to ring on my phone, but I doubted Eli would be calling so soon. It was Griffin.

I answered the phone. "Hey."

"Hi. Just checking on you."

"I'm fine. We've finished the operation for tonight, so you can quit worrying."

"Yes, ma'am. How did it go?"

I sat at my desk and swung side to side in my chair. "Good. We were able to set up a meet with Eli. Hopefully we can get a better handle on how this crossover process works."

"And Dalton?"

"If he helps us solve the case, then I can live with it for now."

Griffin paused for so long I thought I'd lost the connection. "Are you still there?"

"Promise me you won't do anything...ill advised, Kyle."

I wasn't sure if he was referring to the case or something else, but I didn't want to dwell on it. "I promise. I've got to go meet with the team to do some planning."

"Okay, my sweet. I'll talk to you tomorrow."

I turned back to face my desk and jumped, dropping my phone. Dalton was leaning on my office doorjamb.

"Who were you talking to?"

He was eavesdropping on my conversation and had the nerve to speak to me in that tone? The new and improved Kyle McKinley had left the building. "None of your damn business."

He took a step into my office. "It is my business if you compromise the case. Do I need to explain again that I'm in charge of this case?"

I jumped to my feet. "I've been working these types of cases for ten years. I'm not a novice."

"Well, telling someone outside the team about our operation is a novice move."

"He's my..." *Partner? Boyfriend? Lover?* "...boyfriend, and he worries about me."

"Is he human?" His gaze tightened on me.

"What does it matter?" I glared at him.

"It matters, because another supernatural will keep the secret, right?"

"I keep the secret. You and Captain Morrison don't go around plastering it on billboards, either. And we're all human."

"I would still appreciate it if you didn't tell him about the specific details of the case."

"Give me a break. You never told Lauren about your cases?"

Oh, shit.

His jaw tightened. "How do you know about Lauren? We haven't been together for years."

How the hell did I know about his ex?

He practically shook with anger, or was it indignation? "Did you do a background check on me?"

"Umm. Yes. We needed to know who you were. You aren't the only one worried about exposure. Don't tell me you didn't drill Morrison about all of us before you took on this case. Hell, you watched us in the interrogation room at the police station like animals in a zoo."

His eyes widened slightly. Apparently I had hit the bullseye. He backed out of my office. "Get changed and come up front. Let's get this over with."

I shut my door and leaned against it, my heart beating a staccato rhythm as I tried not to cry.

By all means, let's get this over with.

Forty-five minutes later, we finished the team meeting and Dalton left. When the door shut behind him, I slumped and scrubbed my hands over my face.

"You okay, little one?" Misha watched me warily.

"He's..."

"Demanding?" Talia supplied.

"That's an understatement. He was cautious before, but now he's driven by regulations."

"You're not the only one with demons, Kyle." Misha laughed at his own joke. "You know what I mean."

Jean Luc sat next to me at the table. "Do you remember two years ago, when your car skidded on black ice and ended up in the guardrail?"

"Of course. But I'm not sure what it has to do with anything."

"After the accident, you drove under the speed limit for months."

I sat up straighter. "It was cold and icy, and I didn't want to end up in another guardrail."

Jean Luc smiled. "Exactly. You were overly cautious and followed the rules. Misha is right. Joe almost died, and he is still recuperating. Still facing his demons."

I dumped my dress and shoes on my couch, fully intending to consume the entire quart of mocha swirl I kept in the freezer for emergencies. Today had been a mocha swirl kind of day.

While I stared into my empty freezer, I bit my lip to keep from bursting into tears. Son of a pup. When had I eaten the emergency quart? And why the h, e, double-hockey-sticks hadn't I restocked it? Before I could launch into even more colorful expletives, someone knocked.

I peered through the peephole and did a brief happy dance before opening the door with a straight face. "Hey, Tony. What brings you here tonight?"

Tony was about my height and twenty years my senior. He owned one of the best Italian restaurants in Little Italy and was part empathic demon, which he used to select perfect dishes for his customers. I had become his pet project, and he brought food to me, or sent his son with it, when I was upset.

"Kyle. I have a delivery here for you." He held up a white paper bag, and I gave him a quick one-armed hug.

"What do you have for me tonight?"

"Some biscotti and a pint of spumoni."

"I could kiss you on your empathic lips, Tony."

He chuckled. "I am old enough to be your father, and I don't think my Anna would approve of you kissing me."

"I know. Thanks so much. As usual, you showed up with exactly what I need."

Tony gazed at me for a moment before nodding. "Do you also need a friendly ear?"

I gave him another quick hug. "I'm good, Tony."

He raised one eyebrow at me, and I sighed. "Fine. I'm not good. But I'll be okay. Honest. You better get back to the restaurant before Anna sends out reinforcements." I hugged my bag of spumoni and biscotti. "Thanks for watching out for me. I'll come see you if I need to talk."

Tony left grudgingly, and I pulled the lid off the spumoni and set it on the counter. Then I shook my head. Who was I kidding? I picked up the lid and flipped it into the trash. There would be no leftovers.

Back in the living room, I plopped into my comfy chair. Even though I didn't want to talk to anyone, there was one person who deserved to know Dalton's whereabouts.

"Marie!"

I waited for a second but still got nothing. I scooped up a large spoonful and moaned as the icy goodness exploded in my mouth. Then I took another bite and closed my eyes in bliss.

"Should I leave you alone with your ice cream, Kyle? It looks like you two are having a moment."

I opened my eyes. Marie stood across the room, watching me with a smirk.

"You're not funny."

She floated over in front of me. "I am funny. Isn't this how our conversation started the other day?"

"Not exactly." I set the ice cream container on the coffee table. "Dalton is back."

Her grin faded. "What?"

"Joe is here, Marie."

Her face paled. Which was pretty scary, since she was a ghost and melanin was no longer her friend. "I just checked on him a couple of days ago, and he was working a case in Chicago."

My stomach dropped. "Did you talk to him?"

"Of course not. I watch over him. He doesn't know I'm there."

"Well, he's working a case here now. With me."

Marie reached her hand out and then dropped it, as if remembering she couldn't touch me. "Oh, Kyle. Are you okay?"

"I've been better."

"He doesn't remember you?"

I set down the ice cream, no longer hungry. "No."

"Do you think he will?"

"I don't know for sure, but I have to try to avoid it."

Marie frowned. "Maybe you should try to make him remember."

"He almost went insane from the memories of his torture, Marie. I can't risk it. He's moved on with his life."

Marie huffed. "If you consider working all the time and spending the rest of his time alone as moving on with your life."

"What?" I sat up from my slouched position on the couch. "Why the hell didn't you tell me?"

Marie sighed and floated back and forth in front of me as if she was pacing. "When should I have done that Kyle? When you ran away to Nevada and wouldn't talk to me? Or when you were lying to everyone about the Key possessing you? Or when you moved on and seemed to be happy?

"And now, finally, you've let people get close to you again. You're starting to act human again. I couldn't tell you about Joe. What could you have done, anyway?"

"I don't know. This is such a mess, Marie. He's cold now. He has no spark in his beautiful eyes. I took the spark from his eyes."

"You saved him."

I walked over and stared out the windows at the wet street below. "You know everyone keeps telling me that, but if he's unable to live his life, then what's the point of saving him?"

"My grandson may be a little lost right now, but he won't be defeated by this. He'll bounce back. Just like you did."

I laughed harshly. "God help him if you're using me as a gauge for bouncing back."

CHAPTER 13

Morning already, and I needed coffee with a capital "C." I poured some java into a traveler's mug and flinched when my cell rang.

"Hey, Mish, what's up?"

"Cynthia Hamilton called. She wants us to come to the museum."

"How far away are you?"

"About ten minutes."

"Okay. I'll meet you there." I pulled on my coat and stuffed my phone and wallet into the pockets before grabbing my aluminum mug and loping down the stairs.

Even though it was damp, the smell of fresh baked goods filled the air. I loved living in Little Italy for many reasons, but the food was definitely at the top of the list.

I made a quick detour into the bakery and ordered a dozen fry cakes for Misha. Then I climbed into my car and drove to the art museum. Even with the bakery run, I still beat Misha.

The museum hadn't reopened yet, but there was a great deal of activity all along the route one of the security guards used to escort me to Cynthia's office. Today, she seemed much more put together than the last time I saw her. Her hair was pulled into a tight bun, and she had on a steel gray business suit.

She nodded to one of the guest chairs. "Where's your teammate?"

I sat down. "He should be here any minute. There's a lot going on in here today."

"We're set to reopen tomorrow, and we need to make sure everything is ready to go."

Cynthia looked past my shoulder just as the swish of the office door alerted me that someone else had come in.

"Sorry to keep you waiting," Misha said.

"And who's this?" Cynthia asked.

I turned in my seat at the question and stifled the urge to grumble.

"I'm Special Agent Dalton with the FBI."

"Captain Morrison told me an agent had been assigned to the case," Cynthia responded.

Dalton nodded. "I apologize for the delay in contacting you. I've been working the case for two days and had planned to come and speak with you today, so when Misha got your call, I decided to tag along."

"No problem. Take a seat, gentlemen."

Misha pulled over one of the chairs from the large conference table across from Cynthia's desk. Dalton sat next to me in the other guest chair.

"I assume you must have found something, or you wouldn't have called us in today," I blurted, my curiosity getting the better of me.

Cynthia grinned at my enthusiasm. "I followed your hunch, Ms. McKinley, and we examined the items we'd not yet unpacked for the special exhibit. I almost didn't catch the missing items, since we'd decided not to use these particular pieces in the exhibit after all."

"What are they?" Dalton asked.

"We believe they're religious artifacts. But we couldn't authenticate them as being Mayan, so they weren't going to be used."

"Can you describe them?" I asked.

"I can do better than that." She opened a folder. "When we receive artifacts on loan, we photograph them for insurance purposes. We're missing two pieces."

Cynthia pulled a photo out and placed it on the desk for us to examine. I leaned forward to study it. It was a stone tablet that appeared to be quite ancient. There was some sort of print on it, but the wording was too obscured to read what it said. As I stared at it, the base of my brain buzzed as if waking up from a deep sleep. I resisted the urge to rub the back of my neck.

Dalton leaned forward as well. "Do you know what it says?"

"No. It's in a dialect we haven't been able to translate. It was found in a Mayan ruin, but it's unlike any Mayan artifact excavated in the past."

The buzzing grew louder, like a swarm of bees in my brain, and I glanced over to see if anyone else could hear it. Misha's eyebrow rose at my look, but I shook my head slightly to stop his questions.

Misha picked up the photo. "Why would someone want to steal this?"

Cynthia shrugged. "I'm baffled. With all of the priceless pieces that could have been stolen, I'm amazed they chose this tablet."

"What about the other item?" Dalton asked.

Cynthia pulled out a second photo from the folder, and I flinched before I could stop myself. *Holy shit.*

I exchanged a startled glance with Misha.

"What is it?" Dalton asked Cynthia while Misha and I sat there mute.

"We believe it was used to ward off evil. A talisman. We haven't been able to interpret the symbols on the box yet. But neither of these pieces are worth breaking into the museum for."

I bit my lip to keep from exclaiming how wrong she was. There was every reason to take this piece. Even though my brain insisted it was impossible for the museum to have it. Because it looked exactly like the box Jean Luc kept locked in our office safe. The box that had held the Key of Knowledge.

Several minutes later, I mumbled goodbye to Cynthia and rushed out of the museum, not waiting for Misha and Dalton to finish their conversation. I stumbled toward the parking lot, but when I looked at my shaking hands, I knew I wouldn't be able to drive for a while. Instead, I went to the other side of the museum to look out over the lagoon. A body of water I was becoming way too familiar with.

What the hell was I going to do? How could there be another box? And what was I going to tell Dalton? All the things I was trying to protect him from kept raising their ugly heads and threatening to attack.

"What was that?"

I spun. Dalton frowned at me from the sidewalk. Had he smiled even once since he'd been back? I stared at him.

"I saw the way you reacted to the box. Have you seen it before?"

Misha walked up and stood beside me, as if to lend support.

I closed my eyes for a moment. How much of the truth could I afford to tell him?

"Well?" he pushed.

"We'll meet you back at the office," Misha growled.

Dalton opened his mouth, and Misha got right up into his face. "This is not the place to talk about it." He pulled out the keys to the van and held them up.

Dalton glared at Misha, grabbed the keys, and then took a step back. "Fine. I'll meet you at the office. Collect yourself, McKinley, and then I want to hear the truth." He strode away.

Misha pulled me into his embrace. "Are you okay?"

"Yeah. But the sucker-punches just keep on coming. What the hell?"

"I know, little one. What are we going to tell him?"

I leaned away from him and looked up into his eyes. "As much of the truth as we can. We tell him about the Key, and the fight for it, but we sure as hell don't tell him it's possessed him or me."

"Do you think it's safe to tell him even that much?"

"He didn't react to the picture, Mish. No recognition at all. If he was going to remember, don't you think the Key receptacle would have forced the memories to surface? I have no idea what we can risk at this point, but if this is about the Key, then all hell's going to break loose. We tell him what we can to appease him, and then we pray that we get a call from Eli very soon so we can locate this demon. Then we send Dalton back to Chicago where he'll be safe."

And then, maybe I'd be safe.

CHAPTER 14

I gazed absently at Dolly as I followed Misha into the reception area.

On the ride back, Misha called Jean Luc and Talia and filled them in. I'd never heard Jean Luc swear profusely in French before. It sounded much prettier than those same words in English, which had been going off like fireworks in my mind ever since Cynthia Hamilton pulled out the second photo.

Misha was so upset he didn't eat any of the pastries. Dolly's and my eyes widened simultaneously at each other when he placed the unopened box on the reception desk.

"I'll be out for some later."

At least it sounded like Misha planned to recover from his anxiety fairly soon. I couldn't say the same about me. I reached for the doorknob to the office and hesitated. I prayed that what we were about to tell Dalton wouldn't trigger his memory. But I had to tell him something. Misha patted my back and then reached around me to open the door.

Inside an antsy FBI agent and two grim vampires waited for us. I walked into the kitchenette, poured a cup of coffee, and went over to sit at the table.

"Are you going to tell me what's going on?" Dalton demanded.

I wrapped my fingers around the mug, the warmth grounding me. "Yes. But you have to sit down and stop pacing."

His eyebrows hiked up. Maybe he was surprised that I wasn't going to fight him, or maybe he didn't like someone telling him what to do. Either way, I couldn't handle his agitation. He sat down across from me. And I looked into his turquoise eyes.

"The reason I was so shocked today when I saw the picture of the box is because we've seen it before."

"Where?"

"It turned up during a case last year, and the museum director is right. It's a talisman to ward off evil."

"And you think it's the same box?"

"No. It can't be." I nodded to Jean Luc, and he walked over to the wall safe and opened it, pulling out the box.

Dalton's eyes sharpened on the box for a few moments, and then his gaze homed in on me.

"*This* is the box from last year's case," I said.

"What does it do?" he asked.

Now things were going to get tricky. How much did I tell him? "It protects some sort of artifact that supes have been fighting over. Whoever controls it supposedly tips power in their favor."

"What type of power?"

"*The* power, as in the power of good and evil."

He frowned. "And we're sure this thing is legitimate?"

"Well, considering the fact that angels got involved last year, I would say it's pretty serious."

Dalton jerked up straighter. "Angels are real?"

"You have no problem believing in demons and vampires, but you struggle with angels?" I asked.

"Captain Morrison never talked to me about angels, and I haven't had to cover up for them in past cases."

"Normally, angels stay out of the limelight. When they do get involved, that means it's pretty damn serious."

"And all because of this artifact this box protects?"

"Yes."

Dalton held his hand out to Jean Luc. "May I see it?"

Jean Luc hesitated, but after a few moments, he placed the box in Dalton's hand. I don't know what I expected, but the box didn't change in any way, and Dalton didn't stand up and scream, "I remember!" So I let out the breath I'd been holding and took a sip of my coffee.

"Do you think the demon stole the other box to try and figure out where this artifact is?"

"That seems to make the most sense," I responded.

"And the tablet?"

Jean Luc spoke up. "It could be a description of the artifact. It may be connected to the boxes."

"Does this artifact have a name?"

I swallowed hard before answering. "The Key of Knowledge."

"And you never found this Key?"

I stared at him, praying my face showed no emotion. "No."

Dalton turned the box over. "Sounds pretty cryptic to me. *Looks* pretty cryptic, too."

"Last year, we almost had a supernatural war over it, so it's very real." I picked up the photos from the table. "We need to find these artifacts and get them back."

"When I was saying goodbye to Director Hamilton," Misha added, "I asked her to send the .jpeg files to me so I can blow them up and we can get a closer, more detailed look."

"When—"

Misha interrupted me. "You'd run out of her office by then."

Dalton set the box on the table. "You're pretty easy to read, McKinley. You might want to practice your poker face a little bit more."

I bit back my retort and looked down at the box sitting on the table. If that were the case, the ugly truth would already be out there for all to see.

Now that I was sure the Key was part of this case, I had a few missions to accomplish. First, I drove to John Carroll University. We needed more information about the Key, and Father Brown was my best source. I dialed Father Brown's office and was told he was hearing confessions at Gesu Church. Somehow I always ended up meeting the good Father in the confessional. The irony was not lost on me.

I sat in the back pew of the church, waiting for the confessional door to open. After a few minutes, an elderly lady came out of the room and bobbed her head at me before she knelt in the pew across the aisle and began to pray.

I slipped into the confessional and closed the door. The room still looked the same. Two chairs and a small table with a Bible were all that could fit in the tiny space. Father Brown stood up as soon as he saw me, tall and lean and reminding me of Jimmy Stewart. Not the frazzled Jimmy Steward in *Rear Window*, but the Jimmy Stewart at the end of *It's a Wonderful Life*, when he got his family back.

"Hi, Father."

"Kyle! It's been a while."

"Did you have a good sabbatical?"

He gestured to the chair on the other side of the table. "I did. I arrived back last night, in fact. But somehow I don't think you're here to talk about my trip to Greece. What's wrong?"

I pulled out the photo of the box from the museum and handed it to him.

He nodded. "You showed me this picture last year."

I shook my head. "This isn't the same box."

His eyes narrowed on the picture. "Do you have the other picture from last year so I can compare them?"

I pulled the small box from my pocket. "I thought it might help if you could compare it to the real deal."

His eyes widened as he held out his hand, which was shaking slightly. I set the box on his open palm, and he ran his fingers over the carvings reverently. I didn't say anything while he examined it. After a few moments, he seemed to come out of his musings and set it on the table by the picture. "You're right, the carvings are similar, but not exactly the same."

"Can you interpret it?"

"Most are wards against evil."

"Why do you think there's another box, Father? Is it some sort of backup?"

Father Brown stared at the picture again. "I don't know. Do you think the Key moves from box to box?"

"Maybe there are extra boxes, so if the person who's absorbed the Key is killed, it goes into one of these receptacles and the next Key is chosen?"

"Possibly." Father frowned. "But if that were the case, and if it held the same Key each time, wouldn't the wards look the same?"

I rubbed my hand over my face. "Do you think there could be more than one Key of Knowledge?"

His eyebrows drew together. "The prophecy reads as if there is only one path for Knowledge."

"So then what's the other box for?"

Father locked his gaze on me. "Maybe there are other types of Keys?"

"Holy crap." I cringed. "Sorry, Father."

He smiled. "No apologies necessary. What I just said was a 'holy crap' in the making."

"Have you been able to interpret any more of the prophecy?"

Father Brown pulled out the small book of scriptures he always carried. He extracted a folded paper from the book and opened it, flattening it on the small table next to me. The folds in the paper were worn, as if he opened it constantly. Maybe he did.

At the top of the sheet the prophecy was written in a language no one except Father Brown had been able to interpret. At the bottom of the page was what he had translated so far. I gazed up at him, and he began reciting it without looking at the paper.

"'Evil thrives among us
Angels descend, preparing for battle,
Key of Knowledge in hand
With it the tides turn
And light will triumph.
"'The war will be long
And fraught with treachery
Lives will be lost
And the Key will change hands
Only the true keeper will
Save us from annihilation.'"

"You memorized it?" I asked.

"I had to memorize the mass in Latin, Kyle. Learning two stanzas of the prophecy wasn't difficult."

"What about the third stanza?"

"Nothing yet. Now that I'm home, maybe more will come to me."

I held the tattered page and stared at it until the characters blurred. I had hoped maybe the Key would clue me into something—anything—that might help us. But as usual, when I needed the rolodex to start spinning in my brain, it was quiet.

"I can't read it either."

He blinked at me. "Why would you be able to read it?"

"I...ah..."

"Kyle. What haven't you told me?" And he gave me The Priest Stare, the one that made most people fall all over themselves to confess each and every one of their sins. Good thing I hadn't been raised Catholic.

I sighed at my slip-up. Father Brown knew the Key had possessed Dalton, but I'd never told him it had transferred to me. He took the paper from me and grasped my hands.

Looking up into his Jimmy Stewart-esque face, I blurted, "I have the Key in me now." So much for not crumbling under The Stare. Maybe I could blame the ambiance. I was in a confessional, after all.

He jerked back as if I'd smacked him. "You have the Key in you? How does it feel?"

I shrugged. "I don't feel much different, if that's what you mean. Except when my brain goes haywire when the Key tries to tell me something."

"And what does it tell you?"

"Not much, really. I see names periodically, and I can read Latin now."

"And how are you faring with this additional responsibility?"

Leave it to him to go right for the hard questions. "I'm okay with it. I just wish I understood what it was trying to tell me. I don't seem to be hardwired to receive the messages the right way."

To stop him from asking any more questions about how I was doing, I pulled the second photo from the envelope I'd brought with me and handed it to him. Misha had blown the picture up so the writing was easier to see. Jean Luc had said the writing was in the same language as the original prophecy, so I wasn't surprised when Father looked at it and gasped.

"Is it the prophecy?" I asked.

"The beginning looks the same, but there are some different symbols here. This may help me finish translating the prophecy."

"Sorry to throw more work at you."

"Don't be ridiculous, Kyle. I'm happy to help. May I keep this photo?"

"Yes. And Father, remember, you can't tell *anyone* about this. You aren't supposed to remember anything."

"Absolutely. I'll call when I have more translated for you."

I thanked him, picked up the box, and left the confessional. The old woman from before was still praying, and when I didn't kneel, she pursed her lips at me.

I'm not sure if she thought I was shirking my penance duties or if she was jealous because I didn't have to say a gazillion Hail Marys. Either way, I didn't feel any lighter as I left the church and headed out into the rain.

CHAPTER 15

My next mission was to check on Doc at the lab. She'd been spending a lot more time there lately. Sabrina had always been dedicated—she was a doctor, after all—but now she was bordering on obsessed. Was it because Jason had shut her out?

She'd scolded me plenty of times about not drowning in self-pity. Maybe I needed to give her the same speech. I found her in the lab scrubbing the exam tables.

"What are you doing, Sabrina?"

She stopped. "Isn't it obvious? Is something wrong?"

"No, I'm avoiding the office. Now don't you avoid my question."

She started cleaning again. "I answered your question."

"So we're going to be literal girl today, huh? Fine. We can play it your way. Why are you spending so much time at work?"

"I'm not spending too much time at work."

"Call him." I held up my hand when she opened her mouth. "Before you pretend to be obtuse, I'm referring to Jason. Call him."

"Obtuse? Is that your word for the day?"

"Maybe. Is yours *bitchy*?"

Her mouth tightened. "He doesn't want to talk to me."

"It's been long enough, Sabrina. Call him and don't take no for an answer. You didn't even know about his shifter side. He can't blame you for keeping secrets. And he needs someone in his corner."

"I've tried to get him to talk to me, but he won't listen."

"Then make him listen. With all due respect, you're older than the hills. I think you can get a thirty-something male to listen to you."

Sabrina's mouth quirked. "I am older than Methuselah. I can try again."

"That's the spirit."

"And what about you?" Sabrina asked, wiping the table again.

"What about me?"

"Please don't make me use your word of the day. How are you doing?"

I decided to go with the truth. "Dalton's a control freak, and I'm having a hard time coming to grips with pretty much everything right now."

"How's Griffin doing with all of this?"

"He's being very supportive."

"That's a good thing, right?"

"Of course."

Sabrina stopped cleaning and leaned her hip against the table. "But?"

"But everything feels wrong right now. And he can tell because of his damn shifter senses. It isn't him. It's me. And I know it sounds lame coming out of my mouth, but it's true."

"Not to repeat the advice you gave me, but you should talk to Griffin about it."

"What do I tell him? My previous boyfriend is back in my life and I'm mourning what could have been. That's not fair to him."

"Griffin is a big boy. He'll tell you what's fair and not fair. Don't shut down again, Kyle."

"I'm not going to shut down again. Wasn't I just warm and fuzzy with you?"

"You called me bitchy."

"That's what tough love is all about."

She glared at me.

"Fine. I'll talk to him if you get the hell out of here and find Jason."

Doc peeled off her gloves and threw them in the biohazard bin. "Deal."

"I'd shake on it, but first you have to wash up."

I was going to be an adult. I'd left the office earlier so I wouldn't skewer Dalton, but now I was in a better frame of mind. I decided to go back, and if he was still there, I wouldn't let my emotions get the better of me. While I was being an adult, I called Griffin to talk, but got his voicemail, so I left him a message that I wanted to see him. One item crossed off on my adult check list.

My *I-can-handle-this-mantra* repeating resoundingly in my head, I took a deep breath and walked into the office with a confident bounce to my step.

Misha and Jean Luc were sitting at the table, and Talia was busy in the kitchenette. All three studied me, concern etched across their faces.

"Is Dalton here?"

"No, *ma petite*, he left right after you did."

I let out my breath in relief. Maybe I wasn't as confident as I thought.

Talia set two mugs on the table for me and Misha. "Coffee for you two. French roast."

I looked at Misha, who in turn looked at the mugs like they were going to explode. We had been down the coffee-as sludge road with Jean Luc many times before.

When she saw our hesitation, Talia laughed. "No worries, unlike Jean Luc, I make good coffee."

"*Excusez-moi*? I know how to make coffee."

Talia wrinkled her nose. "Your coffee smells like something that could raise the dead, Jean Luc. I can't even imagine what it tastes like."

Jean Luc sputtered in an adorable French kind of way. "I do not make bad coffee. I have never had any complaints." He glared at Misha, who suddenly became very engrossed in his computer. Then Jean Luc's gaze swung to me.

"Ah. Well...your coffee is a little strong."

Misha snickered.

I glared at him. "Help me out here, you chicken-shit demon."

"I'm sorry, my friend, but your coffee is abominable."

I nodded my agreement.

"*Mon Dieu!* Why have you not said anything before?"

Talia walked over to Jean Luc and ran a soothing hand down his arm. "Because they love you and didn't want to hurt your feelings."

He narrowed his eyes at her. "And yet you have been on the team for two weeks and felt the need to announce it?"

"I would have done it sooner, but it took me a while to figure out." Talia turned to me as if to change the subject before Jean Luc could sputter again. "How are you doing with everything, Kyle?"

"I'm okay. This Key business has me a bit freaked out. I'm worried it might trigger Dalton's memories."

"We cannot hide everything from him," Jean Luc replied. "Maybe he is here for a reason, like Running Wolf said."

"Running Wolf?" Talia asked.

Jean Luc squeezed my shoulder and then sat next to Talia.

I bit my lip and heard Doc's voice in my head telling me to get on with it. "When I realized I had absorbed the Key," I told Talia, "it directed me to a man named Running Wolf, who is kind of a spiritual welcome wagon. He told me the names the Key shares with me are people who have done or will do something important. The problem is, I have no clue what to do with the names once I receive them.

"But the real kicker was when he told me I wasn't the one he had been expecting. He had been given visions of a man with turquoise eyes."

"Dalton," Talia whispered.

"Right. Even though my brain has all the info from the Key, I apparently don't have the actual power, which is probably why I short-circuit when it tries to tell me something. We don't know if the power's been lost, or if Dalton still has it locked inside him."

Talia grimaced. "God, this is..."

"A disaster in the making?" I supplied.

Misha came around the table and hugged me to him. "You can't think that way, little one. We'll figure this out. You're not alone."

"I know, big guy. It helps to have you three here backing me up." I pointed to the table and the running laptops. "Have we learned anything new about the case?"

Misha sat again and started typing. "My father said the elders of our clan might have some information for us about the demon clans who don't live on earth."

"Oh, good," I said.

"Yes. They've asked to meet with me tomorrow."

"Do you mind if I tag along?" I asked.

"Let me call my father to see if we can all be part of the meeting."

"You mean we finally might get to meet your elders?"

"You are an official part of the clan now, Kyle."

"True, but I didn't think it meant I get to ride on the rollercoaster. I thought I was still relegated to the kiddy rides."

Misha chuckled. "Father has been asking to see you."

I grinned. "Who would have guessed that Boris would actually come to like me?"

"You grew on him."

"You make it sound like I'm fungus."

Misha's chuckle blossomed into a full belly laugh.

CHAPTER 16

All this talk of Running Wolf and the names the Key teased me with reminded me about the most recent name the Key had given me—Marlene Thompson. She had to be connected with the case. Maybe if I concentrated on her name, I would be able to see her face, or flash on something else about her.

It was worth a try, and Jean Luc, who closed my office door behind us with a definite *click*, was here to help with the experiment.

He reached for my hands. "Are you ready to try, *ma petite?*"

I grasped his strong fingers, closed my eyes, and took a deep breath. I tried to clear my mind of the museum, and the realm, and demon crossovers, and Dalton. Dalton who'd come back as a different person.

Focus!

Deep breaths again, and I concentrated on one thing: Marlene Thompson. I pictured the name and let it float around inside my skull. Jean Luc's hands grounded me, and the warmth of his thrall inched up my arms.

Come on...show me something. Muted light flittered in my brain, and blurry images appeared like old-timey movie newsreels. But the reel picked up speed and slammed my cerebellum with too many images to process. My head snapped back.

My chair was wrenched to the side, and someone grabbed me.

"Kyle!"

I opened my eyes and looked up into Jean Luc's worried face. He stood in front of me, hands cupping my cheeks.

"Are you okay?"

"Yeah." I blinked a couple of times. "I was close, but the Key tried to tell me too much, too fast. I can't interpret it."

He nodded. "We will figure it out, Kyle. It is only a matter of time."

Except, now that the realm demons were after the Key, I wasn't sure we had the luxury of time.

I answered my cell as I walked toward my apartment building. "Hey, Mish."

"Little one. We have a green light about meeting with the elders."

"Great. What time?"

"9:00 am tomorrow. We'll pick you up at eight."

I unlocked the building door. "I'll be ready. I'm getting antsy waiting for Eli to call. Hopefully they can give us some info to break this case. 'Night."

"We have a break in the case?"

I jumped at the voice. Dalton stared down at me from the landing. Memories of him carrying me up these very stairs flooded me. But that had been another lifetime.

I stopped myself from groaning, jogged up the steps, and passed him on the landing. Dalton followed me. I was sure he would, but a girl could dream.

I opened the door and flipped on the light. "Why are you here?" I asked, not bothering to ask how he knew where I lived, since he was a cop. I stood in the doorway, blocking the entrance to my apartment.

He frowned. I was being rude, true, but 1) he had shown up unannounced, and 2), I didn't know if my heart or sanity could handle having him in my apartment.

After a second, common sense prevailed, and I stepped back and let him in. Whatever we had to talk about shouldn't be discussed in the hall. Most of my neighbors were elderly, but they had supersonic hearing when it came to gossip, or what they called scuttlebutt.

"Who were you talking to?"

"Misha. The elders of his clan want to talk to him about the demons who live in the demon realm. They might be able to help us figure out what type of demon robbed the art museum. We're supposed to meet them tomorrow morning at nine."

"I'm coming, too. No more leaving me out of this case."

I stared at him, and my internal radar started beeping. "How are we leaving you out?"

He moved further into the living room. "You're not telling me everything."

I pulled my coat off to give myself time to settle my nerves. "Like what, exactly?"

"Why were you at Gesu Church today?"

My nerves jumped to attention. "You followed me?"

"Yes."

"Why?"

"Because this case reeks! Tell me what I'm supposed to think when one of the items stolen from the museum looks exactly like the box you have stored in the office safe? How much coincidence do you think I can take?"

"This case does stink. We have a dead human, and a demon that's too dangerous to live on earth, yet it's somehow crossing to our world."

"So why did you go to Gesu?"

I crossed my arms. "For a personal reason, which is none of your damn business."

He started to pace, ignoring my indignation. "Then you go to some run-down building by the river. What the hell aren't you telling me?"

"That building houses our lab and storage facility. We keep it looking run-down on the outside so people"—I narrowed my eyes at him—"don't come snooping. I stopped in to see Doc. She's the ME we told you about. Are you happy now?"

He scowled. "You're acting awfully jumpy. If you've been doing this for ten years, I wouldn't expect you to be this jumpy."

"*If*...I have been doing this for ten years. Maybe I don't like the Feds sniffing around our case."

"What does that mean?"

"Trust goes both ways. How do we know you aren't going to spill all this to your FBI buddies in Chicago? Our job is to solve this case and stop humans from finding out the truth about the supernatural. If they find out, how do we know the government won't turn supes into lab animals?"

"You've seen too many conspiracy movies."

It was hard not to scoff at his naïve response. "We still have people who hate others for the color of their skin, for the Gods they worship, and the gender they want to sleep with. Do you honestly think humans can cope with learning about the supernatural? Races that are more powerful than they are. That live centuries longer than they do and can travel to and from another realm!

"I'm not the one living in a dream world, Special Agent Dalton. The government would try to control them, and we would have a bloodbath."

His eyes widened at my tirade, and I plowed on before he could say anything. "So forgive me if I don't trust you with the whole truth. You haven't earned it yet."

I yanked open my apartment door and gasped at Griffin, who stood in the doorway.

He glanced over my shoulder and focused on Dalton, his eyes flashing amber for a split second before he subdued them. "Am I interrupting something?"

"No. He was just leaving."

Griffin walked into the room and stood to the side, so Dalton could make his exit. I simply waited with the door open. No more words needed to be spoken. I had spewed enough for one day.

"I'll see you in the morning," Dalton announced on his way out.

I shut the door, my back to Griffin, and closed my eyes for a second.

"Kyle?"

I turned to face him and tried not to lose it. One false step, and the ice would crack...and I would fall through. "I'm fine. Dalton is being a control freak about this case. He thinks we're keeping things from him."

Griffin's eyebrow rose. "You are, aren't you?"

I rubbed the back of my neck. "For his own good."

"I'm not questioning why you're doing it, but he obviously can sense something is wrong."

"Everything is wrong." I paced into my living room. "He's so suspicious and closed off now. Jean Luc thinks it has to do with the memories I implanted in him last year. I erased the torture only to replace it with other things that have screwed him up." I stopped pacing and turned to him. "You don't want to hear this."

Griffin opened his arms, and I just stood there. Trying to breathe. After three shaky breaths, I launched myself into his arms, and he held me. His warmth wrapped around me even though my insides felt frozen. "I'm sorry." I whispered.

"Shhh."

"I'm sorry." And I was. Sorry for Dalton, and sorry for Griffin. Neither of them deserved this. Why did I have to inflict pain on everyone I cared about?

CHAPTER 17

It had actually stopped raining, so I waited on the sidewalk to soak up any stray UV that *might* make its way through the clouds. Jean Luc pulled in front of my apartment building at 8:00 am sharp. Talia nodded at me through the front passenger window, eyes smiling. The back door of the van opened, and I handed Misha a bag of apple turnovers fresh from the nearby bakery. He grinned like a silly schoolboy, and I grinned right back. At least I had figured out how to make one male in my life happy.

I climbed in and sat next to Misha, relieved to see Dalton wasn't in the van. Maybe he'd decided not to go with us.

Misha had the bag open within seconds and groaned. "They're still warm. Thanks, little one."

Jean Luc pulled away from the curb. "We have to pick up Dalton at the art museum."

And with those words, my bubble of relief officially burst. "He called you?"

Jean Luc looked at me in the rearview mirror. "Yes. He wanted to make sure he was included today. Did something happen with him?"

"He showed up at my apartment."

Talia twisted in her seat. "Why? Does he remember you?"

"No. He's suspicious of me. He followed me yesterday, to Gesu Church and then the lab."

Misha stopped in mid bite. "Whaad di you..."

I grimaced at him. "Finish chewing, Mish."

He swallowed hard and then frowned. "What did you tell him?"

"I told him about the lab."

"And Gesu?"

"I told him it was none of his damn business. If he was to ask anyone, all they could tell him is that I went to confession."

Misha snorted.

"Father Brown is back in town?" Jean Luc asked.

"Yes. I gave him pictures of the box and tablet. He thinks they might help with the translation."

A few minutes later, we drove up to the museum. Dalton was waiting next to the entrance. Jean Luc pulled up and stopped, and Misha yanked open the van door. Dalton froze in mid-step, and I stared at him in confusion. Then I glanced at my other teammates. Jean Luc and Talia were scowling, and Misha actually growled a little bit.

From the looks on their faces, they were going to open up a can of supernatural whup ass on Dalton.

Jean Luc turned in his seat, angling toward the back. "Before you get in, Agent Dalton, we need to establish some ground rules. If you have a question about what we do, in the future you should ask us. Following Kyle or any of us, or accosting us at our private residences, are breaches of confidence that will not be tolerated."

Dalton opened his mouth and then closed it again as if he was rethinking his response. "You're right." He turned to me. "I apologize for following you and for barging in when you were off duty."

I gazed into his eyes. He looked sincere, but this Dalton wasn't the one I'd known. At that moment, it would have been great to have shifter senses so I could smell if he was being truthful. But since I couldn't, I had to trust my human gut. I nodded. He climbed into the far back seat.

Misha shut the door, and we were off. Awkward silence descended. After a few minutes, I decided someone needed to break the tension. "Where are we going?"

"Our compound," Misha answered.

My eyes widened. "Boris agreed to let us into the super-secret compound?"

"Yes. Many of the elders do not leave the compound anymore."

"How many elders are in your clan, Mish?" I asked.

"We have several, but father said we would be meeting with two today."

Dalton leaned forward. "Do your elders run the clan?"

"No, my father runs the clan. The elders are part of his council that discusses issues and helps him resolve disputes."

"And you think they'll have information about the different demons in the demon realm?" Dalton asked.

Misha mumbled "yes" around another bite of turnover.

"Where's the compound?" I asked.

He swallowed before answering. "Solon."

"And you're okay with me knowing where your compound is located?" Dalton asked.

Misha shrugged. "Our compound security is top notch. And you would not be allowed into the clan compound unless you were accompanied by a clan member—me or Kyle, for example."

Dalton frowned at me. "You told me you're human."

"I am. I was inducted into the clan. Long story." A long story I wasn't about to tell Dalton, since he'd witnessed it.

"No word from Eli yet?" Talia asked.

God love her for changing the subject. "Nope. It's been two days. I'd think he would call soon."

Forty minutes later, Jean Luc drove up to a tall metal gate. Misha opened the door, clambered out, and punched a bunch of numbers on a keypad. After a few seconds, the gate opened slowly. Once Misha hopped back into the van, we traveled a long driveway.

When Misha had used the word compound, I'd gotten a totally different image in my mind. More like a campground with rustic cabins. Instead, the vibe was ritzy, gated community. We drove past several very nice homes and continued toward a large building sitting next to a man-made lake.

"Good grief, Mish. Your clan's not hurting for cash."

Misha chuckled. "No one can ever accuse you of being subtle, little one. Not all of our clan members live here, but everyone can come here when they like. We have emergency housing, and a medical facility, too."

"Why do you have an apartment by the Steelyard then?" I asked.

"I like my independence."

"And Boris doesn't want you to live here?"

"Oh, he wants all his sons to live here. Sergei, my youngest brother, doesn't stay still for long. The last time I spoke to him, he was in Hawaii. Only Aleksei has remained at the compound. But it makes sense, since he's next in line to lead."

Misha's jaw tightened when he spoke Aleksei's name. Bad blood, maybe? Now was not the time to ask, though I was dying of curiosity. After we parked, Misha led us into the white clapboard community building and down the hall to a large meeting room. From the size of it, I was pretty sure they conducted clan meetings there. The elders we were going to speak with sat at a table at the far end of the room, with chairs arranged across from them, as if they were holding court.

I gaped at the two females for a moment. The female on the right had short, curly gray hair and sharp blue eyes. Her companion's white hair was pulled into a bun, and she wore one of those sweatshirts with pictures of various flowers and their Latin names.

Your average octogenarians. Except they were demons. If they looked this old in their human form, then they were very, *very* old demons. Misha's father was eight hundred, and he looked like he was in his fifties.

As if my thoughts conjured him, Boris entered from a side door and beamed at us. He strode over to me, hauled me into his arms, and gave me great, smacking kisses on both cheeks. "So good to see you."

"You too, Boris." I grinned at his flamboyant style and peeked at Dalton, who observed the exchange closely. "Boris Chesnokov, let me introduce you to Special Agent Joe Dalton. He's helping us with this case."

Misha had warned Boris to act like he didn't know Dalton, but since Boris could be a bit of a loose cannon, I held my breath.

The two exchanged formal guest-host greetings, and I breathed again.

Boris turned to Jean Luc. "Good to see you, vampire. And this is your mate, Talia?"

Jean Luc nodded.

"You're as gorgeous as Misha said. I hear you're smart and feisty as well. How did this uptight vampire win you over?"

Talia grinned at both Boris's quip and Jean Luc's glower.

The female elder on the right cleared her throat. "Enough of your bluster, Boris. Let's get this meeting started."

Boris winked at me and then gestured for us to follow him up front and take our seats. "May I introduce you to our elders?" He bowed slightly to the female on his right first. "Irina." Then he motioned to his left. "Katya, this is the BSR team I told you about."

Jean Luc bowed his head slightly. "Thank you for meeting with us. We appreciate your time."

Irina's eyebrows rose slightly at his formal greeting. "Boris wasn't exaggerating. You are a bit uptight, vampire."

Misha coughed next to me, but I was pretty sure it was to cover up a laugh.

She continued, "I'm not one for pomp and circumstance. Let's jump in, shall we? Boris has explained that the BSR needs help. What do you need to know?"

"We want to learn about the demon realm. How many clans live there?" I asked.

"Five that I am aware of," Irina replied.

Dalton spoke up. "Who decides which clans are allowed on earth?"

Katya smiled tightly. "Centuries ago, all the clans moved freely between earth and the realm. There were fewer humans then, and more places for us here on earth. But we were still not happy. The clans battled for dominance. And when the bloodshed finally stopped, a coalition was formed. The clans who agreed to peace formed an alliance, and the demon council was established. The five clans who wouldn't agree to peace were banished to the realm."

I frowned. "I thought the strongest demons were placed in the realm because they couldn't be trusted on earth."

Katya shrugged. "And history is usually written by the victors. I'm sure if you spoke to them they would tell a different story."

"And the border patrol?" Talia asked.

"The patrol are demons," Irina answered. "Pulled from the various clans centuries ago, they enforce the peace and ensure the banished demons do not escape the realm."

"But demons are escaping," I said.

Irina nodded. "There is only so much the patrol can do. The border fluctuates, since the realm is in another dimension than ours. Things are in a constant state of flux. I do not envy them their jobs."

"Is there any way we could meet with the border patrol?" Jean Luc asked.

Irina continued. "Not easily. Only their leader is allowed to visit earth a few times a year. The rest are not allowed to enter the earth realm. They can exist either in the realm or in the in-between."

Dalton frowned. "What's the in-between?"

"It's the space between worlds. It's where those who patrol spend their time watching to make sure no one can breach the portals."

"Well that sucks for them," I blurted. "They protect earth for the rest of us, and yet they don't get to come here?"

"No. They don't have the power to come to earth," Irina explained.

"Then why can these other demons manage it?" I pushed.

"There is a conduit between the worlds that ebbs and flows like electricity," Katya answered. "Some demons are in tune with it and can manipulate it. They've made a lucrative business out of transporting other demons back and forth."

"Abstatholm," I said.

Katya's eyes sharpened on me. "Yes."

"The demon who burglarized the art museum had multiple powers—invisibility, telekinesis, and the ability to suppress the security cameras. Do any of the five clans have demons who could have all three of these abilities?" Misha asked.

Irina pursed her lips. "The realm demons are dangerous. But even there, it's not common for demons to have that many powers. Only two of the clans might have someone who is this powerful."

"Is one of them Majock?" I pushed again.

"Yes," Irina said. "It could be a Majock. Do you think it's the Majock Boris asked me about last year, when everyone was hunting for the Key?" Her wizened eyes tightened on me. "Has the hunt started again?"

Dalton tensed next to me, and I stifled a groan. He probably believed we were keeping things from him again. More explanations would be in order later.

Irina sat waiting for my response. She was a smart old broad. There was no point in lying. "Possibly."

Katya picked up a folded piece of paper and held it out to me. "Irina and I composed a list of the five clans and what we know about them. Demon skin, eye color, powers, etc."

I reached for it, and Katya pressed it into my palm.

"Can demons have different eye colors within their clan?" I asked.

"I've not seen it before." Irina answered. "What about you, Katya?"

She frowned. "No."

"Then I don't think the demon was Majock. Majocks' eyes aren't white, are they? The demon's eyes glowed white."

Irina and Katya exchanged startled glances. "His eyes were white?"

"Yes."

"And don't forget about the green blood, Kyle." Talia said.

"That changes things," Irina mumbled.

Dalton frowned. "Why?"

"Because no demon on earth or in the realm normally has white eyes while in their demon state."

"Normally?" Jean Luc asked.

"There is one possible reason for the white eyes. If a demon forms a bond with another demon, they borrow powers. It's a dangerous situation, because it puts the demon who has borrowed those powers into something like an indentured servant relationship with the other demon."

Before I could ask another question, a tall male stalked into the room. He glared at all of us before turning to Boris. "What's going on here?"

"We're meeting with the BSR to discuss a case," Boris answered.

The demon glared at Misha. "It is one thing if Mikhail wants to associate with outsiders, but it is quite another when he brings them here."

I snorted at his high and mighty intonation, and his piercing glare turned on me. But I wasn't intimidated. I had been glowered at by supes way scarier than he was.

"Did I say something amusing?" he asked, and actually looked down his nose at me.

"No," I replied.

He started to look away in triumph, so I decided to enlighten him a bit. "What you said was rude."

"Excuse me?" He pulled himself up even taller and crossed his arms. He was wearing a designer suit and a pair of shoes he or some suitably humble minion obviously buffed daily.

"Rude. You might think we *outsiders* aren't worthy to shine your incredibly shiny shoes, but you shouldn't say so in front of us. That. Is. Rude."

He opened his mouth to bluster something, but Misha interrupted him. "As usual, Aleksei, your first impression

leaves much to be desired. You have just insulted your ses-
tra."

This was Aleksei? While Misha didn't look like Boris except for their matching ice blue eyes, Aleksei looked just like
his father, except his eyes were moss green.

Irina sighed. "They came here so Katya and I would not
have to leave the compound. Would you rather have us meet
them outside these walls and be vulnerable?"

I doubted either of these females was ever vulnerable, but
I had to hand it to Irina for putting Aleksei in his place. He
unfolded his arms and moved to the side. I was fine with that.
Again with the glowering, though. Seen that, done it myself.
So last year.

"How do you plan to locate this demon with the white
eyes?" Katya asked.

How much could I say without sending Dalton into a
conniption fit? "We're working on some connections who
may lead us to the Abstatholm. If we can get a handle on
how demon trafficking works, we hope to stop it and find
the white-eyed demon in the process."

There. That should be generic enough to avoid Dalton's
wrath. I glanced at him to find him frowning at me. Okay,
maybe not.

Aleksei scowled at Misha. "This is dangerous. You bring
this trouble into our clan?"

Misha scraped his chair back, but before he could stand,
Irina held out a staying hand.

Irina pinned Aleksei with a glare. "Aleksei, leave us.
Mikhail did not bring trouble to the clan. I do not have time
for your squabbling."

Aleksei stalked from the room in much the same way he
had entered it. The tension sucked out the door with him.

Boris placed his hands on the table, palms down. "I must apologize for my son. Aleksei can be a bit zealous when it comes to protecting the clan."

"A chip off the old block?" I winked at Boris, who laughed out loud.

"I'm afraid so."

There didn't seem to be anything further to discuss, so we began our goodbyes. Katya nodded and left the room.

Irina gestured to Misha. "Mikhail, come closer and bring the smart-mouthed one with you."

"I'm in trouble now," I muttered.

"You're not in trouble."

I stared at her.

"I might look like I'm about to bite the dust, but my demon ears are working just fine."

Misha bent down to kiss Irina's cheek. "*Babushka*, this is Kyle."

"Ah, that explains it. Boris told me you have a tendency to talk back."

"I would say it's more a matter of speaking my mind than talking back."

She smirked. "Like right now, you mean?"

I smirked right back. "Exactly."

"Well, I find it refreshing. And I would expect nothing less from my granddaughter."

My eyes widened. "What?"

"Boris is my son. As much as I love him and my three grandsons, I am happy to have a woman in our family."

"Why didn't he introduce you as his mother?" I asked.

"Because I was serving as an elder for our meeting, not his mother."

So in one fell swoop, I had met practically the whole fam-damily.

Irina examined me for a moment in silence before speaking. "Are you and Misha an item?"

Misha winked at me.

"No, ma'am. Misha is one of my best friends, but we're not involved romantically."

She sighed dramatically. "It would be nice if my grandsons would marry and give me grandbabies."

I chuckled at Misha's sour face. "Maybe we can work on that together."

CHAPTER 18

Was there a pain reliever for demon information overload? Jean Luc drove out of the compound gate, and I glanced back at Dalton. It was best to let him think we were being upfront about everything. Even if it wasn't exactly true. "Before you pop a blood vessel, let me fill you in on the Majock Irina referenced."

Dalton leaned forward on his elbows, looking attentive, and I continued. "Last year, we had several supernatural factions looking for the Key. One was a pair of evil-ass vamps who, I am happy to say, are both dead. As in really dead, not vamp dead. Another was a Pavel demon. Pavels are a clan living on earth. And we also had a Majock demon that was somehow mixed up with the vamps. Misha didn't recognize him in his demon form, so Boris checked with the elders to see if they could help identify him. Irina told us about the Majock and the demon realm."

"What about the angels?"

"They have a tendency to stay detached from what's happening on earth. Until last year when one of them...detached...a vamp's head to stop him from finding the Key."

Dalton rubbed his hand over his face. "No wonder you were freaked out when you saw the Key box. And now someone is after it again."

I swallowed hard. "Looks like."

"Do we have any idea where this Key could be?"

I schooled my face into a blank expression. Or at least I hoped I did. "No."

"What happens if they find it?"

"I'm not sure. Certainly they'll want to control it and use the power for their own gain." I picked at the fraying knee of my jeans. This conversation was making me sweat. 'Cause the bottom line was, *it* was technically *me*, and I didn't want to be controlled by anyone.

Misha interrupted the barrage of pointed questions Dalton was lobbing my way, thank God. "Let's discuss this demon list Katya gave us so we have an idea of what we might be up against." Misha unfolded the paper.

"Good idea," Talia chimed in from the front seat.

"We know about the Majock, but let me bring Joe up to speed. In demon form, Majock are blue with black stripes and orange eyes. They have the ability to manipulate energy, and the more powerful of them can read minds. Next are the Kelmar. Orange skin and yellow eyes, they can manipulate matter and move through space. The third are the Dragans."

"There are dragon demons?" I interrupted because, seriously, dragon demons would be awesome.

"No, these are spelled *an*, not *on*. Although the myth surrounding dragons probably originated from them, since Dragans control fire and heat. Their demon form is green and brown skin with red eyes.

I glanced at Dalton, and the *holy shit* look on his face more than likely mirrored my own.

"And the other two clans?" Dalton asked.

"The other two are the Palthat and the Lagfel. Palthat are light blue with green eyes, and they are telekinetic. Lagfel have gray skin and purple eyes, and their primary powers are brute strength and speed."

Jean Luc stopped at a light. "It sounds as if the demon at the art museum had several powers at his disposal."

"Yes," Misha answered. "If Irina is correct, he's borrowed several clan powers."

"To what end?" Talia asked. "Irina made it sound as if these clans warred against each other. Why would they be willing to do this?"

"Because whatever they're after is worth the clans working together," I answered.

Dalton leaned forward again. "They want the Key."

I jerked when my phone rang, interrupting the onset of my mental breakdown. "It's an unlisted number guys, so keep quiet for a sec." I clicked accept. "Hello."

"Carly, it's Eli."

"Eli. I hope you're calling me with some news."

"I have someone who'd like to do business with you. Can you meet tonight at eight?"

"Yes, tonight works. Where?"

Eli rattled off the address, and I repeated it back to him so Misha, aka Mr. Perfect Memory, could memorize it.

"If everything goes smoothly, we'll expect an electronic transfer of funds at that time."

"Why wouldn't it go smoothly?" I asked while the tiny hairs on the back of my neck started doing the mambo.

"I don't anticipate any problems."

"Neither do I." I hung up. "It's on."

"We need to discuss the plan," Dalton said.

Misha held up his phone. "The address he gave us is a warehouse building on St. Claire. It looks like it hasn't been used for a while."

Talia turned around. "How did you figure that out so fast? Are you tied into the database?"

"Nope. Google Earth. Big brother is watching at all times."

I interrupted. "So Talia and I will go in with Misha, and Dalton and Jean Luc can stay in close proximity as backup. We'll wear earbuds and trackers so you two know where we are at all times. It sounds like they'll want to make sure we have the money and that Misha is legit before we can do business."

Dalton frowned. "No offense, Misha, but I would think you are pretty well known among the demon population, especially with that accent. Can we risk sending you in?"

"Losing the accent is not a problem," Misha replied, and then dropped into a perfect southern drawl. "I'll use the name Michael for tonight, y'all."

I bit my cheek to keep from laughing. "You are one talented demon."

What was it with supernaturals and abandoned buildings? Their MO was usually to conduct shady business in the most out-of-the-way places, the dumpier the better. This building was literally falling apart, right down to rainwater dripping from the high ceiling, plopping loudly on the cement floor.

Eli and bouncer Johnny stood in the center of the warehouse. I skirted a couple of collapsed boxes. Based on the rustling sounds underneath them, they were serving as rodent condos. I made a bigger circle around the next set of boxes until I came to a stop in front of Eli. Talia and Misha stopped next to me.

"Eli."

"Carly. Is this your traveler?"

"Yes. Eli, this is Michael."

Eli looked Misha over for a few awkward seconds.

"Are you ready to wire the money?" Eli asked.

I shook my head. "Not so fast. Explain to me how this is going to work."

"We'll open the portal, and Michael can step through and do his business."

"How much time does he have in the realm?"

"That's a bit relative," Eli answered with a smirk.

I frowned. "Can you clue me in on the joke?"

"Time is different in the demon realm. For us it will feel like he is gone for an hour, but in the realm it could be a day or more."

"And how does he get back here?"

Eli arranged the cuffs on his shirt. "I was getting to that. One of the Abstatholm will go with Michael, and then open the portal on the other side when it's time to return. Any other questions?"

"Where are the Abstatholm?"

Eli nodded to Johnny, who texted something on his phone. "They're on the way."

Misha asked, "What if we need to have someone come back with me from the demon realm? How would that work?"

"I don't handle those types of transfers," Eli answered tightly.

"Who does?" Talia asked.

Eli scowled. "This is starting to feel like an inquisition."

"It's a business arrangement. We want to know how we can bring someone over from the other side," I persisted.

"It can't be done."

The side bay door opened, interrupting my argument. Two males, assumedly demons, lumbered in our direction. This meeting was turning into a scene from a bad cop movie.

The demons were twins, with shaved heads and tattoos of various symbols wrapped around their bulging arms. If they were this badass in their human form, I didn't want to imagine what they would be like as demons.

Eli jerked his chin in the direction of Tweedle-scary and Tweedle-scarier. "Your transport team has arrived."

They both scowled in our direction, taking in Misha first and then Talia. When their eyes stopped on me they both growled. What the hell?

Eli jerked and looked over his shoulder at them, then ran for the door. Talia took a running leap and tackled Eli while Misha squared off with Johnny the Body-Building Bouncer. The spooky-ass demon twins stalked in my direction, and I yanked Stanley from his holster and pointed it at them. "Don't even think about it."

A rush of air blew the scattered packing peanuts across the room as Jean Luc appeared from his flash. The twins took off running, splitting up, one careening to the right down a hall, the other skidding left behind a pallet of boxes. I motioned to the left and Jean Luc nodded, flashing toward the back loading dock.

Why didn't anything go smoothly, ever? I ran after the other demon. The back door crashed open. I raised my gun...and came face to face with Dalton, or more specifically Dalton's gun. We froze for a second and then lowered our weapons.

I gestured toward the hall. Dalton and I walked together slowly, guns ready, as we checked the empty rooms.

When we got to the last room and found nothing, I looked around again, carefully. "Where the hell did he go? We need to talk to him."

Energy shot across the back of my neck down my spinal column. It was like static electricity times one hundred. And from the frown on Dalton's face, I wasn't the only one feeling it.

"We need to get out—"

A demon appeared in front of me in full demon form. Orange skin with tattoos circling his biceps. His yellow, glowing eyes stared at me defiantly.

"Freeze," Dalton yelled.

The demon smiled. Who smiles like that, pointy teeth and all, when a gun is aimed at them? Someone with a plan, that's who. He grabbed my arm. The air in front of me rippled like water. The ground shook, and I fought to get away from him, but it was like pushing my way through pudding.

Dalton yelled and lunged for me as I dropped through the floor, like Alice in freaking Wonderland tumbling down the rabbit hole.

CHAPTER 19

I landed hard on packed ground, which knocked the breath out of me. Dalton landed next to me with a hard thud and met my panicked look after a moment. He scrambled over to me on his hands and knees and checked me over while I tried to pull air into my lungs.

"Relax, McKinley. Stay still, you'll be okay in a minute."

A minute? Hell, I would be dead in a minute.

He grabbed my hands. "Look at me. Calm down."

I nodded even though black dots were dancing and multiplying in my peripheral vision. After a few more seconds, the tightness let loose, and I sucked in a gulp of glorious air.

"That's it. Take a deep breath, don't hyperventilate."

After a few more seconds, I attempted to sit up, but Dalton put a steadying hand on my shoulder.

"Does anything else hurt?"

"No. Are you okay?"

"Yeah. Where the hell are we?"

He finally helped me sit up. "If I was a betting woman, I would say we went through the demon portal."

Dalton's eyes widened. "Are we in the demon realm? Or maybe the in-between?"

"I don't know."

"Okay. So now what?" he asked.

"I don't know."

He scowled at me. "I thought you've been doing this for ten years."

"I've been dealing with supernatural cover-ups on *earth*. I wasn't trained in Demon Realm 101. Although I think we might be in for a crash course."

I looked around. We were in a cave the size of a large room, with walls made of some sort of crystal. Light shone through the stones, bathing everything in a reddish hue.

Dalton examined the ground. "Do you have your gun?"

I frowned. "No. I must have dropped it when we came through the portal."

"I don't have mine either."

"I'm not sure it would have worked here anyway. Objects from earth might behave differently, if they work at all, in other dimensions."

Dalton held out his hand, and I grabbed it, pulling myself up. I took out my cell and clicked it. Nothing worked.

"I guess my calling plan doesn't extend to the demon realm."

Dalton rolled his eyes and brushed his hands on his pants.

"What? We could use some levity right now. Don't you laugh anymore?"

"Anymore?"

Crap. "I mean I don't think I've ever seen you laugh, or smile for that matter."

"How about once we get to earth we talk about smiling? God, I can't believe I just said that. We're not on earth anymore."

I blew out a hard breath. "Don't freak out on me, Dalton, or I'll lose it, too. We need to scope out this place first and make sure we're the only ones in here. Jean Luc, Misha, and Talia will have us out of here in no time."

At least I hoped they would.

Ten minutes later, Dalton and I picked our way through a narrow tunnel. It was barely wide enough for Dalton to get through without having to shift his shoulders sideways. I sucked in a breath through my nose and let it out of my mouth to keep the walls from closing in on me. I was too busy breathing and reminding myself claustrophobia would not defeat me that I didn't notice when Dalton stopped. I ran into his back and grabbed his arms so I wouldn't fall on my butt.

"Sorry."

He looked over his shoulder at me and said in a low voice, "This opens into a larger cavern. Hold on." He took a couple of steps and peeked out. "It's empty."

He walked into the cavern, and I scrambled behind him to get out of that damn tunnel. The space was bigger than the cavern we had landed in, and the opposite end had an opening to the outside. Wherever outside was.

Dalton spoke. "So the question is, do we stay here or go outside the cave?"

I opened my mouth to answer, but he plowed on.

"Basic survival training says stay put. If they open the portal again, odds are it will open here, and we probably won't have much time to get through it."

I shrugged. "Maybe. Or maybe the portal will open up wherever we are. Plus, I'm not liking the idea of us being in this cave with only one way out. Kind of makes us sitting humans for some demon to stumble across."

"Where the portal reactivates again might have been a helpful question to ask Eli earlier."

"It never occurred to me we'd need that bit of info. We didn't exactly plan to end up here by ourselves. We weren't going to let them open up a portal *at all*. As you stated in our planning session," I said as my fingers formed air quotes, "we were supposed to engage the perps, extract the data, and capture them for further questioning."

"You're right."

I shut my mouth against the responses I had been preparing to fling back at him. "Huh?" Not smooth at all, but my tongue was still in scathing mode, and I hadn't had time to readjust.

He rubbed the back of his neck. "I said you're right. This wasn't part of the plan."

"It's the way life works. Someone or something will always find a way to muck up the plan."

"Don't I know it," he replied, pain flashing in his turquoise eyes.

Finally, some type of emotion from him. If only it hadn't been pain. "It must have been hard last summer for you."

He flinched slightly, and it was my turn to plow on.

"You were splashed all over the news. Decorated cop almost dies stopping serial killer. You were a hero. But people forget there's more cleanup to do after the headline fades, isn't there?"

"Yes."

"But you have to move on." I swallowed hard. "You have to—"

He slammed his hand over my mouth, and I gasped. Or at least I tried to, but was stopped by his palm. He leaned close, his breath tickling my ear. My heart thumped. *What the hell?*

"Someone's coming," he whispered.

My heart's thumping exploded into full-blown gymnastics. Some*one* or some*thing*? I nodded, and he let me go. He leaned over and picked up two sturdy-looking rocks, handed one to me, and motioned toward the cave wall next to the entrance. I walked as quietly as I could to the wall, and he moved to the other side of the entrance.

We were going to take on a demon with rocks as weapons. The only other thing I brought to the equation were rusty self-defense moves Jean Luc taught me eons ago. That and my sarcastic wit.

We were so screwed.

CHAPTER 20

I took a shallow breath so I wouldn't give us away and gripped the stone so hard it bit into my fingers. Dalton's gaze latched onto mine from across the entrance, as if to encourage me. This was the Dalton I remembered. Why did it take a crisis to make us band together?

The demon who'd sent us here came through the entrance, his orange skin taking on a reddish cast from the crystal walls. He circled Dalton slowly, shooting a sideways glance at me.

"Here you are." He tsked his tongue at us like a kindergarten teacher. "You slipped away during the transfer."

"Send us back to earth, right now," Dalton demanded.

"I don't think so."

"What are you planning to do with us?" Dalton asked.

"I'm not planning to do anything to you unless you try to stop us." He smiled. "She's coming with me."

The hell I am.

"The hell she is," Dalton said, and I would have cheered at his word choice if I hadn't been so damn freaked out.

The demon lunged. Dalton sidestepped and used the demon's momentum to push him away. The demon spun and kicked out, almost making contact with Dalton's legs, but he backed away in time.

Dalton swung the stone in a powerful arc, but the demon blocked his punch and knocked him to the ground. He leaned over Dalton and grabbed him by the shirt. I bit my lip to keep silent and ran forward, slamming the rock against the back of the demon's head. He staggered, cursing in demon tongue.

He looked over his shoulder at me and growled.

"Don't hurt her!" Dalton yelled, jumping up.

The demon swung his fist, connecting with Dalton's face. A sickening *thud* echoed in the cave, and Dalton stumbled. I kicked out, hammering into the demon's knee, and then crashed the rock down on his head again. He howled and fell to his knees. Dalton knocked him out with another blow of his rock, and then grabbed my hand. As we ran out of the cave, I gave thanks again for steel-toed work boots.

Outside seemed normal...if you were on a mission to Mars. Lots of dirt and rocks mixed with red crystals from the cave, and the sky had a washed-out blue cast to it. It seemed to be daytime here, even though we had dropped through the portal after dark our time.

After a few minutes, we stopped running. Dalton let go of my hand and turned in a circle, slowly casing the landscape. "I don't think we should stay out in the open like this, in case our friend comes after us again." He pointed to a cluster of trees, and we jogged in their direction. We finally slowed once we were several feet into the forest, far enough that the trunks and branches hid us.

We maneuvered farther into the trees, and I slowed and deepened my breathing to calm my heart. The air was stale and a bit dusty, like the inside of an old attic. I switched to shallow breaths instead.

Dalton picked up a large branch and tested its strength. Apparently satisfied, he carried it while we walked between the trees.

I did a double-take when I looked at Dalton again. "You're going to have a heck of a shiner. Are you okay?"

"I'll be fine."

"Thanks for protecting me back there."

"You're welcome. But you were the one who returned the favor by getting us out of there." He stopped. "Why do you think that demon was after you in particular?"

"I don't know. Maybe he was pissed that I set him up."

Dalton scowled. "What happened in the warehouse to set them off?"

"Nothing. They came in and looked at me, and then all hell broke loose."

"Do you think they recognized you as BSR?"

I shrugged. "I don't know how. I've never seen them before."

We continued on in silence for a while, my thoughts hopping around in my brain. Why *were* they so damn interested in me? Could they sense my power? I stopped. Or maybe they could sense the Key? *Shit.* Who knew what beings from the demon realm could sense?

"You okay, McKinley?"

I nodded, not wanting to open that supernatural can of worms. A couple of seconds later, Dalton raised his fist in the air. I stopped immediately and waited quietly. Good thing I had seen enough military movies with Misha to know what the heck he was doing. He cocked his head and listened. I held my breath, hoping my heartbeat couldn't be heard. It sounded like a bongo drum in my ears.

Rustling sounds reached us, and Dalton motioned for me to get behind a giant tree. He held his branch like a baseball bat and waited.

I saw a sharp-looking staff first, and then my eyes tracked back to the demon holding it. He was covered in some sort of black armor from head to toe, which was bad enough. But then another, even bigger demon came up behind him.

Dalton swung the branch and knocked the staff away. The second demon lunged for Dalton, and the branch shattered in a dozen pieces when it connected with the second demon's armor. The demon grabbed Dalton and held his arms behind him.

The first demon pulled out a sword from the sheath on his back and pointed the sword at Dalton's chest.

"Stop! Don't hurt him!" I screamed as I ran up.

The demon jerked around when he heard me and pointed his sword at my chest, stopping me in my tracks. He spoke in some unintelligible demon language, but his voice was strangely...feminine.

"I don't understand you," I said.

The demon waved his sword, and I backed further away from the blade. When I was far enough away, the demon yanked off his helmet and hair cascaded down his—no, definitely her—back.

Even though she was a female demon, it didn't make her any less intimidating. She reminded me of an Amazon. She was very tall, with long, black hair and violet skin, like a purple *Xena: Warrior Princess* brought to life. Misha would be rocking this reality.

She glared at both of us for a moment before she spoke in perfect English. "I am Naya of the Demon Patrol." She pointed to a symbol engraved in her chest armor. Was it some sort of badge?

"What are you two doing here?" she asked.

"Where's here?" I blurted, ridiculously relieved to be talking to a demon version of the police. Maybe we weren't screwed after all.

She frowned. "You do not know where you are?"

"We have an idea," I responded. "Either the demon realm or the in-between?"

"You are in the realm. How did you get here?"

"We were chasing a demon on earth, and he sent us here," Dalton replied. "We left him back in the caves."

"Why would *you* be chasing a demon?"

Dalton said, "Because we work for law enforcement on earth. We're working a case, trying to stop demons from crossing from the realm to earth."

"And the demon who sent you here. What did he look like?"

I jumped in. "From his orange skin and yellow eyes, I think he was a Kelmar demon, which is one of the clans in your realm. There were two demons. Twins, I think."

Naya scowled. "Did you see their human form?"

"Yeah. They're scary big as humans. Their heads are shaved, and they have dark brown eyes and tattoos that wrap around their arms."

"Tattoos?" Naya asked.

"Permanent ink markings on their skin. They looked like demon symbols."

"These markings are used to hide the demons from our kind. And these tattoos are permanent?"

"Most are. Some are temporary, and they can either be washed off or fade away over time."

"I know the two you speak of. We suspected they were participating in crossings, but we have not been able to catch them."

Naya spoke to her partner in demon tongue, and he took off in the direction we had come from. "Marrick will track the demon."

"Well, we might have the other twin in custody on earth," I said.

"How? You are here?"

"Our team includes a Shamat demon and two vampires. They probably captured some of the demons involved."

"Let us hope so, or you will have a difficult time getting home."

"Can you help us?"

"I cannot send you back to earth, but I can take you to the in-between until we find a way for you to get home."

Dalton frowned. "Shouldn't we stay here so our team can track us?"

Naya shook her head, sheathed her sword, and then knelt down to pick up her staff. "No, it is not safe for you here. In fact, we have already spent too much time in this location. We need to move on so others cannot find you."

"Thank you for helping us," I said.

"Luckily you spoke in English instead of demon-tongue so I realized what you are. Otherwise, I would have killed you."

I gulped. "So now what?"

"Now you follow me and do as I say. I will take us to a jump point where we can transport to the in-between."

I looked at Dalton, who nodded. "I'm Kyle and he's Dalton. Thanks for um...not killing us earlier."

She smiled. "You are welcome."

Naya put her helmet back on and led us further into the forest, through dark trees towering above us and blocking out the light. It appeared similar to a forest on earth, same colors, same kinds of trees, but for some reason it gave me the creeps. After a few minutes, I realized why. There were no sounds. No birds singing, no animals running or rustling through the forest. Only the sound of our footsteps, which echoed loudly in my ears, so loudly I cringed, thinking we were going to summon every nasty demon in the realm.

Dalton stumbled next to me, and I reached out and grabbed his arm. We stopped for a moment, and he braced his hands on his knees and took some shallow breaths.

"Are you okay?" I whispered.

"Yeah. I'll be fine. I'm just having a hard time catching my breath since it's so hot."

I opened my mouth and then closed it again. It was not hot. It was cold. So cold that I had been wishing for a heavier coat. I studied him and noticed a sheen of sweat covering his forehead. Something was wrong. Was he getting sick?

Naya walked back to us. She held up a metal bottle to Dalton. "Drink this. It is safe." She pointed to a tree that had been cracked off at its roots and was lying on its side. "Rest for a moment."

Dalton didn't protest, just accepted the bottle and sat on the felled tree. If he was listening to orders and not com-plaining—for sure he felt even crappier than he was letting on. Naya moved away and watched the forest. I followed her.

"What's wrong with him?" I asked quietly.

"From the signs he is showing, the demon realm is toxic to his system."

"How can we help him?"

"We need to get him to the in-between, but it will not cure him. He needs to be returned to earth quickly."

"How sick is he going to get?"

"Fever, sweats, horrible thirst. How long were you in the realm before I found you?"

"Less than an hour."

Naya frowned. "He is getting sick faster than I would expect for a human."

"Why am I not getting sick?"

Naya's eyes practically pierced me. "What do you think?"

I looked over my shoulder quickly to see if Dalton was listening, but he was leaning forward, his head in his hands. "Maybe my powers protect me?"

Her eyebrow lifted in surprise. "He does not know about your powers?"

"No, and I would like to keep it that way for now."

She nodded. "Let us move on. The gate to the in-between is half an hour from here. Hopefully moving him there will slow his symptoms, but it will not stop them."

I swallowed hard, and Naya grabbed my arm. "Try to hide your concern. Undue stress will exacerbate his illness."

"You mean like falling into a demon realm with no way out didn't stress him out enough? How exactly am I going to top that one?" I scrubbed my hand over my tangled hair. I could do this. I had been hiding my feelings since he came back into my life. I could do this.

"You must school your features. Your feelings for him show on your face."

Crap. So much for hiding my emotions. I closed my eyes and took a long, deep breath and relaxed my face.

"Better. We should travel now while he is still able."

And while I could still keep it together.

CHAPTER 21

I felt like a walking tube of toothpaste, one that had been squeezed in the middle and then folded on the ends. Or that was the closest I could come to describing it.

I steadied my legs and shook my head like a wet dog once the portal plopped us in a field. I checked on Dalton, who was leaning forward, hands on his knees again.

"You okay?"

He nodded and straightened up shakily. "Feel like I'm getting the flu or something."

Naya paused next to us. "I will take you to a place where you can rest until your team is able to call you back. It is not far."

We walked for about a mile before we saw several small buildings. On closer inspection, they reminded me of English cottages.

As we approached, two demons dressed in armor similar to Naya's stepped into the clearing and stared at us. Or rather glared at us. Dalton tensed and positioned himself slightly in front of me. God love him for his protective streak, but what did he plan to do, crush them by collapsing on top of them?

The taller demon crossed his arms and moved in front of the middle cottage's door to block our path. He spoke in demon-tongue, that reminded me of Klingon, which officially meant I had been spending way too much time with Misha and his *Star Trek* marathons. First the green blood, now this. There was a ridiculous pattern forming.

Naya frowned and answered the other demon sharply. Nothing made sense to me, but I didn't care at that moment, since I could tell Dalton was indeed ready to fall on his face. I wrapped his arm over my shoulder and my arm around his back. Then I reminded myself to be nice so I wouldn't land us in demon jail.

"I'm sorry to interrupt, but he needs to lie down right now."

Naya glared at the mammoth demon until he stepped away from the door. We entered the cottage, and Naya directed us through a door into a bedroom with a double bed, a small table and chair, and a trunk as the only furnishings.

I helped Dalton sit on the bed, and then I pushed his shoulders until he lay flat.

"I'm okay, McKinley."

I smiled to hide my worry. "I know you are. Just rest for a bit. There isn't much to do right now anyway. We have to wait for the team to get us out of here."

He sighed and closed his eyes. "Just give me a few minutes. I'm sure I'll be fine once I rest."

"I'll be right outside."

I went into the living area and closed the bedroom door. Naya was not there, so I snooped a bit. A hearth filled one wall, with pots hanging nearby, and a kettle hung from a hook next to the fire. A small table and chairs were clustered in the corner, and in the other corner were piles of books. Hundreds of books. I read a few of the spines. They were all classics: Shakespeare, Tolstoy, Byron.

The outside door opened, and Naya came back in. She removed her armor and placed it on a low table next to the door, along with her sword. She was wearing some sort of one-piece jumpsuit under the armor, and now that the armor was gone, there was no mistaking that she was a she. Why I kept meeting—and having to stand next to—tall, drop-dead gorgeous women was a question my ego continued to badger me about.

"How is he?"

"He's resting for now."

She pushed the kettle over the flames. "I'll heat water for a special tea for him. It should help with some of the symptoms."

"But it won't cure him?"

"No. His system will not be fully restored until he returns to earth."

"How will we get back to earth? Can my friends find us here in the in-between?"

"If they have one of the demons you spoke of in custody, he should be able to sense both your energy and Dalton's. You will stand out from the other energies here in the in-between."

I hoped so. "Did you calm down your friends outside?"

"Yes."

"I hope we didn't get you into trouble."

"After I explained that you were sent to the realm by a rogue demon, they stopped asking me why I had not locked you up. I would introduce you to our leader, but he is on patrol now."

"Is this your home?"

"Yes."

"Thank you for bringing us here."

She shrugged. "It is for purely selfish reasons. Very little changes here. This is the most excitement I have had in decades."

I laughed. "I like your honesty." I pointed to her books. "May I?"

She gestured for me to go ahead, and I picked up a leather-bound edition. It was *Beowulf* which, if I remembered correctly, was about knights battling a monster. Which seemed very fitting. "How did you get these books?"

"The demon council meets with our leader several times a year. He brings back items we can use."

"So mechanical and electrical items don't work?"

"Correct."

"What is the in-between?"

"The border patrol lives here when we are not on duty in the demon realm. It is the space separating earth and the realm."

"Most demons don't have the ability to escape the realm. How do you move around?" I asked.

"The patrol has been given a device that allows us to pass back and forth between the in-between and the realm, but not to earth."

"What happens if a non-patrol demon gets ahold of the device? Can they use it to escape?"

Naya shook her head. "The device is implanted in us. They cannot take it. If they try, we will die, and it will be useless to them."

"And you're stuck here. That sucks."

Naya's eyebrows raised. "What does 'sucks' mean?"

"It means it isn't fair that you protect earth from harm but you aren't allowed to see it for yourself."

"I see it through my books."

I set the book back down and joined her at the table. "From what I understand, demons from the twelve clans on earth are part of the border patrol. You must be Pavel?"

She frowned. "Why would you assume that?"

"You have purple skin, which is what Pavel demons have on earth. Although your black eyes threw me."

"The patrol is one clan here, Kyle. There is no separation of clans for us. We protect each other."

It was my turn to frown. "But your parents are from one clan, right? On earth, the demons can't have children unless they marry within their clan. And there are the small few who have mated and have children with humans."

"In the realm, they cannot procreate across clans either. We do not know if any of the realm clans have ever mated with a human, or if it would be possible to do so. But here in the in-between, we can procreate regardless of clan. Before we combined clans, my father was Shamat and my mother was Pavel."

"What does your human form look like?" I cringed. "I apologize if that was rude. You don't have to answer if you don't want to."

"It was not rude to ask, but I do not know the answer to your question. I cannot bring out my human side. Most of the patrol are unable to do so. We have never been to earth, so there is no need for our human side in any case."

"You give up a lot to protect us."

"It is what I do."

"Maybe we could help each other?"

Her eyebrow lifted haughtily. "And how exactly could you help me?"

She was cocky, but then so was I most of the time. "You are not allowed to go to earth. We could be your eyes and ears there."

Naya got up to pull the kettle off the flames with long metal tongs. She wrapped a thick cloth around the handle and poured boiling water into a mug, then dropped some leaves into the steaming liquid. "How long have you been hunting the demons who cross over?"

"A week," I answered.

She smirked while she stirred the tea. "A whole week? I have been on this patrol my entire life. I was born to protect the border."

"Then I would think you would want to help stop this," I said.

"In less than a week you have been trapped here by a demon. I am not sure you would survive the fortnight if you continue on your quest."

I laughed. "You aren't afraid to speak your mind, are you?"

"I have a feeling the same can be said of you."

I opened the door to check on Dalton. He was worse. Sweat streamed down his face and neck, and he had kicked the blankets off and was moving restlessly in his sleep. I put my hand on his forehead and he was very hot.

He opened his eyes at my touch and tried to sit up. "No, McKinley," he mumbled.

"What's wrong?"

"I don't want you to get sick."

I tsked him. "You silly man. You've already exposed me to your cooties. If I'm going to get sick, it will happen whether I help you now or not."

His eyes widened. "Cooties?"

"Yep. I need you to drink some of this tea. It should make you feel better." I braced his shoulders up a couple of inches, and he took several sips before his face scrunched up.

"Tastes awful."

"Take another sip for me."

Naya brought me a basin of water, and I dipped a cloth in, wrung it out, and ran it across his forehead and down his cheeks. I laid the cold cloth up against his black eye.

"How does that feel?" I asked.

"Better. Thanks." He stared at me with those ridiculous turquoise eyes of his. "You don't strike me as someone who forgets much. I'm going to owe you big time when we get back to earth, aren't I?"

I ran the cloth over his face again. "I won't make you squirm too much."

He closed his eyes and took a shaky breath, and I blinked to stop a tear from escaping. I sponged his face and arms for a few more minutes until I could tell by his even breathing that he had fallen back to sleep.

Damn it. I couldn't forget anything. Seeing him this weak was too much like last year and the torture he endured. He was not going to die in some demon dimension. He needed to get back to earth so he could get his life together again.

We both did.

CHAPTER 22

I stared at the flames dancing in the hearth until my eyes burned. Or at least that's what I told myself when I wiped the tears from my cheeks.

Naya blocked my view of the flames as she stirred the pot cooking in the hearth. "Tell me your story, Kyle."

"What do you mean?"

"I sense powers in you, and you keep them a secret from Dalton. Yet he is aware of the supernatural."

I blew out a harsh breath. "I'm human, but for some reason I have the ability to manipulate memories. I use my powers to stop humans from finding out about supernaturals living on earth."

"And how does Dalton fit into your world?" Naya asked.

I looked back at the fire and bit my lip.

"When you leave here, we will never see each other again, Kyle. Your secret is safe with me." She ladled some stew on a plate and handed it to me. "You love him."

"Yes. I did, or I do... Oh, hell, my life is too damn complicated. Even the explanation is too damn complicated. I met Dalton last year on a case. He was tortured to the point of insanity, and the only way I could save him was to erase his memory of the case and of me. And he went away and started a new life. But the Fates brought him back into my life on this new case, and now I have to pretend like I don't know him."

"And that you don't love him."

"Yes," I said, my heart pinching inside my chest.

"It sounds like one of my Russian novels."

I smirked and then studied the stew on my plate.

"Don't worry, you can eat it. It's just vegetable stew."

"You're using contractions. Before you were speaking differently. Now you're using contractions."

She tilted her head slightly as if puzzling my words.

"Before you said 'do not' and now you say 'don't.'"

"Ah. Yes. I adjusted my speech after I listened to you and Dalton. I learn languages through my books. Speaking it can be very different from reading it."

"Wow. How many languages can you speak?"

Naya shrugged. "Maybe a dozen or so."

"Amazing. I would love for you to meet Jean Luc. He speaks seven, but refuses to use contractions in any of them. He sounds like he's from the Middle Ages half the time."

"I wish I could meet him as well. Now eat while the food is hot."

I took a bite. The stew was rich, the vegetables reminding me of carrots and potatoes. "It's good."

"Tell me of your case on earth."

I leaned closer. "You mean we can work together?"

Naya sat across from me with her own plate. "I haven't agreed yet. Tell me what's happening."

As we ate our dinner, I told her about the demon in the art museum and what we'd learned so far.

Naya picked up our plates and set them next to the washbasin. "And the demon had multiple powers?"

"Yes. The clans on earth don't have multiple powers. And the blood sample didn't match any of the demons found on earth."

"What did his demon form look like?"

"He never turned into his demon. Stayed human. But his eyes glowed white."

Naya frowned. "White?"

"Yeah, it confused us, too. Does it mean anything to you?"

"No." Naya busied herself with the dishes. After a few moments she spoke again. "I'll help you with the case. But it will be difficult since I can't come to earth."

"Difficult, but not impossible."

She walked to a shelf and picked up a bowl that she brought to the table along with a small metal hammer. Naya extracted a piece of red crystal the shape of a quarter from the bowl.

I leaned closer to look at it. "What is it?"

"It will allow me to communicate with you." She placed the crystal on the table and rapped it once with the hammer. The crystal broke into two, jagged, half-moon pieces, like the forever friend charms kids wear.

"Why did you break it?" I asked.

"Because you need to carry half and I'll keep the other half. It will connect us so we can communicate telepathically."

"And you think it'll work on earth?"

"Yes. I believe so. I've never tried to communicate as far as earth before, which is why I'm giving you the crystal to provide a conduit."

"So you're telepathic."

"Yes. I'm surprised you didn't ask me what my power was before now."

I shrugged. "On earth it can be a touchy subject, and I didn't want to alienate you."

Naya chuckled. "Why do I get the feeling you don't normally worry about alienating others?"

"You're right. But I'm trying to be a new and improved Kyle McKinley. Think before I open my mouth. Unfortunately, it hasn't been working very well with Dalton."

"Because your feelings are involved. You'll figure out what to do with him."

I stood. "I better go check on him."

"And I'm going to leave for a few minutes to check on some things as well."

When I entered the bedroom, Dalton was sleeping, and the sound of his even breathing settled my nerves. I touched his forehead lightly. Still hot, but no worse than before. When I ran the washcloth over his face, he didn't stir, so I sat in the chair and watched him sleep. After a couple of minutes, my eyes drooped, and I crossed my arms on the bed and lay my head on top of them.

A tingle ran along my neck. Someone was watching me. I opened my eyes slowly and found Dalton staring at me, his eyes almost iridescent in his pale face.

"That doesn't look very comfortable."

I sat up and cringed. "It's not."

"How long have I been asleep?" he asked.

"A couple of hours...I think." I stared out the window into the dark sky and then at the burning lamp next to the bed. "I'm not sure how long I was asleep."

"Naya brought the lamp in here a couple of minutes ago and made me drink some more of her nasty tea. You were sleeping so soundly she didn't want to disturb you."

I kneaded my stiff neck and shoulders. "How are you feeling?"

"Weak. Leave it to me to get the damn flu when we're stuck in a demon dimension."

"Bad timing for sure."

His eyes sharpened on me. "What's wrong?"

"Nothing," I answered, looking away from him.

"Has anyone ever told you you're a bad liar?"

"Yeah. You. Two days ago." Except I couldn't be that bad a liar, or he'd already know the whole truth, so help me God.

"What's going on, McKinley?"

"Naya thinks you're sick because this dimension is toxic to you."

He frowned. "It's poisoning me?"

"Kind of. Humans aren't exactly made to live here."

"What about you? Are you feeling okay?"

"I'm okay so far. And Naya said once we get back to earth, you'll be fine."

"Have we heard anything from the team yet?"

"No, but I'm sure they'll be coming for us any minute now. Misha, Jean Luc, and Talia won't rest until they find us."

"You have a good team."

I jerked back in shock and then tugged on my ear like it was waterlogged. "I think I heard you compliment us. It must be the fever talking."

He smirked. "Maybe."

Naya came into the room in time to interrupt my heart palpitations triggered by Dalton's almost smile. Almost.

"I thought I heard talking. Your friends are coming for you. The patrol has sensed an energy disturbance for several hours now. Usually it means someone is attempting to pass through the portal. You will need to be ready to move quickly once the portal opens. I've set a chair outside for Dalton.

"I should be fine." Dalton sat up and swung his legs to the side and swayed forward.

I grabbed him before he face-planted. "Whoa. Maybe a chair is a good idea."

Naya and I each took a side and draped Dalton's arms over our shoulders.

"You ready?" I asked.

"Yep."

We walked slowly through the cottage and out the door. The night air was warmer, almost a thick blanket, compared to what it had been during the day. A glow lit the sky in purples and pinks and blues, reminding me of the aura borealis.

We sat Dalton down slowly, and he took a couple of deep breaths once he was sitting.

"Is that your normal sky?" I asked.

"No. Those colors mean the portal is forming. Normally, we don't know where it will show up, which is the biggest stumbling block in our battle against the traffickers. This time, we have a pretty good idea it will be here."

"Knowing my friends, I think you're right."

Naya gestured for me to follow her. I leaned down for a minute and checked Dalton carefully. He didn't look like he was going to pitch out of the chair, but I wanted to make sure. "You okay to sit for a minute while I say goodbye to Naya?"

"Yep, I won't flop onto the ground."

I walked over to join Naya a few feet away.

Naya spoke softly. "When he gets back to earth, it's going to be a shock to his body. He may get worse before he gets better."

"Okay. Is there anything we can do for him?"

"Fluids to flush his system. Also, strip and bathe him right way, so anything remaining from the realm and in-between is cleared out completely."

"Thank you for helping us. You could have simply killed us back in the forest."

"And miss all this fun?"

I chuckled. "The next time your leader comes to earth, I'm going to make sure he brings you some reading material that is more recent than the 1800's. I've got some interesting stories in mind."

Naya smiled and grasped my hand, pressing the crystal in my palm. The air started to sizzle with energy, and warm tendrils danced across my skin.

"It's time."

I went to Dalton and pulled him from the chair as the air in front of me started to undulate. We stumbled forward, Dalton leaning heavily on me.

"I wish we could meet again sometime, Kyle."

I looked over my shoulder at Naya and smiled. "Me too."

I stepped into the shimmering light and held tight to Dalton while we catapulted into the void.

CHAPTER 23

My breath hitched as if I was on top of a rollercoaster hill right before the car plummeted. After several seconds, I dropped, my screams stuck in my throat until we landed with a *thud* on the ground, Dalton sprawled on top.

Dalton rolled off of me with a moan, and I pushed myself up from damp grass. I shook my head to clear it, trying to focus on where we were, but our surroundings were still blurry, wavering as if we were underwater. Finally, the air stopped shimmying. I blinked. We were on a lawn outside a high fence. It was night, but floodlights illuminated the area.

Multiple shouts rang out, and I looked behind us. Doc and Jean Luc ran in our direction while Misha guarded one of the demons from the warehouse. He must have been the one to open the portal for us.

"Are you okay, Kyle?" Doc asked.

"I'm fine. It's Dalton."

"Is he hurt?" Doc turned to him and ran her trained gaze over his body.

"The realm was toxic for him. We need to get him out of these clothes and scrub him down. We also need to flush his system."

Doc knelt next to him. "I'm Doctor Miller. I'm going to take care of you. How are you feeling?"

"Like I have some super-flu bug. I'm weak and achy, and I'm pretty sure I'm running a fever."

"Let's get you cleaned up and start an IV to flush that demon toxin out of your system."

"Okay. But check McKinley over too."

Doc smiled at him. "I'll do that as soon as we get you settled."

Dalton attempted to sit up, but he was as wobbly as a newborn colt. Doc nodded at Jean Luc, who picked Dalton up and carried him to the open doors of a van.

"Where are we?" I asked.

"We're outside the Shamat compound. Irina wanted you close to their medical facility so we could help when you returned. She was afraid of what the demon realm would do to you. But we didn't want to risk opening the portal inside the compound walls."

Sabrina gave me a quick ER-Doc-mode exam as well.

"I'm fine."

"I'll be the judge of that. Let's get you in the van and up to the facility as well."

I didn't bother arguing. After I climbed inside the van, Talia drove us through the gate into the demon compound, turning right toward a building I hadn't noticed the last time we were there.

We stopped in front of the facility, and the doors opened to a group of people in scrubs pushing two gurneys. Jean Luc placed Dalton on the first one.

I shook my head when one of the orderlies came up to me. "Nope. Take care of Dalton, I'm fine."

Doc said, "I'll check you later. But I still want you to shower and bag up all your clothes. Boots too."

Talia spoke up. "I'll make sure she does."

A nurse led us down a hall to a lounge area with a large shower. She took towels from a cabinet and set them on a bench; then she gave me a biohazard bag for my clothes.

I sighed. I did *not* want to throw away my steel-toe black work boots. This was the second pair this week. They went with everything and let me wade through the messiest supe cleanups unscathed.

"Did you guys find Stanley?"

"Yeah, Misha has Stanley, and Dalton's gun, too. You steady enough to shower, Kyle?" Talia asked.

"Yeah. I can scrub my own back."

She chuckled. "I'll sit out here and wait for you."

I washed my body and hair twice before toweling off and dressing in the light blue scrubs and canvas shoes that had appeared on the bench while I was in the shower.

When I went into the lounge area, Talia looked me over. "At least you've got some color back in your face." She held up a cup. "Orange juice."

"I want to see how Dalton's doing."

"We'll go find out, but drink this first."

I took the cup, gulped it down, and then found Dalton's room. There were a lot of people coming and going, and I had to stand on my tiptoes in the doorway to see what was going on. Dalton was lying on a gurney. He was stripped with the exception of a towel draped across his manly parts, and nurses were bathing him. His eyes were closed, and his head lolled to the side. An IV ran to his arm, and he was wearing an oxygen mask.

My heart hammered and I had trouble swallowing. "What's going on?"

Doc pushed me into the hall. "He's been having trouble breathing, Kyle. We're giving him oxygen, and we're washing him down a second time. Then we'll transfer him into a clean room."

I started into the room again, but Talia steered me a few feet down the hall to a set of chairs.

"You'll be in the way. Sit. You're white as a sheet again."

The backs of my knees met a chair, and I folded onto it, resting my head in my hands. The orange juice churned in my stomach. He couldn't die.

"Kyle!"

Griffin ran down the hall toward me and I stood. He grabbed me and pulled me against him. "Are you okay?"

"Yes."

He held me away to look me over, his hand still grasping my shoulders. "You're not okay. You're in pain. Where's Sabrina? Why isn't someone taking care of you?"

"I'm not hurt. I—" I stopped talking when I caught sight of Sabrina coming out of Dalton's room. "Is he okay?" I blurted.

She put her hand on my shoulder and nodded to Griffin. "Joe's fine, Kyle. The oxygen helped. And the IV is flushing his system. His fever is also going down. Irina has some ideas to help him as well."

I took a deep breath, and my heart started up again.

Griffin stood quietly next to me. I didn't know what to say to him. My emotions were in the nuclear meltdown stage, so there was no hiding anything from him right now. His shifter senses were more than likely begging for a hazmat suit.

"I want to check you now, Kyle."

"I'm fine."

Griffin grasped my hand. "Please, Kyle. Let her examine you."

I stared into his green eyes. Sparks of amber broke through his pupils, and I squeezed his hand. He was trying so hard to control his emotions.

"Okay. I'll do it for you."

I loosened my grip and tried to take a step away from him, but he held on for a moment longer. I smiled at him and he slid his hand away from mine. I flexed my fingers, closing my hand into a fist to try to hang onto the heat of his touch, to keep it from bleeding away as I walked down the hall away from him.

CHAPTER 24

"I'm fine," I said for the third time.

Griffin simply stared at me. We had moved to the main building to meet with Irina. We were waiting in a small sitting room, Griffin on a chair across from mine. Why wasn't he sitting next to me? Maybe he'd decided that chair gave him a better angle to glare.

He had tried to get me to lie down, but there was no way I could relax. Talia had thankfully found me some real clothes, but I was still wearing the canvas shoes they had given me earlier. At least Dalton was doing better. According to Doc, he could breathe on his own now, and she had given him a mild sedative when he insisted he was fine and wanted to get up. His stubborn streak was in full force.

Irina walked into the room and patted my shoulder. "It is good to see you, Kyle."

I smiled at her. "Thanks for your help."

She batted her hand in an *it-was-nothing* gesture before sitting next to me. "You had no ill effects from the demon realm?"

"No. I was lucky. If I'd gotten sick like Dalton, I don't know how we would have gotten back."

Irina stared at me for a moment and opened her mouth to say something, but was interrupted by Misha, who rushed into the room.

"Kyle!" Misha yanked me into his arms like a rag doll.

I let out a squeak from the depths of his bear hug. "I'm fine, Mish, honest."

Irina tsked. "Put her down, Mikhail."

He plopped me back down in my seat and then sat next to Griffin. "Glad you could get here, Griffin."

"I was an hour away when you called me, or I would have been here sooner."

I frowned. "Why did you wait to call him, Mish? We were gone for a day."

Misha shook his head. "No, little one. You were only gone for a couple of hours. Remember Eli said time is different in the demon realm."

"You can say that again. We got sucked into the portal at night, but it was daytime there."

"What was it like?" Misha asked.

"It started out like a trip to Mars with dirt and red rocks, then the realm went all scary woods vibe. It reminded me of purgatory on *Supernatural*."

"Great show," Irina chirped.

I gawked at her.

Irina chuckled at my gaping fish imitation. "Honey, even though demons get a bad rap on that show, it's worth putting up with that part so I can watch those two mouthwatering brothers."

Misha clutched his forehead. "*Babushka!*"

"I'm not dead, Mikhail."

I grinned. I should introduce Irina to Marie. They would get along *really* well. "The in-between reminded me of a small English village, but with no modern conveniences."

Irina tilted her head slightly in question. "How did you get to the in-between?"

"We fought off the demon that sent us to the realm and then ran into a border patrol demon. She took us to the in-between to protect us until you could open the portal again."

"Did Dalton get the black eye fighting the demon?" Misha asked.

"Yeah."

"Damn. I owe Jean Luc twenty bucks."

"What are you talking about?"

"I bet you'd clocked him one."

"I didn't clock him!"

Irina scowled at Misha and then said, "Tell us exactly what occurred, Kyle."

"Mish, could you go find Jean Luc and Talia so I don't have to repeat this a gazillion times?"

Misha stood to leave, but Irina held up her hand to stop him. "You better find Boris, too. If your father misses Kyle's story he will pout for days."

Twenty minutes later, I had finished telling the story to a small room chock-full of people. Irina, Misha, Jean Luc, Talia, Boris, and Griffin listened intently to my story without interrupting until I mentioned what Naya had told me about the mating across clans.

Misha sat bolt upright. "That isn't possible."

Irina shook her head. "I have lived a long time, and so I can tell you with certainty that anything is possible. It is fate's way of giving back."

"What do you mean, *Babushka*?"

"She means that the border patrol got the short end of the stick. They spend their lives protecting us, and yet they can't come to earth. So they've been given the ability to mate between clans as a way to continue their purpose."

Irina nodded her agreement.

"Naya says she was born to protect the borders, and she'll help us any way she can."

"If she cannot come to earth, how does she plan to help?" Jean Luc asked.

"She can communicate telepathically. She's going to keep an eye out on her side and tell us if anything happens there. She gave me a crystal to help link us telepathically. I'm supposed to keep it close to me."

"Where is it?" Irina asked.

I pulled the crystal out of my canvas shoe, running my thumb over the jagged edge.

Irina held out her hand. "May I see it?"

I gave it to her, and she stared at it in silence for a long moment, turning the stone over and over in her hand.

She gestured to Boris, who went to stand next to her. Irina placed my crystal in his palm.

"What are you going to do with it?" I asked.

"No worries, Kyle. I will bring it back to you shortly." He left the room.

A lull filled the room before I blurted, "What are our next steps?"

Griffin frowned. "Don't you think you should take a break?"

"Doc said I'm fine." When Griffin opened his mouth, looking ready to protest, I rushed on. "I need to do this."

He stared at me for a moment before nodding slightly.

I turned to Misha. "Did you guys capture Eli?"

"Yes. He and bouncer Johnny are being held in a cell in one of our outbuildings."

"What will happen to them?" Griffin asked.

Irina answered. "They'll face charges in front of the Demon Council."

"And the demon from the realm?" I asked.

"He'll be returned to the realm once we've finished questioning him," Misha replied.

I rubbed my hands together. "So let's go interrogate us some demons."

CHAPTER 25

Griffin, Misha, and I entered the one-story facility where the demons were being held, and Misha led us down the hall to a room with a table and monitors displaying live feeds of the cells. The monitor on the right showed Eli and Johnny, and the monitor on the left showed the realm demon.

"Pretty fancy setup, Mish."

He grinned and sat in front of the computers. "It was easy to do. Since Father is one of the Demon Council leaders, he has a responsibility to be vigilant in guarding against those of us who break the rules."

I stared at the realm demon pacing back and forth in his cell. "How did you get him to help you?"

"We persuaded him that it would be in his best interest."

"How could you tell he was opening the portal and not trying to trick you? What if he'd lied to you?"

"Jason would have been able to tell if he was lying."

I spun to face Misha. "Jason's here, now?"

"Yes."

I couldn't have heard that right. "He's helping with the investigation? What made him come?"

Misha smiled. "You. I told him you were stuck in a demon dimension, and he came to help."

My throat tightened. "I'm surprised he didn't say good riddance."

Misha clucked his tongue at me. "Kyle. He cares about you. That's why he was so hurt when you kept the truth from him."

"But I wasn't trying to hurt him, Mish! I just wanted to have more information before I told him the truth. If I'd been able to tell him more about his background, it could have helped with the news that he's part shifter. Instead, he was blindsided. I should have never kept it from him."

Griffin shook his head. "I was the one who told you not to tell him the truth."

"It's still my fault."

Misha held up his hand. "Talk to Jason, Kyle, and explain."

"I tried to before, but he wouldn't listen."

"He'll listen," Misha answered in a tone that brooked no argument, and his gaze flicked away from my face to focus over my shoulder for a split second.

I glared at Misha, who winked at me before I turned and saw Jason standing in the door.

"Good to see you, Jason," I said, my voice cracking at the end like a pre-pubescent boy.

He nodded, his face not showing any hint of emotion. "Glad you're okay."

"Thank you for helping." I took a tentative step in his direction while I steadied my breathing. "I wouldn't have blamed you if you'd steered clear of us forever, but I want you to know I'm sorry I didn't tell you the truth sooner. I thought I was doing the right thing at the time, and I certainly never wanted to hurt you. In fact, it's why I waited."

"Of course you didn't mean to hurt me, Kyle. But you know trust isn't easy for me, and you broke that trust."

"It's not easy for me, either. And it was wrong of me to not tell you the truth as soon as I found out about it."

Griffin walked over and stood next to me. "And I apologize for keeping it from you, and for the pain you suffered at my brother's hand. If you ever want to learn more about your shifter side, I'm available to help. Or if you don't want to deal with me, I can find someone else to work with you."

Jason cleared his throat. "I'll keep that in mind."

Misha stood and clapped his hands together. "Now that we've made up, can we decide which demon to interrogate first?"

I studied the monitors for a moment. "I think Johnny does what he's told to do. Not sure if he'll be a font of information. Of the two, I think we'll get more information out of Eli. What do you think, Jason?"

"I think we split them up and interrogate Johnny first. Make Eli sweat a little bit."

"You're devious," I chuckled. "I like it."

Jason grinned. "Takes one to know one."

I grinned right back at him. Things were going to be okay between Jason and me. I hadn't screwed it up. "Then we go talk to the realm demon."

"The realm demon is a slippery bastard. I'm not sure how much we're going to get out of him."

"Hopefully Eli will give us something we can dangle in front of him to persuade him to talk." Plus, I wanted to find out why he and his brother had reacted to me the way they did at the warehouse.

Twenty minutes later, I'd been proven right. Johnny knew almost nothing about the operation. He simply went where Eli told him to go and served as his guard. If he'd been smart, he would have listened and learned so he could use it himself in the future if he needed to. But Johnny wasn't smart.

Jason and Misha returned Johnny to his cell, and I went into the surveillance room where Griffin had stayed to observe. Griffin was just ending a call.

"Problem?" I asked.

"No. I was getting a status report from Tim."

"If you need to be somewhere..." And like that, the proverbial light bulb went on. "Today was your quarterly board meeting. I pulled you away from that? Crap, Griffin, I feel terrible about this."

"Tim handled it. It's not an issue."

"Well, I'm still sorry I worried you."

He frowned. "You can't stop me from worrying about the people I care for, Kyle. It's not part of my DNA...or yours, for that matter."

I started at the vehemence of his tone, but quickly recovered. "I know."

He closed his eyes for a moment, and when he opened them, the storm had subsided. "I think I'll leave you to your work now, if you're okay."

I nodded. "Yes. You being here means a lot to me." I reached for him, but before I could touch him, Boris bustled into the room.

"Here you are!"

Griffin said his goodbyes and left. Boris wrapped his big arm around my shoulder. "I didn't get to tell you earlier, Kyle, how happy I am that you're okay."

I grinned up at him. "Considering we didn't like each other much when we first met, I'm happy that you're happy."

He barked out a laugh. "I have something for you."

Boris opened his hand and let a silver chain dangle from his fingers. Attached to the bottom of the chain was the crystal Naya had given me. He gestured for me to turn, and he fastened it around my neck. I ran my fingers over the cool stone, and it quickly warmed to my touch.

"Thanks."

He bowed in his over-the-top way. "We couldn't have you carrying it around in your shoe all day. It would have gotten quite uncomfortable."

Misha poked his head into the room. "We have Eli in the interrogation room. Are you ready to ask some questions?"

I tucked the necklace under my shirt. "Absolutely."

Eli was an actor for sure. His facial expression might have said "I could care less," but the stiff set of his shoulders said otherwise. Plus, his normally slicked-back hair was sticking up at odd angles. He was in trouble with a capital "T," and he knew it. And from the amount of perspiration gathering on his upper lip, his brain was doing mental gymnastics to figure out how to get out of this situation.

I couldn't blame Eli for his anxiety. I sure wouldn't want to have to face the Demon Council. From what I gathered, demon trafficking was bad—as in breaking one of the top three commandments, bad. But I had no sympathy for him. He was greedy, and greed made even the smartest beings' IQs take a nosedive.

I sat across from him. Misha crossed his arms and stood to my right while Jason stood to the left. Both glared at Eli. It made an intimidating picture, but that was the point.

Eli swallowed and tried not to look at the intimidation squad. Which meant he stared at me.

I gave him my toothiest smile. "I'm baa-ack."

Eli's eyes widened at my words. Both Jason and Misha would get the *Poltergeist* reference, but it wouldn't hurt to throw Eli off a bit.

"How?"

"Your friend the realm demon helped my friends out. I think he's trying to cut a deal. Make things better for himself with the Demon Council."

Eli's wide eyes narrowed into slits. "I had nothing to do with sending you to the demon realm."

I tapped my fingers on the table. "No, but you brokered the deal, which makes you an accessory to attempted murder."

Eli jerked upright. "Attempted murder? What are you talking about?"

"Sending humans to the demon realm is a death sentence."

"And the demon that did it got away! That's his twin you're holding in the other cell. Ask him where the bastard is who transported you. I'm not taking the rap for what he did."

"Even so, the Demon Council isn't going to go easy on you. I know the saying is 'Go Big or Go Home,' but demon trafficking is a big no-no."

"What do you want from me?"

"The recent art museum break-in was done by a realm demon. We want to know who helped him."

Eli shook his head. "I don't broker deals from the other side. I deal with earth demons who want to go to the realm."

I stared at him for a moment until his eyes darted away. "You might not broker the deals, but there have to be demons on this side that help the realm demons. When they come here for the first time, they can't be left on their own. Hell, they wouldn't have any idea what to do with our technology, how to drive a car, or how to buy food and clothes. Do they even know how to change into their human form when they first arrive? Who handles that for them?"

"You should talk to Sylvia Reynolds. She runs a motel on the west side, helping the demons acclimate to earth. Takes them in and teaches them how to survive here."

"Like a demon halfway house?"

"Pretty much, yeah. Are we done?"

I stopped myself from huffing. "Far from. We want to understand how this process works. We want names and locations. Anything that can help stop the trafficking."

Eli scowled. "The circuit is too big. I only know how it works here in Cleveland."

I shrugged. "That at least is a start." I stood and gestured to Misha. "Fill my friend in here with the rest of what you know."

Jason followed me out of the room. "You did a good job in there."

"He was ready to sing. I didn't even have to push him hard. Was he telling the truth?"

"Yeah. I'll go and listen to the rest of his story to make sure he isn't lying."

"I'm going to check on Dalton. We can question the realm demon once you guys finish with Eli."

I walked out of the detention building and across the lawn. The air was chilly, but at least it wasn't damp, and I stared up at the dark sky for a moment. Lampposts illuminated the area, and I sucked in a lungful of air to help clear my groggy brain. The demon-dimension-jump business was finally getting to me. I needed a hot bath and a day's sleep.

Once inside the hospital building, I searched for Doc. I found her writing some notes on a computer tablet.

"How's Dalton doing?"

"He's bouncing back. Still weak, but getting snarky. He's not happy I sedated him earlier. If he keeps it up, he might be a worse patient than Misha."

"Wow, that's saying something. Is he up for visitors?"

"Yeah. Just don't blame me if he bites your head off."

I walked softly down the hall and peeked into Dalton's room to make sure he wasn't sleeping. He was awake, and he scooted up farther in his bed when he caught sight of me and beckoned for me to come in.

"How are you feeling?"

"Fine. Fill me in on what's going on," he demanded.

Well, Sabrina hadn't been exaggerating about Mr. Surly. But I wasn't going to go down the el destructo path I always did with him. I would be the bigger person. "We interrogated the bouncer and Eli. Misha and Jason are finishing up with him now."

"Who's Jason?"

"He's another member of our team. He's very good at interrogations."

"You brought someone else in on the case without consulting me first?" Dalton growled.

"He was brought in while we were in the demon dimension. I only found out myself a little while ago."

"What have you learned?"

"Eli gave us the name of someone who helps acclimate realm demons that come to earth. He's also giving Misha information about how his part of the trafficking operation runs."

"And what about the realm demon?"

"We're interrogating him next."

Dalton threw the covers off and moved to the edge of the bed.

I rushed over and held my hands up like a traffic cop. "Whoa. You're not ready to get out of bed yet."

"I'm fine."

"You were passed out earlier and breathing through an oxygen mask. You're not fine."

"You're not a doctor."

"No. I'm the one who took care of your weak ass in the in-between. Now stay on that bed, or I swear I'll handcuff you to it."

He opened his mouth, but his retort was drowned out by an alarm bell. I ran to the door and looked cautiously up and down the hall. Was it the fire alarm?

Doc came racing into the room.

"Sabrina, what's going on?"

"Something's happening at the detention center. They're locking down the hospital as a precaution."

Shit! I ran down the hall, ignoring Dalton's shouts, and slammed out of the side door before the locks clicked. I kicked off the canvas shoes I was wearing and bolted for the center, the wet, cold grass freezing my feet. But the cold didn't stop there. It shot up my spine. What the hell was going on, and were Misha and Jason okay?

I careened around the edge of the building and skidded to a stop in the grass when I saw Jason standing out front, guarding the door.

"What's going on?" I yelled over the alarm.

"A portal opened in the realm demon's cell, and he got away," he hollered back.

"Shit, his brother must have tracked him here. Why are the alarms still on?"

"Misha's sensors are detecting energy spikes."

The air between us wobbled like gelatin, and my stomach bottomed out. *Not again.* Jason pulled his gun and fired at the demon twins as they emerged from the portal, hitting one in the arm. The demon screamed and scurried backward. The other demon reached for me, but invisible hands grabbed me first and carried me on a wave of speed, away from the portal and across the grass. Jason fired two more shots as the portal closed around the last demon.

My stomach lurched as we came to a halt. "I could kiss you, Jea..." Except I didn't finish my sentence because Jean Luc ran past me with Misha following close behind.

A feminine chuckle sounded behind me. "You might not want to kiss me, Kyle, it would overly excite the menfolk."

"Talia?" I squeaked. "Oh, jeeezzz. I thought—"

"Not surprising. Jean Luc does have a tendency to save the day a lot."

"Thank you."

She set me down, and while we walked back over to the building, the alarms finally stopped.

Jean Luc took a step toward us, his pupils flickering red. "Are you both okay?"

Talia rested her hand on his arm. "We're fine."

"How did the other twin find his brother?" I asked. "Some freakish demon twin connection?"

Misha scowled. "That would take a lot of power. The better question is why would they risk appearing again after they'd already escaped?"

"Because they tried to grab Kyle," Jason said.

All four of them stared at me for a moment, while I tried not to squirm. "What?"

"Do you have any idea why they were after you?" Jean Luc asked.

"No. But when Dalton and I were in the demon realm, one of the twins tried to grab me there, too."

"Why didn't you say anything about this earlier?" Misha asked.

"For two reasons. One, I didn't want Griffin to freak out. And two, I didn't know if they were grabbing me because they wanted to use my power, or if they could maybe sense something else in me."

Talia's eyes widened. "The Key."

"Right. How do we know what the realm demons might sense that we can't? Since I was relating the story to a room full of people, some of whom don't know about the Key, I didn't think it was wise to mention it then."

Misha nodded. "Jason, Jean Luc, and I will check the perimeter as soon as Doc gets here. I called her a few minutes ago."

"I'm fine."

"She's coming over to check on one of the clan guards who was banged up a bit when the demons escaped."

"She's locked in," I argued.

"Once the alarms stopped, the buildings came off lockdown," Misha explained.

I smacked my thigh with my palm. "Damn. I should have stayed and questioned him earlier."

Jean Luc pinned me with his stare. "Which means you would have been in the room when they escaped the first time. No one would have been there to stop them from taking you. My heart is old, *ma petite*, and you have been testing it quite frequently lately."

I chuckled. "Your heart could stop beating, and you would still be here to grouse at me."

"And you are lucky for it."

"I'm not sure we would have gotten much from the realm demon anyway," Jason added. "Especially since he was biding his time until his brother could find him."

"What else did you get from Eli?" I asked.

Misha answered. "Some names of minor players and the process he follows to set up most of the portal jumps. That should help the demon council shut down the trafficking here in Cleveland, at least."

"When do we go talk to Sylvia Reynolds?"

Jean Luc frowned. "I think we should regroup as a team tomorrow and plan our next steps. We do not need to charge over there tonight."

I sighed. "There will be no charging from me. I'm more than done today."

I jumped slightly when I noticed Doc next to me with her medical bag in hand. She was one stealthy demon.

"I'm glad to hear it, Kyle. I was going to suggest you call it a night but was afraid you would fight me on it."

"Dalton's not with you?"

"He tried to come, but he almost took a header when he stood up. I ordered some food for him and promised someone would be over to report in ASAP." She grinned at me. "He was especially irritated when you took off."

Pissed was more like it. "You guys can fill in *Mon Capitan*. I don't think I should try to deal with him right now. I'm going home."

"What if the demons come after you again?" Jean Luc asked.

I shook my head. "I should be safe for now, Jean Luc. They don't know where I live, and Jason winged the one. They'll need to lie low for a while."

He opened his mouth to protest, but I held up my hand. "Please don't. I can't live like I did last summer, afraid of my own shadow. I'm taking Stanley with me and calling it a night."

CHAPTER 26

I dragged myself up the stairs to my apartment, fumbling with my keys. Bath, ice cream, bed. Bath, ice cream, bed. My mantra for the evening—well, technically the middle of the night. But my bed was calling ever so loudly, which made me rethink things. I could eat my ice cream while I was in my bath. That would shorten the timeframe between wakey-time and REM.

Two steps into my apartment and a voice called through my door.

"*Knock, knock.*"

My plan had just been blown to hell.

I laid my forehead against the doorjamb. "What do you want?"

"Aren't you going to open the door and see who it is?"

"I know it's you, Marie. I recognize your voice, and everyone else actually knocks."

A disgusted huff sounded. "I can't knock, Kyle. I'm a ghost, remember?"

"I remember. You're the one who keeps hanging around on earth. Isn't there some resort cloud you could be chilling out on instead?"

Marie floated through the door and brushed my shoulder, sending cold shivers along my skin. She turned, placed her hands on her hips and glared at me. "Where have you been? I couldn't sense you earlier."

"Dalton and I were in the demon realm."

Marie gaped. "What? Where's Joe now?"

"Your grandson is fine. Got a little sick in the realm, but he's bouncing back. Doc is watching over him."

"How in the world did you let yourself get sucked into a demon realm?"

"The case we're working involves demons traveling from the realm illegally. We set up a sting, and it went south."

"South is Miami Beach, Kyle. You ended up in a *demon realm*."

"We're getting closer to figuring out what's going on. Once we do, Dalton will return to Chicago."

"Is that what you want?" Marie asked.

The words stuck in my throat like a piece of hard candy, choking me. "I want him to be happy, and from the way he's been acting, he's not happy."

She frowned at me. "Maybe he's not happy because he's away from you."

"Don't, Marie. We're not doing this again. He doesn't remember me. He doesn't like me, and I can't risk that he might remember his torture. He barely made it through the last time. I'm sorry, but you have to leave now. I have to get some sleep."

"Kyle—"

"Later, okay?" I must have had a pathetic look on my face, because she faded away, leaving behind the smell of roses.

I blew out a breath and headed for the bathroom when someone knocked. I stomped back to the door, jerked it open, and hissed. "Cut it out!"

Except it wasn't Marie standing in the door. And if I'd thought about it for a second, I would have remembered that Marie, *duh*, couldn't knock.

Griffin stared back at me, eyebrow raised.

"Sorry, I thought you were someone else." I stepped back and let him in.

His stared at me hard. He didn't speak, but his eyes pierced me, as if he was attempting to reach inside my brain to discern the truth. My throat tightened as the silence stretched on. He ran his fingers through his hair.

"Forgive me for showing up without calling. I needed to be sure you're all right."

"I'm okay."

Griffin walked further into my living room, running his hand over a stack of books. It was my mystery stack. He picked up the top book and flipped it open.

He was scaring me. He was avoiding eye contact, and he'd avoided touching me. Not Griffin's style. My stomach twisted.

"Tell me what's wrong, Griffin."

He glanced up at me, and for a moment, I wished he had kept avoiding me. His eyes flashed amber, sharp sparks of fire that seemed to burn me. I was not going to like this conversation at all. He opened his mouth, but nothing came out.

Waiting for his words was slow torture.

"You're breaking it off with me," I blurted. I couldn't stop myself. Maybe if I threw the words out there in the ozone, ripped off the Band-Aid so to speak, it wouldn't hurt so much. Or maybe he would tell me how ridiculous I was being.

But he didn't. Instead, he dropped the book and came closer to me. My instinct was to step back, to turn away from him. But I wouldn't do that. I couldn't do that to him or to me.

"The first time I saw you sitting in the tree house with Trina, I wanted you. I knew you were dangerous for me. But back then you were with Joe, so I didn't pursue you. Then you were alone, and my alarms were going off telling me to stay away, but I couldn't." He stopped for a moment as if to gather his thoughts.

"The biggest risk in starting a relationship with you wasn't because you're human. It's because you were still in love with someone else. Someone who was no longer available to you. If he had died, you could have eventually moved on and let him go. But this? This terrible limbo state you live in was—is—torture.

"Your passion is what attracted me to you in the first place, Kyle. It takes a lot for someone to gain your trust. And to gain your love? That is the ultimate prize. I took the risk, and I'm happy I had my time with you. But I can't be your consolation prize."

I opened my mouth to argue, and he held up his hands.

"I know you don't think that way. But I can sense your emotions when you're around him. They are volatile and soul-driven. I can't compete with that."

"Do I get to talk now?"

He nodded.

"I won't lie to you. I love Dalton. There is a part of me that will always love Dalton. And I haven't been able to fully let him go." I swallowed. "When I lost him, in typical Kyle fashion I ran away. From everyone and everything who meant anything to me. I ran, because it was easier than facing the truth. Easier than letting anyone else help me. I decided I'd rather be by myself than allow anyone else to hurt me. But then you came along. Let me tell you what you did for me."

I stared hard into his green eyes, trying not to let the tears fall, but it was a lost cause. "You made me a stronger person. You called me to the table and wouldn't take any of my I-am-an-island bullshit. And you were right. I couldn't have done it without you.

"It was time to grow up and move on, and I was doing that with you." My voice wobbled, so I took a shaky breath. "But he came back. Before I had finished repairing my heart. Instead, he ripped the wound back open again. And the pathetic thing is, he doesn't even know I love him. That he wields such power over me.

"He's going to leave again, and I am going to have to say goodbye again. But as much as it will hurt me, I can survive it. You helped me see that I can survive it. And I love you for it."

"But you're not *in* love with me like you are with him."

A sob lodged in my throat, and I had to clear it before I could continue. "No." I grabbed his hand. "But I have *never* thought of you as a consolation prize, and if I ever gave you that impression, I beg you to forgive me. And you know me well enough to know I don't beg."

He swiped his thumbs along my cheeks, brushing away my tears. Then he leaned and ran his lips lightly over my eyelids the way he had the first time we kissed. The way he'd greeted me every time since then. It seemed an appropriate way to say goodbye. An aloha kiss.

"You have never made me feel anything but special, Kyle."

His last words echoed in my head long after he left.

CHAPTER 27

Talia and Doc barged into my apartment while I lay like a lump on the couch. They were on their way down the hall before I spoke to get their attention.

"I'm right here."

They slammed into each other like a beauty queen version of the *Three Stooges*. And turned to stare at me.

"How'd you get in?" I asked.

Talia looked chagrined. "Misha gave me a key."

"And how did Misha... Oh, never mind. It doesn't matter."

Talia walked around the coffee table, carrying a large cup of coffee and a bag with grease stains on the outside.

"What's in the bag?" I asked.

"Not sure. Guy named Tony stopped me in the hall and asked if I was coming to see you. Said you needed a pick-me-up."

Of course he did.

"Why are you here? Is Dalton okay?"

"Joe's fine," Sabrina answered. "Misha took him home. He's still weak, but he promised to take it easy the rest of the day, and he should be fine by tomorrow morning. We came to check on you, Kyle."

"And you felt the need to tag team me first thing in the morning? You couldn't just pick up your cells and call?"

Talia cleared her throat. "Jean Luc sensed you were in some sort of emotional distress. He and Misha were going to barge in here, and I convinced them to let me and Sabrina check on you instead."

Of course they were.

"Thanks for waylaying them. I love them both, but I can't deal with either of them right now." I sat up, tucked my feet up on the couch, and wrapped my arms around my knees. I might as well take the training wheels off and ride on two wheels like a big girl. "Griffin and I aren't seeing each other anymore."

Talia and Doc stared at me.

"What?" I barked.

"Who decided to end it?" Sabrina asked.

"Griffin."

"And how do you feel about it?"

I huffed. "Crappy. How else am I supposed to feel about it?"

Talia handed me the coffee. "Griffin is one of the good guys. You have a right to feel crappy."

I took a sip and dropped my head back onto the couch. "Aren't you going to ask me why he broke up with me?"

Doc shook her head. "We know why."

"I care for Griffin so much."

Talia set the bag on the end table. "But you're not over Joe, and Griffin knows it."

"Does that make me a horrible person?"

"No," Sabrina answered. "It makes you human."

"I'm so confused."

Talia sat on the coffee table across from me. "Let me ask you this. When Griffin ended your relationship, did you fight him on it?"

"No. I mean I don't want to hurt him. He's helped me so much these last couple of months."

"Well that tells me something important."

I frowned. "Stop being so damn cryptic, Talia, and spell it out for me."

"Because, Kyle, you're a fighter. And when someone tells you no, if you really want it bad enough, you fight them. And your first instinct was not to fight."

My stomach lurched, and I set the coffee on the side table.

Doc sat next to me on the couch. "Ask yourself this. If you hadn't erased Joe's memory, would you still be with him?"

"I don't know!"

"Yes, you do. If you hadn't erased his memory or run him off because you are such a stubborn pain in the ass, would you still be with him?"

I hesitated even though I knew the answer.

"Kyle?" Doc persisted.

"Yes. But it doesn't matter."

"Why?" Talia asked.

I flung my arms up in exasperation and jumped to my feet. "Oh, I don't know. Because he doesn't remember me? Because I'm in love with a man I don't even like anymore." I paced. "He was overbearing before, but it was okay."

"He was overbearing because he wanted to protect you. He loved you," Doc said.

"*Loved*. Past tense." I paced over to the window. "He seemed different in the demon realm, like I was starting to see the old Dalton again. But as soon as we get back here, he reverts back to Mr. No Personality. All he wants is to solve the case and trip on back to his life in Chicago."

Doc looked me in the eyes. "Does he? Or does he want to solve the case and move on to another case and another group of people he can keep at arm's length. I was a psychiatrist for a while in the 1900's, and humans haven't changed much. As a species, you need companionship. When someone fights it, there is a damn compelling reason why."

"Then how do I help him?" I swallowed hard. "To get him to live his life again. Because I don't know what to do next. I'm not a therapist."

Doc smiled. "No, but you're an expert in pushing people away. Or at least you used to be. Dig deep and find a way to break down his walls. Do you honestly want him to spend the rest of his life this way?"

"Of course not."

"What do *you* want, Kyle?" Talia asked.

"I want him to be happy. I don't want him to live his life for work." I hesitated and then choked out, "I want him to find someone to love."

"Maybe that's you," Doc said.

"Don't, Sabrina. My life isn't a damn supernatural Lifetime movie. He's going to leave. And I know I can survive when he does. I've done it before, and I'm a stronger person now. So I have two missions. Solve the case and knock down Dalton's walls before the concrete sets and no one can break through. Then we can both move on."

"That's your brain talking, not your heart," Doc responded.

I looked out the window and didn't say a word. Because even though my heart was indeed protesting, it needed to shut the hell up.

CHAPTER 28

As fate would have it, or maybe the Fates would have it, I didn't have long to wallow in my Griffin/Dalton misery. After several hours I finally convinced Talia and Doc to leave and settled in for a restless night. I stumbled out of bed in the morning and was on my second cup of coffee when Father Brown called. Now, I was on my way to meet him at the John Carroll campus. Apparently, I was going to join him on what he called his morning constitutional.

I climbed out of my car and zipped up my jacket to stave off the damp air. It was still early in the year to be comfortable outside first thing in the morning. I found Father Brown walking along Carroll Boulevard. He was dressed in normal priest attire, but he had on florescent blue tennis shoes. I smiled at him, and he wagged his finger at me.

"Not a word about my foot attire, Kyle. I can't do any serious walking in loafers."

I nodded and we resumed walking. "Got it, Father. So you've found something?"

He smiled broadly. "Yes. I've been able to translate some of the tablet. It's a history of the Key. An instruction manual on how the Key works, so to speak."

My heart accelerated, and it had nothing to do with the walking. "What does it say, Father?"

"It talks about the Key being absorbed into a person. A guardian—although I don't think that's the right word, I'm sure it's something close to that. I was up half the night trying to figure out the right word."

I stopped and pulled my phone from my pocket.

"What are you doing?"

"Looking up synonyms for guardian on the Internet. Here we go...sentry, guard, watchman, sentinel."

"That's it! Sentinel. The Sentinel is the keeper of the Key. You've been chosen by heaven to protect it and use it to fight evil."

I shook my head. "The angels chose Dalton, and then it got bounced to me by accident. I'm definitely not their choice."

"How can you be sure?"

"For one thing, they don't know it's in me. They're a little worked up in heaven right now, trying to find the Key."

"And you are aware of this how?"

"Let's just say I have my sources. Does the tablet talk about how to control the Key?"

"Not anything specific. It talks about working in harmony with it."

"Well the Key didn't get that memo. I'm all for harmony. Hand-holding, singing around the campfire, whatever it takes to stop it from drilling a hole in my head when it wants to share."

"There's also some text about the receptacles."

"The box the Key was held in?"

"Yes. It says the box was fashioned and warded by the angels. Which means when an angel draws near, it will recognize them."

"What do you mean by recognize?"

"I'm not sure. Maybe it will vibrate when an angel is close by."

"Maybe I should carry it with me at all times. Angels are wily bas...buggers. If we could get one to talk to us, it might help."

"What if they realize you have the Key inside you?"

"It's a risk I have to take, Father. But I'm not convinced they would tell us the truth regardless. They're big into the not-interfering thing."

Father gaped at me for a moment. "It's so strange to hear you talk about angels like they live next door."

I smirked. "Not next door. My next door neighbor is Mr. Morelli, and he's pretty crotchety. Too mean to be an angel."

Father chuckled. "There are more sections I've not been able to translate yet. I'll keep working on it." He started walking again, and I hurried to catch up with him. "Have you considered telling Joe the truth?" he asked.

"It could hurt him," I said.

"It could hurt you, if you don't. What if he's supposed to be the true Sentinel, Kyle? If the Key is not meant to be in you, I can't imagine what the long-term ramifications will be."

"Another risk, Father. There are some demons after the Key, and I can't let them have it."

"You talk as if the Key is a separate thing. You *are* the Key."

"I know, Father. I'm just trying not to dwell on that part."

I walked into the office a little while later, not knowing what might be waiting to pounce. A hovering Misha and Jean Luc?

An angry FBI agent? Instead, I was greeted by an empty room.

Where was everybody?

After a few seconds, I heard voices down the hall and followed them till I peeked inside Misha's office. Misha was sitting at his desk, working on his computer. Both Jean Luc and Jason were standing behind him, looking over his shoulder at the screen. All three of them looked up when I cleared my throat.

Jean Luc circled the desk and laid his hands on my shoulders. "Are you okay, *ma petite?*"

"I'll be fine, Jean Luc."

He stared at me for a moment as if he could read my thoughts before letting me go.

"So what's the plan, guys?"

Misha smiled at me. "We're getting to know Sylvia Reynolds before we pay her a visit."

"What have you found out so far?"

"That her name is an alias."

"How do you know?" I asked.

"When I track her history, it only goes back a few years. Before then, Sylvia Reynolds didn't exist."

"What's she hiding?"

"Good question," a voice sounded behind me.

I jumped and spun to face Dalton. He still looked a little pale to me, but at least he was steady on his feet.

Misha grabbed his laptop and stood. "Let's take this into the main office so we have more space."

In the main office, Jason and I plopped onto the lime green sofa, and Misha and Jean Luc sat at the table. Dalton walked over to the whiteboard and studied the case notes.

"Before we talk more about Sylvia, I need to fill you in on what Father Brown told me." I spent the next few minutes getting them up to speed on the newest information.

"So these Sentinels protect the Key?" Dalton asked.

"Yeah."

Jason tapped his fingers on the table. "And the Key box is some sort of angel radar?"

I nodded. "Good way to think about it, I guess."

Misha typed away on his keyboard. "Too bad we can't get an angel to talk to us."

Dalton picked up a marker from the whiteboard. "Don't you have some connection to the angels?"

I gulped a bit as I shook my head. Couldn't exactly tell him the only contact we had was his ghost of a grandmother.

He wrote Sylvia Reynolds on the board with a question mark, then he turned to Misha. "So what have you found out about her?"

"So far, not much. She took over the motel five years ago and keeps a pretty low profile."

"How do we find out more about her?" I asked. "Do we charge in there and grab her for questioning, or do we send in someone undercover?"

Talia came into the room with a cardboard carrier filled with four large coffees. "Who's going undercover?"

"Not you or Kyle," Jean Luc answered. "If the realm demons are still on earth and Sylvia is protecting them, they would recognize you."

Talia frowned. "They would recognize all of us."

"So who can we send in then to get a feel of the place before we invade it?" Misha asked.

I sat forward. "I have an idea, but you aren't going to like it, Mish."

Dalton folded his arms over his chest. "Another team member I don't know about?"

"Not an official team member, but he's helped on some cases before and saved my butt a while back."

Misha groaned. "Oh, Kyle. No..."

I smiled. "It's perfect, and you know it. He can sneak in and check things out for us first. No one will be the wiser." I turned to Dalton. "Before you kibosh the idea, let me make a phone call."

Dalton checked his watch for the tenth time. "When is your guy going to show up?"

"He should be here any minute. Trust me, this is going to work."

Before Dalton could respond, Dolly opened the door from the receptionist area and walked into the back office with her coffee mug. Behind her pranced Booger. I'd told him he would have some convincing to do with Dalton, but I hadn't expected him to pull out the big guns. I stifled a giggle when he jumped up on the couch and sat right next to Dalton. He stared up at him with his big yellow eyes and bumped his cat head against Dalton's thigh.

Dalton frowned for a second and then patted him. "So what makes this Matthew guy so good at undercover work?"

"He's unassuming and can get into most places without any fuss."

"Does he have a military background or something?"

"Nope. But his supe abilities are especially well suited for undercover work," I said.

Dalton frowned. "Well, he's late. We don't need someone who is unreliable on this case."

Booger purred and bumped his head against Dalton's thigh again, and I couldn't stop myself from laughing. "Actually, he's right on time. Dalton, meet Matthew. I call him Booger when he's in his cat form."

Dalton jerked away from the cat, his eyes as big as saucers. "You're telling me *this* is Matthew?"

The little shit held up his paw as if he wanted to shake Dalton's hand.

Misha growled. "Knock it off, you showoff. Time to shift back to human now."

"Wait!" I raised my hand. "Please tell me he left clothes in the lobby."

Dolly smiled. "Yep. I'll go get them for him." A minute later, she came in with his clothes and headed down the hall with Booger right behind her.

Dalton appeared to be recovering from the shock, so I sat next to him. "Sorry about that. I never thought he'd show up in his cat form. I should have expected it, though. Matthew can be a bit over the top sometimes."

"*Sometimes?*" Misha grumbled. "He's a menace."

"He's good at what he does, Mish, no matter how much he annoys you." I turned to Dalton. "Now do you see why we should send him in to gather intel for us?"

Dalton nodded. "As long as he can convince someone to let him into the motel."

"No worries," Matthew answered as he walked into the room, pulling a T-shirt over his lanky frame and smoothing his blond hair. "I can get someone to let me in."

Dalton stood and gawked at Matthew. "You're..."

Matthew smiled. "I'm...the cat who's here to save the day."

"Tell me he didn't really just say that!" Misha groaned.

I laughed as Matthew gathered me in his arms for a hug. "It's good to see you Matthew."

"You too, Kyle. Jean Luc, Talia. Jason"—he shook Jason's hand—"glad to see you back in the fold." He grinned wickedly. "It's nice to see you, too, demon."

Misha glared without answering him.

Matthew slapped his hands together and rubbed them. "Fill me in so we can get down to business."

Two hours later, I chuckled as I watched Matthew worm his way into the motel. It had taken all of ten minutes of his pathetic meowing before someone let him in.

"That didn't take long." Dalton announced from the front passenger seat. Misha had parked the van a little way down the street with a view of the front door.

"He suckered me into letting him into my apartment the same way."

Dalton's eyebrow rose in question.

"He was hired to watch out for me. Ended up living with me for months before I knew what he was."

Misha growled. The three of us had taken the first shift for the stakeout. If necessary, Jean Luc, Talia, and Jason would do second shift.

"Oh, Mish. Get over it, already. If he hadn't been around, that vamp would have finished me off last summer."

Dalton frowned. "Was this about the Key?"

My heartbeat kicked up in my chest. "Yeah, it's all related."

"Maybe we should have just gone in there and dragged Sylvia out for questioning," Dalton said.

"What if the realm demon twins are staying there now?" I said. "We don't want to lose them again. Matthew knows what they look like in both their human and demon forms. Let him poke around a bit. He might find out something about the demon from the art museum, too."

Misha tapped his fingers on the steering wheel. "I wish we could hear what was going on."

"Our earbuds aren't made for cats, Mish."

"Maybe I could create something he can use the next time he goes in."

I smirked. "You work on that while we wait for him."

"Good idea. Let me in the back so I can get to my tools."

I moved to the driver's seat and smiled at Dalton. "At least I distracted him. Normally, he talks nonstop when we're on stakeouts. If he isn't talking about police shows, he tells you stories about past cases, like delivering babies in elevators."

Dalton's mouth actually tipped up a bit on one corner, as if he wanted to smile but was out of practice. "Stakeouts can be extremely stressful and boring at the same time."

"I know what you mean."

We sat in silence for a while. Finally, Dalton cleared his throat.

"McKinley...Kyle. I uh, wanted to thank you for your help in the demon realm. I'm sorry that I have been somewhat—"

"Of a jerk," I supplied.

The corner of his mouth quirked up again. "I don't know if I would have gone with that exact word. I was going to say overbearing."

"Overbearing jerk works for me too," I said with a smile.

"Okay. I get it. Anyway, I apologize. I should have given you guys the benefit of the doubt instead of taking over. But this case is important, and the last thing you need is to have the government come in here and find out about the supernatural."

I stared at him for a moment. "Aren't you the government?"

"Partly. I'm a cop on loan to the Feds. If I can prove myself, then I'll become a permanent member of the task force. This case could help me achieve that."

I took a breath. "And that's what you want? To leave Cleveland?"

He stared out the window for so long I didn't think he was going to answer. Finally, he nodded. "I don't have anything holding me here. So yeah, working on an FBI taskforce could jumpstart my career."

My stomach twisted. "Well, let's see what we can do about that."

CHAPTER 29

Booger scrambled into the van and jumped onto the back-seat next to Misha. I pulled the van away from the curb. A few seconds later, a glow emanated from the back, shining in the rearview mirror and almost blinding me.

Dalton sat in the passenger seat next to me, his face turned to the backseat with his mouth gaping open. "That was..."

"Amazing," Matthew completed his sentence. "I know."

"Damn, Matthew, couldn't you wait until we got to the office to do that?" I stopped at a light and turned to give him the stink eye, until I saw he was still naked. "Put some clothes on!" I squeaked, turning back to make sure the light hadn't turned green yet.

Matthew chuckled. "You've seen me in my naked glory, sweetheart, why so squeamish?"

"I seem to remember I almost shot your naked glory off."

Matthew's chuckle exploded into a laugh as he pulled a shirt on over his head. "So you did!"

I glanced back over at Dalton in the passenger seat. He was frowning again. So much for him lightening up a bit.

"What did you find out?" Dalton asked.

"Sylvia is a hoot. She's like a little general, ordering the tenants around."

"Are they all demons?" Misha asked.

"Not all. There are humans, too."

"Did you see the twins?" I asked while I turned at an intersection.

"Nope. But a couple of the demons didn't smell like any clan here on earth, so I'm guessing they came from the realm."

"What about Sylvia? Is she from the realm?" Dalton asked.

"Sylvia's human."

I jerked the wheel at the news. "What!"

"Keep it on the road, Kyle! Sylvia's human. No doubt about it."

"Why would she be mixed up with demon trafficking?"

"Sylvia's a certified hippie. She fights against injustice based on race, gender, sexual orientation, and what she calls supe-bashing. She believes the realm demons have been unfairly incarcerated."

I pulled into the office parking garage. "Holy shit. And here I thought I'd heard everything."

"I'm still surprised every day, Kyle, and I have two hundred-plus years on you," Misha said. "Sylvia might not be the enemy in this scenario. Which could work to our advantage."

Dalton turned to Misha. "How so?"

"We go in there, not as Big Brother, but as a group concerned about a few of the demons who are giving the rest a bad name."

I parked and turned off the van. "You might have the right idea, Mish. Who's going to go in there and convince her to be buddy-buddy with us? It can't be Dalton. Sorry, but you don't come across as buddy-buddy."

Dalton nodded. "Fine, but I'm not sure you're the ideal candidate either. You don't strike me as the Kumbaya type."

"Agreed. Let's get Jason, Jean Luc, and Talia up to speed on this, and we'll decide next steps."

Forty-five minutes later, the consensus was that Misha and Talia would run the interrogation with Sylvia tomorrow. But first, we'd have Matthew go in again to scope things out.

In the meantime, Jason, Talia, and Jean Luc left to stake out the motel overnight, in case the twins or the demon from the museum showed their faces.

I went back to my office and sat in front of my laptop to deal with my neglected email box. As I cleared out the junk, Matthew walked in and sat across from me. He stared at me for a moment, and I stared right back at him.

"What's up?"

"Sorry about you and Griffin."

I jerked at his words, my stomach bottoming out. "Well that news didn't take long to spread. Did he post it on the shifter Facebook page, or something?"

Matthew held up his hands. "Wow. Displaced aggression, much? You know Griffin better than that. I saw him yesterday. He didn't say a word." He touched his nose. "I could sense something was wrong, and now that I've been around you for a while, I can tell you're sad, too. I just put two and two together."

I nodded, my throat tightening a bit. "Now, I'm sorry."

"No worries. How's it going with Joe?"

I glanced toward the open door.

"It's okay. He left. He went to brief Captain Morrison about the case and where we stand with everything."

I blew out a hard breath. "It's been a bitch. I'm scared one of us is going to let something slip and Dalton will remember."

"Did you give him that shiner?"

"No! Why does everyone keep asking me that?"

Matthew smirked at me. "The Fates are using you as a plaything right now."

I rubbed the back of my neck and snorted. "Ya think?" Just as quickly, the humor left me. "I'm worried about him. He's not the same."

Matthew leaned forward. "Do you want me to tell you?" He tapped his nose again. "The truth?"

"Yes."

"He's wound very tight. He's got this anger simmering just below the surface, all the time. I also sense he's conflicted about you. Not full-blown attraction, but he sure wasn't happy when I mentioned you'd seen me naked before. There's something there, Kyle, but he's way too closed off to read much."

"You're just reinforcing what I already know."

Matthew reached across the desk and placed his hand over mine. "Hang in there. I'm a firm believer that things work out for the best."

"A closet optimist, huh?"

"Absolutely. Why look for trouble ahead of time? You spend your life waiting for the other shoe to drop, and you don't enjoy the good things that happen along the way."

I shrugged. "I see your point to a certain extent, but you have to admit my life has been more than a little out of control lately."

Matthew smiled, which made his lean face even younger-looking. "Yes. But what if all of this hadn't happened? You wouldn't have met Joe or Griffin. Heck, you wouldn't have met me, either, and that would have been a crying shame."

I chuckled and stood up. "That's for sure, Morris."

Matthew stood too. "Oh, boy, you're dragging out the cat jokes. It's time to call it a night."

We walked into the main office and found Misha working on his laptop.

"See you tomorrow, demon." Matthew winked at me and left.

"That cat is shifty," Misha mumbled.

I sat down across from him. "Mish. You need to let it go. Even you have to admit Matthew's been a great help."

Misha shut his laptop and stared at me, hard. "How are you really doing, little one?"

I sighed. "I'm doing okay. Or I will be. I miss Griffin. But he deserves better."

"Don't talk that way about yourself."

"I'm not. I only mean that he deserves someone who'll love him and isn't carrying all the ridiculous baggage I have. Especially when my baggage carries a badge and tries to boss everyone around."

"I heard Joe apologize to you in the van today."

"If you heard that, then you also heard he's using this case to further his career. He can't wait to leave Cleveland since, and I quote, 'there's nothing holding him here.'"

Misha got up, walked around the table, and pulled me up from my seat. "So give him a reason to stick around."

I squeezed his hand. "I want to help him, Mish. But all the lies have turned this into a convoluted mess right now. Let's get through the case and we can talk about it then. Now let's go get something to eat. You pick."

Misha rubbed his hands together, and his eyes lit up. "Oh, boy."

I laughed at the glee on his face. I felt a little guilty for using food as a distraction, but I couldn't bear another discussion about Dalton. I had already surpassed my quota for the day.

CHAPTER 30

I should have known better than to let Misha choose dinner.

I dropped my keys and cell phone on my entry table and pulled off my jacket before sprawling on my couch. The Indian restaurant had been phenomenal, and Misha had ordered way too much food, which meant I had eaten way too much food. I groaned. I'd learned years ago not to try and keep up with him. Maybe it was nervous energy that made me reach for the naan multiple times. I was a sucker for bread, no matter the culture.

Misha had wanted to come back to my place and watch over me. But I talked him out of it. I refused to live scared again. I rubbed my belly and stretched my legs out, letting myself settle into the cushions. Peace and quiet.

"Whatcha doin', Kyle?"

My head banged against the couch arm, and I bit my lip to stop the expletive from erupting. Maybe if I ignored her she would go away.

Marie floated into my line of sight. "Are you asleep?"

I scowled at her. "No."

"So how's the case going? Is Joe feeling better?"

"Dalton's feeling fine. He's back to his closed-off self."

"And the case?" Marie asked.

"We're interviewing someone tomorrow who's been helping realm demons acclimate to living on earth."

"Why do they want to live on earth?"

"I don't know about all of them. The one we're chasing is after the Key."

Marie's eyes widened. "You mean they're after *you*?"

I sat up, the Indian food rioting in my stomach. "Yeah. Have you heard any chatter in heaven about the Key lately?"

"Nothing much. The angels keep mumbling about it, but no one knows where it is."

"Have you heard them talk about other Keys?"

Marie floated higher in front of me. "No! Why would you ask me that?"

"Because I think there's more than one Key, and if that's the case, then someone else in this wild world may be like me. Carrying a Key inside them. And maybe they've learned how to control it better than I do."

"I'll dig around some and see what I can find out."

"Thanks. I've got another question for you. How is it that you're allowed to spend so much time out of heaven?"

"What do you mean?"

"I mean, it looks to me like you have carte blanche when it comes to traveling back and forth between heaven and earth. Why is that?"

"I don't have any special privileges, Kyle." Marie answered, her eyes darting away from me.

"Now that I think about it, Marie, I believe you have a lot of pull. Why don't you talk to your angel buddies and see if one of them will tell you the truth about the Key? No more subterfuge. Just ask them, straight out."

"Ah. I'll see what I can do, Kyle. As a matter of fact, I actually have to get going. I'll talk to you later."

Marie disappeared so quickly papers lifted up off my coffee table into a small whirlwind that lost its momentum moments later, scattering the pieces across the floor.

That was the fastest I had seen Marie leave in...well, ever.

I'd definitely touched on a sore spot, and she was lying about not having privileges. But why? I rubbed my forehead with my palm. I wouldn't hold my breath about getting the truth out of her any time soon. I leaned back again on the couch. Deep breath in. Peace and quiet.

And then my cell rang.

I refused to whimper. And sat up again. Zen was not my friend tonight. Hell, it hadn't been my friend for quite some time. I got up and grabbed the phone before it went into voicemail. It was Dolly.

"Well, hello, Dolly."

A groan answered me. "That wasn't funny when Misha started it. Not sure why you think it's funny now."

I chuckled. "I don't think it's funny. But it irritates you. A girl's got to get her kicks somewhere."

"Where are you?"

"At home. Why?"

"Have a call for the BSR, and you're the closest one. Java Café on Euclid. Trevor called it in. Said nothing dangerous, but they have a containment issue."

Great. That's all we needed. Trevor was a vamp who'd been in a minor scrape a few years ago. Since then, he'd been a model supe. Hopefully he wasn't backpedaling now. "I'm on it."

"Jean Luc and Talia are on their way, but they're across town, so it'll take them awhile to get there."

"Got it."

I picked up my keys, jammed my arms into my jacket, and headed out the door. Fifteen minutes later, I walked up to the small coffee shop, the sign on the door flipped to 'closed.' I tried the handle, and the door opened, a small bell ringing above my head.

Trevor stood behind the counter wearing a Beatles T-shirt and a scared face. "Kyle! Thanks for coming."

"What kind of trouble are you in this time, Trevor?"

"It was an accident, I swear."

He motioned for me to come behind the counter, and I followed him into a small kitchen area. A woman sat slumped on a kitchen stool. A young woman was standing next to her, her fangs peeking out slightly when she saw me.

I knelt in front of the unconscious woman and placed my fingers on her neck. I was relieved to find a pulse.

I looked up at the two vampires. "Did you bite her?"

"No!" The female stuttered, turning paper-white. "She's my boss. She passed out when she saw my fangs."

I frowned at her. "Why are you showing your fangs in broad daylight?"

Trevor answered. "Sandy's a fledgling. When she gets upset, she sometimes shows her fangs."

"And she was upset why?"

Trevor's mouth tightened. "We were having an argument."

"In the coffee shop?"

"No we were in the alley out back. Connie opened the door to take out some trash and heard us arguing. When she caught sight of Sandy's fangs and glowing eyes she passed out."

"My eyes were glowing?" Sandy squeaked.

"Yep. Red."

Sandy staggered, and Trevor grabbed her arm.

A vampire with the vapors. How perfect. "Sit her on the floor and put her head between her knees."

Trevor did as he was told. Smart vampire.

"Did anyone else see you in the alley?"

Trevor nodded.

"Spit it out."

"Her daughter was there. I don't know if she saw Sandy or was just scared when Connie fainted."

"Crap. Where is she now?"

"She ran down the alley and up the back stairs to Connie's apartment."

"How old is she?"

"Hannah is five. I went to the apartment door, but she wouldn't let me in."

Smart little girl. "Okay. Here's what we do. I'm going to erase Connie's memory." I pointed to Trevor. "You stay up front and keep people out of here. Some of my teammates will be here soon. Let them in and tell them what's going on." I pointed at Sandy. "You, suck it up, since I'm going to need your help."

Trevor hustled to the front of the shop.

Sandy got up from the floor and came up next to me. "What do you need me to do?"

"Show me the alley and where the apartment is."

I followed Sandy out and stared up and down the small alley, memorizing it, from its rusty blue dumpster to the old metal chair next to the door. Then we walked through the alley until we came to a door that opened to a set of stairs up to the apartment. We returned to the kitchen, and I knelt in front of Connie.

I concentrated and latched onto her synapses. They were moving languidly, interspersed with small surges of power, as if her conscious mind was trying to jumpstart her brain. I rolled with the motion of her thoughts and imagined Trevor and Sandy in the alley having an argument, and then grabbing each other and kissing passionately just as Connie and Hannah opened the back door.

Her brain accepted my suggestion easily, and I thanked the powers that be that she hadn't fought my intrusion. I then pushed a suggestion into her subconscious that she was tired and needed a nap. Her breathing slowed and a light snore filled the room.

"She'll sleep for now. You stay here. I don't think Hannah needs to see you right now."

Sandy blinked back tears. "Hannah's a great kid. I feel so bad about scaring her."

"I need you to watch over Connie for me until I send Hannah back down. When Hannah comes in, wake Connie up. She shouldn't remember being asleep. Both she and Hannah will remember seeing you and Trevor argue and then kiss in the alley. Got it?"

Sandy nodded. I jogged up the stairs and ran my hands around the doorjamb, looking for a key. Nothing. Picking up the mat, I didn't find a key on the floor either. But when I let the rubber mat plop back down, it made a plinking noise.

I turned it over. The key was taped to the bottom.

The apartment was small but tidy. A living room with a couch and chair opened to a kitchen with a table piled with crayons and coloring books. After a quick canvass of the area, I went and checked the two bedrooms thoroughly, even crawling under the beds and digging through the closets. No little girl. I finished off the search in the bathroom, which was also empty.

I hurried back into the living room and peeked behind the couch. Nothing. I returned to the kitchen and stopped when the table wobbled slightly, a crayon rolling off and landing on the linoleum.

I moved closer and hunkered down. Hannah sat under the table, clutching a doll. Twin pony tails stuck out on each side of her head, and large green eyes watched me warily.

"Hi, Hannah. My name's Kyle. Your mommy sent me upstairs to find you."

Hannah bit her lip and blinked as a large tear rolled down her freckled cheek. I waited for her to yell, "Stranger danger!"

She sniffled and whispered, "Mommy fell down."

The door opened behind me, and I held out my hand to stop Jean Luc or Talia from coming in any further. I didn't look away from Hannah, hoping she wouldn't spook about having more strangers in the room.

"Your mommy's fine, Hannah."

She shook her head and squeezed the doll tight to her. "The monsters got her."

"There are no monsters, honey. If you mean Trevor and Sandy, they aren't monsters. They were playing around in the alley. Being silly."

I held out my hand to her. "Let me take you to your mommy."

When I touched her arm, she screamed. I went down on my hands and knees, crawled under the table, and swept her into my arms. She squirmed, and I held her as close as I could while I rubbed my hand over her forehead. Touching her would help strengthen the connection and hopefully help me to implant the memories quickly.

Her synapses were scattered and unlike any I had touched before. But then I'd never changed a memory for someone so young. I searched for the memory, weaving between the tendrils until a thin black string twisted in front of me. It had to be the one. I grasped it and fear shot through me. Bingo. I imagined the couple in the alley teasing each other and kissing. Then I pictured Connie taking Hannah's hand and pulling her back into the restaurant as they both giggled at the pair in the alley.

After a few more seconds, warmth blossomed in my brain, and heat flowed through my hand into her forehead. The transfer of memories was complete.

I set Hannah down and she looked at me, her head tipping slightly as she wondered who I was.

"Hi, Hannah. Your mommy is looking for you. She's down in the café." I stepped away from her, and she skipped across the room, smiling up at me before she slipped through the door.

"How did you do that?"

I spun at the sound of the voice, having forgotten that anyone was behind me. Instead of Jean Luc, it was Dalton, his eyes wide and unblinking.

"What are you doing here?" I barked.

His wide eyes narrowed with suspicion. "I called the office, and Dolly said you were on a call. She told me where to find you. I thought maybe it was about our case."

"It's not."

Dalton crossed his arms. "Funny thing happened when I got here. I told Trevor and Sandy that I was with the BSR, and they explained what happened. When I asked them why they didn't just make the woman downstairs forget with their thrall, they looked at me like I was a serial killer. Explained what thrall really was and how it worked. It was quite enlightening."

"I bet."

"Plus, they told me you were taking care of the issue. So are you going to tell me the truth, McKinley? What did you just do to that little girl?"

"I made the monsters go away." I sighed. "I'll explain, but let's get out of here before someone sees us." I locked the door and retaped the key to the mat before we headed down the stairs. As we walked into the alley, he glanced over at me and frowned before grabbing me by the arms.

"What?"

"You have a nosebleed."

Damn. This was happening a lot more often lately.

He guided me over to his SUV, opened the passenger door, and helped me inside like I was about to fall over.

"I'm fine."

He opened the glove box and pulled out a handful of napkins. "Lean forward just a little bit. Now pinch your nostrils."

"I know the drill," I said, my voice muffled by the napkin. Déjà vu swamped me. Dalton had taken care of me the first time I had a nosebleed.

We sat in silence until the bleeding stopped. I leaned back and turned to him. He was staring at me like I was a puzzle. It was as if his cop brain was chugging away behind his turquoise eyes, trying to determine what exactly to make of me.

"Are you okay?"

"Yeah. The nosebleed is a side effect of what I can do. I work with the BSR because I have the ability to manipulate memories."

"How?"

"I don't know exactly. I can create a memory in my mind and insert it into someone else's brain. I use it with humans to cover up supernatural exposure. I erased Hannah and her mother's memory of seeing Sandy's fangs."

"So you were the one who erased David Heller's memories of the museum events, not Jean Luc."

It didn't take him long to make that leap. "Yes."

A hard rap on the window made us both jump. Jean Luc and Talia were looking in. Dalton rolled down his window.

"Everything okay, Kyle?" Jean Luc's nostrils flared slightly, and he looked at the wadded-up, bloody napkins.

"Had another nosebleed. The case is contained. I erased the norms' memories."

Jean Luc's eyebrows lifted in response.

Dalton unlocked the car doors. "Why don't you two get in? I think we need to discuss a few things."

They climbed into the backseat, and we sat in silence for a moment, the tension thick like fog in the air.

"I know the truth about her power now. Why the lie about your thrall?" Dalton asked, getting right to the point.

Jean Luc answered. "Because Kyle's gift is unique. And I will do anything to protect her. Last year, she was stalked by someone who wanted to abuse her power. We will not allow it to happen again."

"Are you worried what I would do with the knowledge?"

"I have been alive for more than four hundred years, Detective. I have seen what governments do in the pursuit of power. While I think you are a man of honor, you work for the government. I will not let Kyle become a victim of their avarice."

I smiled at Jean Luc. It took a lot to get him worked up, but when he was, it was spectacular.

I spoke quickly when it seemed like Dalton was going to protest. "Please don't take it personally. Nine out of ten humans who know about my power have tried to use me."

He stared at me. "Well, count me as the one out of ten who won't."

I nodded. I had no doubt the old Dalton would never have used me. But this new Dalton was a wild card. I wanted more than anything to believe him, but I wasn't sure if his drive to solve this case would overshadow everything else.

CHAPTER 31

I watched Dalton on the monitor. He prowled the hotel room, making sure the camera Misha had set up worked correctly.

"Can you hear me?" he asked.

I spoke through the open door between the adjoining hotel rooms. "You come through loud and clear. We should be set now."

We were in a hotel one street away from Sylvia's motel. A neutral place to talk to her. Dalton followed me into the room with the monitor and shut the door just as my phone rang.

I clicked on the speaker button. "Yeah, Jean Luc?"

"Misha and Talia are on their way with Sylvia."

"They didn't have any trouble?"

"No, they picked her up as she left the motel. There were no confrontations with any of the demons. Jason, Matthew, and I are going to keep watching the motel."

"Okay, talk to you later."

I hung up and checked the monitor and recording equipment one last time. Silence descended, choking the air out of me. Dalton had been all business since he found out about my powers. And while awkwardness had buzzed around us in the past like a worrisome gnat, it had now morphed into a flock of crows, dive-bombing us and squawking incessantly.

Did he think I was a freak?

After a few more minutes of choking silence, I cleared my throat. "I hope Sylvia can give us something to work with."

Dalton nodded, his expression tight. "We're getting closer, McKinley."

Closer to when he left again after we solved this case.

The negative mental path I'd been stumbling down the past few minutes was waylaid by the sound of the hotel room door opening. We watched the monitor as Misha, Talia, and Sylvia entered the room.

Sylvia was small, but she had the presence of a larger person. Her silver hair was long and in a braid that hung down the middle of her back. She wore a loose sage green jumpsuit that must have been made of natural fibers...probably great for the environment, but hopelessly wrinkled within five minutes of putting it on.

Talia gestured to the loveseat, but Sylvia stood in the middle of the room with her arms crossed.

"Why don't you tell me who you are and why I'm here?" she asked.

Misha answered her. "We told you, we're with the police and need to speak with you."

"I heard what you told me, and the shiny badges are a neat trick, but I need the truth now. The only reason I didn't yell my head off at the motel was because I didn't want my tenants to get pulled into whatever this is. Now, I will have no problem at all screaming."

Misha and Talia exchanged a look while Sylvia plowed on. "I've been arrested more than once in my life. First time was at a peace rally when I was seventeen. You two aren't normal cops."

I chuckled. "This old broad is smart."

"We're from the BSR." Misha answered. "The Bureau—"

"I know what the BSR is. Supernatural Fuzz."

Misha smiled at her. "I haven't heard that term in a while, Sylvia."

"Don't try to charm me with those icy blue eyes, demon."

Misha's icy blue eyes widened. "How did you know I'm a demon?"

"I can see auras. Yours is bright green with flecks of gold. Screams demon." She nodded in Talia's direction. "Just as the deep purple aura for your lady friend here tells me she's a vampire."

Talia grinned. "Very impressive."

"I'm not here to impress anyone." Sylvia held up her hands, wrists together. "If you're going to arrest me, then get it over with."

Misha shook his head. "We're not going to arrest you, Sylvia. We want to talk to you about the demons you help cross over from the realm."

Sylvia blew out a hard breath and glared at both Misha and Talia. "Who ratted me out?"

Talia answered. "Your name came up as part of our investigation."

"Let me guess." Sylvia sat on the loveseat. "You're trying to stop the crossovers, right? Typical government, going about this the wrong way."

Misha sat in the chair across from her. "You don't know what our plan is."

Sylvia snorted. "Don't I? You want to stop all of these *hardened criminals* from coming to earth. Ask yourself this, Mr. Demon. Is it fair to incarcerate demons for millennia? To stop their children and grandchildren—who had nothing to do with their parents' decisions—from living on earth?"

Sylvia lifted her chin and glared at Misha. "Most of the demons I've helped want nothing more than to live on earth and blend into society. And I teach them how to live here. Some are so screwed up that they have a hard time forming their human side when they first arrive. Do you know their realm is like living in the dark ages? No electricity. No modern conveniences."

"I've never been to the realm."

"Of course you haven't. But you still judge them and tell them they can't live here among us." She shook her head in disgust. "It always comes down to us and them. I've heard their stories. Talk to me when you've experienced their world."

The tough old hippie had a point. I walked across the room and reached for the door.

"What are you doing?" Dalton hissed.

"Giving her what she wants." I opened the door and walked into the room. "I've been to the realm. Are you willing to talk to me?"

Sylvia squinted at me, looking me over from head to toe. "Good Lord, girl. You're like a walking glow stick."

I blinked at her, since words escaped me. That was not the reaction I'd been expecting.

"What are you?" she asked.

"Human."

Sylvia's mouth quirked up and she studied me some more, like I was a science experiment. "Whatever you say, kiddo. You've been to the realm, huh?"

"Yep. And the in-between. You're right. They don't have much of anything there. The border patrol lives the same way."

"You've met the patrol?" She sighed. "I almost feel worse for them. They've been programmed to stop demons from coming to earth, giving up their own freedom in the process. All subterfuge."

She plowed on before I could speak. "Ask yourself this. How exactly were the more powerful demons forced from earth by the less powerful ones? It doesn't make sense."

"Maybe they were defeated by sheer numbers. There are twelve clans here on earth and five in the realm," I argued.

"Maybe. Or maybe someone helped tip the scales. And if so, why?"

"I don't have the answer to that, Sylvia."

"Well, it's what you *should* be investigating. Not how to send demons back to the hellhole they've been living in for millennia."

Okay...I had to bring her back to the crux of the issue. "I'm not here to argue whether the realm demons should be allowed on earth. If most of these demons are living on earth minding their own business, then I don't have a problem with them. But when one comes here, breaks into the museum, steals something, and kills a guard, then we need to deal with the ramifications."

Misha opened the folder on the coffee table and put the composite picture on the side table next to Sylvia. She looked at it, and her eyes widened slightly before she could hide it.

"You know him?" I asked.

"What makes you think he broke into the museum?" she asked, which pretty much meant she did know him.

"I saw him run out of the museum, and a witness saw him kill the guard."

Sylvia stared hard at the picture without looking up at me.

"He snapped the guard's neck. Carl Willis was married with two kids."

Sylvia flinched slightly. "I didn't acclimate him to earth. But I've seen him before. When he showed up at the motel, he told me someone tried to rob him. He'd been shot in the shoulder."

My heart sped up. "I shot him when he tried to hurt me using his telekinesis. So you've seen him in the past couple of days?"

Sylvia finally met my eye. "I helped dig the bullet out of his shoulder."

"Do you know where he is now?"

She shook her head. "No. He took off shortly after I cleaned him up."

"We're also looking for twin demons, heads shaved with arm tattoos," I said.

Misha pulled the drawing out of the folder, and Sylvia waved her hand like she didn't need to see it.

She scowled. "I know exactly who you're talking about. I kicked those two out months ago. Troublemakers, both of them."

"Do you have any idea where they hang out now?" Misha asked.

"No. The demons who stay with me try to steer clear of them."

"Do you think you could ask around a bit and see if you can find out about the three of them?" I asked. "Nothing too risky, maybe a couple of feelers?"

Sylvia looked between the three of us. "So you aren't going to shut my business down?"

I smiled. "Not right now. Especially if you'll help us out."

She opened her mouth as if she was going to disagree, so I decided she could use some added incentive.

"And if you help us, we won't ask your real name, even though we know Sylvia Reynolds didn't exist five years ago."

Sylvia pursed her lips. "I can do a little digging for you. Give me a day or two, and I'll get you something."

I nodded. "You're not going to run, are you?"

She huffed. "I'm too old to run. Plus my tenants need me."

"Good." I sat on the chair across from her. "I'm really curious about your ability to see auras. Are you human?"

"I'm human. Always have been able to see them. My parents used to have conniption fits when I talked about it as a child...before I knew better."

"And different supes have different-colored auras?"

"For the most part. Humans, too."

"So what does your aura look like?"

She stared at me like I was speaking in demon tongue. "I can't see my own aura. That would be weird."

I had to smile. After everything she'd told us, that's what she thought was weird?

Talia and Misha ushered her out of the room, and I walked back into the adjoining room to find Dalton turning the recording equipment off.

"Thoughts?" I asked.

"She's a bit...eccentric."

"She might come across that way when she's on her soapbox, but she's whip smart. And if she can connect us to the realm demons, all the better. That little eccentric might be the break we've been waiting for."

"You were real interested in her ability."

I sat in the chair next to him. "Yeah. I haven't met many humans with powers like me before."

Dalton cleared his throat. "Are you feeling better?"

I looked at him in confusion.

"From yesterday. Have you recuperated from using your power?"

Ah. "Yeah. I bounce back pretty fast."

"If it hurts you, maybe you shouldn't use it."

It was hard not to gasp. Dalton had said the same thing to me last year. He had been more concerned for me than what my powers could do. And here he was again, thinking about me first. *Damn.* I closed my eyes. That very statement demonstrated why I had fallen in love with him in the first place.

"McKinley? Are you okay?"

"Yeah. I can't stop using my powers. There's a reason why I have them."

He stared at me for a moment. "Does it make it hard fitting in?"

"The truth? Yeah, it does. Or it did. I thought I was a total freak for years. Then when I found out about supernaturals, my powers actually came in handy."

"You make the monsters go away. That's why you're so adamant about keeping supernaturals hidden. You've experienced how humans react when they're faced with the truth."

I studied his eyes for a moment. There was no judgement peeking out at me from those turquoise depths. Just curiosity. After a few more seconds, he blinked, and the connection was lost.

"Sounds like this job was tailor-made for you."

"Nicholas, my boss, would agree with you. He's always said my working for the BSR was meant to be."

"What do you think?"

"I don't know if it's a destiny thing or not. I'm just glad that when it comes to my powers, the Fates let me use them for good." I took a deep breath. "What about you?"

"What about me?"

"How are you doing, really doing, since the serial killer case last summer?"

Dalton busied himself with putting away the equipment. "I'm fine."

"Hmm."

He looked up from what he was doing and frowned at me. "What's with the hmm?"

"You don't seem fine."

He placed some cords in the equipment case and closed it with a loud snap. "What exactly are you basing that on?"

"I know you need to get back to your life in Chicago. Your nice, orderly life. Where you work non-stop, and...?"

"And?"

"What else do you do, Special Agent Dalton?"

"What do you want to know?"

"I want you to tell me you don't work all day and then go home with your case files at night and review them. I want you to tell me you have friends in Chicago. I want you to tell me you aren't afraid to live."

He glared at me, his iridescent eyes sparking with fury. "I don't need a pop psychology lesson from you. How, exactly, are you an expert on my pain?"

His words stabbed me like shards of glass. I swallowed hard on the retort I wanted to make. So much for our touching moment mere seconds ago. "I've experienced what it's like to have your world pulled out from under you and not know where to turn. To wonder what the hell to do next. When it happened to me, I ran away. Is that what you're doing, too?"

He picked up the case from the floor and stalked across the room. "We're working a case together. It doesn't make you an expert on me or my past." He opened the door and pinned me with those turquoise eyes. "You don't know me."

The door shut behind him, and I blinked back tears.

That went well.

CHAPTER 32

We were in a holding pattern, waiting for Sylvia to give us some info, so when Trina called and asked me to her house for breakfast, I immediately said yes. It had been a while since I'd seen her, and I wanted to check how she was doing, plus it didn't hurt that her mom was cooking. Stephanie was an amazing cook.

I called the office to let them know I would be in later. I'd hoped Dolly would answer, but of course, as luck would have it, Misha picked up the phone.

"Hey, Mish. I'm going to be in late today. I'm having breakfast at Trina's house."

"Trina? Is something wrong?"

"No. She and Stephanie want to thank me for helping Trina shift for the first time."

"Stephanie? How are they thanking you?"

"Um..." This was why I had wanted to talk to Dolly. "They invited me for banana stuffed French toast. Apparently, it's Stephanie's specialty."

Misha whimpered.

"Sorry, buddy. Maybe next time. I'll tell you all about how they taste."

"You are a cruel woman, Kyle McKinley. A cruel, cruel woman."

Thirty minutes later, this cruel woman knocked on the door of the Connors' two-story house in the heart of suburbia. Trina answered the door with a huge grin on her face, a girl of twelve going on thirty, with long dark hair and twinkling brown eyes. I was surprised to discover I no longer needed to look down to meet her eyes. She was starting to catch up with me already, and we would be eye-to-eye soon.

"Hi, Kyle! Still blonde, huh?"

I chuckled. "Trina. Yep. Still blonde."

She opened the door further, and I followed her into the entry. "Mom's working on the French toast now. Come on in."

Trina led the way down the hall to the back of the house. When we entered the large, homey kitchen decorated in sunflowers, there was Stephanie, standing by the stove. Her long blonde hair was pulled back in a ponytail, and she was wearing an honest-to-goodness apron. I think I gaped for a second before I could stop myself. I'd never experienced anything like the Connor family. Hell, my mother was the antithesis of Stephanie. The closest thing I could compare this to was a *Leave it to Beaver* episode. If Beaver had been a wolf-shifter, that is.

"Hello, Stephanie."

"Kyle! So glad you could come today. Would you like some coffee?"

"Sure." I waved her off as she moved to get it for me. "I can pour my own." I selected a mug from the mug rack on the counter and poured a cup, the aroma of vanilla teasing my nose.

Trina plopped into a chair and motioned for me to sit beside her.

"Why aren't you in school today?" I asked.

"Teacher conferences."

I took a sip of the coffee, and the flavor burst on my tongue. "Wow, Stephanie, this is delicious."

Stephanie smiled as she flipped the toast and placed it on plates. "French vanilla. One of my favorites." She put a plate in front of each of us. "Whipped cream?"

I moaned a little bit. "Sure, why not?"

Trina giggled. "It is a celebration."

Stephanie topped both of our dishes with whipped cream and sat across from us with a mug of coffee.

"Aren't you having any?" I asked.

"No. Too rich for me this early in the morning."

"Where are Tim and Molly?"

"Tim had a meeting this morning, and Molly's kindergarten didn't have conferences today, so she went to school."

I cut a corner of the toast off and took a bite of it, my eyes practically rolling to the back of my head as the warm banana and toast melted in my mouth. "Oh my God, this is amazing. I told Misha I would report back about these, but I'm afraid if I tell him how good they are, he'll camp out on your front lawn until you make him some."

Stephanie laughed. "Misha can come over anytime."

"Mom will just have to buy double the supplies."

I grinned. "Triple. Okay, time to tell me how school is going."

Trina regaled me with stories that had me flashing to my own pre-teen angst. When I set my fork down a few minutes later, I sat back and tried to decide if it was bad manners to rub my stomach and groan a bit. "That was amazing."

"Would you like some more?" Stephanie asked.

"No. I have to be able to function today. Thanks for inviting me."

Stephanie carried the plates to the sink. "It's the least we can do for you. You've helped our family in so many ways."

I smiled and cleared my throat to break up the lump that was forming. Trina was a well-adjusted example of what could happen when my powers got rid of the monsters. "It was a pleasure."

Stephanie smiled back at me, and if I wasn't mistaken, blinked away moisture from her eyes. There would be no crying today. I wouldn't be able to handle it. I didn't want to think about what they had been through only a few short weeks ago. The entire shifter population had been on the brink of civil war. Griffin almost died. Griffin. Nope. Not the time to dwell on what could have happened.

Trina took my hand, and I looked into her too-knowledgeable eyes. "I want to show you something, Kyle."

"Okay."

"Can I, Mom?"

"Sure, honey. Go on."

I followed her out of the kitchen and up the stairs to her bedroom, where I stopped and stared for a moment. I had been in her bedroom last year, and it had obviously belonged to a little girl. Now her room was painted gray and lavender, with matching abstract swirl patterns on the comforter and chairs in the room.

"This is great, Trina."

She smiled. "I'm going to be thirteen in a couple of months, so Mom and I redecorated."

"Makes sense to me. You need a room for a teenager."

"Right! Plus, I wanted to get it done before the baby comes."

I stared at her. "Your Mom is pregnant?"

"Yes."

"That's great. Why didn't she say anything?"

"She doesn't know yet."

I frowned. "What do you mean, Trina?"

"She doesn't know she's pregnant yet."

"How do you know?"

She shrugged. "I just do. Daddy will figure it out soon, too. Shifter females' scents change when they're pregnant."

Trina did have the strongest scenting ability I had ever encountered in a shifter. Maybe that was how she knew what was going on.

"Why don't you tell her your suspicions, Trina?"

"It's not my place." She turned away from me and sat in her desk chair, giving it a spin, as if to change the flow of conversation. "I'm sorry about you and Griffin."

I swallowed. Her words spun me around like she'd done to the chair. "Griffin and I will always be friends."

Trina smiled. "I know. You're both sad right now, but things will change. You both will be stronger for it."

Where did a twelve-year-old get this stuff? I let the subject drop and walked to the shelving unit that now took up one wall. On the shelves were a clutter of books, a jewelry box, a skateboard, hair bands, and art supplies. On the wall was a poster of a bunch of small, abstract shapes close together.

I leaned closer to it. "What's this?"

"If you stare at it long enough you'll see another picture inside it."

I frowned. "I've never been able to decipher these."

"You're standing too close." She motioned for me to move farther back. "Stand right here and stare at it without concentrating too hard."

I was about to give up when the picture moved, shapes pushing themselves outward into a three-dimensional picture of a wolf looking up at the moon. "I see it!"

"I knew you would. When you're too close to it you can't see the whole picture."

"Yes, ma'am. Speaking of which, how is your wolf doing?"

"Good. The transitions don't hurt anymore, and I feel stronger when I'm my wolf side. Thank you for helping me set her free, Kyle."

I moved away from the poster. "I didn't do anything."

"Yes, you did. I didn't think I would ever be able to change. But you helped me let go of my fear." She grabbed my hands. "You will always be my friend, Kyle. No matter what."

She squeezed my hands, and I marveled at her childlike enthusiasm coupled with innate, natural wisdom...except when I looked into her eyes. They gazed back at me with a mix of melancholy. As if she had a secret she wasn't ready to tell.

I squeezed her hands back. "I'm not going anywhere, Trina."

CHAPTER 33

I was still buzzing from my banana French toast sugar over-load as I walked through the office parking garage to the ele-vator. A limo pulled up to me and stopped, blocking my path. The back window rolled down, and there was Nicholas. And just like that, my buzz disappeared.

He gave me a slight nod. "Kyle."

"Nicholas. What brings you back to the office so soon?"

His eyebrow rose at my question. "The case. May we talk for a moment?"

The driver got out of the car, circled around the back, and opened the door for me.

"We've been keeping you apprised on what's going on."

"Yes. Misha just filled me in on your interview with Sylvia. Please, Kyle. Get in."

I crossed my arms over my chest.

"We won't leave the garage."

I settled in the seat across from him, and the driver closed the door with a soft *click*.

Nicholas continued, "Do you think this Sylvia will be able to find the demons?"

"I think she has a better chance of locating them than we do. She is part of their world."

"And then what?" Nicholas asked.

"We get the artifacts and send the demons back to their realm."

Nicholas leaned forward slightly. "That's the short-term answer."

I blinked at him. "I'm not following you."

"How do we keep this from happening again, Kyle? How do we protect the Key?"

I frowned. "I won't let you hurt Dalton."

He held up his hands, palms out. "I have no intention of hurting Joe. According to Misha, he hasn't shown any sign of remembering or of possessing the Key. We have to assume the Key has moved on."

I swallowed hard. Was he fishing for information? Did he know I possessed it now? Or, rather, that it possessed me? "What are you saying, then?"

He paused as if to collect his thoughts. "I'm saying you're trying to cure the symptoms without understanding the disease. Why are they after the Key in the first place?"

I left Nicholas in the garage, my mind spinning with his questions. When I entered the office, I found Jean Luc, Misha, and Dalton taking turns pacing like expectant fathers. At least I wasn't the only one going stir-crazy. I poured a cup of coffee, because caffeine was absolutely what I needed right now, and sat at the office table between Jean Luc and Dalton. It was Misha's turn to pace in front of the whiteboard.

"Where are Talia and Jason?"

Jean Luc answered, "Talia is meeting with Sandy, the fledgling from the coffee house. She is trying to teach her how to acclimate to her powers."

"She's got her work cut out with that one."

"Jason's gone to the lab to drop some things off," Misha added.

I sat up straighter. "I hope Doc's there. It's time those two talked," I added for Dalton's benefit. "They're fighting their attraction for each other. Hopefully, they'll both get over their stubbornness." I took a sip of my coffee. "I've been thinking, guys."

Misha and Jean Luc exchanged cryptic glances.

"What?"

"Usually when you start with that sentence we end up in trouble," Misha said.

I scowled at them. "You're exaggerating."

"Case 69742—you had an idea for how to trap that klepto-maniac Traman demon, and I ended up with thirty stiches in my posterior. Case 96832—you came up with a way to track the shifter cage fighting ring, and Jean Luc had to sleep for forty-eight hours to recuperate from ingesting bad blood."

"Okay! This is what I get for hanging around a demon with an infallible memory. You going to let me talk now?"

I took their silent glares and Dalton's slightly amused look as permission to continue. "I ran into Nicholas in the parking garage."

"With your car?" Misha asked.

"No! I mean I talked to him. He brought up a good question. We haven't been thinking about why this demon is after the Key."

"Because of the power associated with it?" Jean Luc suggested.

"Yes, of course. But there has to be a reason why someone wants power. I mean, why would you escape the realm and then rob a museum and kill a guard? If your wish is to live on earth, why call attention to yourself?"

Misha picked up a marker from the whiteboard tray and rolled it between his palms. "He wants the Key to control earth?"

"Maybe. Or does he want the Key to help free the other demons from the realm? I've been thinking about Sylvia."

"I wish she would call," Misha groused. "She'd better not back out on us."

"I don't think she will. I've been thinking about what she said."

"Which part? She was on her soapbox for a while," Dalton said.

"About the demon realm. We don't know whether they're all truly bad or not. None of us know what really happened during the war that forced the demon realm closed. And I would like to have more information about how and why only certain clans were forced into the realm. It doesn't feel right to me. Didn't Katya tell us history is written by the victors?"

Dalton turned to Misha. "Can we talk to Irina again and see what she remembers? Maybe she can shed some light on it."

"I don't see why not. *Babushka* loves to talk about the past."

Sixty minutes later, Jean Luc pulled into the Shamat compound, and Misha directed him to the community building. "*Babushka* will meet us here."

We were greeted by a very pissed off Aleksei. "Why do you keep bringing these people into our private compound?"

Misha sighed. "Aleksei, I don't have time to fight with you. I'm here to see *Babushka* on official business."

"Grandmother doesn't need this stress in her life."

"She has been more alive in the past few days than I've seen her in years. She wants to help, Aleksei. We're trying to stop a killer."

"Yes. And because of you, we had a portal open inside the compound. We don't need any more trouble, *brother*."

Misha stood toe to toe with him and spoke between his teeth. "I'm not here looking for trouble, *brother*."

Whoa. Childhood baggage alert, line one. "Guys...umm. Let's take a deep breath, okay? You're right, Aleksei, the last thing we wanted to do was bring danger to the compound. But right now, your Grandmother might be able to provide us with some information to help stop the killer."

"And how do you think she can help do that?"

I answered, "She was alive when the realm was shut down. We need to hear about what actually happened. You're more than welcome to sit in on the conversation with us."

Aleksei's eyes widened at the invitation. "I'll do that."

I nodded, and we all walked into the community room. Irina was once again sitting at the front of the room at the head table. Misha was right. Her eyes sparkled when she saw us, and she smiled with obvious delight.

"Good to see you up and about, Joe. Kyle."

Misha leaned down and kissed her cheek.

Irina frowned, although it did not reach her eyes. "Mikhail, I am meeting with you in my official elder capacity. No kisses."

Misha winked. "Yes, *Babush*...I mean, Irina."

She gestured for us to sit, and the four of us sat across from her. Aleksei strode around the table and sat next to her. His stiff body language screamed that he would put a stop to the conversation if he could.

"Mikhail told me you wanted to discuss the time before the wars?"

"Yes," I said. "Do you remember what it was like before the realm demons were sent away?"

"Vaguely. I was a small child then. But Katya may be able to help."

The door behind Irina opened, and Katya entered the room. Aleksei jumped to his feet, clasped her hand, and escorted her to a seat on the other side of Irina. He squeezed her hand slightly and smiled at her before taking his seat. He'd just moved one notch lower on my pompous ass meter.

Irina spoke. "Since Katya is older than I am, she may be better able to answer your questions."

Katya grimaced. "I'm not *that* much older than you, Irina, so don't make them treat me like I'm frail."

Irina smiled. "Of course not."

"Go ahead with your questions."

I started. "You both mentioned the last time we spoke that before the wars demons could move freely back and forth between earth and the demon realm."

"Yes. There were established portals then, so you could travel back and forth whenever you wanted. My father went there on business quite frequently. He was the second in command for our clan, and the clan council often met in the demon realm."

"When did the fighting begin?" I asked.

"I was a young woman then. But I heard others talk about it. How the clans had begun to squabble among themselves about land and possessions. And then, one night, several of our males came home bloodied. They'd been attacked by a neighboring clan who had always been friends with us. More stories came to our small village. And as the fighting escalated, humans became part of the casualties."

"Did you interact with humans?" Dalton asked.

"Back then, there were far fewer people, and so much land the demon clans were able to avoid humans. But when the war grew, so did the bloodshed."

Katya looked up slightly, as if losing herself in her memories for a moment. "My father would come home and tell my mother how things were going. We lived in a small hut, and he would wait until my brother and I were asleep to discuss it with her. He told us we were too young to hear about war. But sometimes I would pretend to sleep and listen to his reports.

"And they were scary. How he didn't think the fighting would end soon. How every clan wanted to dominate the others. Then we started hearing rumors that the clans were banding together. The Majock and Kelmar were first. Then the Dragans, Lagfel, and Palthat joined them. They were the strongest clans, and when they came together, they destroyed the weaker ones."

"How did the war finally end?"

Katya frowned. "What do you mean?"

"I mean how were the demons with weaker powers able to force the stronger ones to remain in the realm?"

"One night, several clan leaders came to our village. They met in secret. I followed them to a clearing and hid in the trees. The leaders were standing around a campfire discussing how to stop the invading clans.

"While they talked, a male appeared in the circle. He was unlike anyone I had met before, and I knew he was not a demon."

I sat up straighter. "Another supernatural? A vamp or a shifter?"

"He was not a vampire. Vampires wanted nothing to do with our war. I think they hoped we would annihilate each other so they would not have to deal with us any longer."

Jean Luc leaned forward, resting his forearms on the table. "That makes sense."

"And it wasn't a shifter. Shifters were just evolving back then. They were skittish of anything outside their packs. I think the male I saw that night was an angel."

My breath hitched. "An angel. The same ones who always tell us they don't get involved? Those angels?"

Katya lifted her brows and tilted her head with a small smile. "One and the same."

"What did this angel have to say?"

"He talked about the clans standing up together. He said he could close the portals permanently and trap the power-hungry demons in the realm. But someone would need to watch over the realm to ensure they didn't escape."

"The portal guard," Dalton said.

"Yes."

"Did you see the angel again, Katya?"

"No. But within a year, the wars had ended, and the most aggressive clans were trapped in the realm. Members of the patrol were chosen from each clan to oversee the in between."

"And you had peace after that?" I asked.

Katya and Irina chuckled together before Irina spoke. "We have as much peace as any other species on earth. We still squabble, but the threat of being sent to the realm has squelched many uprisings."

"And do you think the punishment fit the crime?" I asked.

Katya paused for a moment. "I think most who are left in the realm are not the ones who caused the strife to begin with. I think they should be free, as should the portal guards who have given up their lives for generations to protect us."

Irina frowned. "I agree to a certain extent, but a millennia of animosity can build into an ugliness that could explode on earth. If we were to ever consider letting them come here, we would need to proceed with caution."

I said, "I think, after our visit to the realm, I would have to agree with you."

Katya's eyes widened. "Tell me about the realm, what was it like?"

I described it, as well as the in-between. Katya listened, the expression on her face like that of a small child on Christmas morning.

"How long before you got sick?" Katya asked.

"I didn't get sick at all. Dalton got sick within an hour or so."

"You didn't get sick? How long were you there?"

"A day."

"That makes no sense."

"I was thinking it had to do with my power."

Irina glanced at me in surprise, and then over at Dalton. "It's okay, Dalton knows about my ability to change memories."

"That is a formidable power to have, but I don't think it's what protected you." Katya stared at me for a moment and then held out her aged hand, palm up. I reached across the table, and her fingers wrapped around mine in a surprisingly strong grip. She closed her eyes.

I glanced at Irina, who nodded reassuringly at me.

After a few more seconds, Katya opened her eyes. "Well, that explains it."

"What?"

"You are part demon, my dear."

I jerked my hand out of her grip and jumped up, knocking my chair onto the floor. "That's impossible. I'm human." I looked at Jean Luc and Misha, who both stared at me, wide-eyed. I pointed to them. "They would have sensed demon in me. Hell, I had a shifter boyfriend, and there's no way he wouldn't have known I was demon."

Katya tilted her head to the side and smiled. "I'm not wrong."

"I didn't see that one coming," Aleksei blurted.

"No! You have to be wrong. Jean Luc. You bit me, wouldn't you have tasted demon in my blood?"

Jean Luc frowned. "I would think so, Kyle, but I have never bitten someone who is both demon and human."

"Then someone explain it to me," I demanded shrilly.

Katya answered, "They do not sense demon in you because, as far as I know, a human and a realm demon have never produced an offspring before. Your demon side is cloaked beneath your human side."

"Realm demon?" I wobbled on my feet, and Dalton stood up and steadied me before I landed on my butt.

"Sit down, McKinley. It's okay."

He righted my chair, and I plopped down. *Okay? How was this okay?*

"Do you know what kind of realm demon I am?"

Katya frowned. "No."

Jean Luc reached for my hand and squeezed it. "We will figure this out, *ma petite*."

"How?"

Irina spoke up. "You could talk to your parents, Kyle."

I shook my head. "I never knew my father. He took off before I was born."

"And your mother?"

Misha walked over and stood behind my chair, placing his hands on my shoulders. "Kyle's mother is dead, *Babushka*."

I blew out a harsh breath. "Actually, that's not quite true."

CHAPTER 34

After my announcement, Misha's hands dropped from my shoulders, and he moved away from me to stand silently to the side while Irina and Katya left the room.

I didn't have the first idea what to say to him. How to make it better. His face looked like someone had stolen his puppy. I'd never lied to him about my mother, exactly. But I didn't think now was the time to argue semantics.

When the door clicked shut, my quiet teammate erupted. He ranted in Russian and paced in the back of the room. It was as if he was having a conversation with himself. Or more of an argument, really.

Jean Luc patted my hand. "He will calm down shortly, Kyle. We will then plan next steps."

Dalton watched the tirade for a moment before turning to me. "Do you know what he's saying?"

"Oh, yeah. Misha taught me all the Russian swear words. He's being very creative with them right now." I frowned. "I don't recognize that phrase."

Aleksei chuckled. "It translates loosely to pig-headed woman."

"Ah." I nodded. "That makes sense."

After a few more minutes, Misha's pacing subsided, and he finally turned to me and glared, his ice-blue eyes practically pinning me to the wall.

"I'm sorry," I blurted.

"Why would you tell us your mother was dead?"

"The woman who gave birth to me is still alive."

Misha crossed his arms. "Isn't that the definition of a mother?"

"Not in my book." I rushed on. "I never said she was dead. I said she was gone." I guess I *was* going to argue semantics.

"And you knew exactly what we would assume. Why would you do that?"

I looked at Aleksei, and he inclined his head slightly. "I'll take my leave now." He walked out without an argument. And he fell down another notch on the jerk-o-meter. At the rate he was going, I might end up liking him.

I stared at my hands. I'd never told anyone about my mother. Except Dalton, and he didn't remember. The irony was not lost on me, especially when I glanced up and saw the same compassionate look on his face that he gave me last year.

"My mother kept a roof over our heads. She also clothed and fed me until I was fourteen, and then I took on odd jobs to pay for things. She didn't care what I did or where I went. She did expect me to go to school, but that was only so I could graduate, find a job, and get out of her house. I'm paraphrasing that last bit, but it's close enough. I moved out a week after I graduated from high school."

"Does she know about your gift?" Jean Luc asked.

"No." I bit my lip to stop the tears. I wouldn't waste them on her. "She did. I told her when I was sixteen, but I erased her memory a few days later when she made me use my power to cover up something for her."

"Shit," Dalton mumbled.

"Yeah. That about sums it up."

Misha uncrossed his arms and enveloped me in a hug. "This must have been terrible for you, little one."

"I never talk about her because I try not to think about her."

Jean Luc came and put a hand on my arm. "Unfortunately, I believe you do need to talk to her, Kyle. She is the only one who can tell you about your father. Do you know where she lives now?"

"Yeah. She lives in Wheeling, West Virginia. But this is something we can table until after we finish the case."

Misha pushed me to arm's length so he could look me in the eye. "That's a thirty-minute flight from here. Father will let us borrow his jet. We can be back here tonight."

"Mish—"

"*Ma petite*, listen to him. You and Misha should go to Wheeling. The rest of the team will stay here in case Sylvia calls. You will return tonight in any event."

Dalton nodded. "He's right. You need to know the truth."

Says the man I was lying to. That irony was not lost on me either.

The taxi pulled up in front of a small, modular home with tan siding, burgundy shutters, and an old Chevy Malibu sitting in the driveway. I took a deep breath and slowly let it out through my nose.

Misha squeezed my hand and smiled at me. "I can go in with you if you want."

"We talked about this on the plane. It'll be better if I do this alone."

"Well, I'll be right here waiting. I can be inside with you in a heartbeat."

"Got it." I mustered what I hoped was a convincing smile, even though I felt like running in the opposite direction. I got out of the cab and walked up to the small porch. Two steps up, and I was in front of the door. I lifted my hand to ring the doorbell, and my fingers shook. But I pressed the bell and stepped back.

I held my breath, the chicken in me hoping she wasn't home so we could jump back on the plane and scurry home to Cleveland. But the door opened, and my mother stood there, staring at me through the screen door. I hadn't seen her in more than ten years. She looked the same, except her dark hair was in a short bob. No gray hair or wrinkles yet, but she was still in her late forties.

"Whatever you're selling, I'm not buying."

I cleared my suddenly clogged throat before answering her. "I'm not selling anything. It's Kyle."

She opened the screen door and narrowed her gray eyes at me. At least I had gotten one thing from her. "I didn't recognize you with blond hair. What are you doing here?"

"I need to talk to you. Can I come in?"

She hesitated for a second and then stepped back, letting me into the house. I studied the small living room. It was relatively clean, with a couch and recliner sitting in front of a flatscreen TV. Very few knickknacks cluttered the space, except for a collection of wooden and glass turtles sitting on a shelf behind the couch. There were no pictures anywhere.

She gestured to the couch, and I sat there while she chose the recliner. Or rather, perched at the front edge of the recliner, as if to say she wouldn't be getting too comfortable and I shouldn't either.

I decided to jump in with both feet. "I need you to tell me about my father."

Her eyes widened. "You won't find him."

"Is he dead?"

She grimaced. "I hope so. Why do you even care?"

"Because I need to know who he is."

"Your father was a liar. He told me he loved me. That he would never leave me. But he got me pregnant and left me. I was on my own at seventeen. At first I thought he left because he couldn't handle fatherhood. Then I found out he left after his job was done."

"What job?"

"He was supposed to get me pregnant."

"What do you mean?"

She stared at me, as if sizing me up before she answered. "You're old enough to know the truth. Your father wasn't human. He was the devil, and he left his offspring for me to raise."

My heart clattered in my chest like a pinball machine. "Why do you say he was the devil?"

"Because his eyes glowed."

"What color did they glow?"

"What color did they glow? That's the first question you ask me after I tell you your father wasn't human?" She sat up straighter. "You already found out, didn't you?"

"What happened to him?"

"He left me when I was eight months pregnant. But first he told me to keep the baby safe. Which—duh—is what mothers do, right? Except he neglected to tell me that others like him would try to kill me."

"What?"

"Another devil came after me and tried to kill me. Or tried to kill you, and since you were still inside me, I was just collateral damage. And this one spouted some shit about needing to stop you from being born and changing the balance of power."

"How did you get away?"

"He attacked me at the gym where I worked. A couple showed up and saved me. They acted like cops. I think they were some kind of demon slayers or something, but they never said, and I never saw them again."

I blinked at her, wondering if I was imagining this conversation, but I wasn't, and my gut twisted, because apparently this, whatever-it-was, was far from over.

"I had been tricked into being an incubator. And you never did anything normal, Kyle. You did things your own way. Even your birth was on your own terms."

"That's why you weren't surprised when I told you about my power."

Her eyes narrowed on me. "What did you say?"

"Nothing."

"After you were born, a man came to the hospital and told me I was in danger. That I couldn't stay there. I had to go into hiding to save you."

"Do you remember his name?"

"No, but I remember what he looked like. They had given me some pain medicine in the hospital, and I thought for a moment I was hallucinating when he walked into the room. He reminded me of Cary Grant but with blond hair."

Son of a bitch. I clenched my fist and dug my fingernails into my palm, imagining the wind up before I clocked Nicholas right in the face the next time I saw him. I could literally feel my pulse pounding in my temples.

I choked out, "What did you do?"

"I changed my name to Dee Baxter before taking you far away from Indiana and starting over. I even met a man who told me he loved me. Everything was going to be okay.

"Until I heard him one night on the phone talking to someone, telling them the toddler was fine and he was happy his job was almost finished so he didn't have to keep pretending to be in love with me. Couldn't stomach sleeping with a human. Or so he said. I ran again and changed my name to Anne McKinley."

God. "No wonder you wanted nothing to do with me. Why didn't you just give me away then?"

She looked away. "So someone else would die in my place? They had no idea what you were, and if I'd tried to tell anyone they would have locked me up."

"Glad to see your motives were so altruistic."

She shot up from her chair and walked to the front door. "Be happy I took care of you."

I stood as well and followed her to where she held open the door.

"Do you have a name for my father? A picture?"

"He told me his name was Anthony Grayson, but I'm sure it was a lie. And I burned all the pictures of him when he left me."

I stood on the porch for a moment, fully aware that this would be the last time I would ever see or speak to her. My mind frantically tried to think of any last question to ask her.

"Why did you name me Kyle?"

Her eyes softened for a moment. "I named you Kyle after the one man in my life who didn't have an agenda. He helped deliver you...in an elevator, of all places. He told me I should name you after someone I admired. His name was Russian and it sounded like Me-Kyle. So I shortened it to Kyle."

Oh. My. God.

She shut the door before I could say anything else, but it was fine, because I didn't know what else to say. Goodbye? Take care? Have a good life?

I turned on wobbly legs and headed toward the cab and Misha's expectant face. The face of the person who had helped bring me into this world.

"Are you okay, Kyle?" Misha asked as I climbed into the car.

I shook my head, and he pulled me against his side and wrapped his arm around my shoulder. He smelled like the cherry hard candy he'd been eating on the plane. I blinked and breathed slowly, suppressing the tears. If I started now, I wouldn't stop.

"We can talk on the plane," I whispered.

It wasn't like I could explain anything with the cab driver listening from the front seat anyway. Plus I needed to process and decide next steps. The first step was to tell Misha everything. *Wow.* He helped deliver me. Which brought more tears. I looked out the window so Misha would stop asking me what was wrong.

The next step of my plan, flashing continuously in my mind in glorious Technicolor, was KILL NICHOLAS. He had known about me from the beginning. Had told my mother to hide me! Then he found me in Vegas and offered me a job. Had he been watching me all along? Had everything in my life been planned and executed by him?

I was a first-class chump.

Hadn't I just told Dalton I didn't think the Fates were playing me? Hell, they would have had to get in line behind Nicholas, the Grand Manipulator.

I had always believed I was lucky to be able to use my gift for something good. But now? I'd been played.

And I was done with being played.

CHAPTER 35

Misha and I climbed onto the small jet and flopped into the plush leather seats while the pilot shut the hatch and then closed himself into the cockpit.

"Okay, Kyle. Please tell me what happened."

"I'll explain everything to you in a minute. I promise." I buckled my seatbelt, buying a bit more time to decide how best to break it to him.

"I have a question about that story you've told me time and again. The one about delivering the baby."

He frowned. "Kyle..."

"Just let me ask you, okay?"

He nodded. "What about it?"

"Was it in connection to a case?"

"Yes. It was the first case Talia worked with Jean Luc and me. We were tracking a demon who'd been killing people."

"I take it you caught him?"

"Jean Luc and Talia did. The demon tried to kill the young mother, and they stopped him. I went with her to the hospital. She didn't have any family, and the father wasn't in the picture. You've heard the rest of the story."

"Did Nicholas assign you to the case?"

"No. He'd just moved us to Indianapolis a couple of weeks before, and then the case came up."

"You never said what happened to the mom and baby."

Misha's eyes tightened. "I don't know for sure. I went to visit them at the hospital the next day, but they'd been discharged. I always wondered what happened to them."

I took a deep breath. "What if I told you the baby grew up with a smart mouth and a sarcastic disdain for authority?"

It's a damn good thing he'd been sitting down.

"I didn't faint." Misha huffed.

I smiled. "Fine. You didn't faint. You simply decided to take an instantaneous nap."

He growled at me.

"I'm sorry I broke it to you that way, but the whole thing is so surreal, I couldn't figure out a better way to tell you."

He blew out a hard breath. "I can't believe it. I was so scared when your mom went into labor, and then you decided to come out before they could get us out of the elevator. Seems you had to have your way from the beginning." He smiled. "Do you know I was the first person to hold you?"

I smiled back at him. "It sounds like I owe you, Talia, and Jean Luc my life."

"Tell me what else your mother said."

I relayed the entire conversation, with the exception of who I was named after. After his earlier reaction, I didn't know how he would take the news. I decided to save that revelation for when Jean Luc was there to calm him down.

Misha's smile was quickly replaced with a scowl. "I wish I could have helped you, Kyle. If only she hadn't left the hospital, maybe I could have helped you both."

"It's the past, Misha. We can't change it. But I sure in the hell am going to find out how Nicholas knew about the demons that were after me and my mother. And what else he's manipulated in my life."

I didn't so much walk into the office as storm into it. Dolly had just shut down her computer for the evening when I stopped in front of her, picked up her phone receiver, and held it out to her.

"Call Nicholas."

"You have his number."

"I have his main cell number, which I called several times, and he's not answering. You also have another number to reach him, right?"

She blanched at my question.

"I always wondered how Nicholas knew what was going on here before we told him. From your reaction, I think you've been reporting in to him."

"He's our boss. I didn't do anything wrong."

"Call him, Dolly, and tell him to come to the office as soon as possible."

"He's out of town. You know he travels to the other BSR offices."

"Tell him to get back here by tomorrow or I'm going to CNN and telling the world that supernaturals exist."

She opened her mouth...and then closed it again after she studied my face. "Got it."

Misha and I walked into the back office. Talia, Jean Luc, Jason, and Dalton sat at the table with a pizza box sitting in front of them.

Jason moaned. "I knew we should have ordered more food."

Misha shook his head. "I'm not hungry."

Silence descended. The four of them looked at him with varying expressions—skepticism, concern, horror, and bemusement.

Jason dropped his pizza back into the box. "Your news must be bad, Kyle, if Misha doesn't want to eat."

I told the story again, and now they wore similar expressions of shock—wide eyes, slack jaws. It would have been amusing if it wasn't a reaction to my pathetic life.

I smiled at Talia and Jean Luc. "I need to thank you both for saving my mom."

Talia wiped a tear from her eye. "You're more than welcome. It's so hard to take in."

Jean Luc nodded. "*Oui*. At the time, we did not know why the demon had targeted your mother. He talked about your mother glowing. And muttered on about stopping destiny.

"I thought it ramblings as part of his delusions. He must have been able to sense your demon side somehow. *Mon Dieu!*"

"What?"

"When I confronted him, he said he had to kill her. I thought he meant your mother, but his claws were aimed at her stomach."

"He meant me. Maybe the demon wasn't delusional. Maybe he wanted to stop a demon realm half-breed from being born."

Jason grabbed my hand. "I'm sorry, Kyle."

"The irony's not lost on me, Jason."

"Even when I was mad at you for not telling me about my shifter side, I wouldn't have wished this on you."

I looked at Dalton to gauge his reaction, since he was being so quiet. He nodded at me, his eyes filled with compassion. His gaze was like flashing back in time to last year.

"It's a lot to take in. You have to give yourself some time," Dalton said, softly.

"I know, I need time to process it all. Oh, there's one other thing. I asked my mother why she named me Kyle. She said she named me after the man who helped deliver me. Said his name sounded like Me-Kyle so she shortened it to Kyle."

Talia gasped, and Jason let out a low whistle.

Misha froze for a second and stared at my lips as if replaying what I said.

I took a step toward him. "Mish, are you okay?"

He yanked me into a bear hug and spun me around with a shout of glee.

Even with his shout, I heard Jean Luc utter. "*Mon Dieu, she has just created a monster.*"

Misha spun me around a few more times before I could make myself heard over his shouts and tell him to put me down.

Dolly looked tentatively into the back office, interrupting us. "He's not answering," she announced.

I glared at her.

"I swear." She held up her cell phone. "I've left him three messages and just texted him."

I blew out a hard breath. There wasn't much else I could do. Nicholas was an enigma. Even if he was in town, none of us knew where he stayed. Not even Misha's computer skills had ever been able to uncover his secret lair.

"Kyle, I think this will give you an opportunity to calm down," Jean Luc said. "We do not want you to kill Nicholas before you get your answers."

"We don't even know if Nicholas can die," Talia reasoned.

"I bet you if I lopped off his head, he'd die."

"I don't know for sure," Misha said.

"What's the saying? If he bleeds, he can die? I could take him. I'm highly motivated."

Dalton listened to our repartee with wide eyes. "Please tell me you're joking right now."

Dolly's phone beeped, which spared me the necessity of answering Dalton. She read the message and blanched again. "Nicholas responded. Says he can't make it back in town tonight. He'll come here first thing tomorrow morning. Uh..." She looked up at me.

"What else does he say?"

"He respectfully asks you to refrain from contacting Anderson Cooper until after you two have spoken."

I bit my lip. Overnight was not going to be enough time for me to calm down.

CHAPTER 36

"Kyle, stop pacing!" Misha snapped from his perch at the office table.

"I can't." I stared at the case notes scattered around the table.

Dalton, Jason, and Talia sat reviewing them. Jean Luc had the Key box in his hand, attempting to decipher some of the symbols.

"Where the hell is Nicholas?" I grumbled.

Jean Luc sighed. "Take a walk around the block, Kyle. You will feel better."

I frowned and then acquiesced. I was driving myself and everyone around me mad. "Fine, but if he shows up, you text me ASAP, and I'll be right back."

Talia smiled at me. "We will." Which really meant *go away, silly woman.*

I trudged down the hall, punched the elevator button, and waited. *Sunshine, puppy dogs, ice cream...* Nope, happy thoughts were not working right now. It didn't help that the building's elevator was the slowest on the planet. Just as I thought about using the stairwell, the elevator dinged and the doors slid open.

I came face to face with Nicholas.

"I hope you weren't going somewhere, Kyle? You summoned me here. You need to explain why."

"You son of a bitch." I hauled back and punched him, hard. My knuckles slammed into his mouth. I stopped myself from gasping as pain shot through my fist and up my arm.

Nicholas didn't even flinch. "You're going to want to ice that."

I'd hit him with enough force to split his lip, but nothing. No blood, no death? Dang. I would table that thought for later.

I marched into the elevator and let the doors close. Then I hit the stop button and turned to face him. No one would be interrupting us before he told me the truth.

"You've known all along!"

Nicholas shook his head. "I am not all-knowing, Kyle."

"Don't give me that cryptic bullshit. You know what I am."

"I know you're part human and part demon, yes."

"You told my mother to run and hide right after I was born."

He looked away for a moment. "I simply suggested she find another place to live. Since she'd just been attacked by a demon, I didn't have to say much to convince your mother to disappear."

"How did you know about me? Misha and Jean Luc had no idea I'm part demon. That wouldn't have been part of their reports to you."

"I have my sources."

I clenched my fist again, even though pain radiated through my fingers. "What fucking sources?"

He glared at me. "There are things I can't tell you, Kyle. There would be serious repercussions."

My phone rang, and I ignored it. "You sent Misha and Jean Luc to protect my mother. Misha told me they moved there a few weeks before I was born."

"I would say it was a lucky coincidence."

"And what about offering me a job? Was that a lucky coincidence?"

"That one is on you. You were trying to use your powers to cheat in Vegas. My team there identified you as an issue. I thought it appropriate to pair you with Jean Luc and Misha, since they had been instrumental in bringing you into the world. So I brought you into the fold, so to speak."

"And I drank the cool-aid, right, Reverend Jones?"

Nicholas smirked. "Overly dramatic reference aside, you can't tell me that working for the BSR hasn't been the best thing for you then and now. You've used your powers to help people and protect supernaturals."

"And last year, when you had Matthew watching out for me, was that because of your mysterious sources?"

Nicholas nodded. "Yes. I was told you were in danger, so I hired Matthew."

Misha's muffled voice permeated the elevator. "Open the door, Kyle!"

The fight drained out of me. "Why didn't you just tell me what I was from the beginning?"

"Because it was something you had to learn on your own, Kyle. I know you don't believe me, but there are things I can't tell you."

I turned away from him and hit the button. The doors opened to a frazzled Misha and frowning Jean Luc.

"Don't worry, guys. I didn't kill him." I stormed past them into the reception area where Jason, Dalton, and Talia had congregated.

"Are you okay?" Dalton asked.

"Peachy. Still as confused as ever. But that's my constant state of being. You would think I'd be used to it by now."

I walked into the office, and the three of them followed closely behind me. No one said anything. I sat at the table and reached for the small wooden box to run my fingers over the markings. If only we had never found this damn thing and Dalton hadn't touched it.

Low voices came from the reception area. Nicholas was still here talking to Misha and Jean Luc. He needed to go away quickly or I would be unable to resist testing my decapitation theory on him. Jean Luc probably had a sword tucked away in his office.

My bloodthirsty thoughts stopped when the office door opened. "What the..." The box in my hand vibrated and then started to glow.

Nicholas blanched at the sight of the glowing box.

I stood. "Holy Guacamole, Batman. We've got an angel in the house."

Nicholas shook his head. "I'm not an angel."

I held the receptacle toward him, and the symbols glowed even brighter. "Are you telling me this is lying?"

He closed his eyes for a second, and when he opened them he sighed. "I *was* an angel."

"*Was* an angel?" I squeaked. "Are you fallen? As in Lucifer?"

Nicholas' jaw muscle clenched. "No, I'm not Lucifer."

"Then what the hell are you?"

"It's not so black and white, unfortunately. Yes, some angels fell because they were evil."

"And you?" Jean Luc asked.

"I was the angel of prophecy. God bestowed upon me one of his greatest gifts."

Misha stood in front of the door, as if to block Nicholas's exit, and crossed his arms. "How did you end up on earth?"

Nicholas kept looking at me. "Sometimes the greatest gifts also come with the largest burden. I saw what was going to happen to the world..."

I finished his sentence. "And you weren't allowed to warn anyone."

"Yes. When I disobeyed the order, I was reprimanded."

"Your wings were clipped. Seems like a crappy thing to do."

"Kyle!" Talia scolded.

"What? He tries to stop something bad from happening, and he's booted out of heaven?"

"There is a reason for rules, Kyle."

"So now you are what?" Dalton asked.

"I am a being who spends his time on earth trying to help."

I put the box down. "And the sources you mentioned earlier that have warned you about bad things. Those are actually your visions?"

Nicholas lowered his voice. "My prophetic powers were stripped from me, but sometimes I have residual flashes. I flashed on your mother before you were born."

I grabbed the picture of the tablet and thrust it at him. "Are you telling me you could have helped us translate this tablet and the Key prophecy all along?"

"No. I can't translate it."

"Bull." I dropped the photo onto the table.

"I'm not an angel anymore, Kyle. The holy languages are not available to me. And that tablet was written after I left heaven."

Good grief. How long had he been exiled here? "What is the point of you being on earth? You get to live here forever and watch us destroy ourselves?"

His eyes tightened. "I think I've done some good in my time here. But there's a limit to what I can get away with, Kyle. I'm not supposed to have these powers anymore. At some point I'll step over the line and be reprimanded again."

"They threw you out of heaven, what's left?" I asked.

Nicholas grimaced. "That's not something I want to test. I know I don't have the right to ask this of you all, but if you would consider keeping this revelation to yourselves, I would be grateful."

The room went silent, and then heads nodded in agreement. Except mine. "I have to tell Doc."

"That's fine, Kyle." And then he left.

I walked after him, and Jean Luc grabbed my arm.

"It's okay, Jean Luc. I won't try to hurt him."

He stared into my eyes for a moment and then let me go. I ran out of the office and reached Nicholas while he was still waiting for the slowest damn elevator on the planet to arrive.

"I have to know something, Nicholas." I glanced over my shoulder to make sure no one had followed me. I lowered my voice just in case. "Could you have helped Dalton last year?"

"No. I didn't see what was going to happen to him. The Key did not exist when I was in heaven. And I did not have the power to make him better. Only you could do that."

"Why were you so damn adamant that he needed to forget?"

He paused for a moment. "Because I truly believed it was the only way to save him. I also hoped that the search for the Key would stop after Sebastian died. If Joe's memories of the Key were gone, then the Key would be gone, too."

I couldn't fault his logic. I bobbed my head in agreement as he stepped onto the elevator.

Even though he'd revealed a lot today, I still didn't trust him enough to tell him the truth about the Key.

CHAPTER 37

I walked back into the office to find everyone talking at once and huddled together as if they'd just finished high-fiving each other.

"What's happened?" I asked.

Misha's eyes sparkled. "Sylvia called. She wants to meet."

"Thank God. Where?"

"She's on her way here. Said she wanted to check out our digs to make sure we weren't torturing people."

I grinned. "She's a kooky lady, but if she helps us get the realm demons, then she's my new best friend."

Misha laid his hands on my shoulders. "Are you okay, Kyle?"

"Yeah. Hearing Nicholas's story makes me realize we all have crap to bear."

"Then you believe him?" Jean Luc asked.

"For once, I do."

Misha led Sylvia into the office, and she stopped in the middle of the room, her mouth falling open. "This is your super-secret lair?"

I laughed. "This is our office, yes."

She puckered her lips like she'd been sucking on lemons. "Even in the seventies this furniture was hideous."

"I knew I liked you." I pulled out a chair, and Sylvia sat down. "You remember Misha and Talia. And this is Jean Luc, Jason, and Dalton."

Sylvia looked at Jean Luc. "You're a sexy one, vampire."

Jean Luc's eyes widened before he recovered. "*Merci.*"

Next her eyes swiveled to Jason. "You're interesting. Mostly human, but with a little hint of something on the side."

Jason smiled. "Nice to meet you, Sylvia."

Finally, she turned to Dalton, and her eyes widened this time. "Now *this* is a cop if I've ever seen one."

Dalton nodded. "Thank you for helping us, Sylvia."

"Yep, talks like a cop, too."

I decided to steer her back to the reason for her visit. "Sylvia, you have some news for us?"

"Yes. I've been digging around and found out that the demon twins you're looking for have been staying in various abandoned houses. And they've been bringing in quite a few new demons lately." She frowned. "None of them have been filtered through my motel, so I'm not sure how well they're acclimating."

"What about the demon from the museum?"

"This is where it gets interesting. He apparently has been seen with the twins."

"So they're working together?" Dalton asked.

Sylvia shook her head. "I think the twins are working *for* him."

Talia leaned closer. "What makes you say that?"

"Talk from some of the other demons. The demon from the museum appears to be calling the shots. He's the one who has the twins bringing over these new demons." Sylvia paused for a moment. "Were you serious about not sending back the demons I've helped?"

I looked at Jean Luc and Misha, who both nodded. "If they aren't causing trouble and want to live peacefully on earth, then I don't think any of us will be searching them out."

Sylvia's gaze traveled over each of us, as if trying to read our sincerity. Hell, maybe our auras told her whether we were being honest or not.

"I brought someone from the realm with me who could help." She pulled out her phone. "Let me call him up here."

Five minutes later, a thin young male with blond hair and brown eyes stood fidgeting in the office doorway. Sylvia walked over to him. "It's all right, Nate. They won't hurt you."

He took hesitant steps into the room and sat down next to Sylvia. Nate looked around the room at everyone while introductions were made, and when his gaze rested on me, he gasped. "You do exist!"

I sat back in my chair. "What do you mean?"

"I, ah...I..." He turned to Sylvia, his eyes bugging.

"It's okay. Tell her."

"You're part realm demon."

"Yes. How did you know that?"

He shrugged. "I don't know how to explain it, exactly. When I meet other supernaturals, there's a feeling I get." He pointed at Jean Luc. "Vampires feel different to me than demons. I haven't gotten to meet an actual shifter yet, but I'm looking forward to it."

Misha said, "That is similar to how our senses work for us here on earth as well, but we do not sense Kyle's demon side."

"Can you tell what type of demon I am?"

"No."

Jean Luc spoke. "Why did you say 'you do exist'?"

"Because the other demons have been talking about her. About the half-demon."

"And what have they been saying?" Misha asked.

"They say she's proof that coming here to earth is meant to be."

I frowned. "Why?"

Dalton answered. "Because not only can they come to earth to live in a better place, but they can mate with humans and have children."

Nate nodded. "In the realm there are very few females left. The generations born since our exile are mostly males. Unless we can find compatible females, eventually we'll cease to exist. There are factions in the realm who declare we must fight and take back our freedom."

"What do you think?" I asked Nate.

"I think that since I had nothing to do with our clans being exiled, I should be given the chance to prove myself here on earth."

"Can you tell us about the demons from the realm who are involved in this?"

"There are two brothers who have been helping realm demons cross over."

"Did they help you come here?" Jean Luc asked.

"Yes. And there is a new demon. He's trying to organize those of us who have crossed over to join his group."

"Do you know what his demon side looks like?" Misha asked.

"No. I met him on earth. I've only ever seen his human side."

I laid a picture in front of him, and he traced his finger over the portrait. "That's him. He goes by Saul. But I doubt that was his name in the realm."

"We need to locate them. Can you help us?"

"I've seen them spending a lot of time in the neighborhood where Sylvia's motel is, but I'm not sure exactly where they're staying. But there's been talk that Saul is trying to schedule a recruitment meeting. It's supposed to take place some time in the next few days. As soon as I hear the time and place, I'll let you know."

God, this sounded like a demon cult. Hadn't we just dealt with a shifter cult? Could we not catch a break? "And Saul is recruiting demons to prepare for what, exactly?"

"To help bring the demons here to earth."

Misha frowned. "Isn't that what he's doing now?"

Nate sighed. "I'm not explaining this well. Saul is working on a way to open the portal forever. Demons will be able to leave the realm and come to earth all on their own."

"How many demons are we talking about, Nate?"

"Around ten thousand."

The room went silent. How the hell could we stop ten thousand demons from coming to earth?

Dalton broke the silence. "What would happen if all the demons came here at once?"

Nate cleared his throat. "There would be anarchy. When I first arrived, it was days before I could bring my human side out. I didn't know the language. I had never seen technology. If it hadn't been for Sylvia, I would have been exposed to the world in no time."

"Now imagine that times ten thousand," Sylvia said.

"How did you get to earth, Nate?"

He paused until Sylvia nodded at him. "I promised them money."

My stomach twisted. I wasn't going to like this.

His hands clenched into fists on the table top. "I have to pay the brothers fifty thousand dollars." He closed his eyes. "Sylvia has explained that it will take years for me to do so."

"And if you don't?" I asked.

He turned to me, his brown eyes darkening. "Then they will hurt my family in the realm. I had planned to work and bring them all here, but now..." He shrugged. "That is how they are recruiting some of the demons. They're forgiving their debt if they join the group."

Jesus. They were creating indentured demon servants.

"Sylvia said you would help me."

"I want to be honest with you, Nate. If we stop these demons, it might mean your family won't be able to come to earth."

"I understand, but I won't hurt others to help myself."

I smiled. "Thank you. If I told you Saul's blood is green, would that clue you into the type of demon he is?"

Sylvia explained for him. "When demons first arrive, they all bleed green. It takes a while for it to turn red."

"What about glowing white eyes? Does it mean the demon has borrowed another's powers?"

"Never seen that before," Sylvia answered.

Nate frowned. "That can't be."

"Why not?"

"Because the only demons I know of whose eyes glow white are the portal guards."

I stopped myself from groaning out loud at his statement.

Sylvia patted the young demon on the arm. "You were great, Nate. Why don't you wait for me in the car?"

"Can I drive home?" he asked, just like any other teenager with his driver's temps.

Sylvia smiled at him. "Sure. You need more practice."

Nate closed the door behind him, and I grinned. "You're a smart lady, Sylvia."

She placed her hand on her heart. "Me?"

"You brought a demon realm poster child to represent your cause."

"I brought you an example of who I'm helping."

"Were you aware this extortion was going on?" Talia asked.

"I know many of them are struggling, but I didn't know it was because they are giving all their money to these bastards. Once Nate came clean, several of the others told me as well. They're embarrassed that they've been suckered into trading one form of imprisonment for another."

"Let's see what we can do to help them," I said. "I can't make any promises, but I'll certainly talk to the Demon Council about what's been happening."

"As will I," Misha said.

"Thanks."

I leaned forward. "I have to ask, Sylvia. Are you ever going to tell us your real name?"

"I thought the deal was that if I helped you, you wouldn't keep digging into my past."

"And we haven't been digging. This is just for curiosity's sake. You're not in the witness protection program, are you?"

"No. Let's just say I had to escape from a past where I was labeled. I've gone by many names over the years. But the name my parents gave me was Marlene Thompson."

Her words shot up my spinal column and into my brain like I was gripping jumper cables. My head jerked backward, and Jean Luc flashed and caught me before I fell. He'd been doing that a lot lately. Thrall and flash. Flash and thrall.

He ran his hands over my arms, but this time, his thrall didn't penetrate the pain the way it normally did. I whimpered as my brain tried to worm its way out through my ears.

"What the hell's going on?" Dalton asked.

"She's going to seize," Jason said. "Jean Luc?"

"My thrall is not helping her."

"Put her on the couch, vampire," Sylvia commanded.

Jean Luc layed me on the couch, and my back bowed up as pain shot from my spinal column into my nerve endings.

"Let the cop touch her. Put your hands on both sides of her face."

Dalton hesitated.

"Do it now!" Sylvia yelled.

The tremors started, and I braced myself for the sharp muscle pain that would soon follow. Dalton's hands framed my face, and warmth streamed from his fingers into my cheeks and migrated up to my brain. Calm descended. My muscles unclenched, and I took a careful breath and braced for the pain to return.

"Kyle?"

I opened my eyes and stared up into Dalton's concerned face.

He smiled down at me, and it was the first real smile he'd given me since he came back. Even though it was the smile of a man who was simply trying to comfort me, I would take it. I gazed up at him and soaked in the smile and the heat of his hands that still held my face.

A few seconds later, his touch softened to almost a caress, and even though I could tell I was going to be okay, I didn't want the connection to end. After a few more seconds, his eyes widened, and then he let me go and I tried to sit up.

"Take it easy, Kyle," Jean Luc protested.

"I feel fine."

Dalton rested his hands on my arms and helped me. "What happened? Are you an epileptic?"

"No. It has to do with my power. Thank you for helping me."

"I didn't do anything." His turquoise eyes narrowed on Sylvia. "How did you know my touching her would help?"

"Each of us has a unique aura. But also surrounding us are other energy patterns that affect our well-being. You two have similar energy patterns. When Kyle collapsed, the energy field around her dimmed. By touching her, you were able to stabilize her energy, so to speak, by providing some of your own. The Chinese would call it yin to yang. If you believe in that stuff."

It had to be the Key connection. But that was a conversation for another day. "What do you believe in, Sylvia?" I asked.

"I believe there are reasons why we meet the people we do. Each choice we make can lead us down a completely different path. The trick is redirecting yourself if the path you've taken is wrong."

Chapter 38

I sat in my office with the door shut. After Sylvia left and I convinced Dalton he didn't need to call 911, the team started working on a stakeout schedule for the streets in Sylvia's neighborhood. By the time Misha announced something about setting up a command central in the hotel across from Sylvia's, I excused myself, saying I needed a few minutes to myself.

In reality, I had a long distance call to make, and I didn't want to be disturbed. I hadn't forgotten the bombshell Nate dropped right before he left.

I wrapped my hand around the crystal hanging from my neck and concentrated. I didn't know what I was doing, but when had that ever stopped me?

"Naya. Can you hear me?" I sat for several minutes, repeating the sentence over and over like a mantra. After another minute, I was about to give up. But the stone started to heat up in my hand. *Please don't let it be my imagination.*

"Naya. It's Kyle. Please answer me."

I jumped at the voice that responded. It came from inside my head, like I was hearing it through a headset.

"Naya?"

"Yes Kyle, it's me."

"It worked!"

"I'm surprised you could initiate contact as well. Has Dalton recovered?"

"Yes, he's fine now. Thank you for helping us." I hesitated for a moment, deciding what to say. The straight approach was the best. "I have to ask you something. Why did you lie to me?"

"I don't understand."

"When I told you about the white eyes. You said you didn't know what it meant. I spoke to a realm demon today, and he told me the white, glowing eyes are the mark of the patrol."

She sighed, and the sound whooshed in my ears. "Please let me explain. When you told me about it and the multiple powers, I was shocked. I couldn't believe someone from the patrol could be involved in this. I had just met you, and I've worked with the patrol my entire life. You could have been mistaken."

"So the patrol demons have multiple powers?"

"Yes. They inherit them from their parents, who come from different clans."

"So you lied to cover it up?"

"No! I wanted to do my own investigation first."

"Have you found anything yet?" I pushed.

"Not much. Guards come and go for days at a time. This is not abnormal when on patrol. I have to be careful. I don't want to attract suspicion. If it is one of the guards, he could run."

"The one we're looking for is probably still on earth. I can tell you what his human side looks like if it would help."

"No, it won't, Kyle. I've never seen the human side of any of the portal guards."

"He goes by the name Saul."

"That name is not familiar to me."

"Well, crap."

Naya chuckled. "You get right to the heart of things, don't you, Kyle."

"In my opinion, there's no point in wasting time."

"The guard have fought this battle for so long. Why would someone betray that oath?"

"I think you may have answered your own question. The demon patrol has sacrificed their lives to live in a limbo world, fighting demons, and never getting to see the very place they're protecting. Maybe someone decided they'd had enough."

"Maybe."

"Let me ask you this, Naya. Why do you think I didn't get sick in the realm?"

She paused for a moment. "I think you know the answer, but want me to confirm it. There is demon inside you."

"And you couldn't have shared that with me at the time?"

"Kyle, I do apologize, but you have to look at it from my perspective. You and Dalton appear in the realm and tell me you're chasing demons, and I can see you're part demon yourself...which you don't seem to know, or aren't telling me the truth about. You then tell me this demon on earth has glowing white eyes. I wanted to believe you, but I had to confirm it myself first."

"Fair enough. I understand being cautious. I didn't lie to you, though. I didn't know about my demon side then. It appears I may be quite unique in that regard."

"You are unique, Kyle. I've never heard of a human and realm demon producing offspring before."

"Yeah, it's a big news flash on earth, too. Most of the supernaturals here can't sense my demon side. Can you tell what type of demon I am?"

"I can't tell for sure."

"Are all the demons in the realm dangerous?"

"The ones I encounter, yes."

"How many have you encountered?"

"Our patrol keeps track of close to fifteen hundred or so demons."

"I met a realm demon today who said there are ten thousand demons in the realm."

Naya gasped. "That can't be possible."

"Why?"

"Because we have scouts whose job it is to take a census on the numbers in the realm."

"That might be the first group you should look at. If they're lying about the numbers, you have to wonder why. I also know that many of the demons who've come to earth are living law-abiding lives."

"I don't know what to say."

"I'm sorry, Naya. I can imagine how hard this is for you to hear."

"What do these crossover demons hope to accomplish?"

"They want to permanently open a portal so the entire demon population can migrate to earth on a massive scale."

"Even if what you say is true, Kyle, and many of these demons simply want to live on earth in peace, they can't all go there at once. It would create pandemonium."

"I agree. We'd have war on our hands."

I'd relayed my conversation with Naya to the team, and now I was ready to go home. The day had sucked rocks—boulders, actually—and I was exhausted. If we were lucky, Nate would call us tomorrow, and then we could bag these demons and close out the case. Jean Luc and Misha volunteered to set up the hotel room with various cameras pointed at the street to track the demon comings and goings in front of Sylvia's motel.

I rinsed out my coffee mug in the kitchenette sink and was about to announce I was heading home when the office door opened, and Doc came in carrying her medical bag.

My hands jumped to my hips and I growled, "Who called you?"

The office went silent, and I turned in a circle to find the guilty party. Misha refused to look at me and started to hum an out of tune version of *Happy Days*.

"Misha!"

He flinched. "Dalton made me do it."

Dalton frowned. "I wanted Doc to check you over after your incident."

Before I could argue, Doc interrupted, "Humor me, please. Let's go to your office so we can have some privacy."

We walked to my office, and Doc shut the door and sat across from me.

"Let me give you a quick once-over."

"Come on, Sabrina."

She unzipped the bag and pulled out a small grocery bag. Reaching inside, she extracted a plastic spoon and a pint of mocha swirl.

"Just what the doctor ordered." I reached for the ice cream.

She held it away from me. "Ah, ah, ah. I examine you and *then* you get your treat."

"Fine."

Doc pulled out her equipment and brought her chair around my desk so she could sit next to me. "I want to tell you how sorry I am, Kyle."

"Why are you apologizing?"

"Because if anyone should have realized you're part demon, it was me. You've banged yourself up on numerous occasions, and nothing in your tests showed that you're anything but human."

"Except that I can erase memories?"

Doc smiled. "Except that."

"I don't understand it either, Sabrina. Last year, when Misha got shot, the poison bullet made you sick. But I was able to touch it. Why didn't it affect me?"

"I don't know. Maybe your human side protected you."

"Do you think it's why the Key and I don't seem to get along? I can't imagine that the angels ever thought a demon would possess it."

Doc nodded. "Possibly. It might not be able to fully acclimate to you, since it senses your demon side. How are you doing with all of this?"

"At first it was like a punch to the gut. Especially finding out everything from my mother, but now I think it helps me understand my gift."

"I can't believe Misha actually helped deliver you."

"Good Lord, that demon is a Chatty Cathy. He must have told you everything."

"He loves you and worries about you."

"I know."

"Now let me take a look at you before your ice cream melts."

Doc listened to my heart and then shone a light in my eyes...and frowned.

"What's wrong?"

"I don't like how your pupils are responding."

"What do you mean?"

"I don't know for sure, since I haven't run any tests, but we need to find out if the Key is starting to affect your brain function, Kyle."

"With the way it takes over my body, I wouldn't be surprised to learn it's doing something to my brain."

Doc wrapped her stethoscope and placed it in her bag while she gave me her Concerned Doctor glare. "I want to do an EEG on you and run some other tests."

"Sabrina, do *not* say anything to anybody about this right now. This case could be wrapped up as early as tomorrow, and I'm sure the tests can wait a couple of days."

"Kyle—"

"Even if you do find out something from the tests, what are you going to do about it? You can't exactly perform surgery to remove it, can you?"

"No. But it doesn't mean we shouldn't be trying to figure out how to help you. I don't think you should try and engage the Key at all until we have a better idea of what's going on."

"Got it." But I only said that to appease my friend.

Because the bottom line was, when it came to the Key, I wasn't the one in charge.

CHAPTER 39

I sat across the office table from Misha and Jean Luc. With Dalton at the police station updating Captain Morrison, and Jason and Talia taking their shift on stakeout, it was just the three of us. The way it used to be.

"What are you smiling about, *ma petite?*"

"Us. It's hard to believe we've been working together for ten years."

Misha leaned back from his keyboard. "It's even harder to believe we haven't killed each other before now."

I laughed. "I agree. Now we have Jason and Talia as part of the team."

"And you are okay with that?" Jean Luc asked.

"Of course. They both have talents and skills that add to the group."

Jean Luc and Misha looked at each other. Something was cooking.

"What's up?"

"Kyle, Jean Luc and I have been talking. We think you should tell Dalton the whole truth. He's so close to knowing everything now and hasn't shown any signs of a breakdown."

I sighed. "Are you guys doing another intervention? I wondered why Jason and Talia took the next shift."

"We want you to consider it." Jean Luc answered.

"Honestly, I've been thinking about it. But what exactly am I supposed to tell him? So sorry I didn't mention this earlier, but I erased your memory last year because you'd been driven insane and—oh, yeah—you were or maybe still are the Key of Knowledge? That'll go over well."

"So what if it doesn't?" Misha responded. "You have to try. You would have already told the two of us to suck it up."

"He is right, Kyle. I believe it was only a short time ago when you told me to go after Talia and not take no for an answer. You do not strike me as a hypocrite."

I frowned at him. "Wow, you guys were nicer during my last intervention."

Jean Luc grabbed my hand. "You have more to lose this time, Kyle."

I nodded. "I'll tell him the truth. He may never want to speak to me again, but he deserves to know, and maybe it'll help him. But not until the case is over. Once we bag these demons, I'll tell him everything."

Misha smacked his palms together. "Good. Our work here is done."

"Why is there always a comedian in the group?"

Before Misha could respond, my phone rang. I glanced at the screen and answered it. "Hello, Father."

"Kyle, I'm glad I reached you."

"You have something new for me?"

"I've been able to interpret more of the tablet. And I've also been looking at the prophecy again. I didn't interpret it correctly."

"Father, I'm going to put you on speaker phone. I have two of my teammates in the room. Go ahead."

"I told you the phrase in the prophecy was 'angels descend and protect the key.'"

"Yes."

"It's actually 'angels' *descendants* protect the key.'"

"I don't understand, Father."

"Angels' children."

"Nephilim?" Jean Luc asked.

"Some have used that term for fallen angels, although Nephilim are supposed to be the giants who lived before the flood. I'm talking about those angels who have fallen and live among us. Only their descendants can open the receptacle and release the Key."

And then it hit me like a punch to the solar plexus. "Wait. You're saying Dalton is a descendant of the angels?"

"Yes. A Sentinel is an angelic descendent."

"Anything else, Father?"

"Not right now, but I'll keep working on it. The translations are coming easier now."

"Good. Thanks very much."

I hung up and spun my cell phone on the table, waiting for it to stop. I finally met Misha and Jean Luc's concerned gazes. "Yet another thing to tell Dalton. How many more can he handle? He's going to hate me forever."

"We don't even know if Dalton is part angel, Kyle." Misha argued.

"So we get proof, like we did with me. We go to the source. Or, more precisely, we bring the source to us." I stood and walked to the center of the room. "Marie!" I hollered. "Marie! Show yourself. They know about you, so quit hiding, already."

After a few more seconds, Marie appeared in the office. Same yellow sundress, but it looked like she'd gotten her hair done. Did they have beauty salons in heaven?

Marie twinkled at Jean Luc first and waggled flirty fingers at him. "Hello, vampire. It's lovely to meet you finally."

Jean Luc bowed slightly.

"Where is Talia? You didn't break up, did you?" Marie asked, a little too enthusiastically.

Jean Luc's mouth tipped up slightly on the corners. "No. Talia and I are still together."

"Well, I'm glad to hear it." Although she didn't sound very glad. She turned her attentions to her next victim. "So you're Misha."

"Nice to finally meet you, Marie."

She tittered at him. "Your accent is wonderful. If I were forty years younger and had an actual body, I would so go after you."

Misha laughed out loud. "I like you, Marie."

"I'm a wonderful cook. My cannoli are legendary."

Misha moaned.

"Marie, enough. You need to come clean and cut the bull, okay?"

"About what?"

"About your grandson being part angel."

Marie's mouth opened in a perfect circle, and she appeared to be gasping for air, if she'd needed to breathe air, that is.

"How did you find out?"

"I was hoping you would tell me I was wrong."

"Joe's father was an angel. Fallen angel to be exact. Wonderful man, and he loved my daughter with all his heart. They were killed when a rogue demon attacked them."

"That can't be right. Dalton told me they were killed because his father worked for the FBI and he went after a mob boss."

"That's what I told Joe. Timothy was an FBI agent, but the mob had nothing to do with his death."

"God, Marie. How has he not asked more about this? Shit, he could have pulled records at the Bureau."

"Yes, and I would be surprised if he hasn't done it by now. He would find records of the case. Obviously, the FBI couldn't know the truth. BSR teams have been around for a long time, Kyle."

I blinked and looked at Jean Luc and Misha.

Misha held his hands out in front of him. "Don't look at me. We had nothing to do with it."

"He has major issues with his dad, Marie. Blames him for his mother's death."

Marie's translucent hand went to her chest. "No! That was not what was supposed to happen. I raised that boy as my own. And then the angels decide he's going to carry this Key of Knowledge around in him? And be a target? Not acceptable. So I told them I wanted to be their angel liaison. And they said yes."

"And now?"

"Now they think I'm helping them find the Key. They let me watch over Joe to make sure he doesn't show signs of having the Key inside him."

"And you have not told them about Kyle?" Jean Luc asked.

"Of course not. If I told them, they wouldn't let me come here anymore. Plus, they don't need to know. It's their problem if they can't keep track of their own Sentinels, for goodness' sake."

I sat down with a thud in a chair. "How the hell am I going to tell him this?"

Marie's eyes focused on me. "You're going to tell Joe?"

"I was planning to tell him the truth about what happened last year."

Marie clapped her hands. "I would love to be able to talk to him again, Kyle. If you tell him the truth, I'll be able to visit regularly like I did before."

I rubbed the back of my neck. "Yeah, he won't hate *you* once the truth is out."

She frowned. "Once he knows why you erased his memory, he'll forgive you."

"I'm not worried about his reaction to the initial erase. It's the fact that I've kept it from him."

Marie floated closer to me. "Joe is a stubborn man. But he's also a caretaker. He would have done the same for you. Make him see that, Kyle."

"I'll try, Marie, but I'm not a miracle worker."

As Marie faded away, I started hollering again because I couldn't calm my voice or my heart. "Dolly!"

She ran into the room. "What's wrong?"

"Track down Nicholas. I need to talk to him."

"In person?"

"Or on the phone, whichever is faster."

"I'll let him know. Should I attach any CNN threats to the communication?"

"Just get him on the phone, please."

Thirty minutes later, we were still waiting for Sir Nicholas to return Dolly's multiple phone and text messages.

Apparently angels, even watered-down ones, weren't easily intimidated.

CHAPTER 40

I unlocked my door and entered my dark apartment. As the light from the hall landed on my couch, it reflected off a pair of glowing yellow eyes. I squealed and slammed my hand on the light switch. Booger was perched on the arm of my couch and blinked at me, twice.

I banged the door shut and stalked over to him. "Booger! You gave me a heart attack. What are you doing here?"

He jumped down and walked to the center of the room. A vortex of light surrounded him as he changed from cat to man. Gray striped fur gave way to skin, and then he grew to his full size in seconds, like Alice in Wonderland after she drank the potion. I had been making a number of Wonderland references lately. Did that make Booger the Cheshire Cat?

"Didn't mean to scare you, Kyle."

"You're just lucky I wasn't carrying Stanley or you would be one dead cat."

He chuckled as he bent over in all his naked glory, opened the trunk next to the window, and pulled out some clothes.

I couldn't tell if the heat creeping up to my scalp was rage, or...or what. "Why do you have clothes in my trunk? And how did you get into my apartment?"

"Misha gave me a key."

Again? I really needed to have a talk with Misha. "How in the hell does Misha have a key to my apartment? And why would he give it to you? He doesn't like you."

"I think you're exaggerating the animosity."

"Why in the world did Misha give you a key?"

"Because he's worried about you. Ever since the twin demons from hell tried to grab you, he's had me watching the neighborhood."

"Of all the overprotective, overreacting, overbearing—"

"Be glad he did."

I blew out a deep breath. "You need to explain what exactly is going on, but first put on some pants."

Matthew shook his head repeatedly. "You are almost puritanical in your attitudes about the human body, Kyle."

"Keep it up, and I'll go get Stanley."

He pulled on his clothes quickly. "Here's the deal. I saw the demon from the museum skulking around your apartment."

"What! Are you sure?"

"He looked like the drawing you showed me, so yeah."

"Why didn't you call us?" I asked.

"I was going to, but he did that disappearing thing, and I lost him. But not before he met with another demon."

"Did you hear what they said?"

"Only a couple of words. The other demon gave him a package."

"What did the other demon look like?"

"Male. Smelled like a Shamat to me. Dark hair. Ritzy vibe. Suit and ridiculously shiny shoes. I could barely stop my cat side from spitting up on them."

Oh, crap.

And like that, Trina's words came crashing back to me. I was standing too close to see the picture in front of me.

I could blame it on the revelation-palooza coming at me like fastballs. My demon side, Dalton and Nicholas's angelic beginnings. But I should have caught it myself.

When I interrogated Eli, I'd told him the demons from the realm needed help when they first came here. How else would they acclimate? Yet Sylvia hadn't helped the demon from the museum, and now Nate said others had crossed over too. Someone else on earth had to be helping them.

Aleksei had wormed his way into most of our conversations with Irina. Could he have alerted the twins we were after them? Hell, he could have told the one twin where the other was located so he could break him out of the demon compound.

And here Aleksei had dropped down several notches on my pompous-ass meter. But if he was the one responsible for these crossover demons and their plan to invade earth, he had just been transferred to my evil-scary-bastard meter.

"Earth to Kyle! Hey! Are you okay?"

"Yeah."

"I think you should go get Stanley and pack a bag so you can stay somewhere else for a while."

I nodded. "I'm supposed to be heading to the hotel for my shift on stakeout."

"You won't be alone, will you?"

"No. I'll be with Misha."

God. How was I going to tell him about Aleksei?

I paced the hotel room waiting for Misha. What words could make this better? Aleksei's betrayal might actually destroy him. Was Aleksei's disdain for humans enough to motivate him to bring thousands of demons to earth?

Distraction. I needed a distraction. I studied the room. Everything about it was faded, from the blue comforter to the threadbare striped curtains. And the air in the room was stale, like day-old popcorn. I had just relieved Jason and Talia and hadn't said anything to them about Aleksei. I owed it to Misha to tell him first. My phone rang, and I growled at the name on the screen. Really? He decided to call me now?

"About damn time you returned my call, Nicholas."

"What can I do for you, Kyle?"

"You can tell me why you keep lying to me."

"You're going to have to be more specific with your accusations."

"You can't tell me you didn't know Dalton is part angel."

"You asked me if I knew what you were, and I told you. You never asked me about Joe."

"You conniving angel bastard!" I barked.

"As much as I enjoy your colorful, but inaccurate, descriptors of me, we've had this conversation before. It's not my place to tell him what he is."

"Why the hell not?"

"What do you want me to say to him, Kyle? That his father was an angel? That he wasn't killed by a mafia don, instead, he was killed by a demon? How does it help him fit into this world? How does he move forward and not become obsessed with crushing evil? Sometimes knowledge is not power. Sometimes it's paralyzing. He no longer has the Key in him. Let him live out his life as a norm."

"Maybe he isn't supposed to get married with the white picket fence, two point two kids, and a dog. Maybe he's supposed to stop evil in the world. Isn't that why you came to earth a millennia ago? Because you were punished when you tried to stop something evil from happening? Maybe you've been here so long that you've forgotten what it means to take a risk and do the right thing."

I sucked in a deep breath. "I'm the one who erased Dalton's memory of being the Key. You aren't the only one who has to deal with the fallout."

"What the hell did you just say?"

I jerked at the voice behind me and whirled around, my phone slipping from my fingers.

Dalton stood in the doorway.

Chapter 41

Oh God, oh God, oh God. My heart ricocheted. How did he keep sneaking up on me? Were angels extra-stealthy? Anger radiated from him like a tidal wave. His fists closed around the fast food bags he carried.

I took a step toward him. "Let me explain."

"When did you erase me memory?"

"I..."

"When!"

"Last summer."

He dropped the bags on the coffee table. "Last summer? That can't be right. I was involved in the serial killer case last summer."

"Yes. But what you don't remember is that we worked on the serial killer case with you. The killer was a vampire by the name of Hampton. He was beheaded, and his sire Sebastian took up where he left off. They were killing people in search of the Key."

"The Key. *I* was the Sentinel for the key?"

"Yes. You were the only one who could open the receptacle last year. We had no idea what it meant at first, until Sebastian kidnapped you."

"Jesus Christ! Are you kidding me?" He glared at me for a moment, his turquoise eyes phosphorescent in his fury. "Of course you're not kidding. Why the hell did you make me forget? You didn't think you could trust me? Are you going to erase my memory again after this case too?"

"No, I'm not going to erase your memories again. Last year, Sebastian tortured you so badly that you'd gone insane. I changed your memory to save you."

"So you say."

His words were like a slap across the face. "I'm not lying."

He threw his arms out and paced rapidly. "You've been lying to me all along. Acting so damn jumpy, I couldn't figure out what was going on. I'm surprised you haven't been laughing it up behind my back."

"There is nothing funny about this," I said. "I understand how upset you—"

"How can you possibly understand? I don't know what part of my past is real and what isn't. You took the truth away from me. And now we're fighting demons who want the damn Key, and it's been in me this entire time?"

I shook my head. "It's not in you anymore."

"Where the hell did it go?"

I hesitated, and Dalton scowled at me. "Don't you dare lie to me again, McKinley. Where is it?"

"When I erased your memory, I absorbed the Key."

A sharp laugh erupted from him. "Perfect. Just perfect."

"I was going to tell you when the case was done," I blurted, wanting to erase the words as soon I said them. He'd never believe me.

"How convenient."

I opened my mouth, and he held up a hand to silence me. "Don't. I can't listen to this anymore. I told Misha I would take his shift, but I can't be here. Get him on the phone. I need to get out of here so I can breathe."

He marched away from me, then turned and pointed. "Don't think we're done talking about this. You *will* tell me everything. All the memories you stole from me."

He yanked open the door and immediately flew backward, slamming into the wall. I cried out as he landed on the floor, unconscious.

I pulled Stanley from my holster, but the gun shot across the room into the waiting hands of the demon from the museum. He was still in his human form, his eyes glowing white in the low-lit room.

The twins followed in behind him, and the door closed without any of them touching it. "Finally, we found you. You're a tough woman to get alone."

"What do you want?"

"You. The brothers told me you were causing trouble for them." He gestured to his right. "Zachariah wanted to kill you, but you're too important to our cause. I was not happy to hear he had sent you to the realm."

"I wasn't happy either."

He chuckled, low and creepy, in the back of his throat. "You have no idea how special you are."

My stomach flip-flopped. Did he know I was the Key? I moved away from Dalton to keep him out of the line of fire. "Why don't you enlighten me?"

"You are the first. Proof that we are meant to come to earth. Before you, there were no half-realm demons. A grand experiment, if you will. We tried for decades before you were born. We need a carrot to dangle in front of the realm demon population. If they can mate with humans, our numbers would grow exponentially."

"Why does that matter?"

"Because we're dying out. And when we finally break out of the realm, we will need more demons. We'll make the other demon clans pay for what they did to us."

"You're a portal guard! You *are* part of the demon clans on earth."

"No. The portal guards have been abandoned as well. Our parents and grandparents volunteered to protect earth. And what did we get in return? Nothing. We're treated as poorly as those imprisoned in the realm. I have pleaded with the council for centuries to make changes, and it fell on deaf ears. Now it's time to make change for ourselves."

"You're the portal guard leader?"

He nodded and handed Stanley to Zachariah.

"You figured out I was half demon at the museum. That's why you didn't kill me."

"I almost snapped your neck, but thank goodness I realized what you were in time."

"Yes. Thank goodness."

He flattened his lips in a grim line. "You are a disrespectful one."

"In order for me to be disrespectful to someone, I would have to have a reason to respect them in the first place."

He stalked closer, growling, and I braced for some sort of punishment.

"Saul, don't mar her face," Zachariah said.

He took a shuddering breath. "You're right. She needs to stand on the stage tonight and look pretty for the potential recruits. Let's leave before her other teammates arrive. Bring him along too."

"Why?" I asked. "Leave him here. He'll just slow us down."

Saul narrowed his eyes. "He comes with us. Something tells me he'll be a useful tool for keeping you in line."

Dalton moaned and twitched. He was lying on a flattened stack of cardboard boxes that I'd rolled him onto after the twins dumped him on the concrete floor. I crawled closer.

"You okay?"

"Yeah." He sat up slowly. "Where are we?"

"Some sort of abandoned factory. We're locked in an old storage room."

"Why are we here?"

"I think this is where the demons are going to have their next recruitment meeting. I'm going to be their main attraction tonight. The poster child for demon-human fertility."

"We need to get out of here."

"Not possible. I've checked this entire space. There's one door, and other than the cardboard you're lying on, the room is empty. No weapons anywhere."

He reached under his jacket.

"They took your gun."

Dalton ran his hand down his leg and felt along his ankle. "Not my spare."

"Don't take it out now. You'll have to surprise him, or he'll use telekinesis to take it away from you. When did you start wearing an ankle holster?"

"I pulled it out again after we fell into the demon realm. I started wearing it when I was attacked during the serial killer case last summer." He frowned. "Although now I don't know what was real and what wasn't."

Could guilt take up permanent residence in a body? "I promise I'll explain everything once we get out of here."

He got up and paced the room the same way I had, but I wasn't going to argue with him. He was a cop. Maybe he would notice or think of something that I hadn't. But after a few minutes, he sat back down next to me.

Footsteps pounded outside, and we scrambled to our feet. As the door scraped open, Dalton pushed me behind him. Even though he was pissed at me, more than likely hated me, he still placed himself between me and the demons.

"It's show time," Saul announced.

"She's not going anywhere with you," Dalton said.

Saul gestured to the twins, who stalked toward Dalton. The two smiled at each other. An evil twin smile that made you wonder if they were communicating in evil-twinspeak. Even human twins seemed to be able to communicate telepathically. Who knew what these two were capable of?

I rested my hand on Dalton's tense arm. "Please don't. They'll hurt you and take me anyway."

Saul chuckled. "I knew he'd be useful if we brought him."

I gritted my teeth and walked ahead of him out of the storage closet and onto the plant floor. Rusted machinery hulked like sentries in the large space. We walked toward a makeshift stage at the end of the room, and as we approached it, I gasped. The Prophecy tablet and the Key box sat on a table in the middle of the stage.

Dear God, I needed to keep Dalton away from that box. Who knew what would happen if he touched it? I looked behind me. The twins were flanking him and led him over to stand next to the far corner of the stage.

Saul directed me up onto the stage, and as I got closer to the table, the air teemed with power, a magnetic quality that drew me toward the objects. Light shimmered around the table like sunshine reflecting off the pavement on a hot summer day.

Saul stopped beside me. He stared at the box and tablet with no reaction, as if he couldn't see the power emanating from them. A low humming sounded in my ears. I watched him, but he still didn't react.

"Why did you steal these from the museum?" I asked.

"Because they're going to help open the portal forever."

"How?"

He frowned. "You don't need to know."

Which meant he didn't know how to use them. "Then what do you need me for?"

"You're going to entice the realm demons to come to earth. Some of our recruits are going to take you back through the portal and show our brothers what they can have here."

"No!" Dalton yelled. He bolted for the stage, but the twins each grabbed one of his arms.

I closed my hands into fists. "I'm not some damn freak show you can parade around."

"You will be whatever I want you to be. It's your destiny. The reason you were born."

"Is my father part of your team?"

He scowled. "There are a number of realm demons who have been working toward this goal for decades. Your father was one of them."

Was? "Do you know—"

"Enough questions!"

"Fine. How about a statement, then? If you bring thousands of demons through the portal, there will be war."

"Do not underestimate us. A millennia of living like rats has made us very resourceful. And we have powerful connections on earth."

"Like Aleksei."

His forehead bunched in confusion.

"No, dear, he means me."

I turned. Katya walked toward us.

CHAPTER 42

Katya smiled like an actress accepting an award as she stepped up on stage. "I see I've surprised you."

"Why?" I blurted, shock leaving me at a loss for more words.

"Because the imprisonment of the realm demons is a travesty! Over a thousand years of banishment, and for what?"

"And this is, what? A personal crusade to correct an injustice?"

"Our neighboring clan was sent to the realm, and with them, the demon I loved."

I frowned. "But back then demons didn't marry outside their clans. You wouldn't have been able to have children."

"Instead, I spent my life childless *and* alone. My father forced me to marry a male in our clan who left me when I couldn't give him children. How is that any better?"

"Katya, your demon flunky here killed a human to steal these pieces from the museum. If you let demons come to earth all at once, we'll have war on our hands."

She flipped her hand in the air as if batting a fly. "I've lived through hundreds of wars. What is one more?"

Oh Lordy, she was a crackpot. Why did I attract the crackpots? "There has to be a better way to do this. Speak to the Council."

Katya huffed at me. "The Council? They're a bunch of bureaucrats. I need action."

"And you've recruited Aleksei to help?" I asked. "He was seen with Saul here."

"No, my dear. Irina raised her grandsons to respect their elders. Aleksei runs errands for me, and I had him deliver a package to Saul. Aleksei doesn't know about Saul or my little project here." She chuckled. "That's how I got rid of Misha today so we could grab you. He's also running an errand. Such helpful boys."

"Well, I can tell you I'm not willingly going to the demon realm to help recruit."

"I agree."

"What?" Saul barked.

"She has a much more important role, now that I know what she is."

Nerves fluttered along my spinal cord into my brain. "What are you talking about?"

"Don't play stupid, Kyle. You're the Key."

I opened my mouth and closed it. What was the point of trying to deny it?

"I have a unique ability. Through touch I can tell what a being is. The first time we met, I made a point of handing you the paper describing the demon clans. What a surprise to discover you were part realm demon! And when you told me you were working on a deal with the Abstatholm, I figured it had to be with the twins. I made a call and got them to agree to meet with you."

She frowned at the twins. "They were supposed to kidnap you, but they got a bit carried away. But something bothered me about you. Our first touch had been blocked by the paper, and I'd sensed something else was there, but couldn't lock onto it. That's why I held your hand that second time."

"And you sensed the Key?"

"Yes. And the irony was not lost on me. I have spent the last millennia trying to find a way to open the portal again. If an angel was able to close it all those years ago, then they had the knowledge to open it again. And that's where the Key comes in."

She walked over and ran her fingers over the tablet. "I discovered the Key of Knowledge in ancient texts. I think it was God's way of removing power from the full angels. I'm not convinced He was overly happy when they helped trap our clans in the realm. Free will and all that being a big sticking point for Him."

"But he lets angels' descendants carry it."

Katya's eyes narrowed on me. "If that is true, maybe he trusts their human side to provide something a full angel is not born with—a conscience. I knew it was the answer I was seeking, but no one could find where it was being kept until last year, when those egotistical vampires decided they could control it."

"Silly vampires, tricks are for demons." Okay, now I had turned into a crackpot.

Katya barked out a laugh. "I really like you, Kyle. Maybe we can talk more later, if you survive opening the portal. Now do your thing with the Key, and let's get this party started."

I shook my head. "I don't know how."

Katya frowned. "Don't play me for a fool."

"Hey, Crazy-Demon-Lady, I'm not playing you. I. Don't. Know. How. To use your precious Key."

She growled, her eyes turning jet black. "What if I let the twins hurt your human? Would that incentivize you?"

"Don't do it, Kyle!" Dalton yelled.

One of the twins punched Dalton in the stomach, and he folded over.

"Stop!" These SOBs were not going to ruin everything. But how could I stop them? The Key. The prophecy. What good was it, if it did nothing to prevent these bastards from destroying the rest of the world? *What could I do?* The answer came to me like a V-8 smack upside the head.

The tablet.

Father Brown had said the tablet was the instruction manual for the Key. Well, it was time to download the information into my brain.

"I need to touch the tablet."

Katya glared at me for a second and then backed away from the artifacts. I looked at Saul, who watched our exchange from the front of the stage. Then I glanced at Dalton, who still struggled between the demon twins.

I reached for the tablet slowly, letting my fingers brush the cool stone. *Come on, Key. Do your damn job, already.* Tingling answered my pleas. It ran up my spinal column and quickly morphed into razor-sharp pains slicing into my brain. My instinct for self-preservation tried to force me to back away, but I couldn't stop now.

I slapped the palm of my hand down on the tablet.

The room narrowed, graying around the perimeter, so Dalton, Katya, and the other demons were highlighted in vivid detail, like cartoon characters against a gray backdrop.

And then all became clear.

Latin words bubbled into my thoughts and spouted from my mouth. The demon twins froze where they were, wearing matching twin grimaces as they stood stiffly, unable to move. They growled and struggled to free themselves from the energy that wrapped around them like the cloth strips of a mummy. I could see the energy, brilliant and lifelike, as the words tightened the tendrils around them.

Dalton wrenched himself free. Saul gawked for a moment at the twins and then turned to me in shock. While he was distracted, Dalton reached for his ankle holster. But he wasn't fast enough.

Saul spun back around and raised his hand toward Dalton. I screamed, let go of the tablet, and lunged in front of Saul's hand, his energy slamming into me like a freight train.

Shots rang out, and Saul dropped to the concrete floor.

Somehow, I stayed on my feet. The words kept me there. I continued to speak my Latin verse, no longer needing contact with the tablet.

"No!" Katya morphed into her demon form, orange skin with red splotches dotting her face. She lunged for the tablet. When she made contact with it, she shot across the room as if she'd touched a live wire and slammed into one of the big, rusted machines.

She was dead. The Key told me so.

I walked to the table and picked up the box. The energy surrounding it wasn't mine to have. It buffeted my hand until I threw the box into the air and it disappeared with a flash of sparks that showered down onto the wooden stage, catching it on fire.

Liquid warmth streamed down my face. I blinked in slow motion at the flames surrounding me. Ringing erupted in my head like a thousand slot machines announcing the jackpot winner.

I didn't know if I was hallucinating when I saw Misha and Jean Luc race toward me through the smoke-filled room. As soon as I saw them, I collapsed, spikes of icy agony invading my brain through my nose and eardrums. And the words, the words bombarded me, the rolodex on hyperdrive, trying to fill my brain with too much information.

The Key had finally opened its doors to me.

Muffled voices wafted through the smoke and fire. And then I was in Dalton's arms. He carried me away from the heat. I screamed at the motion, at the words.

Make it stop. Please make it stop.

But I couldn't speak. Instead, I gave in to the murky darkness.

I opened my eyes and did a double take at the scene below me. Doc and Jean Luc were performing CPR on someone. From my perch above them, I couldn't see who it was. I ran my gaze down the jean-clad legs until I stopped at the black work boots. I knew those boots. They were my third best pair.

What. The. Hell?

Crap. I was having one of those tacky out-of-body experiences. I looked up and saw the ceiling inches above me. Was I floating?

Doc barked orders at Jean Luc. My eyes flew back down to the scene. Jean Luc moved for a moment, and I saw my face. Blood flowed from my nose and ears. The ground spun below me, and I jerked my gaze away.

Could an astral-projection puke? 'Cause I felt like puking.

But when I saw Misha standing to the side, I didn't feel like puking anymore. He was crying. Tears streamed down his face as he clenched his hands spasmodically, as though he wanted to reach out, to do something.

But what was there to do?

Dalton stood grimacing on the other side. Blood was smeared all over his shoulder and arms. I wanted to scream at them to help him, but I couldn't form words. When he stood there, frozen to the spot, it finally hit me that it was my blood on his shirt.

I looked up at the ceiling again to calm my heart. How could I feel it pounding in my chest when I was ether, floating above a body whose heart wasn't pumping?

This was it.

I hadn't gotten to say goodbye. I sucked at goodbyes, but I still wanted to say something.

The scene around me started to flicker like an old-fashioned television, and dread clawed along my spinal cord.

"How long has it been?" Doc yelled.

"Twenty minutes," Jean Luc replied.

"Let me try shocking her again."

My vision blinked out. When it came on again, no one moved. As if the frame was paused.

Finally, Doc looked down at my body. "Time of—"

"No!" Dalton yelled. "She's not gone."

Misha reached for him. "Joe."

"She's not gone!" He shoved past Doc and grabbed my face. "Don't you leave me now, McKinley. I'm pissed at you, and I haven't had my say yet."

The scene flicked to black again.

Warmth ran over my face, and I felt safe for just a moment, even as the panic in Dalton's voice increased while he yelled for me to come back. For some reason I wasn't scared anymore.

Until the silence descended.

CHAPTER 43

A buzzing surrounded me, circling my head until it entered my brain, the vibrations finally bringing me out of my stupor. Light seeped through my eyelids, and I was forced to open them slowly.

I saw my hands first, resting palms down on an old-fashioned table. The metal cooled my hands and sent a chill along my spine. I blinked at my surroundings. I was sitting in the middle of an empty ice cream parlor.

How had I ended up here? I wandered over to the long glass counter, peering at the tubs of ice cream. Mocha fudge swirl, chocolate almond, toasted coconut, all my favorites. Behind the counter, a metal container of fudge sauce bubbled, permeating the air with its rich sweetness.

On the wall behind the counter was a large sign with the words "Now Serving," and an arrow pointing down to a blinking red number 00. Sitting at the end of the counter was a small ticket dispenser. Maybe if I pulled a number, someone would come out from the back of the store and help me. I reached for the ticket.

"Don't, Kyle."

I jerked at the voice. There was Marie, standing behind the cash register wearing a pink waitress dress with a white apron. I was hallucinating. Had to be. Maybe it was bad sushi. I'd had bad sushi before, and I'd definitely gone to another plane of existence when I did.

"Marie, what's going on?"

"Don't pull the number, Kyle."

"Why are you here? Where is here?"

A bell rang behind me, and Marie disappeared. I turned as the door swung open and Nicholas entered. His eyebrows rose slightly while he glanced around the shop. "This is an interesting interpretation."

"What the hell is going on?" I demanded.

He smirked. "Followed up by even more interesting word choice."

"Nicholas!"

He gestured to a table and sat down. "Please sit and let me explain. We don't have much time."

I sat across from him. "Why am I here?" I threw up my arms. "Where is here?"

He stared at me for a moment. "Do you remember anything?"

"No."

"Think, Kyle."

I closed my eyes and scenes flashed in my head. "We were fighting the demons, and I was hurt."

"Yes."

"Doc and Jean Luc were working on me and Misha was crying and I...oh crap, I'm dead."

He shook his head. "Not yet. But you're on the cusp." He gestured around the room. "This is your holding space until a decision is made regarding your fate. Where you will go next."

I took a steadying breath. "And who's making the decision?"

"I would say, with your background, a number of the bigwigs up here will be brought in to confer."

"Well, that sucks. Don't I have a say in this?"

"Absolutely."

I stared at him in shock. "Are you serious?"

He leaned closer and lowered his voice. "Normally, at this point, it's too late to turn back. But you still have it in you to return. You never had a problem with bucking authority in the past. Don't go soft on me now."

"Funny."

He squeezed my hand. "I've got to go. Decide what you want to do, Kyle, and then hold on to that choice, here." He tapped his heart. "Not here." He tapped his head. "Think you can do that?"

"Hell to the yeah."

"They have no idea who they're up against." Nicholas chuckled as he faded away.

CHAPTER 44

My head hurt. Why did my head hurt so much? Had some-one smashed it with a baseball bat? After I took a couple of deep breaths so I wouldn't throw up, I opened my eyes slightly. The room was dark with the exception of a lamp in the corner, but even that low light was like a lance in my skull.

Then I remembered. I was dead. Wait, if my head was imploding, then I couldn't be dead, right? The pain would be gone.

Unless I was in hell. Oh, crap, was I in hell? I mean, I didn't think so. Could sarcasm and a disdain for authority land you in hell? I moaned.

Movement came from the dark corner of the room.

"Kyle? Are you back with us?"

The disjointed voice made me happy, because I somehow knew it. I tried to say so, but nothing came out.

Light pressure landed on my shoulder. "Don't try to talk. You're okay."

For once, I didn't argue. I closed my eyes and slept. For a long time.

But I wasn't alone.

Voices kept me company while I dozed. So many voices that changed over the seemingly endless time I slept. At first I couldn't put names to them. But I knew they were protecting me.

The first one I recognized was Jean Luc. Lilting tones interlaced with French terms of endearment, followed by Misha's deep bass. Another time Talia talked to me, and Doc's no-nonsense voice spoke to me as well.

Jason, Matthew, and Griffin followed. Trina's young voice also filled my head with stories from school. Sylvia, Irina, and Boris. Even Kevin Doyle teased me about finally being able to get a word in edgewise.

But one voice was missing from my memories. One voice I wanted to hear more than the others. To know he was okay.

I finally opened my eyes and was able to keep them open without feeling like sharp sticks were invading my skull. I blinked and turned my head to the side.

Misha sat in the chair next to the bed. He was leaning with his elbows on his knees, his head in his hands.

"Mish?" I croaked.

He jerked at my voice and leapt to his feet. "Kyle?"

I nodded, and the tension in his face simply disappeared. I opened my mouth and tried to speak again, but it felt like sand and cotton were waging a war in my mouth.

"Don't try to talk." He reached for a button on the wall and pushed it. Seconds later, Doc bustled into the room, followed by Jean Luc.

"There's my girl!" Doc said as she stepped up to the bed. "All right. Everyone out while I take a look at her. Go on, now. No arguments."

Doc spent a few minutes looking me over, listening to my heart and lungs. She reviewed the monitors. Then she checked my pupils with a small flashlight and frowned slightly.

"What?" I choked out.

"Nothing. You're fine." She picked up a pink plastic pitcher and poured a small amount of water into a matching cup and placed a straw into it. "Take just a small sip, Kyle. It should help."

I swallowed, and the glorious cool liquid ran down my throat. How could water taste so good? I took another pull on the straw, and then Doc took it away from me. "Enough for now. I don't want you to get sick." She laid her hand on my arm. "How do you feel?"

"Okay...tired."

"Do you remember what happened?"

"Yes." I whispered. "How long?"

"You were in a coma for twenty-four hours, and then you woke up for a few seconds, and then slipped back under for three days."

"Voices?"

Doc smiled. "Yeah, I can imagine you heard voices. We haven't left you alone. We've been taking shifts with you. Talking to you to try and coax you out of your coma."

"Dalton?"

"He's okay, Kyle. He burned his arm getting you out of the fire, but he's fine. He was summoned back to Chicago to report. We had to make up some interesting case notes for him. He stopped the killer. Unfortunately for the Feds, but fortunately for us, Saul's body was burned beyond recognition, so they couldn't perform a full autopsy. We've sent the twins back to the realm."

"The Key."

"What about it?"

"It's gone."

"You're sure?"

I nodded. I wasn't sure how I knew, but it wasn't in me anymore. "In Dalton?"

Doc shook her head. "I don't think so. He's been calling in to see how you're doing, and says he feels normal." She patted my arm. "I'm going to let Jean Luc and Misha back in before they trigger a riot in the hall. Don't tax your throat. I'm going to give them five minutes to gush, and then out they go."

Sabrina opened the door, and the two of them practically fell through the doorway. They crowded around the bed, each taking one of my hands.

"Little one."

"*Ma petite.*"

They both spoke at the same time, which made me smile.

"We're so happy to see you awake." Misha spoke, his voice rough.

"*Oui.* It is about time you woke up, Kyle. It has been very quiet without you."

"I love you guys," I whispered.

Jean Luc squeezed my hand and smiled at me.

Misha cleared his throat and blinked a couple of times, but he couldn't stop a tear from escaping. "We love you, too."

Chapter 45

"What aren't you telling me, Sabrina?"

"What do you mean?"

I glared at her across the hospital room. "Everyone is walking on eggshells around me."

"You were in a coma, Kyle."

"It's more than that."

"Can't we table this discussion until you're stronger?"

I crossed my arms over my chest. The gesture was probably not very intimidating since I was propped up in a hospital bed, but you have to work with what you've got.

Doc sighed. "When the demon struck you with the energy blast, it hit your head. You have a scar now."

"Is it big?"

"No."

"What's the problem then? Is it giving off Frankenstein vibes?"

Doc chuckled. "No. You're safe."

"Then why has everyone looked a little freaked out when they see me for the first time?"

Doc bit her lip before responding. "It's your eyes. They've changed color."

I gulped. "What? Let me see."

Doc pulled a small mirror out of a drawer in the bureau and gave it to me.

The eyes that widened as I stared at myself were blue. They still had hints of my original gray, but they were predominantly blue. On my right temple was a small scar running back into my hairline.

"Do you think the blue is from the demon blast?"

Doc shook her head. "I don't think so."

"*Sabrina.*"

"You almost died, Kyle. I tried everything. I shocked you and pumped you full of adrenaline."

"Like John Travolta did to Uma Thurman in *Pulp Fiction*?"

Doc huffed. "Misha has not been a good influence on you. Yes, like *Pulp Fiction*, except you didn't wake up like Uma did." She looked away from me. "I was about to call time of death, but Dalton argued with me. He told me you weren't dead yet, and he laid his hands on either side of your face. I was reaching to pull him away when he started to glow. Then you started to glow."

Goosebumps shot down my arms. "He still had the power from the Key."

"Or maybe you absorbed some of his angel essence. I wouldn't swear to it, but his eyes don't seem as vibrant anymore."

I sat up straight. "But he's all right now? You told me he's okay."

Doc waved at me with a settle-down gesture. "He's fine. He was very weak afterward, and I put him on bed rest for a day, but then he got a summons from Chicago. We've had a lot to cover up."

"I bet. How did he know what to do?"

Sabrina shrugged. "He said afterward that he heard a voice in his head telling him to touch you. Since he'd helped you before when you seized, he didn't think he had anything to lose by trying it."

I dropped my head back on the pillow. "Wow."

Doc frowned. "I knew it was too early to have this discussion."

"I'm fine, Sabrina. Just trying to take it all in."

"Well, take your time. It happened days ago, and I still haven't taken it all in yet."

"I want to take her outside!" Misha said.

"It would be better for me to do this, Misha," Jean Luc argued. "I have a medical background."

"I think I know what Kyle needs. She is named after me."

I clapped my hands like a kindergarten teacher calling the class to order. "Guys, enough! I'm fine. I'm not going to relapse. Would someone please take me outside so I can breathe fresh air and see the sun?"

"Are you sure, Kyle?" Jean Luc asked for the gazillionth time.

I clamped my hands on the wheelchair's arms and started to push myself up. "I'm going out by myself, then."

Misha grabbed my shoulders and eased me back into the chair. "Just because you've been taking short walks in the hall doesn't mean you've built up the strength to walk all the way to the garden and back."

They finally compromised by having Misha push me outside onto the terrace while Jean Luc walked beside me, patting my shoulder every once in a while. It was one of those rare, warm, spring days, and I studied the brilliant blue sky and fat, fluffy clouds and sucked in a lungful of air that smelled like new beginnings. The grass was the emerald green that lasts for only a few weeks in the early spring.

Misha rolled the wheelchair over to a concrete bench, and he and Jean Luc sat next to me. "Is this okay?"

"Yes. It's great. Thanks."

The three of us sat in silence for a while, and I closed my eyes and tilted my face up to bask in the sunshine.

"Here," Misha said, handing me a pair of sunglasses.

"I'm fine."

"Humor me, please."

I put the sunglasses on and tilted my face up again. After a few seconds, a shadow blocked my face. I opened my eyes. Dalton looked down at me. His black eye had faded to a pale yellow, and he was smiling.

"I'm glad to see you're out of bed, McKinley."

"I'm glad to be out of bed."

I motioned to the bench. "Join us."

Misha stood. "Here. Take my seat. We have to go check on something. Don't let her get out of that chair. She'll try to do cartwheels if we don't keep an eye on her."

Misha nodded, Jean Luc bowed slightly to both of us, and they walked into the building, closing the terrace doors.

Dalton sat so I didn't have to strain my neck looking up at him.

"I didn't mean to run them off."

"You didn't. They know we need to talk... Doc told me what happened. Thanks for saving me. How is your arm?"

He stared at me for a moment as if choosing his words carefully. "My arm is fine. I should be thanking you. You were willing to sacrifice yourself for me, for all of us. I'm only glad I could help. How are you feeling?"

"Better. Tired. Which is ironic, since all I've done is sleep for days." I took a deep breath to calm my jitters before I pulled off my sunglasses. "I think I owe you for these as well."

His gaze locked on my face, and his turquoise eyes widened. "Oh, my God."

"Not too shabby a color. A bluish gray. Jean Luc told me they're the color of a stormy sea, but he's a romantic at heart."

"How?"

"Doc thinks it's because you shared your energy with me."

Was it my imagination, or was Doc right and his eyes weren't as blue anymore? They were certainly still gorgeous. And then I reminded myself to stop with the stalling and say what needed to be said. "I want you to know how sorry I am."

"McKinley—"

"No. Hear me out. I've been lying around in a hospital bed for days with nothing but time on my hands, time to think. I'm sorry for lying to you. For making you feel like I was trying to control your life."

"Jean Luc explained to me why you didn't tell me the truth when I first arrived. Logically, I get it. Emotionally, it still pisses me off. You took away my memories. For a good reason, but it feels like you've stolen something from me, and I'm having a hard time getting over it."

"I get that," I said. "If I'd been able to come up with any other way to save you, I would have. But we were out of time, and I refused to let that bastard Sebastian destroy you. So I did what I thought was best. If you'd been in any shape to weigh in on the decision, I would have listened to your wishes. But you couldn't."

"I need to know what you erased. But I think that's a discussion for when you're stronger."

I started to protest, and he placed his hand on my arm. "It can wait, McKinley. I'm going back to D.C. today for another case, anyway. When I've finished that, I'll contact you so we can talk."

"How did it go with the Feds and our case?"

"Good. They bought the story. They've offered me a full-time job."

"That's great." *Liar, liar.*

He smiled at me, *again*. "Can you stay out of trouble until I'm able to get back here?"

His hand felt like a hot brand on my arm. "I'll give it my best shot."

CHAPTER 46

"I hear you're going home today."

The voice brightened my day even before I looked up into Griffin's face. "Hey, you."

"Hello, sweet. How are you feeling?"

"I'm good, Griffin. Glad to be going home."

"You gave us all a scare."

"So I've been told. Thanks for coming and spending time with me."

He cocked an eyebrow at me.

"I could hear you talking to me. And Trina, too."

He smiled. "That doesn't surprise me. I understand you saved the day again."

"Yep. And I'm pretty sure the Key has gone bye-bye."

"Thank God. How is Dalton doing with all this?"

I shrugged. "He knows I erased his memory, but I haven't had a chance to explain everything to him yet. I'm not sure he'll ever be able to forgive me."

"Give him time, Kyle."

After everything, how could he be concerned about Dalton? I swallowed. "Can you forgive me?"

Griffin gripped my hand. "There's nothing to forgive, Kyle. You didn't do anything wrong."

Tears threatened to erupt, and I blinked. "You're a wonderful person, Seamus Griffin. Now tell me how you're doing."

"I'm doing better, especially now that I know you're okay."

It was official. In a few minutes, Misha would pick me up and take me home. No more hospital. But before I left, I wanted to spend a few minutes in Irina's garden, so when Doc told me I had one last visitor waiting on the terrace, I figured it was kismet.

I walked outside, and there was Nicholas, sitting at the small iron table on the stone terrace holding a bouquet of purple roses wrapped in cellophane. I stared at him for a moment. Something was different about him. His hair was a bit messy. I'd never seen him with a hair out of place before.

I joined him at the table. "I hoped you'd stop by."

"It's good to see you up and about, Kyle." His gaze tightened on me. "Sabrina told me about your eye color, but it still's a bit surprising."

"Is it a side effect of the energy Dalton shared with me?"

"How would I know?"

"Because you're the one who told Dalton to touch me when I was dying."

He looked at me but didn't respond. For me, his silence was confirmation enough.

"I want to thank you."

He shook his head. "Kyle—"

"Let me finish. Thanks for your visit to the ice cream parlor."

His eyebrows rose. "You weren't supposed to remember the parlor."

I shrugged. "I have a tendency to go against the norm."

Nicholas chuckled. "Tell me something I don't already know. How are you feeling?"

"The old, cynical Kyle would wonder if you are really asking if the Key is okay."

"I do wish I'd known about the Key earlier. But I never sensed it in you."

"Yeah, well. I couldn't exactly trust you with the truth then."

"And now?"

"Now you've moved up a notch or two on my trust scale." I stopped. "Wait. If you didn't know that I had the Key in me, then how did you know Dalton's touch would help me?"

"Lucky guess."

"It's like talking to the CIA with you."

His eyes smiled. "I can neither confirm nor deny that statement."

"Well, how about this statement? I no longer have the Key."

He paused before answering. "It could be that the Key served its purpose for right now and has been put away for the next rainy, apocalyptic day."

"Wow, I didn't realize how sarcastic you could be."

He smirked. "You're usually way ahead of me in that department."

I smiled back at him. "Now you're just sucking up." I stared across the garden for a moment, at the flowers peeking out of the ground, then refocused on his face. "I'm going to ask you something else, and I want you to tell me the truth."

His eyes narrowed. "That sounds ominous."

"How much trouble are you in?"

"What do you mean?"

"Let's see. Father Brown has been struggling for months to translate the prophecy and suddenly it miraculously started to come to him."

"You've always been too smart for your own good. I might have called in an angel favor on that one."

"I think that kind of thing is your normal, sneaky MO. So that wouldn't have caused you strife. Then there was the whole Dalton saving me thing, which you cannot of course confirm or deny. And finally—the big *oh-no-he-didn't*—you sneaked into the ice cream parlor and told me to fight. Haven't you been saying all along that you were only allowed so much leeway before you were reprimanded again?"

He shrugged. "Someone recently reminded me that you have to take a risk in order to do the right thing."

"Since when did you start listening to me?"

"I've always listened to you, Kyle. However, I haven't always agreed with you."

"You just skirted my question again, Nicholas. Are. You. In. Trouble?"

"No. Now tell me how Joe is doing with everything."

"He overheard us talking, so he knows some of what happened, but not everything by a long shot." I frowned. "Something's been bugging me about him being descended from angels. Why didn't the Key boxes glow when they were exposed to him?"

Nicholas shrugged. "The box did respond to Joe. It chose him as the Sentinel."

I nodded. "Do you think I should try to give him back his memories?"

"You could try. But I don't think you can. At least not with your gift. There's always the fear that the pain would return as well. But you can give them back to him in another way. Tell him about them."

He held out the bouquet to me, and flinched as I accepted it.

"What's wrong?" I asked.

"Nothing. Just a thorn. Be careful."

He stared at his thumb. A drop of blood beaded on the tip, and he watched it for a moment before wiping it off with a fingertip.

CHAPTER 47

Father Brown sat next to me in the confessional, and he was frowning. Big time. Not what you wanted to see during confession. And while I wasn't *technically* confessing my sins, I was describing what had happened over the past few weeks.

"I'm sorry, Father."

"I'm just glad you're okay now. I wish I'd known you were hurt."

"Would you have prayed for me?"

"Kyle, I've been praying for you since the day I met you."

"Hey!"

He chuckled. "That didn't come out the right way. You'd been given a huge responsibility to protect our world. I didn't think it would hurt to pray for you."

"Thanks, Father, I can always use the backup. And I want to thank you anyway. The translations helped tremendously with the case. I wish I'd been able to bring the actual tablet and box for you to study, though."

"They were destroyed in the fire?"

"I don't know for sure about the tablet. We couldn't find it afterward. But the box disappeared in a flash of light and sparks when I threw it into the air. And the box we had in our safe has also disappeared."

"Once the Key left you, it had to return somewhere."

"Yep. I think it went back into its box, and the angels have taken possession of it again." I took a deep breath. "And I think your theory about different Keys is spot on, Father. When I touched the other box, it surged with power, but it was different from what was in me. Like polar opposites fighting each other."

He stared at me for a moment. "What was it like when the Key spoke to you?"

How to explain the unexplainable? "At the time it made sense. Like all uncertainty was gone. That all I had to do was think about a question or problem and I would be given the way to solve it. Since my priority at the time was stopping the demons from opening a permanent portal, those are the answers I locked onto. Before it short-circuited my brain, that is."

"Did it tell you its ultimate purpose?"

"I've been thinking about that, Father. Its purpose is to serve as a safety-gap measure when something really bad is about to happen. Like apocalyptic bad. Even though it started out in an evil vampire's hands, it found its way to Dalton, and then to me. It was as if it knew we would need it when the realm demons attempted their breakout months later." I hesitated, uncertain what to say next.

"And?" Father asked.

I shook my head. "You should have been a therapist, Father."

"To a certain degree, priests are therapists, Kyle. Now finish what you were going to say."

"When the Key finally opened up to me, everything made sense. But looking back on it now, it was scary too. That much power should not be in one person for any length of time. The Key doesn't have a sense of time or space. It just *is*.

Katya said the Key was created by God to right the wrongs the angels had done."

Father nodded. "You told me Katya also said an angel was the one who closed the portal to begin with. Maybe she was right. The Key was created to reopen the portal."

I blinked at him. "It was created thousands of years ago."

"You just said the Key has no sense of time." He patted my hand. "I'm happy you've been freed from it. With the help of the tablet photo, I was able to translate the first two stanzas of the knowledge prophecy correctly. I have also finished the last stanza."

"May I hear it?"

He closed his eyes and started from the beginning.

"Evil thrives among us
Angel descendants, preparing for battle
With Key of Knowledge in hand
The tides will turn
And light triumphs.
"The war will be long
And fraught with treachery
Lives will be lost
And the Key will change hands
Only the true Sentinel will
Save us from annihilation.'"

I held my breath as he continued to the last stanza.

"The lost Sentinel will be found.
Knowledge will be embraced
And Faith will erase
The sins of the past so
The worlds become one again.'"

We sat in silence until I had to say something. "That's heady stuff, Father."

He opened his eyes and smiled at me. "Powerful."

"But the prophecy didn't happen."

"Why do you say that?"

"Well, Dalton was the Sentinel, and he was lost, so to speak. But he didn't get the Key back to save the day."

Father Brown shook his head. "Kyle. Prophecies are tricky. They can mean numerous things. Yes, Joe was the Key. And then you were, which represents the changing of hands. But I'm not convinced Joe was the lost Sentinel. I think you were."

"No way. I'm not a descendent of the angels. I'm part demon!"

"Based on what you've described, you stopped a demon invasion from coming to earth, did you not?"

"Kind of."

"And you were willing to sacrifice yourself to do it?"

"Yes, but—"

"No buts, Kyle. You almost died to protect us. Don't downplay what you accomplished."

I studied my hands as my face heated. "I stopped the demons from coming to earth, but it could and probably will come up again. I didn't help solve the problem. If the worlds in the prophecy are the demon realm and earth, I didn't bring them together."

"So what are you going to do about it?"

I looked up at him.

"Who's to say the prophecy is complete?"

"I don't have the Key in me anymore."

"Maybe you don't need the Key. The prophecy mentioned faith. Maybe you just need faith."

I sighed. "Faith is not something I've ever had in abundance, Father. I'm not religious."

The twinkle in his eyes and grin on his face told me he knew something I didn't.

"Okay, spill it."

"Kyle, faith comes in many forms. Faith in God, faith in man, faith in your family and friends. Your loyalty and faithfulness are what make you so special."

I squirmed. "You make me sound like a Saint Bernard."

He laughed. "And there's that wit you use to cover up your emotions."

I opened my mouth and then closed it again. I was being psychoanalyzed by a priest.

"So I'll ask you again. What are you going to do about it?"

He waited quietly for my answer, not rushing me. After only a minute, I knew what I was supposed to do.

"I'm going to rally the troops, Father. I have an idea. I think it's time to shake things up a bit."

CHAPTER 48

The Shamat community room was packed. The crowd had been filing in for several minutes, and they were finally taking their seats. Boris had worked a minor miracle convincing the leaders to come on such short notice, and now demon leaders from the twelve clans sat at the front of the room.

Irina sat in the front row, along with Aleksei, Jean Luc, Misha, and Talia, while Jason stood to the side watching everyone take their seats. Even Kevin Doyle was tucked in the back row.

I had shared the translated prophecy with a select group of people, and they had rallied around my plan to make it come true. Now it was time to get the rest of the supernatural community on board. Piece of cake.

Sylvia walked up. "You ready for this, Kyle?"

"Yes, ma'am."

"You might have to drag them kicking and screaming over to your way of thinking."

I smiled. "I think I'm up for the challenge."

She patted me on the back and took her seat next to Irina, who gave me a thumbs-up. Moments later, Boris strode to the front of the room and the excited, speculative babble petered out.

He smiled his showman's smile and straightened his silk tie. Boris had dressed to impress tonight, in a black suit with an ice blue tie to match his eyes. "May I have everyone's attention, please? We're going to get started as soon as the new portal guard leader arrives."

As if in answer to a summons, the right wall behind the podium undulated, and Naya emerged through the portal, her purple skin vivid against the beige walls. When she glanced my way, I gave her a surreptitious wave.

Boris continued. "Let's get started with this meeting. We've invited you here tonight to discuss a recent event concerning a thwarted breach from the demon realm."

Gasps and murmurs filled the room.

Boris held up his hands. "Please. If you would quiet down so we can continue. I've asked one of the members of the BSR to brief you on what happened."

Boris beckoned to me, and I stepped up beside him. I glanced around the room at the faces staring back at me. Faces that revealed various emotions—concern, distrust, curiosity. Before I began speaking, the back door of the hall opened, and Nicholas walked in. He nodded to me before sitting in the back next to Doyle.

I looked over at Jean Luc, who smiled at me, and then I glanced at Misha. I had expected a smile or wink from him, but instead, he sat slack-jawed, staring at something behind me. I turned slightly to see what had caught his attention. Naya.

Hmm. An interesting turn of events to be explored at a later date. Right now, it was time to get this show started. I took a deep breath.

"Thank you for coming tonight. For those of you who don't know me, I'm Kyle McKinley from the Bureau of Supernatural Relations. Our team recently worked a case that began when a demon broke into the Cleveland Museum of Art and killed a security guard. We learned that the demon was from the demon realm. More specifically, he was from the in-between."

There were gasps from the crowd, but I plowed ahead, telling them about the case and what we had learned about the demons trapped in the realm.

"For now, the mass exodus has been stopped, but this will not stop the demons from banding together and trying again, and potentially succeeding the next time. Tonight, we've brought you here to discuss how we can assist the border patrol and the demons still stuck in the realm."

One of the council leaders spoke up from the front table. "Why would we want to help the realm demons?"

"Because most of the realm demons were born there and are not responsible for what their ancestors did before they were born. The border patrol members have devoted their entire lives to protect earth, and yet they are not allowed to come here. It's time we stopped burying our heads in the sand and expecting things to remain the same.

"We've been working on an idea. Realm demons have been crossing over for a while now, acclimating themselves to earth and living normal lives. If we band together, we can start bringing the demons here on a larger scale. If we work to make living conditions better for the realm demons in general, and then help those who also wish to live here on earth to immigrate, it is a win-win situation."

Voices erupted, and I looked out once again at the arguing crowd. My gaze landed on a lone figure standing at the back of the room. At some point during my speech, Dalton had arrived. For the first time tonight, my stomach did a little jig.

I placed my fingers between my lips and whistled, loudly. "Okay. I know we have a lot to discuss. First, Naya is going to talk to you about the state of the realm. Then we'll follow up with an overview from someone who has been helping the crossover demons acclimate to our world. She has some insights as well."

I moved away from the podium, and Naya took my place. During the next sixty minutes, the crowd heard the truth about the realm and the demons that now lived here on earth. Several members of the council asked questions.

One of the demons spoke up. "I would like to hear what Nicholas thinks of this idea."

I swallowed hard when Nicholas got up from his seat in the back row. The crowd turned toward him.

"I think it's the right thing to do. We can't hide our sins and hope they'll go away on their own. We have to make this right. If we don't, we'll have a war on our hands, and then we won't be able to protect supernaturals from humans."

Finally, after a few more questions, the meeting adjourned so the Council of Twelve could meet independently to discuss the matter. As the Council filed out, the crowd surged forward in a makeshift line to talk to me, like I was the Queen of England or something. Most patted me on the back for calling the meeting. I looked for Dalton, but couldn't find him. Had he already left?

Doyle ambled up with a big grin on his face. "I never thought I would see the day. Kyle McKinley, the concerned citizen."

I chuckled. "How's the used car business, Doyle?"

"Okay. Why do you ask?"

"Because if the clans agree to my proposal, they're going to need someone to oversee the setup. Since you know all the movers and shakers, I thought you would be the perfect choice to help pull together the resources."

Doyle gaped at me for a minute. "You would trust me to do that?"

"Absolutely."

"Yes."

Now it was my turn to gape at him. "Yes? You don't have to think about it?"

"Nope. I hate the used car business."

I laughed. "Your mother-in-law isn't going to give you a hard time about quitting?"

"Nope. She's ecstatic with me right now. Coleen is expecting."

"Holy crap, Doyle! You're going to be a dad!"

He turned a little green, and after a few more seconds, I pushed him toward the door and told him I'd be in touch.

Nicholas was next in line. "You did a good job, Kyle."

"Thanks. And thanks for backing me up earlier."

He nodded. "I'll help the Council any way I can."

"It's time to bring the worlds together again."

Naya walked over when I finally had a lull in the line and gripped my forearm in an old-fashioned handshake. "It is good to see you, Kyle."

"So you're the big boss now?"

She frowned. "After we spoke last, and you mentioned that the realm demon numbers were being underreported, I realized someone at the top had to be involved. It's still hard to believe."

"I'm sorry your friends were involved."

She frowned. "The others are currently incarcerated. The in-between and the demon realm are headed for more turmoil if something is not done quickly. I hope the Council paid attention to what was said here tonight." She smiled at me. "I must go."

"Hold on for a sec." I jogged over to the side of the room and picked up a duffel bag and handed it to her. "Here."

She opened the bag, and beamed when she pulled out a book. "Thank you."

"I think you'll find these interesting. Romance, mysteries, modern fiction. Thought it might help to read something written more recently than the 1800's."

"I'll let you know what I think."

A small hand tucked into mine, and I turned to find a smiling Irina.

"We have our work cut out for us, don't we?" she said.

I squeezed her hand. "Yep. Helping the demons cross over legitimately will be a challenge."

She batted away the notion. "Oh, yes that, too. But I was talking about something else." She pointed at Misha, who gazed after Naya while she disappeared through the portal. He looked gobsmacked.

"So I wasn't imagining things earlier."

Irina clapped. "Oh, no! I've never seen him look at a female that way. Not even his past wives. Do you know if she's involved with anyone?"

I shook my head, and Irina pursed her lips at me.

"Hey. I met her while I was stuck in the demon realm. The topic wasn't high on my priority list at the time."

"I'll forgive you this time, Kyle."

"If everything goes well, Naya will be allowed to visit earth."

"Let's keep our fingers crossed." She glanced over my shoulder, and then back at me again. "I'm sure the Council will not reach a decision for several hours, Kyle. Why don't you get some fresh air? There are several benches by the lake. Someone will contact you when a decision's been made."

I stared at her in confusion. "What?"

She grabbed my shoulders and turned me. Dalton was still at the back of the room, now talking to Jean Luc.

Irina whispered in my ear. "Go get him, Kyle."

Then, she pushed me toward him, hard. I sometimes forgot that beneath her human side beat the heart of a nosy, interfering demon. But then, nothing was as it first appeared in my world.

CHAPTER 49

Dalton and I meandered around the lake. Several geese swam in the middle, and a light breeze blew across the water, leaving ripples in its wake.

"I was surprised to see you here tonight."

"Misha's been keeping me in the loop about what you're working on. Luckily, my case wrapped up two days ago, so I could get back in time to hear your proposal. You did a good job."

"I thought you'd left," I blurted. *Smooth.*

"Nope. Just wanted to let your adoring crowd talk to you first."

"Thanks," I answered, my heart beating triple time.

We stopped next to a bench and sat down, his close proximity making my nerves sit up like a puppy begging for a treat.

He cleared his throat. "I want to know what happened last year."

I took a deep breath and began. "You were brought in to help with a murder at the Erie Bar. An angel, a demon, and a vampire got into a fight."

"Sounds like the beginning of a bad joke."

"You could say that."

And I spent the next hour talking about the case. He asked all the right questions and stayed pretty calm through the telling. I suspected his cop training took over, and he had checked his emotions for the duration of the discussion.

We took a break for a moment, the silence enveloping us like a scratchy wool blanket.

His gaze locked on me. "So we were a couple."

It was more of a statement than a question, but I nodded anyway. "It took a while. We argued at first."

He scoffed. "I can imagine."

"You were overprotective and cop-like, and I was impetuous."

He chuckled. "That's the best word you can come up with to describe yourself?"

"I think the words you used to describe me were smart-mouth and pig-headed."

"Glad to hear I was insightful even back then."

The banter was agonizingly familiar, and I looked out over the lake till I could catch my breath. Two geese were floating next to each other like an old married couple. I had read somewhere that geese mated for life. "If I could have found a way to help you without erasing your memories, I would have. I want you to know that."

"I'm sorry."

I glanced up at him in surprise. "What are *you* sorry for?"

"I was so caught up in what happened to me that I didn't think about what you lost, too."

Oh no, we weren't going there. "I...When do you leave again?"

"Tomorrow. I'm going to Quantico for two months for some training, and then I start officially for the Feds."

"Congrats," I said automatically. And I was happy for him. If this is what he wanted, then how could I not be?

My phone rang, and I pulled it out of my pocket, standing up to answer it since I was too nervous to sit. Dalton got up too, so I flipped on the speaker.

"Hello, Boris."

"Kyle. We've finished deliberating. You did it, my dear. The Council has voted yes."

My mouth opened, but nothing came out.

"Kyle? Are you there?" Boris asked.

"Yeah. I'm here. Wow."

"That about sums it up. Get a good night's sleep. Things are going to get busy around here very quickly."

I hung up and did a little dance, a cross between a touchdown dance and a jig. Dalton laughed, and I looked at his smiling face, and my knees buckled. I landed on the bench as tears threatened, and I blinked, praying they would stay inside my eyes and not embarrass me by running down my cheeks.

Dalton knelt in front of me, his eyes filled with concern. "Are you okay?"

I cleared my throat and rubbed my hands along my legs, the rough denim calming me a bit. "Yeah. I'm just overwhelmed. They actually listened to me. We're going to help demons like Nate and Naya live here on earth."

He placed his hands over mine, stilling them. "That's a very good thing. *You* did a very good thing."

The tears threatened to erupt again at his words. "Thank you for not hating me."

He rocked back a little and his eyes flared. "I could never hate you, Kyle. You exasperate me at times, but hate? Nope, not possible. I expect you to send me reports about how it's going." He stood and held out his hand. "You okay to walk back now?"

"Yes."

I reached for him, and he pulled me to my feet, his warm hand enveloping mine for a moment longer than was necessary before he released me and we walked side by side back to the community building.

CHAPTER 50

Was there such a thing as controlled chaos? If so, it would describe the new office space for the Bureau of Demon Immigration, or BDI for short. Desks were lined up against the wall, and chairs were piled haphazardly on top of a conference table in the corner. Boxes of supplies littered the space as well. In the center of the room stood Doyle, grinning like he'd won the lottery.

"What do you think, Kyle?"

"I...ah..."

"I know, you're speechless. I was too when I first saw it." He spun in a circle. "This is going to be great!"

"I'm glad you're a visionary, Doyle."

"I know, it's a mess right now, but the hard part was getting all these supplies, which I got wholesale, I might add."

I stepped over a box of copier paper and met him in the middle. "It's finally coming together."

"Yes, ma'am. How does it feel to know you started all of this?"

I gulped. "The truth? A bit overwhelming."

Doyle nodded. "Well you should be proud of yourself. Although you might regret it now that you're on the board of directors."

I shrugged. "I've only yelled once, and it was at the first board meeting. Since then I've been the model of diplomacy."

"I bet. I never thought you and I would be working together."

"Me either. How's Coleen doing?"

"She's good. Her mother is doting on her through this pregnancy, and I heard her brag to her friends about her 'son-in-law's important job.'"

"Who'd a thunk it? Both of us becoming upstanding citizens."

A voice sounded behind us. "The jury might still be out on that."

I turned to find Aleksei standing in the doorway. He nodded at me and then looked around the room.

"Where are we—"

Doyle interrupted him. "The furniture and supplies have arrived. I have a group of movers scheduled to be here in an hour to help organize the space."

"What about—"

"The staff interviews are scheduled to start tomorrow morning. I emailed you names and times."

Aleksei stood up straighter. "Very good, Doyle. I'll check in later, while the movers are here."

Doyle nodded. "The drawing of the room layout is sitting on the box to your right, if you want to look at it again."

"No. As long as it's the same one we agreed to, then we should be fine. Thank you. Good to see you again, Kyle." He bobbed his head and left the office.

I watched him depart in shock. "How?"

"I used to deal with criminals, remember? Aleksei is all bark and no bite. I merely anticipate his orders."

"I was a little worried when I suggested him as head of the Bureau."

"No, I think he's the right demon to front this operation. Don't tell him I said this, but under his pompous exterior, he's smart, dedicated, and has a good reputation in the demon community, which will help us with the holdouts."

I frowned. "Are we still getting a lot of pushback?"

"There will always be demons who don't believe the realm demons should come to earth. But they'll just have to suck it up. Change is inevitable."

I snapped a picture of the space and a smiling Doyle with my phone and sent it to Dalton. We had been texting the last couple of weeks since he'd left for Fed training. I'd been surprised to learn that when he had said keep in touch, he actually meant it.

I jumped when my phone rang. Dalton was *calling* me? "Hello?"

"Just got your picture. Is that an office or the aftermath of a tornado?"

I laughed. "It'll be an office once we don't have to climb over the boxes."

"Well, send me another picture once it's set up. That way I can see the before and after."

"Got it."

"I've got to get back to class. We were on a quick break when I got your text, so I thought I'd give you a ring."

"Sure. Ah...thanks for calling."

"Kyle."

He hesitated for a moment and my heart started beating like a mariachi band. "Yeah?"

"I just needed to hear your voice...I mean, I haven't had anyone insult me for weeks."

"Well, we can't have that. I'll start working on some right away."

He chuckled. "Good idea. That way you'll be prepared next time I call."

I hung up and stared at my phone for a second. *Next time he called?* I just had a conversation with Dalton that didn't involve gut-wrenching drama or confessions of wrongdoing on my part. Who the hell had I been talking to?

"Who was that?"

"What?"

"Who were you talking to? And don't tell me it was Misha or Jean Luc."

"Why would you say that?"

"Because of your face. You're grinning like a high schooler with a crush."

"I am not!"

"Now you're blushing like a high schooler with a crush!"

"Cut it out, Doyle."

He stopped grinning and stared at me for a moment. "How is it going with Joe?"

"It's not going anywhere with Dalton. He's in DC, and I'm here."

"A lot of people make long distance relationships work, Kyle."

I shrugged. "A few text messages and a phone call don't make up for the fact that I manipulated his memory and then lied to him about it, repeatedly. That's not something you get over."

Doyle shrugged. "Don't underestimate him. He may surprise you."

I shoved my phone into my pocket as an excuse to break eye contact. "I've had enough surprises in my life, Doyle. I need some predictability instead. Yep. Boring, predictable, Kyle McKinley. That's my new goal."

He smiled. "We'll see how long it lasts."

CHAPTER 51

I parked my car in front of the hall and took a deep breath. It had been two months since I'd addressed the supernatural community and hatched the plan to help bring the realm demons to earth. And so far everything was coming together.

"Hello."

I jumped at the voice, my hand slamming to my chest as Marie materialized in the seat next to me. "Jeez, Marie! You almost gave me a heart attack."

"Which is why I waited until you parked your car to say anything. I didn't want you careening into oncoming traffic."

"How safety-conscious of you."

"I thought so."

I took a deep breath to slow down my heart. "I haven't seen you in months. I was afraid you'd gotten into trouble for helping me when I was..."

"In ice-cream parlor limbo?" She grinned. "Nah. They didn't do anything to me. And you're welcome, sweetie."

"Have you been able to spend some time with Dalton?"

"Yes. My grandson is doing much better, thanks to you."

"I don't know if I did all that much for him."

Marie shook her head. "I have a few choice words to say to you on the subject, but we'll have to talk later."

"Wait!" I growled, but Marie faded from the passenger seat.

A knock sounded on my driver's side window, and I jumped. It was a good thing my heart was part demon, or I would have expired at some point dealing with all these supes scaring the crap out of me.

I rolled my window down, and Nicholas leaned in slightly. "Kyle, can I talk to you for a moment?"

"Sure." I unlocked the car doors and he went to the other side and climbed into the seat Marie had vacated. "What's up?"

"Do you remember the night at the community center you told me you were working to bring the worlds back together again?"

"Yes."

"Well, I've been thinking about the prophecy. While I think what you're doing is wonderful, I wonder if allowing the demons to come here is what the prophecy intended when it talked about bringing the worlds back together again."

"What else could it mean?"

"I think when Dalton touched you, he shared a part of his angel essence with you. That's why your eyes are the color they are now. And if that's the case, then you are part angel, part demon, *and* part human. *You* might be the worlds coming together again."

"Good Lord, Nicholas, put a little pressure on me, why don't you?"

"That's not my intention. I just want you to keep it in mind. You're special, Kyle. There is definitely more to come in your future."

My nerves danced along my spinal column. "Did you have another flash about me?"

"No."

"I'm surprised you've shared even this much."

He shrugged. "Things have changed for all of us. And they're going to get even more interesting as we bring the realm demons to earth."

I stood next to Doc and Misha drinking a glass of wine to try and calm down from my earlier talk with Nicholas.

The hall was packed. Appetizers were heaped across large buffet tables. And it was the primo stuff, too, no mini hot-dogs on toothpicks for this crowd. Tony's restaurant had catered some of the food...stuffed ravioli, meatballs, all my favorites. A bar ran along the back wall serving all types of drinks, and on the dance floor couples swayed to the music.

"Boris sure knows how to throw a party."

"Are you surprised?" Doc asked while she studied the scene as well.

"No. It was good of him to do it."

"Father wanted to thank everyone," Misha said.

Doc nodded. "Everyone's been working so hard to get the new demon immigration process in place it was time to blow off a little steam. I can't believe the first set of demons will be arriving next week."

A lump clogged my throat. "I know. The first group may be small, but it will be a test run before we increase the numbers. Aleksei's been doing a great job running everything."

"I was surprised when you suggested him," she said.

"I knew we needed someone who would be able to lead the project and not take no for an answer."

"That's Aleksei," Misha mumbled.

Doc squeezed my hand. "You did a good job, Kyle."

Her praise made me uncomfortable, so I hunted for a way to change the subject. "I can't believe you talked me into wearing this dress again." I frowned down at my burgundy dress and heels.

Doc smiled. "It's a special occasion that calls for a special dress."

"Well, the trip to the beauty salon certainly wasn't necessary."

"I don't agree, I think your new hairstyle and the color suit you."

I reached up and touched my hair. I'd been growing it out from its pixie cut over the last couple of months. Now it was long enough for the hairdresser to cut it in what she called a "messy style." I could run my fingers through it and go. Which was good, since it was about all the patience I had for my hair. She'd dyed it black again, with a few burgundy highlights to match the dress.

I took another sip of wine, my gaze moving to the dancers. Jean Luc and Talia swirled around the floor like they'd been dancing together for years.

"I should have known Jean Luc would be a good dancer."

Doc chuckled. "He's too sexy not to be."

"Don't let Talia hear you say that."

"Believe me, she knows."

I glanced over at Doc. "How's it going with Jason?"

She frowned. "It isn't going anywhere with Jason. Even though he's back on the team, he's closed himself off to our friendship."

"I'm sorry, Sabrina. Maybe it's just a matter of time. I never thought he would forgive me, but he did."

Misha frowned. "Do you want me to talk to him?"

Doc shook her head quickly. "No, Misha. Please don't." She turned to me. "What about you and Dalton?"

"What do you mean?"

"I mean how are things going with you two?"

"We're just friends. He asked me to let him know how things were going with the demon immigration."

Doc crossed her arms "It might be where it started months ago, but you can't tell me it's not more than that now. You talk to each other and text all the time."

Misha gushed, "Like Tom Hanks and Meg Ryan in *You've Got Mail.*"

"It's more like being around horny teenagers," Doc argued.

Dalton's messages and talks had become part of my daily life. Every communication helped me understand the man Dalton had become since last year, but I wasn't ready to tell her that. "We do not act like teenagers."

My phone beeped, and Doc and Misha both laughed out loud. I pulled it out of my purse and checked the screen. Of course it was Dalton. I clicked on the message.

Surprise.

I read it again, my befuddled brain not processing the word. The phone beeped a second time.

Turn around.

I turned slowly. Dalton stood a couple of feet away from me. He wore a dark suit that fit him perfectly. My mouth went dry. Holy crap, my mouth went dry. I didn't think that happened in real life. *We're just friends. We're just friends.*

I turned to gauge Doc and Misha's reactions, but they'd disappeared.

Dalton strode over to me. "Hello."

I smiled. "Hi. What are you doing here?"

"I was invited. Decided to surprise you."

"You did. How did you get away from DC?"

"I got the weekend off. This is quite the shindig. Do you want to get something to eat or drink?"

I paused. "Not right now." My stomach was arguing with the contents now. I didn't want to risk adding anything else to the mix.

"Have you danced yet?"

"No. I'm not much of a dancer."

He held out his hand. "Let's give it a try."

I looked up into his turquoise eyes, and he winked at me, and I let him lead me onto the dance floor. Within seconds, a slow song replaced the fast-paced music. I glanced over at the DJ. Misha was standing a few steps away from him looking everywhere but at me, so I couldn't give him the stinkeye. Why did I think there was matchmaking going on here?

Dalton grasped my right hand, and his other hand rested on my lower back. My bare lower back. I shivered at his touch. He pulled me a little closer, and we swayed to the music. The other dancers faded away, and I had one of those surreal, Cinderella moments. The song ended way too quickly, and I had to congratulate myself for not stepping on his toes once. He leaned down and spoke in my ear, his breath caressing my neck. *Dial it back, girlfriend.*

"I know I just got here," he murmured, "but would you be okay if we left the party? I need to talk to you."

"Sure," I said. But I was feeling far from it.

A few minutes later, we climbed into his SUV, and the smell of roses tickled my nose. Marie apparently had been quite busy tonight. "I'm glad you and your grandmother have been able to hook back up again."

"How did you—"

I tapped my nose. "Roses. That's what gave her away last year, too."

"Right, you told me, I remember now." He started the car. "Grandma and I have been talking quite a bit lately."

"Marie's a talker, all right."

"She was giving me some advice on the way here."

I laughed. "Whether you want it or not, right?"

"Yes."

I wanted to ask him what her advice was about, but I didn't feel right asking, and he didn't volunteer. We lapsed into silence until we pulled into his driveway a few minutes later.

"I didn't realize the hall Boris had rented was so close to your house."

Dalton's mouth quirked up at one corner. "Pretty convenient."

When we entered his house, I had trouble sucking air into my lungs. I hadn't been here since last year. The living room had boxes piled to the one side. Which was a blatant reminder he was moving away soon. Time to start getting used to it.

He set his keys on the coffee table and pulled off his suit coat before he turned to me. "I wanted you to be the first to know I've finished my training. I'm a full-fledged Fed now."

"That's great!" my mouth said, but my heart deflated. I gestured to his boxes. "So where are you moving? Chicago?"

He shook his head. "No. Those boxes are from my apartment in Chicago. I'm moving back here. I'm going to be based in the Cleveland office."

I locked my knees so I didn't drop to the floor. I blinked a couple of times. My damn tear ducts were on the verge of overflowing, so I turned away and walked to the fireplace to stare at the picture of Marie he kept there, hoping to pull myself together. "I thought you wanted to live in Chicago."

"I changed my mind. Come on. I'm hungry. Let's go into the kitchen."

"Wait—"

But I found myself standing alone, slack-jawed in the living room. He couldn't just drop a bomb like that and not answer my questions. No sirree Bob, Jim, Mike, and anyone else who cared to listen.

I stomped into the kitchen and was about to launch a volley of questions, but something else caught my attention. A quart of Mocha Swirl sat on the kitchen counter.

I stared at the ice cream like it was a rattlesnake. Dalton was a vanilla guy all the way. What was going on? All the questions I was going to ask him evaporated, and instead I stammered, "B-but this is my favorite. How did you know?"

He smiled and came closer to me, holding a spoon in each hand. "I asked Doc. She also told me in order to enjoy it in 'true Kyle fashion' we had to eat straight from the carton."

The hard shell I'd erected around my heart since I lost Dalton cracked open. And Talia's words rushed back to me. "*You're a fighter. And when someone tells you no, if you want it bad enough, you fight them.*" I wasn't letting him go this time. I couldn't.

His hands were full, so I took advantage. I grabbed his face and pulled him down into my version of a sneak-attack kiss.

He froze for a moment until I bit his bottom lip lightly. Spoons clattered to the floor, and he wrapped his arms around my waist and hauled me up against him.

I had forgotten how soft his lips were, and I gasped with delight. Dalton took advantage and slid his tongue inside, and I was gone. Certifiably lost to the sensations of lips and tongue and desire.

I don't know how long we stood there kissing, but Dalton finally loosened his grip on me and stepped back.

His eyes had darkened, and he ran his fingertips along my lips. "I knew it was going to be good, but that was beyond good."

I opened my mouth, but he placed his fingers over my lips. "Shh. It's my turn to talk now. In the past two months, I've felt like a whole person again. And as much as I would like to say it has to do with my new job, the truth is, it's because of you. Every sarcastic text you send me makes me grin. Every conversation makes me want to talk to you again.

"In the past week, I've received texts or calls from Misha, Jean Luc, Talia, Jason, Irina, Boris, Sabrina, and Nicholas, all wanting to confirm that I would be coming to the party tonight. Even Doyle, the used car salesman, called to tell me how great you are."

"Are you telling me you think they threw this elaborate party to set us up?"

"You know your friends and family better than I do, what do you think?"

"Those sneaky supes."

"I've also had several long talks with my grandmother. She explained everything you went through this past year and told me I was being a horse's ass if I let you go."

"That's what she thinks. What do *you* think?"

"I think you are an amazing woman, Kyle McKinley. You have so many people who love you. So let me ask you a question. Do you think you have room for one more? Because the more time I spend with you, the more I fall in love with you."

I grabbed his face and stared hard into his eyes. "You've forgiven me for erasing your memory?"

"You made the monsters go away, Kyle. And you're still doing that for me. Could you find a way to love me again?"

I rested my forehead to his. "You've always chased my monsters away."

"Then I think that answers my question."

He kissed me lightly on the lips, and I pulled back, turning so my back was to his chest.

"What are you doing?" he asked.

"Making sure we aren't disturbed for a while...Marie, I know you're around here somewhere, so show yourself."

Marie appeared in front of us, smiling.

"Go back to the party and tell everyone their plan worked."

She chuckled. "About daggone time."

"I should have never introduced you to Jean Luc and Misha. Now leave us alone for a while, Marie, and tell everyone else I love them, but I will hurt them if they contact either of us tonight. Got it?"

Marie faded from the room. "Yes, ma'am."

"You are a smart woman." Dalton turned me in his arms, stroking his hand down my bare back. "This dress should be illegal. And your hair is beautiful."

"You scowled at me the night I wore it to the bar."

"I scowled at you because I was having an argument with myself. I had to bite my tongue to keep from saying you couldn't go to the bar dressed like that. You are the sexiest woman I have ever met. I kept you at arm's length because you scared the crap out of me. I knew within two seconds of meeting you that if I let you anywhere near, you would own me."

I laughed out loud. "*Own you*? Is that right?"

He moaned. "I shouldn't have told you."

"That's okay. I won't use it against you."

"You're a bad liar, Kyle." And then he turned serious. "I have to ask. Am I very different from the first time you met me?"

I looked into his eyes. They were full of love, but hidden in their depths was vulnerability.

"You are a little different. A bit more serious and cautious."

He frowned slightly, so I rushed on.

"But that's a good thing. We can balance each other out a bit." I leaned in and kissed his nose. "And I've fallen in love with you all over again."

He hugged me to him and sat on a kitchen chair, setting me in his lap.

"Is there anything else we need to get out in the open while we're coming clean?"

I ran my fingers along his chin. "There's one thing we haven't talked about yet."

"What's that?"

"Our sex life."

Dalton's eyebrows rose. "What about it?"

"Well, it was pretty good. As a matter of fact I think you told me it was the best you ever had."

"*Seriously?* The best, huh?"

I grinned. "Yes."

He cocked his head. "I'm not sure I believe you."

I batted my eyelashes at him like a heroine from a silent movie. "What do I have to do to prove it to you?"

His turquoise eyes danced. "Give me a second. I'm sure I'll think of something."

Thanks

Thank you for taking the time to read *Sentinel Lost*. While this is currently the last book in the Mind Sweeper series, don't despair! There is a spin off series that follows Misha and his family as they find love in the midst of the demon immigration.

I hope you enjoyed the fifth book in the Mind Sweeper Series. Please consider telling your friends about it or posting a short review. Word of mouth is an author's best friend, and much appreciated. Thank you!– AE

If you would like to know when my books will be released, please join my newsletter at aejonesauthor.com

Please turn the page to find a list of my other books.

ACKNOWLEDGMENTS

So many to thank once again! To Faith, my editor extraordinaire. This book was a labor of love. Thanks for helping me through each step.

To Melissa, thanks for taking on this project and creating covers for this entire series. I love them!

Sandra Owens, a wonderful friend and writer, thanks for agreeing to beta read this book for me at the last minute and turning it around in a day! Your support means the world to me.

To my CP Becky Lower who kept asking me "how many words did you get done today?" Thanks for being a taskmaster when I needed one.

Helen, Jayne, Lara, Karen, Ruth & Trish, thanks for sticking by me on this rollercoaster ride. Hard to believe we're five books in, right?

About The Author

Growing up a TV junkie, AE Jones oftentimes rewrote endings of episodes in her head when she didn't like the outcome. She immersed herself in sci-fi and soap operas. But when *Buffy* hit the little screen, she knew her true love was paranormal. Now she spends her nights weaving stories about all variations of supernatural—their angst and their humor. After all, life is about both...whether you sport fangs or not.

AE won the prestigious Golden Heart® Award for her paranormal manuscript, Mind Sweeper, which also was a RITA® finalist for both First Book and Paranormal Romance. AE is also a recipient of the Booksellers' Best Award and is a National Readers' Choice Award Finalist, Holt Award of Merit Finalist and a Daphne du Mauricr Finalist.

AE lives in Ohio surrounded by her eclcctic family and friends who in no way resemble any characters in her books. *Honest.* Now her two cats are another story altogether.

Learn more about AE and her books on her website aej onesauthor.com

www.ingramcontent.com/pod-product-compliance
Lightning Source LLC
Chambersburg PA
CBHW070636180626
46817CB00006B/2136